After The Deluge

by Chris Carlsson

1st Printing

ISBN 0-926664-07-7

Full Enjoyment Books
2844 Folsom Street
San Francisco, CA 94110

www.fullenjoymentbooks.com

cc@chriscarlsson.com
www.chriscarlsson.com

Cover and maps by Hugh D'Andrade
www.hughillustration.com

printed on recycled paper

Acknowledgements

Writing a novel has been a surprising experience. While it is mostly a rather solitary effort, this story would not be finished without the help of many friends, some old and some new.

Thanks go out to two writers' retreats that allowed me to hide out from the incessant chatter of daily life and see if there was really a novel kicking around in my head. The Mesa Refuge in Pt. Reyes Station, California, gave me two glorious weeks in October 1999, when I first took a stab at creating some of the characters and scenes for *After The Deluge*. Nearly two years later (Aug.-Sept. 2001), I practically started over when I was blessed with a whole month at Blue Mountain Center in New York's Adirondacks. I was delighted to make many new friends at both retreats, and look forward to future encounters with great anticipation.

I give thanks to the readers who gave me the most detailed and useful feedback: Kurt Lipschutz, Elizabeth Creely, Jim Fisher, Daniel Steven Crafts, Laura Lent, Glenn Bachmann, Karen Franklin, Jon Christensen, Hugh D'Andrade, Jeff Mooney, and my parents, Dick and Bente Carlsson. Adam Cornford, Marina Lazzarra, Pete Holloran, Giovanni Maruzzelli and David Rosen gave me crucial encouragement, as did my amazing daughter Francesca Manning.

Special thanks to Jim Swanson, my business partner, for all the hours, days, weeks and even months I was able to squeeze out to work on this book. Couldn't have done it without his holding down the fort in my frequent absence.

Special thanks too to Hugh D'Andrade for the maps and the wonderful cover. I'm honored to have his work gracing this book.

Lastly, thanks to my love, Mona Caron, for her ongoing enthusiasm for my crackpot ideas and her warm support and steady encouragement for me to go the extra mile to make things as strong as possible. Mona is a great muse and inspiration; this book is inconceivable without her.

All those thanks aside, none of these people should be held accountable for the flaws and inadequacies of this work. Failures in this book are all mine!

I did not conceive this book as a blueprint, but more as a stab at describing the world I'd like to wake up into. And I wanted to spin a good enough yarn to transport you, dear reader, into that world with me. Having been involved in radical politics for my entire adult life I felt it necessary that I make some effort to articulate and describe how much better life really could be. Think of it as a starting point for a more detailed discussion rather than a full-fledged "answer." If you are left wondering, pondering, scratching your head, and trying to answer such questions for yourself, this book will have exceeded my fondest aspirations.

—Chris Carlsson, August 25, 2004

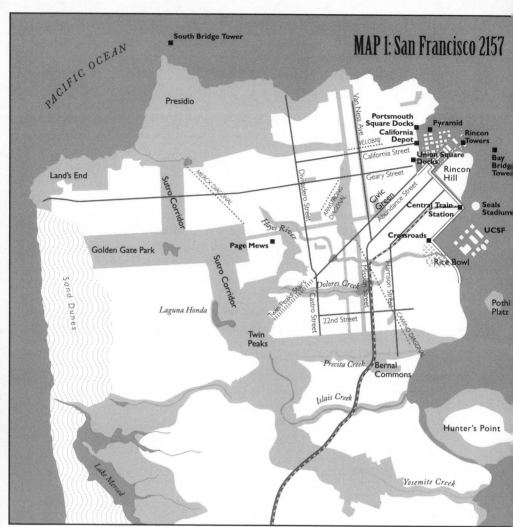

MAP 1: San Francisco 2157

PACIFIC OCEAN

South Bridge Tower

Presidio

Land's End

MERCY DIAGONAL

Sutro Corridor

Golden Gate Park

Sand Dunes

Sutro Corridor

Laguna Honda

Page Mews

Hayes River

Twin Peaks Stairs

Twin Peaks

Castro Street

22nd Street

Dolores Creek

Mission Street

Van Ness Ave

VELOBRIJ

Divisadero Street

ARMSTRONG DIAGONAL

California Street

Geary Street

Abundance Street

Civic Green

Portsmouth Square Docks
California Depot

Pyramid

Rincon Towers

Union Square Docks

Rincon Hill

Bay Bridge Tower

Central Train Station

Seals Stadium

Crossroads

Rice Bowl

UCSF

Harrison Street

CAMINO DIAGONAL

Precita Creek

Bernal Commons

Pothi Platz

Islais Creek

Hunter's Point

Lake Merced

Yosemite Creek

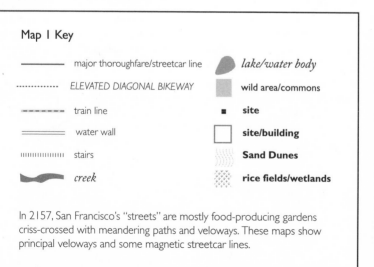

Map 1 Key

———	major thoroughfare/streetcar line
··········	*ELEVATED DIAGONAL BIKEWAY*
≡≡≡≡	train line
═══	water wall
⡇⡇⡇⡇	stairs
∿∿∿	*creek*

lake/water body

wild area/commons

■ **site**

□ **site/building**

Sand Dunes

rice fields/wetlands

In 2157, San Francisco's "streets" are mostly food-producing gardens criss-crossed with meandering paths and veloways. These maps show principal veloways and some magnetic streetcar lines.

Map 2

Map 3

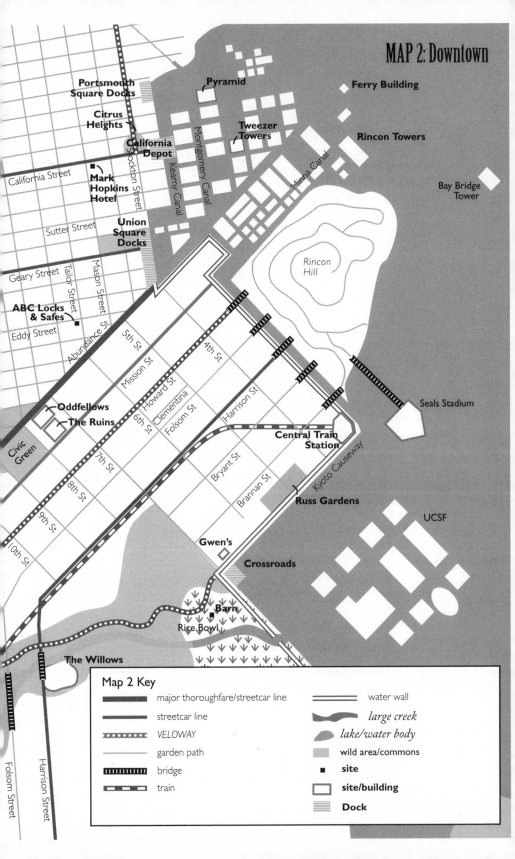

MAP 2: Downtown

Portsmouth
Square Docks

Citrus
Heights

California
Depot

Pyramid

Ferry Building

Tweezer
Towers

Rincon Towers

California Street

Mark
Hopkins
Hotel

Montgomery Canal

Kearny Canal

Stockton Street

Sutter Street

Union
Square
Docks

Minna Canal

Bay Bridge
Tower

Geary Street

Tailor Street

Mason Street

Rincon
Hill

ABC Locks
& Safes

Eddy Street

Abundance St.

5th St

4th St

Seals Stadium

Mission St.

Howard St

Clementina

Folsom St

Harrison St

Oddfellows

The Ruins

6th St

Central Train
Station

Civic
Green

7th St

Bryant St

UCSF

8th St

Brannan St

Kyoto Causeway

Russ Gardens

9th St

Gwen's

10th St

Crossroads

Barn

Rice Bowl

The Willows

Folsom Street

Harrison Street

Map 2 Key

▬▬▬	major thoroughfare/streetcar line
▬▬▬	streetcar line
✕✕✕✕✕	VELOWAY
▬▬▬	garden path
▥▥▥	bridge
▦▦▦	train

▤▤▤	water wall
〰〰	*large creek*
⬯	*lake/water body*
▨	wild area/commons
■	site
☐	site/building
▨▨	Dock

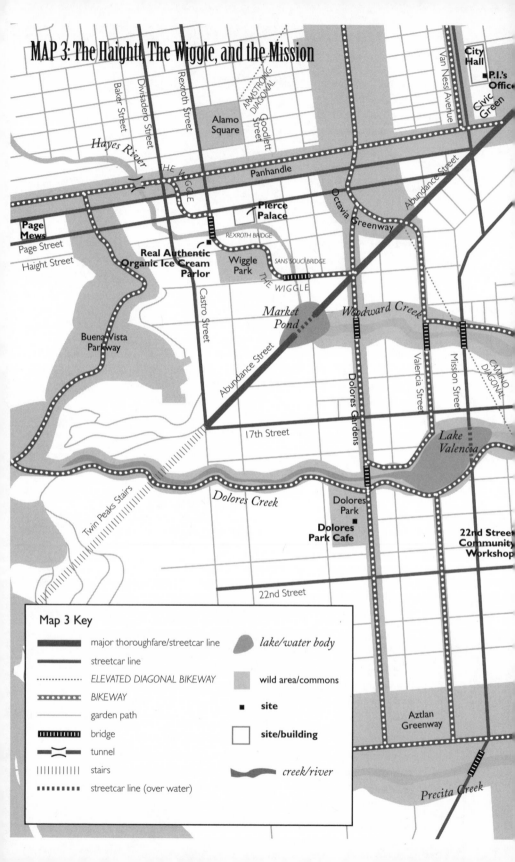

Prologue

He picked up a toy car from the desk and turned it upside down. Hard to imagine a time of freeways and streets, avenues and lanes, each and every one fully covered in asphalt. Spinning the wheels, he imagined driving, sun-glassed and expressionless. He tossed the toy into a corner.

A faded poster caught his eye. He squinted and read "Farewell to the Shoreline" in huge electric blue letters ghosted behind the stacked names of bands, names that meant nothing to him, and the date: June 15, 2031. He swallowed a laugh, wondering if they knew back then it was more than an amphitheatre they were taking leave of...

The lid lifted from the gas can without much effort. He spilled a good fourth of the contents just by tipping the can, a wet stain spreading across the floor. Then he soaked the bed, the moth-eaten curtains, saving the perimeter of the room for last. Well, almost last. The room sagged in the center like an old mattress, and made a small lake bed which he gladly filled, backing out and exiting through the window into the darkness outside.

The sky betrayed a hint of morning in the east. He untied his skiff and moved through the pre-dawn gloom for 90 endless seconds or so, before retying beside another nearby house, this one looted long ago, its upstairs mostly stripped bare. Hurrying now, he saturated the room like an old pro, donating the empty can to the elements. His gloves stunk, his nostrils burned. His rubber boots reeked with the evidence, the same fuel that had powered all those vanished movie cars.

Trembling with excitement back in the boat, his hands were numb with cold as he pulled off his gloves. He fumbled with several moldy cardboard matches before striking a light. Holding it to one of the gloves, he threw the flaming rubber mitt and incredibly, missed. The glove smacked the wall and sank hissing into the water. "Unbelievable," he muttered into the void. The second burning glove made it through the window and the room ignited, a ball of heat roiling out the window, almost knocking him over. He collapsed in the skiff, his heart racing, pounding in his ears. He retraced his watery route to the first house, glancing over his shoulder to admire his handiwork as flames leapt from the roof behind him. He lit a small rag and threw it through the window. Before the rag hit the floor, the room went off like a bomb, one hot wave of glorious explosive power set free. Blown backwards, he nearly fell into the Bay. He kicked the flipper switch near his foot and the boat churned away from the inferno. He reached into his pants and stroked himself, hardened with excitement, climaxing immediately.

Wiping up with a rag, he surveyed the fruits of his labor. The smell was intense. He steered his craft out in to the open Bay, still mesmerized by the flames jumping now from roof to roof. After a few minutes more there was nothing to see but smoke in the dawn light. He headed north, his ears still ringing. His face burned. Rubbing his forehead he realized he had no eyebrows.

Full daylight now. The gray smoke behind merged harmlessly with the fog that was barely retreating in the face of morning. He was thoroughly, teeth-chatteringly chilled, high on adrenaline and without regret. Looking towards the East Bay, he hoped for sunlight, for warmth and luck. It would be a half hour before the sun cleared the hills.

He pointed his boat homeward and decided to bleach his hair.

I.

The train was gliding along through endless rows of suburban apartments, but Eric could see water down various streets that led to the Bay. He was two days out of Chicago and he'd read every sign in the car at least a dozen times, from the fire extinguisher to the emergency exit to the toilet and luggage rules. The paintings adorning the train's walls had interested him at first, but after two days they receded into anonymity.

Now Bay waters licked the sides of the train's causeway, further east hundreds of buildings were semi-submerged in their original locations. Across the Bay rose Oakland. He saw watercraft of every size and shape, skiffs, launches, gondolas, barges. Hundreds of them.

Blue skies had emerged from the morning gloom. Pelicans, seagulls, sparrows, hawks, and many others whose names he could not place cavorted, sailed and soared. He spotted wispy gray smoke drifting up a ways off. Some kind of fire.

The map of San Francisco appeared on the wall display and a glowing red line indicated the route for the short remainder of the journey. The train station sat in the Bay surrounded by water on three sides.

That map is the dew, he thought. His apprehension briefly passed as he enthused about a future in cartography, and contemplated the curious outlines of 22nd century San Francisco. The Bay itself was huge, having spread uphill over urban landscapes in all directions.

"Downtown San Francisco, 15 minutes" came the announcement. He ran his hands through his hair and wiped his face, clearing the overnight crusty grime. His sinuses ached from the cool controlled air. He opened his window inhaling the salt water smell through the damp foggy air. Leaning out made him dizzy as the buildings blurred by like mysterious colored boxes.

He was cautiously hopeful and he tried to hold on to that feeling, despite a pit in his stomach competing for his attention with a persistent headache that had plagued him since the day before.

Coffee, I need coffee. And a big fat cinnamon roll... I should be happy, excited, he thought, morose. He needed a change in scenery and a change of luck. He'd left Chicago unnoticed. The old guy at the corner fruit stand, Virgil, was the only friend he said goodbye to. *Something good is going to happen.*

During eight bleak months in the Windy City he had sampled a half dozen work situations. A stint at the Museum of Natural History, two weeks at the Zoo. He thought he'd like the science, but he hadn't clicked with any of his co-workers, or the work itself. Then another short stint at the University as research associate on a study of the area's water usage. That's where he'd fallen for Cynthia and at first she seemed friendly enough, until they went out a couple of times. *Can't blame her.*

He forced the thought away as the train emerged from a tunnel and rolled onto a long curving bridge. In the distance he could see tall buildings, the famous orange Pyramid and the rest of the San Francisco skyline.

He sank back into his seat, leaning on his hand—all his fears came roaring back.

What the hell am I doing here?! I don't even know anybody.

Virgil—it was his casual remarks that had led to this moment.

"San Francisco! Man, that's the best city in the whole world. The hills, the canals, the beautiful buildings... and the ladies!" He leaned over a carton of apples between Eric and his perch. "I tell ya Eric, you get yourself to San Francisco, and you'll find love there, Virgil guarantees it! The ladies by the Bay are wild!" He leered at Eric suggestively. At the time, it had seemed a stupid conversation, typical of Virgil's exaggerations and unreconstructed sexism. But it haunted Eric, and San Francisco started to seem like the only solution for his aching heart. "You can leave your heart in San Francisco." Virgil chortled as Eric inspected strawberries on that beautiful Spring day two months ago. "See if you find mine. I left it there."

He made his way to the bathroom, where he hurriedly washed up. In the mirror, Eric watched himself paw greasy hair out of his hang dog face and stare at his scars. Great, he was breaking out.

The train braked noticeably and Eric slammed the hand towel back against the wall and left the bathroom, dragging, dreading his imminent arrival, wondering where he'd go.

Minutes later, light-headed, he descended to the train platform and was hit by the pungent, concentrated smell of salt water and decay. The screams of gulls rattled around the station, but he saw no birds. Clanging metal and groaning piers were close by but out of sight. Grabbing his backpack, he walked up the platform to the Central Train Station, an elegant Spanish Mission-style structure. He stopped just outside the soaring arched entrance, awestruck by the elaborate stonework and intricately tiled floors and walls.

Inside the terminal, people were passing back and forth, but with an unhurried feeling to it all. Knots of people gathered, talking, laughing. Small café tables ringed the main pavilion and were packed with waiting passengers. In the far left corner, a small crew in wildly paint-splattered coveralls was on hands and knees, working on the mosaic floor. The aroma of marijuana and coffee overpowered the ocean smells outside.

Eric turned to a clamor at the door to the platforms. A train conductor wheeled in a hand-truck stacked with bundled magazines, and a mob surged toward him. Eagerly they tore open the parcels and began sharing out copies of the new *Free Radical* magazine.

"Hey, hey, take it easy," the conductor admonished. He was used to this ritualized dance and had to restrain the eager throng from taking all the copies before he could pass half the bundles to a waiting woman with her own wagon. Off she went with them through the doors.

Eric spotted an empty seat at one of the tables and dropped his belongings. At the window he ordered a double espresso and a muffin. An oddly grumpy boy behind the counter diffidently slid a muffin onto a small plate and thrust it at him, and then turned to make the coffee. Moments later he brought it back, scowling.

Eric assumed he'd done something wrong. "I'm sorry, did I—?"

"Huh? Oh, no, nothing... forget it," the boy spat and turned away.

Shrugging, Eric took his breakfast back to the table. Not exactly the cheery San Franciscan welcome Virgil had promised.

"Are they always so testy behind the counter here?" he asked the woman at the next chair.

"Oh him? He's pissed—who knows why. Don't take it personally. It's not you, it's the world."

"Okay, thanks." Eric sipped the coffee, savoring its bitter strength. The muffin was sweeter and nuttier than breakfast pastries back East where they were leaden and tasteless compared to these. He polished it off.

He was wiping crumbs from his lap when they burst into the station. An oversized red wagon rolled through the door. On it two women were piercing the station's buzz with inspired trumpet solos while a chubby giant oompahpah'd a steady bass tuba. Up front, steering the slow-moving vehicle, sat a man and a woman in clownish costumes: bright yellow suits with long tails. White and yellow lines spiraled up their improbably tall stovepipe top hats.

"We're late, weeee'rrreeee laaaaaaaaate!" they sang, "but you're NOT!" The two in front jumped down from the wagon and began scurrying from table to table around the mezzanine, running zanily as they tossed small papers on each table, exchanging a word or two at each spot. Regulars seemed to barely note the arrival of the Welcome Wagon but fresh arrivals like Eric stared open-mouthed.

The yellow-suited woman came to Eric's table, tails swirling behind as she spun like a dervish toward him. The stranger at the next chair didn't even look up, so the Welcome Wagon lady directed her words to Eric. She tossed a small brochure on the table that said "Welcome to San Francisco," with an illustration of the city's skyline, flags flying in a full breeze from every rooftop.

"You're invited," she leaned into Eric, her garish clown face obscuring any real expression she may have had, "to the First Night at the Top of the Mark!" And she swirled away, her partner matching her progress on the opposite side of the station.

Me? Eric was confused. He opened the brochure. "San Francisco's Welcome Wagon invites you to spend your first night in old-style luxury at the top of Nob Hill. If you're new to San Francisco, please join us for a night you will always remember. Proceed to Pier C and board the ferry."

Virgil, why did I ever doubt you? He gathered up his bag and found his way to a dock with a dozen piers extending into the Bay. He headed to Pier C, as instructed, and stepped into a 30-foot peapod-looking green vessel with a translucent canopy hanging above a golden cross-hatching of branches. A small host of other newcomers was already aboard. The man in the yellow costume with the huge top hat joined them, but the rest of the Welcome Wagon team was nowhere to be seen.

"Friends of all genders and preferences. Welcome to our fair city," he bowed with a flourish and waved his hand over the cityscape behind him. "I am Fernando Ramirez, your host for the journey to the Top of the Mark. If you have any questions they will not go unanswered. Meanwhile, take a seat and feast your eyes. We'll be making a few routine stops before we arrive at the California Street depot. Now I know it's early, but you are invited to reach under your seat." Amidst general shuffling champagne glasses were discovered and displayed. Fernando made a brief show of hunting through a cabinet along the side of the ferry, and feigned discouragement at not finding anything. Then he smacked himself in the forehead and carefully lifted his hat to reveal a big bottle of champagne on his head. He popped it open and made his way through the happy tourists, pouring champagne and making suggestive remarks as it fancied him.

"Do we need to show our workbooks for this?" asked a leathery-skinned man next to a matronly woman behind Eric.

Fernando stopped and stared. His jaw flapped but no noise came out. He began waving his arm like a windmill, sputtering and gasping. "Work—workbooks?!? Why sir, whatever are you talking about?" Fernando looked all around, in feigned exasperation, as if he needed some help. "Can someone help me here? *Workbooks?*"

Eric certainly knew about workbooks. In Chicago, and most places back east, the local Hiring Halls still tried to keep track of who was and wasn't doing their Annuals, and for certain purposes you had to show your workbook—at major sporting and cultural events. He'd heard that San Francisco and the West Coast had abandoned any system of account-ability, and that it had been surprisingly easy. Still, he kept his mouth shut.

Some girls that had been on his train were giggling in the back, enjoying Fernando's show. One raised her hand and stood up. "Workbooks, you know, it's the place you keep track of your Annuals or whatever work you're doing." No one seemed to really believe Fernando didn't know about workbooks, and she offered her explana-tion in the spirit of participatory theatre more than a real explanation.

"Aaaaah, Gracias, senorita!" He spun around on cue, his foil provided, to the leath-ery-skinned man and his wife. "I'm terribly sorry, my goood sir. We have no workbooks here. All work is voluntary and goods and services are distributed without any check-ing. . . Everything here is free." He had his hands on his hips now, like he'd given this little talk many times. He directed himself to one and all. "You're in San Francisco. There is plenty of everything for everyone. You come, you relax, you have a good time. If you stay," he shrugged, "you will see what to do to help. Meantime, enjoy yourselves. You are our guests."

A happy murmur floated through the newcomers. The declaration combined with the champagne to produce an excited euphoria as the ferry disembarked from the Central Train Station.

The skipper, a salty, heavy-set, dark-haired woman named Maude, bellowed "All aboard, we're heading DOWNtown!" A flapping noise began at the rear of the boat, and slowly they floated out into the Bay. Maude coughed violently as she steered the peapod northward around a red brick stadium. Jutting out of the water in front of the stadium was an old green-tarnished statue of a baseball player gazing at an invisible ball in the proverbial distance, his bat wrapped around behind him at the end of his mighty swing. The waves lapping at his knees gave it a ghostly, strangely elegant look. A great brown pelican landed on his ballcap as they passed.

Out in the Bay dozens of floating structures seemed to be anchored in place. Where they were near each other, tall masts rose and vines swung from one to the next. Tall, straight palm trees dotted San Francisco's slopes in every direction.

They turned further northward and an island became visible in the middle of the Bay, covered in flashing bright lights, and what looked like roller coasters and carnival tents. A steady stream of small water craft were heading back and forth from the docks at its near shore.

"What's that?" Eric asked an elderly man with a tray of green seedlings in his lap.

"Oh, that's Treasure Island. If you stay here long, you'll have to go there eventually. It's where we try to manage supply and demand, if you know what I mean." He winked conspiratorially, but Eric didn't know what he meant. He decided not to ask, for now.

San Francisco loomed up out of the fog, the sun working hard to burn it off. It was almost 10 o'clock. To the left, round hills were covered in dense foliage with houses and paths running down them to small piers along the shoreline. Large glass buildings, dozens of stories high, stood in the water, the old downtown. Many were covered in ivy and vines. Thousands of birds flew about the buildings and in and out of the fog canopy slowly lifting above the tops of skyscrapers. A loud squawking sound unlike anything Eric had ever heard suddenly erupted. A flock of over two hundred bright green parrots tumbled between the shore and the ferry. He laughed, for the first time in days.

A family he'd seen on the train sat across from him, facing the city. Dad and Mom grappled with three young children too excited to sit still. "Look look!" the smallest, a boy, squealed, pointing at seals bobbing along in the water. "What are those fish, Mom?" asked his sister, pointing to three sleek creatures jumping away from the ferry. She turned to the man behind them, hopeful that he could tell them. "Dolphins. The Bay is full of 'em." Eric looked more carefully at the Bay, where shiny silver streaks filled the clear water, dense schools of fish circulating below. A small flock of pelicans glided inches from the surface of the Bay. Eric felt like he was visiting a tropical island. Life pulsed all around him.

To their right they approached a huge tower rising out of a cement platform. The skipper Maude announced in a bored, routine voice, "Bay Bridge, first stop." It wasn't a bridge anymore, having been destroyed in the Earthquake of 2044. People had carved out living spaces on the tower, and it was a routine stop for various water routes. Brightly colored sails with ornate lettering billowed from its upper reaches, while the ubiquitous ivy and vines wove all around, criss-crossing in every imaginable configuration.

Maude steered her vessel into the canyons of downtown. Gondolas, rafts, and small boats commingled, people using long poles to move along while a few still had oars. Most had customized bioboats like Maude's, with structural fins for propulsion.

"Next stop Rincon Towers, then the Dominos, the Tweezer Towers, the Pyramid, and California Street Depot. If you need another address, you can transfer at any of those places to a watercab."

The ferry pulled up to a pier at Rincon Towers where the dock's façade was covered in murals, lively colors with an angular style, apparently chapters of old California history. Three passengers got on, among them a stunningly handsome man with long flowing blonde hair in an intricately embroidered dark blue tunic.

On they went. The Dominos were large gray towers that leaned crazily, giving them their nickname. They had been that way for over 100 years and were fully occupied, the interior floors redesigned to accommodate the tilt. Visible to the north was the great orange Pyramid, with a giant eyeball at its apex. The ferry churned slowly up the California canal, ruins piled amidst towers, water lapping over everything. Tiny skiffs darted in and out of traffic, while barges and taxis clogged the main channel. It wasn't quite gridlock, but the dense mass did occasionally come to a complete stop. Groaning and squeaking boats provided an undercurrent to the sing-song calls and hollers of boatmen and women. "Get that thing outta my way!" "Watch out!" "Hey, you can't do that!" "On your left, on the left, careful now…" Eric grew dizzy watching the chaotic water traffic, but San Francisco was working its seductive charm on him, even so. Meanwhile, sky-bridges soared through the air connecting buildings at all heights and angles, many of them transparent tubes full of people moving back and forth.

"Citizens and Comrades." Ramirez called everyone's attention. "We are almost to our stop now." The ferry was reaching the end of the canal where California Street rose like a vertical wall before them. The tourists pointed at the cable cars scaling and descending the hill. The Depot itself was a spit-polished wooden structure with room for a dozen boats to tie up. Several taxis were docked on one side under a big sign reading "NO BARGES—Barges must use Union Square or Portsmouth Square docks." Baroquely curving wooden eaves, windows and doors gave the Depot a look that was more in keeping with a chalet in the Alps than the Pacific Rim. "You'll notice the exquisite woodwork here in the Depot. This was built in 2048 but had to be moved uphill twice as the waters rose, most recently in 2122. It is made entirely from redwood lumber scavenged from the ruins of the 2044 quake. Please follow me."

The ferry came to a halt. With a flourish, Ramirez jumped onto the gangway, his yellow tails dancing behind him as he ducked his big hat under the ferry's canopy. The First Nighters dragged their bags across the gangway and into the station, up a wide spiral stairway to the second floor mezzanine where a huge shiny black object made up part of the wall. Ramirez stopped to regroup. He leaned against the marble surface, slapping one hand against it as the 14 fresh arrivals gathered around him.

"What, my friends, do you suppose this is?"

A child offered "Broken marble?" which provoked light laughter. Ramirez smiled. "This is a telling piece of old San Francisco. See that huge building?" He pointed up through the skylight at the tower which stood back in the water, mostly dark brown, but with splashes of color. Ten floors up the walls had been removed to make a large opening on the corner, green vines pouring from it, café tables perched along the edge. "That is the old Bank of America building, once the headquarters of the world's largest bank. And this," he slapped it vigorously, "this is the Bankers' Heart." The older people in the group laughed, but the younger ones, including Eric, just stood there.

"I don't get it," one of the younger women in front admitted.

"Aaah, of course, allow me to explain. Bankers handled money, and they decided who would be allowed to build homes, start factories and businesses, even to eat. Bankers decided who would carry and who would ride." He paused, aware that he was not yet making his point. "Well, the men—because they were mostly men—who ran banks were famous for their lack of pity. Thus, the dead, dark stone, the Bankers' Heart."

The young people nodded tentatively, but the whole idea of money and banks was completely alien. Ramirez had seen this many times before, but he always gave it a try. "Follow me, please." He led them out the door to the slope of California Street where it ended in a big circular plaza. Excitement gripped the tourists while they waited for the California Street cable car to ride up the hill. Eric looked up and down Kearny: a canal one block north and two south, ferries and barges clogging the waterways.

Clangorous bells rang as the cable car shuddered into action and began crawling uphill. Eric was standing on the running board, clutching a support railing. A large outdoor sign featured an abstract painting, bold slashes of red and blue across a black object that might be a tree or perhaps just a blotch. A small forest wound up the hill behind the sign, skirting through empty lots and behind apartment buildings. An ancient red brick church stood on the corner of Grant, a sign proclaiming that it had been rebuilt in 2115. Down Grant Street hundreds of people milled about among booths, banners in Chinese crisscrossing the air above it all.

At Stockton, sweet smells of citrus filled the air. On either side of California Street groves of oranges and lemons softly shivered in the rapidly warming mid-summer air. The sun was breaking through now, the fog finally releasing its biting grip on the morning. A flock of parrots noisily passed over as they waited amidst the lemon trees while passengers got on and off.

"Look Dad!" said a boy next to Eric, pointing through the trees down Stockton towards the Union Square docks where a gleaming golden oblong boat was docked. "What kind of boat is that?" The cable car conductor leaned over to save the father from embarrassment.

"That's a golden beetle. Just designed over at the Biomanufactury at the University of California. They're trying it out as a ferry, but it's only a prototype. It's the dew, ain't it?"

The father smiled gratefully and turned back to his son, sharing the excitement of discovery.

Eric carefully stepped to the back of the cable car where there was an open spot at the railing. He joined some San Francisco regulars there. Two burly fellows in orange vests and hardhats were debating the fate of the local baseball team, the Seals.

"I don't care—they could be 25 games out. They could still make it back. The Oaks can't last. They're playing WAY over their heads."

"Chingado! The Oaks are gonna take it. Five hours says the Oaks go the distance. "You're on."

Eric squeezed between them and a threesome to reach the back railing. The threesome were arguing too, about a fourth person, not present.

"I don't think he's done anything about it," said the tall dark-haired woman against whose back his shoulder was lodged.

"Well, it's not his fault," answered a lanky guy, and then another man chimed in, "What about the rest of his department? There's a lot of people who are responsible for this, not just Duvall."

Competing conversations blurred into the background when he realized they were going practically straight up the hill. The cable car ride was far from smooth, but he felt no fear, only exhilaration. The shimmering waters danced amidst dense boat traffic as far as he could see down California, beyond the old Ferry Building they'd passed on the way in. The orange Pyramid with its zany eyeball stood garishly to the northeast. Flags fluttered in the increasingly unfiltered sunshine and the ubiquitous parrots darted in and out of alleys between tall buildings planted in the water below.

The cable car tilted forward and stopped. The passengers packing the back platform with Eric all disembarked, then the car continued up another less steeply sloped block. A massive white building appeared directly opposite an equally imposing tan structure. Eric leaned out the right side of the cable car to admire the old hotels and apartments that filled the top of Nob Hill. At the crest of the hill, the Mark Hopkins Hotel appeared, its courtyard providing a flat surface next to where Mason Street plunged southward. Ramirez led the troop off the cable car and towards the hotel's imposing doors. Standing in the flower-filled courtyard, Ramirez gave a quick history of the elegant old hotels, and the even earlier history of Nob Hill as home to the original railroad barons of the 1860s. "That half-circle entryway full of horse-drawn carriages across the street at the elegant

Fairmont Hotel, is right next to the rust colored brownstone you see, which was once James Flood's mansion.

"So while you're here, appreciate that you are getting a taste of an opulent life once reserved for only the very few."

"Who lives here now?," asked a nondescript guy in a brown turtleneck shirt, beads of sweat forming on his brow as they stood in the sun.

"I do." Ramirez smiled and bowed. "A community of about 1,300 lives in the old hotels. We keep up the tradition of bringing visitors and newcomers here. Mostly you are expected to leave after the first night, but if you would like to stay longer, make a request at the front desk."

Ramirez smiled mischievously. "Perhaps you'll be inspired by tonight's show. Or by something you see or hear." He looked into each of the fourteen faces. "There are not fast rules but I can assure you, it does take a combination of luck and inspiration."

"Please follow me." They filed into the lobby surrounded by massive chandeliers, plush sofas, old polished wooden tables, huge oil paintings, and a very long bar at the rear, already crowded with dozens of people. Or were they still there from last night?

An ominous noise filled the air, humming . . . getting louder and louder. Eric looked around alarmed, but saw that no one outside their group was particularly concerned. Suddenly a very loud crash of bowling pins made him cover his ears. Three huge silver metal circles came rolling into view, each with a human splayed out inside, rolling over and over, forming a circle, tighter and tighter, until they whipped around in a small loop. An acrobat leaped out of each loop.

Two short men, swarthy and in need of a shave, with matching handlebar mustaches and unkempt hair stood at either side of a woman whose hair was the same length and had a matching physique. All three had massive arms and shoulders, the woman's breasts and waist setting her apart from her brothers. She thrust one arm into the air in a traditional gesture of "tah-daahhhh," and they smiled and bowed. They ran through several choreographed routines, tossing each other into the air, jumping and falling in turn, and finally grabbing trapezes that had lowered from the high ceiling. They were lifted up and disappeared into a round hole in the ceiling.

Ramirez reappeared, having changed out of his yellow tails into casual attire. "Folks, let me show you to your rooms. We'd like to give you a few hours to get settled, explore the place, have a bite and get your bearings. Later, there will be more fun and games with some of my colleagues. There's a luncheon banquet from..." and he looked around to peer at a big clock behind the front desk, which showed five minutes until noon, "... about now until 3 p.m. Grab lunch whenever you'd like. Dinner will be at 7:30, followed by some entertainment, a bit of history, a medley of film clips, and if you still need it, more Q & A... Follow me."

They were joined by two associates of Ramirez's, and divided into groups and showed their rooms. Eric's was a huge suite with a sweeping view. Squinting in the midday sun, he could make out the Central Train Station where he'd come in, the ballpark near it. *Must be where the Seals play.*

Late that night, Eric was dizzy and drunk. The show over, he headed toward his room. The banquet and endless supply of wine had done the job. All the guests were drunk and/or happy. Eric had suffered through a show that seemed to go on forever. A Snow White character in search of "true love" had traveled the world, meeting silly characters from every corner of the planet. Dozens of singers had presented a show called "Babylon by the Bay"—full of double entendres, satirical songs about local politicians and famous historical characters. They came on stage wearing outlandish hats bedecked with landmarks and topical jokes, towers of fruit, a rainbow, all manner of mega-props. But Eric didn't like it much. He tried to laugh along with everyone, but inside he was chafing. It wasn't funny to him. *I'm not a tourist. I'm getting out of here first thing!*

2.

Hey, Nwin, coming to the party tonight?"

Nwin was leaving his apartment when his neighbor appeared, as usual.

Groggily, he tried to focus on Lupe without betraying his irritation.

"Nwin, we need you. We're planning our costumes for the Carnival, and there's a lot to figure out."

"Lupe, I—"

"I'm thinking of a yellow and pink combination, with lots of gold trim. We need to plan the float, you know, and design the favors, you know, and the music, and—"

Nwin moved down the hall. Lupe stopped when she realized he was blowing her off.

"Hey, you don't have to be so rude, you know." Nwin shrugged and waved his arm behind him dismissively when the elevator arrived.

Jesus, what does she think? Is everyone supposed to be all hot about Carnival? All those chingin' house parties, everyone sitting around pretending to like each other. I oughta move.

Worked up now he fidgeted while more people got on at the 7th floor. He nodded 'hello' to Renato and Luisa, a Brazilian couple he'd met at dinner once. He squeezed into the back corner of the elevator, impatient to be out of the building.

Water taxis and launches pulled up outside the front door docks. Nwin, almost 18, stood well over six feet with chocolate-colored skin. His hair, usually black but newly bleached blonde, flopped over his narrow eyes. Big lips and a prominent broad nose marked him as a typical striking San Francisco hybrid: the gaze of an Asian with African features. He strode directly to the first shuttle heading south and got on. It was midday already. A warm breeze dissolved his grogginess and he turned his face to the sun, soaking up heat. He fingered a magnifying glass in his shoulder bag.

A sign hanging from the shuttle's rafters proclaimed "NOBODY WANTS TO SO WE ALL HAVE TO. DO YOUR ANNUALS . . . IT'S EASY, IT'S FUN, IT'S FAIR." Nwin scowled and squinted at a water taxi speeding by.

Parrots squawked noisily over the sounds of skippers and mates shouting instructions back and forth. It was hard to discern any rules to water traffic when you were out on the Bay. Accidents were rare, probably because the Pilots Guild insisted on a two-year apprenticeship for skippers.

The shuttle stopped at Rincon Hill north, the Bay Bridge, and Rincon Hill south. Screams and laughter filled the air from Treasure Island. Nwin barely noticed, staring intently towards smoke billowing from somewhere on the Oakland shore.

After crossing the mouth of Mission Bay and making a stop at the 19th Street Potrero Hill viaduct, the shuttle set out for the Precita Creek dock, not far from his parents' place. It was a nice hot San Francisco afternoon now, over 25° as Nwin disembarked. The breeze he'd enjoyed near North Beach had not followed them southward. He pulled off his black leather jacket and threw it over his shoulder, but his black shirt and pants drew the heat even still. As he climbed the hill, his shirt darkened with sweat.

He stopped under the shade of a sizeable n'oak tree he'd spent countless hours sitting in as a boy. Chattering voices caught his attention. Up ahead he could see several girls he knew—and couldn't stand—coming his way. He clambered up the tree, sliding onto one of the sturdiest branches. The girls passed below, Nwin going unnoticed.

"And he told me he'd be there, but when I saw him—"

"You mean he actually had the nerve to show up?"

"Oh sure, but you wouldn't believe. . ."

The voices trailed off as the three girls clomped down the street in their platform shoes, snapping gum and swinging trendy shoulder bags, shimmering and reflecting light around them.

Nwin scowled and lay back on the branch, glad to have escaped. They had been classmates and now when he ran in to them there was always this friendly conversation that he hated. *Everything is so chingin' fake.*

A dog barked urgently, but Nwin couldn't see anything from his perch. The street was quiet, without movement. The dog was in some backyard out of sight. A coyote bolted across the street below the tree, and a trash can clattered on its side and began to roll in a great semicircle downhill. Nwin smirked, feeling an affinity with the outlaw urban scavenger.

A sign in the yard across the street filled his view, like that lame sign he'd seen on the shuttle: "No one wants to so we all have to." *Says who?!* He pulled out his magnifying glass, and began focusing sunlight through it on the outer edge of the branch he sat upon. Soon the concentrated heat caused the bark to smolder. At the smell of smoke his pulse quickened. He put the magnifying glass back in his bag and quickly climbed down.

Glancing furtively back and forth, he crossed the street. The metal trash can that the coyote had upended still lay in the street. He approached the sign in the yard. Whipping out his magnifying glass, he focused its beam on the sign and coaxed a flame into existence. He repeated the act on the sign's other end and soon it was engulfed in fire. Standing in the shade of the tree he admired his handiwork.

Flames consumed the sign, it crashed to the ground, the charred remains continuing to smolder as Nwin continued on up the hill.

He reached the open space at the top of the hill and entered the path that led to his parents' backyard. Breathing hard, his heart was racing, both from the climb and the excitement. He rounded a dense thicket of blackberry bushes and observed someone sitting up the slope, a woman or maybe a girl. He looked at her and saw that she was staring at him intently. He turned back to his path and moved along.

"Hey."

"Huh?" He stopped and squinted up at her, the sun in his eyes as she sat with the sun directly behind her.

"You do that shit all the time?"

'What?"

"Kicking over a garbage can and setting a fire in someone's yard?"

"I don't know what you're talking about." Nwin shot back and started away, pissed, confused and not in the mood for a lecture.

Like a gazelle, the woman sprang up and in three great diagonal leaps had Nwin's arm in a grip of steel.

"Hey, what th'ching?!" He pulled his arm as hard as he could, but couldn't get free from her grasp.

She spun him around to face her. Most unusually, she was taller than Nwin, with long black hair and a thin muscular body. Her face was hard, rather masculine in a way, but with full lips and big cheekbones. Her thick eyebrows were arched over flashing eyes.

"I don't care what you *did*... I just want to know why."

Her grip tightened on his forearm. He thought about kicking her in the knee and making a break for it, but the pain in his arm and the speed with which she had jumped him left him shaken. "Shit, I don't know... for fun I guess... I hate those chingin' Annuals signs... I hate—"

She gave him a tight smile. "Hate, eh? I like hate. There's a hate shortage around here, and yet there's so much to hate, you know?"

He looked at her, bewildered, and said nothing.

"What's your name?"

"Nwin."

"OK, Nwin. I have a proposition for you.

He looked at her expectantly, his heart pounding. She relaxed the hold on his arm.

"I have some friends I'd like you to meet. Can you come? Tonight?"

"Uhh, yeah I guess so. Where?"

"Café Hurricane, on Polk Street, at 10 p.m., around back."

"'Kay. What for?"

"Explanations come later. Let's say we have a project you might be interested in."

He was intrigued now. He looked at her with a conspiratorial smirk.

She grabbed his arm again, digging her fingers into it.

"OW! What're you doin' that for?!?"

Tight-lipped, she glared at him. "This is no chingin' game. If you think it's all fun and games, don't come."

Recoiling, he rubbed his now released arm. "Shit, you didn't have to do that." He looked at her wide-eyed.

"Ten p.m.—don't be late." and she strode down the path through the blackberry bushes.

"Wait! What's your name?" Nwin called after her.

"Nance, like Nancy but lose the 'y'," she shouted over her shoulder. "I'm expecting you. Don't disappoint me."

"I'll be there," he muttered, sounding unconvincing even to himself.

3.

Eric was going to the Tweezer Towers, where a youth hostel promised communal rooms. The Top of the Mark was no place to stay after the first night. The people there were always "on," entertaining visitors and tourists. He wanted a place to relax, a base. He wanted to explore, and maybe, hopefully, make some friends.

He disembarked at the 2nd story lobby, waves lapping against the building. Down through the water he saw what must have once been a plaza at the original front doors. Ruptured sidewalks and exotic underwater foliage were a playground for animals and fish of all sizes and colors. A roar greeted him from across the California canal, where sea lions romped on the cement rubble of a collapsed building rising out of the water. Amid the broken cement, covered in wet moss and seaweed, the huge beasts lay on the drier parts, stretched out and absorbing what little heat was making it through the fog-bound sky. Some were already airing out their virility, like Sumo wrestlers pushing and maneuvering until one fell off the rocks. Eric did a double-take when he realized that the rubble just 40 feet away was itself covered with sculpted walrus heads, tusks and strange molded cement wreathes. Shaking his head at this latest marvel, he went in to the Tweezer Towers.

There had originally been two towers with large antenna at the top. Glass-enclosed walkways joined the top 25 stories, making it one building from the inside, but from a distance it looked like a big set of tweezers. Eric waited for the three people behind the information desk to finish their animated discussion. They were laughing heartily when one of them, a middle-aged woman, finally turned to him. "Yes?"

"I'm looking for the youth hostel."

"Go to 2755, the 'vator is there to your left."

"Thanks."

The elevator was open and when he stepped in it didn't close although a translucent material fell across the entrance. The walls and floor sank slightly as it began to ascend. The elevator seemed to shudder. He leaned back away from the door and found himself surprised at the soft, organic surface of the walls, its wood paneling actually a kind of skin.

It eased to a stop and a young woman covered in paint stood there with a bucket and a bag of brushes. Stepping in, she announced "Thirty-three please." She turned to Eric, placing him as a stranger to the building. "Did you tell it where you're going?"

"Uh, no, I uh..."

"Goin' to the Hostel?"

He nodded.

"Twenty-seven please," she sang out, settin her bucket down carefully in the corner. She looked at Eric for a second. "You know what this is?"

He admitted that he didn't. "Seems like a biodevice. Obviously it's not a regular elevator."

"Good. They're calling it a 'biovator.' Turns voice commands into impulses to drive the pod up and down. The lab jockeys cobbled it together at Mission Bay from the genes of several species. It uses vines as cables. Somehow it connects to the vyne for navigation. I think it's the dew," she said in a confiding tone. "There are some who think it goes too far. Anyway, this thing has only been installed in a few places."

As they passed each floor, the doorless 'vator provided a quick glimpse through translucent film of soaring gardens, intricate staircases and rope ladders, circular landings around great open spaces. Haunting music grew louder as they climbed higher. Finally the biovator eased to a halt at the 27th floor. "Thanks," he said softly, and stepped out.

The building seemed to be tilting, its internal geometry askew. A circular ramp wound down through 15 floors. It was about 25 meters across an open airshaft to the other side of the curving ramp. Light streamed in from all sides through glass panels set at different heights. Not far from where he got off the biovator two women were hanging in mid-air, their thick tangled hair cascading behind them.

Baroque singing echoed through the space, accompanied by the sounds of a strange quartet: a harp, a berimbau, and flute and an oboe. The singers—a dozen people of different ages suspended by twos in odd hanging chairs or hammocks—were singing while they worked on a complicated hanging needlepoint. Diaphonous fabric stretched over a three-sided structure. The singing artists were scattered about it, working on various parts of an elaborate series of embroidered murals. Guidelines held everything in place and they raised and lowered themselves with pulleys.

Eric stared in wonder. He moved slowly around the ramp, following the numbers up from 2700. His heart beat rapidly as a sense of vertigo hit him. At various points doorways appeared on the wall, or set back into small cul-de-sacs. He came to 2755 and knocked.

The door swung open onto the Youth Hostel. Smelling garlic and a tantalizing fish stew, Eric felt ravenous.

"Hi, you looking for a place to stay?" asked the cheerful redhead who opened the door and urged Eric in. "I'm Jack, welcome."

"Thanks, yes, I was hoping you had an available bed for..." and he paused, realizing he didn't have a clear idea of how long he'd be staying, or what he was going to do exactly.

Jack had returned to the front desk and checked the vyne open behind him. "Well, we've got openings the next two weeks, then it's all reserved for two months. So you can stay until July 25th, okay?"

"That's fine, great, thanks," said Eric earnestly. He signed the register and Jack led him back into the hallway, up the winding staircase to Room 2920. "Okay, there are about 13 people here now, and ten bunkbeds, so find yourself an empty bed and make yourself at home. There's space in one of the closets, and you can take any available drawer in the dressers."

"Thank you," said Eric, relieved. He walked to the huge windows and stared at the mid-morning light falling on the buildings and water. Far below, dozens of small watercraft plied the canals between buildings. To the west fog billowed, obscuring visibility. He stood with his hands on hips, zoning out, and didn't notice Jack was still there, and had joined him at the window.

"Quite a view, eh?"

"Yeah."

"Where're you from?"

"I was living in Chicago, and before that Connecticut."

"And what brings you out here?"

"I'm still trying to figure that out," he said, embarrassed, looking at Jack, who returned a friendly gaze, warm and steady.

Jack laughed which made Eric blush. Sagging, he turned back to the window.

"Oh, don't worry man. Everyone comes here looking for something. You'd be amazed at how often they don't know what it is… Hey listen, I've got to get back downstairs to the desk. If you want, there's a fierce *marisco* being served for lunch. Hungry?"

Eric relaxed a bit and smiled gratefully. "Hell yes I am. What time is it?"

Jack checked the wall clock, which read 10:40. "It's about noon, but you can come as early as 11:30. It's worth the wait. Paulo is amazing, we're lucky to have him."

"I'll be there."

"See you," Jack said on his way out. Before he closed the door he called back, "Don't hesitate to ask if you need any help with anything. But of course you can find most everything on the Vyne in your room."

"Okay."

Eric dumped his rucksack on an empty bed near the floor-to-ceiling windows. He stuffed his folded clothes into a drawer, hung up his jacket and shirts, and found a hook for his rucksack, then flopped on his bed to gaze at the view.

He propped himself up on his elbow, fascinated by the gondolas below. Bay waters shimmered amidst the buildings where streets once ran, swamping hundreds of buildings. But that had happened long ago, and San Francisco had learned to insulate the underwater floors and establish entryways higher up, what with nearly a century of rising waters. Transportation had evolved with the climate. A lot of the technology for adapting flooded urban areas had developed right here in the Bay Area.

He closed his eyes and felt a self-loathing as familiar as an old shoe.

Just then a small horde burst in, as though a bus had dropped them at the door.

"I love it there. Have you checked it out?"

"I heard about it, but I haven't been yet."

"—free classes."

"—a cool plaza with all these great—"

"—tomorrow!"

They didn't notice Eric on his bunk as they continued to blurt out their enthusiasms and discoveries. Eric listened disconsolately. He didn't think to introduce himself. Instead, he lay there listening, making guesses about them, pigeon-holing each, lost in his thoughts and assumptions.

An "oh hi" broke the spell, as one of them observed him, a short, stocky woman with brown hair and a cherub's face, in a beautiful embroidered skirt and vest.

Forthrightly, she strode over, extending her right hand. "My name's Victoria. What's yours?"

Eric struggled to sit up, and limply extended his hand. As he tapped hands, he muttered his name.

"Glad to meet you, Eric," she announced to the room. The rest called out their names while waving to him, but Eric immediately lost track. He sheepishly waved back, and then flopped back onto his bed. The others resumed their chatter, changing clothes, brushing teeth and combing hair.

Soon they were headed out to the dining hall. Eric put his shoes on and walked over to the now empty sinks, combed his hair and straightened his shirt. *Ugh*, was all he could think looking at himself. He returned to his bed and sleep suddenly seemed very inviting. He pinched himself behind his ear, a quirk he'd picked up to force himself out into the world at moments like these.

Two floors below, the Dining Hall was jammed, and Eric shrank before the bustle of full tables. Sighing, he made his way to the buffet, where he served himself a heaping mound of rice, then on top of that the *marisco*, local bay seafood floating profusely throughout. Eric let the burnt orange color and strong smell of garlic and spices hypnotize him, as he awkwardly sought out a place to sit. He scanned the room until he noticed a seat by the window in the far corner.

"This one taken?" he asked as he drew near.

"Nope," replied a sullen older man.

"D'ya mind?" asked Eric.

The man, white-bearded and wrinkled, his face red against the white hair, looked up at Eric like he was wasting the last moments of his life. He pointed at the seat and said nothing, though he shook his head.

The old guy's taciturn demeanor kept Eric from conversation. Two people across from them were silently eating also, apparently unacquainted with each other. Eric dug in.

He hadn't taken three bites before someone called the room to attention. It was Paulo, the cook.

"Oh, eskoose me. I have happy to see all eating strong. Please, can some body say 'thanks to food'?"

A woman across the room rose. "Thank you Paulo for your great cooking. Thank you to each of the animal lives we are eating tonight. Thank you to the friends who spent time growing, harvesting, delivering and preparing our food. Thanks to Earth for keeping us all going."

"Amen," came a choral response.

Eric muttered disapprovingly and resumed eating. The old man looked sidelong at him, noting his undisguised negativity over the common Food Prayer.

They continued to eat in silence.

Scraping his plate and finishing off the last few mouthfuls, the old man cleared his throat. "Uhh, umm, you new in town?" he gruffly addressed Eric.

Eric had just taken a mouthful, so he nodded.

"Don't like prayers, eh?"

Eric shook his head, choking a little at the question.

The man lowered his voice. "Listen, there's not many of us 'round here. If you want," and he slipped a card to Eric, "here's a place that you might enjoy Trying Out."

With that, he got up, took his dishes and said goodbye.

Eric looked at the card: Public Investigators Office, 15 Civic Center Plaza. On the back it read: Katherine Fairly, Chief, and under that, Ron O'Hair, Assistant Chief.

He put the card in his pocket, and continued eating.

4.

Nwin hit the stairs running.

His father was out back, probably mom, too. He ran up to his room and paced around it, a caged lion. Eventually he sat down on the stuffed chair that he'd spent untold hours in growing up. He put his feet on the windowsill and clutched the chair's arms, mentally racing over the last few minutes.

His heart pounded in his ears, the sense of danger casting a reddish hue over his vision. "Nance," he whispered and unconsciously began rubbing his arm where she'd held him with what seemed like vice grips.

"Hi sweetie! I thought you came in." His thoughts were interrupted by his mom at the door.

"Hi," Nwin greeted her without emotion.

Smiling, she came over and touched his head lightly, then squeezed his shoulder. "What have you done to your hair? Did you shave off your eyebrows?!?" she asked with motherly concern.

"I thought I'd try blonde for a while, and my eyebrows are so black, it looked weird. Hey—it's *my* hair!" He tried to laugh but was irritated, brushing off the questions.

"You hungry? I've got soup on the stove…" she offered hopefully.

He looked at her but shook his head. "Nope," and turned to the window.

"I'm going to Treasure Island later this week. Do you want anything?"

He whipped back to her, suddenly interested. "There's a Peruvian hat they're supposed to have now—it's the dew—can you get me one?"

"I'll try," she promised. "I'm out in the garden with Dad. You should come and say hi to him before you leave."

"Mm-hmm," mumbled Nwin, too preoccupied to respond.

His mother went back downstairs. Nwin got up and turned on the radio, found one of his favorite dance tunes, and began gyrating with the beat. He spun around the room, arms flailing, smacking into furniture and walls.

After two fast tunes he flopped back into his chair. Catching his breath, he got up and crossed the room, opened the closet door and took a folder from a box. He spread the contents on his desk; diagrams, charts, notes and press clippings. Pawing at the papers he couldn't find what he wanted. His jaw tightened and he unconsciously clenched his teeth. Rapidly he flipped over sheet after sheet, hoping to find the papers he was sure he'd left here.

Damn! Where the ching did I leave that?!?

He didn't have any stuff at his apartment. He kept few things in his locker at the farm. Dismayed, he shoved the papers back into the folder, and returned the box to the closet. He covered the box with old clothes, carefully shut the door, and looked out the window. Below, his dad was hunched over his vegetable garden. Nwin felt a slight dread as he tried to invent a reason to walk out without stopping to say hello.

He kicked the desk as he turned to leave his room. He struck himself square in the forehead with his fist several times, trying to loosen a memory, jog a circuit. *Where is it?*

At the foot of the stairs he hesitated, finally turning and walking into the backyard. "Hey, dad."

Jeffrey Roberston turned from his knees at his son's voice and saw a blonde man, and was disoriented briefly before he realized it was Nwin.

"Hi there. Hey c'mere and give me a hand," he proposed, knowing Nwin would have an excuse to not help.

"I've gotta go. Just wanted to say 'hello', okay?"

"What's your hurry? Can't take a minute to help your old man?"

Nwin's muscles tensed. *Can't he ever just say 'hi' and 'goodbye'?*

"Dad, really, I'm already late for my afternoon shift. Maybe next time, ok?"

Jeffrey muttered to himself, "—*much* more interesting work than *that!*" but Nwin was already out the door and heading down the hill. Jeffrey turned back to his garden and resumed his weeding, his shoulders sagging deeper. He was freshly disappointed every time Nwin confirmed that he was still working at the farm.

Nwin let the hill pull him downwards, spitting on the ground. "Shit!" He shoved his clenched fists into his pockets, his jacket wedged between his arm and his stomach. Immediately forgetting his father and the familiar tension between them, his thoughts turned to the missing diagram.

He came to the bottom of the hill, where Precita Creek rushed by, and started over the polished wooden Harrison Street Bridge, one of several serving pedestrian traffic between Bernal and the Mission District. It curved dramatically up and over, loosely patterned after traditional Japanese bridges. Nwin stopped in mid-span and leaned over the railing, looking down at the rushing water. Along the banks grew dense willows, small pools eddied alongside the main stream. Fish flitted about in the creek. Old-timers and kids were fishing from the bridge, boisterously teasing one another and telling jokes. He had once been one of those kids, but he didn't like to fish. He preferred to watch the river rush by, tossing in an occasional stick to catch the current. Now he stood over the water, not seeing anything, lost in thought.

Who the hell was that 'Nance' woman anyway? "There's not enough hate around here, and yet there's so much to hate…" The words echoed in his head.

He hated his father. He hated San Francisco. He hated lots of things. The things he liked? He didn't think about it. He liked sitting and looking at the river, watching the fox in its den near his flower beds at work, sleeping in the grass under a hot sun. But he never *thought* about liking these things, he just did.

He looked at the fishermen and scowled. They were doubled over laughing, and Nwin knew it was some dumb joke or prank. One kid was poking at something in his bucket, probably they'd dumped in a crawfish or something like that.

He walked across the bridge and when he passed one of the buckets, he gave it a vicious kick, bouncing it against the railing, spilling the water and one forlorn fish, which flopped helplessly on the polished planks of the bridge.

"Hey, what the hell you doin'?" yelled the bucket's owner, striding towards Nwin.

Nwin glared at him and walked briskly off the bridge and on his way. The man turned to retrieve his fish, shaking his head and looking after Nwin angrily.

5.

O f course you can take a vacation!! We WANT you to take a vacation!" shouted a tall man with a splotchy beard and glasses, standing up to speak to the mass at the northeastern corner of Washington Square Park. Eric sat nearby watching.

"Fine! But who is going to keep track of this stuff? Who will plan ahead and make sure we don't run out of basic supplies? It's fine for you to tell me to leave, but I don't see anyone stepping up and taking responsibility. How are you going to do it if I'm not here?" A woman who didn't look as old as she sounded sat down violently and folded her arms, an enraged sneer on her face.

An older woman, back bent after years of arthritic pain, rose from her seat. The audience, which had been buzzing like a swarm of bees, suddenly quieted. The woman raised her arm from her shawl, and pointed up to the hill above them. "You know I've been here a long time."

"Yeah!" shouted someone in the front rows. Eric observed that most of the people in the meeting were looking expectantly toward the speaker, who was ancient compared to everyone else.

"I've seen a lot of people come and go during the past 53 years. There have been crises and lots of times when things just seemed to take care of themselves." She paused to breathe deeply and gather her strength to project her voice. "I want you all to stop for a moment. Tempers are up and you're all taking yourselves WAY too seriously."

Applause skittered across the lawn from various spots.

"Now Susan, you need a vacation. Trust the garden! You can go and we can take care of it. You aren't the only one who worries about continuity, even if you sometimes think you are. I know a lot, even if I'm not always available to help anymore, and there are others perfectly capable of filling your shoes. And yes, your shoes are VERY LARGE! We love you and we want you back. But take a deep breath and remember: no one is indispensable. If the work here is important—and it is—people will do it. It's that simple."

More applause and cheering for Jane Johnson, the "conscience" of Telegraph Hill according to many.

Susan rose again, and said, "OK, look, I'll go. Hell, I want to go too!"

"HAH!" someone yelled from the back, and many laughed.

Susan glared towards the laughter, but put up her hands until everyone was listening again.

"I'll be here another week before I can arrange my life enough to go. Let's organize the hand-off so there's no gap when I go. I'll be gone for at least six months, maybe longer, so you'll have your hands full, believe me!"

Eric got up and strolled across the park. A painting crew lay sprawled under a tree, a picnic spread out on a tarp. The painters weren't talking much, two dozed while two played chess, and the final two quietly stared at the trees. A corner lot was full of bikes, and a small shack next to it bustled with activity. Eric headed over, thinking maybe a bicycle ride would be just the ticket for the next couple of hours.

At the perimeter of the bike lot he found himself behind two people turning in their bikes to the mechanic in the shack under a sign identifying it as "Washington Square Velome." He waited patiently, admiring the passing streetcars, and tapping his foot to the contagious dance music pouring out of a bar across the street.

Soon enough came his turn. "What can I do for you?" asked the grizzled mechanic, an old guy with missing teeth and dirty tangled hair barely hidden under a cap.

"Do you have loaners?" asked Eric.

"O'course we do. Take your pick," he said, pointing to the fleet parked in the corner. He turned back to his work bench.

Eric selected a beautiful silver machine with red trim, called a Silver Fox. He started to wheel it out and then turned back, calling to the mechanic. "Hey do I need to bring this back here, or—"

"Nah, man, drop it off anywhere, there're velomes all over the place."

"Great, thanks!" Off he went.

He cycled a block up Columbus and became immersed in a multitude. Café tables cluttered the sides of the avenue leaving little room to proceed, so he dismounted and began to walk. Elegant couples arm in arm promenaded along the center of the street, while people scurried about on all sides. Intense aromas assaulted his nose—roasting meats, perfumed flowers, tantalizing sauces, fermenting hops, and the natural smells of humans and animals that were somehow more pronounced than he normally noticed. Children ran among adult legs, chasing each other, yelping with delight as they caught their prey.

Eric stopped short as a man pushing a hand truck loaded with bundled magazines appeared in his path. Jugglers hurled bowling pins back and forth to his right, while down the street to the left he could see an outdoor dance underway, couples in costumes from ballgowns to the latest fashion, knit leaf smocks. These garments were in hot demand. Invented by San Francisco designers in the past year, they had been embraced enthusiastically not just here, but across the world. Leaf smocks were thrown over the head like a poncho, consisting of intricately woven leaves designed for durability, resilience and water resistance Once the seed formula was published, variations had begun appearing. On the dance floor in front of him, Eric could see a half dozen types of the leaves, beautiful greenish blends next to chaotic arrangements of yellows, reds and oranges.

Seeing his opening, he pushed off to his right up Vallejo, a cool curving path lined with small trees and bushes. Laundry lines crisscrossed from one side to the other, attached to the upper floors of the building. Hanging from the lines were drying clothes and colored banners, including one of a great tree reading simply "Gardens Grow . . . Grow Gardens!"

Eric rode slowly up the path, skirting small children building castles out of mudpies in front of a very elegantly painted 3-story Victorian. At Stockton he bumped quickly over the streetcar tracks to the veloway heading south towards the hill in the distance. Now he was in a distinctly Chinese neighborhood. Vegetable and fruit bins lined the sidewalks, while a dense mass of people maneuvered along. The smells changed too, though he couldn't identify any of the strange new odors. He noticed clusters of bikes and pedestrians waiting at a side street as he crossed, and after another block he came upon a pack of already stopped cyclists, as they waited for a cable car to cross in front of them, joined by several dozen cyclists and pedestrians. The vehicular traffic included more and more freight bikes of all sizes and shapes, some with big closed containers in front between two wheels, others towing substantial trailers laden with fabrics, boxes of produce, and in one case, stacked with a number of bicycle frames.

He inched forward to get a view up and down the cross street. On his right the street seemed to climb almost vertically. A cable car slowly ascended, as a few bicyclists held on to the sides, getting a free ride up the hill. Other cyclists soared down the incline, flowing locks of hair streaming behind them. Eric self-consciously ran his hand over his short brown hair.

On he went, past a long stretch of sentinel-like palm trees. Nearing the top of the hill he came to a crumbled cement ruin with a sign on it: "Former Stockton Tunnel:

Destroyed in Quake of 2044." Vines and ivy grew densely over most of it and the near-by building ruins too. He proceeded up the hill. After a short curve the paving gave way to a hardened gravel surface, passing through more gardens. The sweet smell of the orange and lemon tree grove lightened the climb, and he waved to some friendly young women who were pruning trees and singing.

Near the top he noticed a cluster of small shops around a courtyard filled with tables. Busy movement in the courtyard sparked his curiosity, so he pulled off the road to take a break and investigate. He parked his bike with some others, and went in to the adjacent café.

"Hi, what can I get you?" offered an eager young man, looking up from a book.

"Oh, an iced tea, please."

The fellow glided to the cooler and poured a tall glass from a pitcher, an unusual, fluted glass. In the wide top Eric found his tea graced with several slices of fresh orange and lemon.

"Sure you wouldn't like to try one of these?" offered the proprietor, holding out a dish of small puff pastries and candied lemon slices.

Already halfway out the door, Eric turned back politely, and took a puff pastry, not wanting to be rude. When he had settled into a corner chair in the courtyard, he took a long quaff of his drink, then a nibble of the pastry. It was surprisingly light, with a delicate lemon cream in the middle. *Mmmm!* The iced tea, too, was good.

At the next table sat several ink-stained, aproned workers, going over a large volume. "Here, look at this," said a woman with her gray hair drawn back in a long ponytail. "We can't have this kind of sloppy trimming going on, look what it does to the binding."

"Yeah, I noticed that the cutting yesterday was really bad. We can't keep having anyone come traipsing in thinking they can help. I've said this before, but don't you think we could do our whole operation between us and the apprentices?" The speaker, his back to Eric, was a heavyset guy with a head of very thick jet black hair. When he looked to his left Eric noticed a dense beard to match. The unflattering view from Eric's seat revealed the man's spreading lower back spilling from his t-shirt and jeans. *How come guys like that don't notice the air on their butts?* He himself was so self-conscious that he couldn't imagine being that oblivious.

"Where are we going to get apprentices, Henry, if we don't give people a chance to try out? I think we should stop giving Annuals workers anything that requires real training. And let's face it, even running that trimmer takes some skill," argued the third person at the table, a gaunt man whose deepset eyes and etched cheekbones reinforced the intensity of his speech.

"You guys!" sighed the woman. "We've had this conversation a million chingin' times!"

"Marta—" but Henry was cut off by Mr. Cheekbone, who put his hands up and rose from the table. "Hey, you're right, and I really don't want to do this again. Let's put it on the agenda at the staff meeting, ok? But you know it'll come down to what we want to do, since we are the lifers here." He glanced over as he finished, and noticed Eric was paying attention to their conversation.

"Pretty interesting huh?" he said self-deprecatingly.

"Oh sorry, didn't mean to eavesdrop," protested Eric, blushing deeply.

Henry turned around and grinned, reaching over and slapping his thigh.
"Don't sweat it kid. We do this all the time. No state secrets here, that's for sure!"
"Are you guys publishers?" asked Eric.
"Yeah," said Marta. "Here, have a look, this is what we're working on right now."
She gestured to the prototype on the table, inviting Eric over.

He rose and joined her as Henry and Mr. Cheekbone turned to leave. Marta introduced her mates: "This is our talented founder, Henry Chadsworth, and his loyal if argumentative associate, Bernie Wadsworth. I'm Marta Rivera, the third, but necessary, wheel on this wobbly enterprise," she smiled and extended her hand.

Eric still felt sheepish about being caught overhearing them, but he took his cue, and slapped hands with Marta, "I'm Eric Johanson, just got here yesterday from Chicago. Nice to meet you."

After a quick look over their beautiful volume, with its elegant full color plates of artwork interspersed with poetry and stories, he accepted an invitation to see their workshop. They crossed the courtyard and entered under the sign of "Worth While Books."

On one side Eric saw Bernie hunched over a sprawling countertop, engraving in a big wooden block. An old letterpress dominated the floor, surrounded by old wooden desks and chairs, a huge dictionary on a pedestal, and several rolltop desks along the back wall. Henry had donned a green visor and sat at one of the desks examining a manuscript. The smell of ink, metal, and wood almost triggered genetic memories in Eric; he knew his ancestors had been newspaper workers. Family diaries described workshops that this place seemed to replicate down to the blotter pads and metal type drawers.

He looked around, awed by the ancient equipment and aura of deep craftsmanship. "This is gorgeous!" he exclaimed.

"You like it?" Marta smiled. "Truthfully, I didn't invite you here without a small hope. . . Recruiting new people to keep this kind of place going is one of our more difficult responsibilities."

"Well," Eric balked, "I don't think I'm ready to make any commitments. But thanks, I mean..."

Marta looked slightly crestfallen, but rallied and said, "Oh of course, no problem. Remember us when you're ready, ok?" And with that she turned to her work. "Have a look around," she gestured.

"Thanks, I'd like to." Marta pointed to the back corner, where an open door led to another room.

Eric admired shelves full of musty books, dozens of unfamiliar tools and machines. He entered a clean white room where two women in smocks sat incongruously at decades-old computers. Large plotters and printers dominated the back of this room, and a huge central work table was covered with stacks of papers. A bored young woman slowly ambled around the table, gathering one sheet at a time from the stacks, making up a new stack with the collated pages on a separate table. She nodded to Eric as he appeared at the doorway.

The two women at the computers were both intently staring into their monitors and didn't notice Eric. He took a quick look around and left, retracing his steps through the old workshop, thanking his new acquaintances for their time and hospitality. Once out into the courtyard again, he noticed that all the shops surrounding it were publishers or booksellers.

It was getting to be almost 5. As he mounted his bicycle, a number of people streamed out of the various workshops, some flopping into seats at the café tables, others heading towards their bicycles, or walking out into the evening light. "End of the day," he thought.

On two wheels again, he proceeded a half block and came to California, much to his surprise. Looking down to his left the Bay surged a few blocks downhill behind the California Depot. And a short ways out into the water rose the Tweezer. He coasted downhill through the cooling evening air, braking all the way, terrified that he might lose control and end up smacking into the Depot. But he made it without incident, dropped his bike at the Depot velome, and boarded a taxi leaving with a dozen passengers in the general direction of the hostel.

6.

The shovel and rake clattered to a halt where Nwin tossed them into the corner. He took off his work apron and hung it inside his locker door along with his work belt, and walked over to the sink to wash up.

Angelo, Tina and Beth came through the barn door, laughing boisterously. Angus followed a minute later, his face set in a permanent scowl.

Tina couldn't stop howling, and Beth was playfully punching Angelo. "I can't believe you! I'm gonna get you for that... You know I will!"

Nwin gazed in the mirror as he stood over the sink, observing his workmates impassively. Angus was putting his tools away, carefully washing the trowels, clippers and small shears. He noticed Nwin in the mirror and nodded his way. Nwin nodded back and looked down to finish washing his hands.

He stood at his locker again when Angus walked by and asked, "Did you check out the south pond today?"

"Nah. I was working on the roses along the causeway." He gestured to the bucket he'd left on the table, full of long-stem beauties destined for the table at the Crossroads.

Angus examined the roses, grunted something noncommittal and headed to the sink. "I found trampled plantings in the west pond ... pisses me off!" He splashed water in his face. "You haven't seen anyone playing around on the edges have you?" he asked accusingly.

Nwin knew what was coming. "No, man, I haven't seen a thing," he shrugged, closed his locker and started for the door.

Tina and Beth saw it too. "Hey Angus, come over and smoke a bowl with us, would'ja?" But Angus was sure Nwin knew who had been damaging their work over the past few weeks. To Angus, all teenagers were in a vast conspiracy to mess things up, and when inexplicable damage appeared, he always knew who to blame.

"Nwin, you tell your friends to stop. If I catch them they'll regret it!"

Nwin had already protested Angus' accusations several times these past weeks. "You're an asshole!" he declared and on that note, Nwin departed the workroom into the golden light of early evening, the fog just starting to rush over the hilltops to the west.

He got on his bike and started pedaling along the winding veloway into the Mission District. *Shit! I forgot to take those flowers to the table... Oh well, Angus will do it. Gives him another excuse to be mad at me.* Frustrated he pedaled harder. The wind off the fog was bracing, he felt refreshed. The Willows loomed on his left, the lawn full of seated people listening to live jazz in the ornate gazebo. The smell of roast chicken rose out of the public kitchen, and a small line of folks waited to join the party and snag a plate of one of the city's best *pollo asados*. Suddenly hungry, Nwin pulled off the veloway and crossed Mission Creek on the rustic little bridge. He dropped his bike among a few dozen others in a small parking area and headed for the chicken.

"Hi Nwin!" waved a couple he knew, Hank and Susan, lounging with a group halfway across the lawn. He spotted a few other familiar faces. Not feeling social, he waved back and considered a hasty departure. But hunger was now raging under the prompting of his nostrils, so he decided stay and eat. The audience erupted into applause and whoops as the ensemble broke into a classic.

Nwin waited for the cooks to load his plate up with salad and chicken. "Hi friend! Light or dark?" called out a jovial bearded fellow in an apron and chef's hat.

"Give me that juicy breast there!" pointed Nwin.

"Enjoy!" exhorted the cook, dropping the choice piece on Nwin's plate. A table to the side was covered with flyers about the chicken farm providing the meal, and the restaurants and kitchens around town that they supplied. There were photos of the farm, smiling chickens amidst pyramids of eggs in a bucolic Sunset farm, backlit by a pink and orange sky.

"Hey man, what's the latest?" asked Hank as Nwin sat down.

"Oh, not much . . . spent the afternoon weeding and trimming rose bushes. Then I got some shit from this old lifer at work 'cause someone's been trampling his rice plantings. He knows all! Or so he thinks... Problems are caused by young people and since I'm young . . . well . . ." Nwin took a big bite of chicken.

"My grandmother is like that!" exclaimed Susan. "Always blaming youth for everything, like when anything breaks, or it takes a while to fix or replace. I guess they need a scapegoat."

"It's a ruin. I'm not going to hang around much longer if he keeps jumping on me," said Nwin. "Too bad, too, it's a pretty good scene. I've already put in six months and . . . my roses. I'll miss them, along with the fox who moved in some months ago. You should come and see her with her babies."

"Where's the fox?" asked Hank.

Gulping his chicken and washing it down with a big swallow of water, Nwin continued. "She's got a lair under the big buckeye near where the Causeway runs into Potrero Hill. She had them a month ago—the three little ones have started exploring now."

"Dew! I'm going to come over soon to have a look. It's not too far from my house," said Hank.

The music stopped again. Applause. Nwin finished his salad as the band started up with another crowd favorite. He leaned back and burped. Dusk fell. Warm lights lit the gazebo and around the edge of the green. Little storm lights and candles began to glow creating a cozy effect, small orange flames dancing all around the audience of about 150 people. The band was good, but soon Nwin had had enough. Plus it was getting cold and windy as dusk extracted the last force from the encroaching fog.

Rising to his feet, he tapped hands with Hank and Susan and said goodbye. On his bike he recrossed the bridge to the veloway where a blur of cyclists passed in either direction. He waited for an opening and joined the flow, heading west.

A few minutes later he turned from the creekside veloway onto Dolores Street. A dense lemon orchard stretched along one side of the street in front of the houses, stately old palms lining the center. On the other side a narrow veloway twisted and turned through beautiful impatiens bushes. Uphill, beyond a multicolored sidewalk packed with mosaic tiles lay Dolores Park. He was about to turn into the park when exuberant cheers and raucous brass instruments echoed from 19th Street—an impromptu parade of fire-eaters, stiltwalkers, people strewing flowers from baskets, a small chorus of singers almost inaudible behind two trombones, four trumpets, a tuba, and a half dozen French horns. The singers had their arms over each other's shoulders, and practically everyone in the zany parade was weaving back and forth, lost in the moment..

This was not unusual. Some days you couldn't cross the city without running into two or three parades. He saw a familiar face or two in the swarm, but no one he was close to, so he turned uphill and walked his bike to the park's café. The parade followed him and after fifteen boisterous minutes of clapping and dancing it disbanded. The café soon filled with post-march euphoria.

Nwin settled into a corner sheltered from the wind to nurse a dark espresso and gaze out at the fading deep purple in the distant sky. A large poster torn loose on the side of the café's wall flapped in the wind. 'Who is the Monarch of Cappuccino?' shout-ed the big headline on the poster, advertising an upcoming competition for San Francisco's best barista.

Two young men appeared next to him. "Hey Nwin, what's twirlin'?"

Nwin vaguely recognized one of them from somewhere. "Uuhh, hi," he said non-committally.

"Hey, don't you remember me? We were in that bike repair class together at the Precita Levee, remember? Serge. And this is Tran," he said, introducing the shorter guy. He had straight black hair and blue eyes, tawny skin, flat eyelids.

"So, you in a bike club?" asked Serge. He wore the jersey of the Billy Goat Hill Club, Kelly green, a white goat inelegantly straddling a large tricycle hurtling down an anonymous hill.

"No, man, I never did join. I'm a gardener these days."

Tran looked away and put his hands on his hips. He exhaled rather loudly, and Serge was embarrassed.

"Oh… Hey, well, we gotta go, it was good to see you. See ya!" Off they went.

The political fight between the Garden Party and the Transit First-ers left Nwin cold. He had heard arguments from each faction, but never found himself swayed either way. He liked his gardening job, and thought of his bicycle as practical. He wasn't both-ered by the normal traffic flows, nor did he think open space and gardens were in short supply. As far as he was concerned things seemed just about right—which earned him the scorn of militants on all sides. He really didn't care. He had his own ideas.

His incipient irritation was quickly forgotten when he observed Valentina and a friend enter the courtyard of the café. Valentina had worked the Rice Bowl for a few days, then left. During those few days Nwin developed quite a crush on her, and when she stopped coming, he had wondered how to find her. Here she was.

With a drink in hand she took a seat on the other side of the café. She was laughing, showing all her teeth, sending a lightning bolt into Nwin's heart. He gazed across at her long legs, lush and wavy chestnut hair. She wore a small, black satiny jacket and snug jeans that accentuated her legs. Next to her sat a round cheerful girl in red overalls and a yellow shirt, her long black braids decorated with feathers and bits of colored fabric.

He knew he had to go over there, talk to her, find out where she lived. But he couldn't move. Looking down into his coffee, he thought about leaving quickly.

Still he sat there. Furtively he looked towards the girls absorbed in conversation but Valentina never looked his way. If she did, what would he do? He grabbed an abandoned newspaper from a nearby table and buried himself in it. Reading without absorbing anything, he eventually put the paper down. Valentina and her friend were disappearing through the bushes as his eyes found them.

"Chingado!" He threw the paper back on the next table, folded his arms and stared at nothing in particular. His heart was beating too fast, but fear defeated desire and he did not get up.

He felt stupid. *Why didn't I go and say hello?*

He had been riding around for a while, hoping to cross paths with her again. It was completely dark now, so he stopped to don his reflective vest and turn on his bike lights. His own get-up was rather modest next to some of the wildly-lit bikes around the city. He only used bright purple flashers in the rear and a small headlamp up front. But others lit up the veloways with screaming neon tubing, light shows crisscrossing their handlebars and frames. One guy had created a small projectile system from which his bike hurled little sparkler clusters. As as he pedaled, they would float up sparkling, then douse themselves before reaching the ground.

Nwin barely noticed as he rode along aimlessly. He skirted Market Pond and made his way up to the Wiggle. Passing through a green arching gate he rolled along next to a long aging wall that had seen better days. On the other side of the wall used to be some kind of warehouse or big store. Now it was a grassy knoll sloping down to Market Pond.

On the crumbling 110-meter long wall was an old mural from the late 20th century. A clever mural within the mural showed the city, starting from a pre-deluge downtown full of cars and bikes and heading past itself to show Hayes River turning into a path to the west to the beach where a huge snake became a bicycle tire track. The mural was considered a civic treasure from the time before and a lot of trouble had been taken to save it after successive quakes and major storms.

At the end of the wall he went over the rushing creek and the high-arching Sans Souci Bridge, steering clear of oncoming cyclists. The veloway followed the winding course of the Hayes River, willow and laurel trees studding the banks, along with impatiens and lupine bushes. Many spots along the creek were open to the surrounding homes, mostly old Victorians that had elegantly stood along this waterway since it had been buried in cement culverts long ago. The lush gardens that filled the small valley gave off a wild variety of sweet and organic smells in the moonlight.

He had another hour before he was supposed to be at Polk Street. At the busy intersection of Haight and Rexroth streets, veloways crossed. He pulled over and dropped his wheels in the velome next to the Real Authentic Organic Ice Cream Parlor. A young woman inside the shack paid him no mind, and he barely glanced at her.

He joined a short line at the ice cream parlor, wrinkling his nose at the strange combination of sweetness and sweat that permeated the place. "What can I getcha?" asked a cheerful gray-haired woman when his turn came. "Let me have a scoop of Old Gym Socks," he smirked.

She smiled worriedly. "Still that bad, huh? We've been trying to get rid of that smell, but with all the cyclists stopping by, it keeps coming back. Sorry!"

"Yeah, it smells pretty weird. Hey, but I'll have a scoop of strawberry."

The woman handed him his cone as she called over her shoulder, "Frank, will you turn the fan up to high, please?"

Nwin went back out into the night air, only to be blasted by the exhaust from the shop, a concentrated dose of the same sweaty sweetness. He quickly walked down the street to a bench along the creek. He felt cold as he ate his ice cream, between the chill from the creek and the fog swirling overhead. He couldn't finish, and tossed the leftovers into the bushes.

"That's disgusting!" scolded an old man ambulating along with a cane.

Nwin just kept walking, ignoring the man's demand that he retrieve his cone from the bush. On the next block he came to the Laughing Horse Bar and ducked in. Boisterous chatter charged the smoke-filled bar. Nwin didn't see anyone familiar so he quickly backed out. Across the creek a noodle bar looked inviting. He stood at the edge of the creek and tried to find a way to hop across, but the creek was running strong and he'd gotten wet from this kind of maneuver in creeks all over town. Cold as he was, laziness lost out.

Downstream, he crossed a footbridge and doubled back to the Noodle Bar. Inside it was dark and empty, but smelled good. He threw his jacket over a seat far from the door. A woman emerged from the kitchen and approached him. When Nwin finally looked at her he did a doubletake as she looked an awful lot like his mom.

"What can I get you honey?" she said, cracking gum with her hand on hip, swinging a hand towel. Nwin grinned up at her, feeling immediately at home. "Noodles with mushrooms," he suggested. "Got it." She spun back to the kitchen and moments later returned with a steaming bowl of noodles in a rich broth, scallions and shitakes bubbling in the soup.

"Thanks, smells great!" gushed Nwin. "Hey, what's this place called?"

"Niggle Woodles," she offered, and seeing his confusion, continued with a hint of resignation, "you know, Wiggle Noodles—my kid reversed it."

"Aaah, I get it," Nwin smiled, and turned to slurping up his delicious soup. "Dew!" he called to her as she was disappearing back into the kitchen.

"I'm glad honey, there's plenty more if you want it."

Three people came in and sat down across the way, chortling over some private joke. Nwin returned their familiar nod though he'd never seen them before. He slurped enthusiastically over his soup.

Looking at the big wall menu, one of them, a woman, brayed loudly, "Well, it sure sounds like good soup!" and her companions joined her in good-natured laughter. Nwin scowled. *Idiots!* Didn't they understand the culture of noodle appreciation? But he kept to himself and finished his bowl. Warmth restored, he soon bolted back into the night, carefully leaving his dishes in the bin and thanking the proprietress again, marveling anew at her resemblance to his mother.

Jasmine vines perfumed the air outside. Buzzing with the hearty fullness of home-made noodle soup, Nwin breathed deeply, shoved his hands into his pockets and strode up the path towards the footbridge. It was time to head to the Café Hurricane and find out what this strange, scary woman was all about. He rubbed his arm unconsciously where she'd held him in a vise grip.

He retrieved his bike and started northward on Rexroth, past Alamo Square, plunging down into the Western Addition. At Golden Gate he cut in to the Armstrong Diagonal, through the arched gates and up the ramp that took cyclists above all the houses, gardens, creeks and streets. Its well-worn wooden planks rattled and groaned as he raced along, rooftop to rooftop in a long straight line towards Cathedral Hill. Treetops and roof gardens gave the sense of travelling through a forest, but this was a rapid transit veloway for getting crosstown in a hurry. Nwin pedaled furiously, occasionally swinging out and around meandering cyclists. The Diagonal wasn't heavily traveled at night since most people stayed in their neighborhoods. Also there weren't many entrances or exits to the throughway.

Rising up to meet Cathedral Hill, the Diagonal ended at the east end of Japantown. A three story spiral ramp took him down to street level. Nwin's bike began to wobble in that telltale fashion. *Shit! Not another flat! That's the third one in two weeks!* His tire hissed as he dismounted and he pulled a huge nail from the sidewall. "Chingin' road crews," he cursed aloud, assuming some maintenance crew had thoughtlessly lost the nail on the Diagonal. He looked around and found a velome only a short distance uphill. Pushing his bike in the door, he approached the counter in a rush. Two guys rose, laying down their smoking pipe.

Exhaling a big cloud of pot smoke, a tall black guy came over grinning, took Nwin's bike, reassuringly. "A flaht? No worries, mahn." The skilled mechanic threw his bike on the rack and his tire was off within a few seconds. Before he knew it, the guy was pumping up his repaired tire, and he was on his way. "Here, take this," Nwin said, and put a nice green bud on the counter as he turned to go. "Oh, yas, verrry nice mahn, tankya," said the mechanic warmly as he returned to his perch and his smoking companion.

Slightly stoned from inhaling the dense air in the velome, Nwin made his way over the hill and rolled down towards Van Ness. Yet another parade was passing through, horns blaring, a drum corps bringing up the rear on a cycle-drawn flatbed float. Banners and flags flying, this particular celebration included dozens of cyclists clamoring for more elevated veloways. The streetcars had piled up, and Nwin waited while the clogged street slowly untangled itself. Hundreds of pedestrians jammed the intersection, coming and going from the numerous theatres and movie houses in the area. Eventually Nwin made his way through the chaotic intersection with the rest of the cross traffic.

At Polk Street he turned left and deposited his wheels at the nearby lot. The Café Hurricane was in Cedar Alley. He had to fight his way through the thick mass at the alley's entrance, bouncing from jostle to shove, even at one point feeling a hand grazing his pants copping a feel. He spun around but it was impossible to tell which of the dozens of leather-clad men had felt him up. "Bearrrr," he groaned to himself as he squared his shoulders and moved on.

He stepped inside the dingy bar, adjusting to the dim light. Patrons lounged at the bar and along the walls, mostly men, mostly wearing black leather. Ancient dance tunes came thundering from a jukebox.

Suddenly both his arms were pinned. Hands grabbed him from behind and he was pushed forward to the back of the bar. He thrashed against the restraint but could not escape. He observed Nance on one side and a mysterious short, stocky man with a big moustache and thick black eyebrows on the other. Each arm was in its own vise grip.

A small door opened in the back wall and he was pushed through, his arms at last released. He stumbled into a table, nearly sprawling over it. A spiraling blue neon tube hung over the table, and even dimmer blue lights lined the back wall. The eerie glow in the room did not cast much light on the dark shapes in the shadows.

Nance appeared again at his side. In a low, almost growling voice, she addressed him. "My associates weren't sure you were going to show up. But I knew you would. Sit down." She pushed him into a chair. He tried to maintain a calm demeanor, frightened and fumbling for breath.

7.

I should have gone out. It was 22:15 and he'd had an uneventful dinner at the hostel, eating alone in a deserted dining room. Nothing like the crowd that had come "home" for lunch. Eric lay in his bunk, exhausted but restless, the sights of the day racing through his mind. Hard to believe he'd only arrived yesterday morning.

An old guy snored on the far end of the room, on top of one of the ten bunkbeds, but otherwise he was alone. He stared out at the city's twinkling lights for what felt like hours. The next thing he knew he heard laughter and shushing noises as people stumbled drunkenly into the room. He pulled the covers over his head, trying to stay at least half-asleep.

At breakfast he took a seat at a long table, munching toast and studying his city map. He planned to spend the whole day seeing the Haight-Ashbury and Golden Gate Park. He looked up to see Victoria, Liz and Fred heading his way.

"Howdy neighbor," Victoria said warmly as they plopped down at his table.

"Sorry about last night," offered Liz. "These guys were really drunk."

"Why do you have tell the world?" protested Fred.

"Hey, don't worry, I practically slept through it all," said Eric. "Was there some big party or what?"

"Nah, we just went to this bar, The Pond. I guess we had a few beers," Fred recounted.

"Fred!" Liz's eyes flashed. "Sorry, what was your name again?"

"Eric."

"Oh yeah, sorry, I'm terrible with names."

"Forget it. You're Liz, right?"

"Yes. Look, Fred must've had a dozen beers while we watched this great band. The Pond is the dew. It's got an outdoor terrace overlooking a pond, and the band played on a beautiful stage set across on the opposite bank. They have speakers on the terrace, so it's like they're playing right in front of you. Plus you can see them really well because the pond is tiny."

"Sounds great. Can you show me on this map?"

Victoria leaned over. "Dew map! Here, it's right here, see? There's Market Pond and the bar is on this side of it. See?"

"I'm heading up that way, maybe I'll stop off and have a look. You going up there again?"

"Those guys," she said, gesturing at Liz and Fred, "are planning to go to the Hiring Hall to see about working already. I'm not sure what I'm doing today, but I heard about a historical walking tour. I'm not much in the mood to work yet," explained Victoria.

"That sounds good, too," said Eric, still examining his map.

One by one they turned to breakfast, passing fruit and cereal back and forth. Eric hastily gobbled his last bite of toast, drained his coffee, and got up to go.

"Rushing off?" asked Victoria, a mischievous smile twitching at the corners of her mouth.

"Uh, yeah, gotta go," said Eric uncomfortably. "Have a nice day!"

Back in his room he quickly gathered up his bioptic camera, journal, a hat and sunglasses, ate a sunblocker, and hurried out the door. Driven by discomfort, he wanted to escape before Victoria either invited him to join her or decided to join him. She seemed perfectly nice, but not his type, and anyway, he didn't know what to say.

In the circular walkway he passed some women getting into their harness preparing to float out to work on the grand hanging triptych. The warm-up sounds of tuning instruments filled the airshaft from somewhere below. He walked briskly to the biovator and touched the call switch, a warm pale green depression that sent a small tingle into his finger. Moments later the translucent door lifted when the biovator arrived. He stepped in, disconcerted again by a squishy sensation as the floor gave a bit. The sheer door material fell and at his command, the device took him to the lobby. Out on the dock he searched for a gondola heading to Russ Gardens, where he planned to get a bicycle and head west. Watercabs bobbed in front, freight skiffs groaned alongside the loading dock. Sea lions sprawled amidst the ruins across the canal. Above, seagulls screeched, twisting and turning among sunbeams that sent bright shafts of light against walls and into the water. A warm day was in the making, sure to increase the already strong smell of animals and seawater.

A peapod much like the one Eric had ridden in on the first day, pulled up to the dock. The skipper was another salt-of-the-earth type, barking out destinations even before they'd tied up: "Line number 6, service to Rincon Towers, Central Train Station, Russ Gardens, Mission Bay, Crossroads, The Willows, Lake Valencia."

Eric waited while some elderly men disembarked, followed by a young man leading a noisy group of small children. The ferry was empty but for a couple with backpacks. Eric boarded to retrace his incoming journey. He recognized some of the sights, including the historical murals at Rincon Towers and the palm-covered avenues on the hill rising behind the Towers. In what seemed a much shorter time than before, the peapod rounded the old ballpark and nosed into the Train Station docks.

"Next stop, Russ Gardens!" called the skipper, and the ferry, flipping furiously, slipped out of the Train Station and headed north along the channel, then west at the face of the seawall. Flags flapped in the distance. As the peapod drew closer, they turned out to be the signature decoration of Russ Gardens, sitting at the edge of Mission Bay and the remains of the South of Market neighborhood, according to his map. (SOMA, South of Market, was the neighborhood's historic name, dating from the pre-revolutionary time when Abundance Street was still known as Market Street.) He got up and found his legs wobbly even after such a short ride, but quickly regained his balance, tipped his cap thanks to the conductor and strode up the pier into Russ Gardens.

The seawall stood solidly at the edge of the Gardens, and he bounded up a staircase and down the other side. The wall's interior proved a remarkable contrast to the gray, granite slabs that made up its defensive outer shell. The inside wall had built-in benches here and there, colorful paintings, moody, abstract and bold, climbing vines, dense flower-filled boxes, and delicate curving lamps intermittently along its length. Admiring it from the steps, it looked like nothing so much as a classic English Garden. Flower beds and hedges lined expansive green lawns. Miniature fruit trees comprised tiny orchards, and berries grew abundantly in raised beds. In the middle of it all stood a large stone pavilion with an outdoor café and a small carousel to its side. Eric walked down the stone path through the big lawn. *What is this place?*

As he entered the perimeter of the café, a bald portly fellow with a huge 19th century handlebar mustache loudly greeted Eric. "Hello young man! You're here quite early," he boomed, wiping his hands on his green apron and lumbering out from the indoor kitchen. "What can I get you? Breakfast? Coffee?"

"Thanks, but actually I just came to have a look on my way across town."

"Lovely! Glad you came! Do you know about Russ Gardens?" he continued enthusiastically.

"No, not really," said Eric cautiously, wondering what he was in for.

"Well, come on in! We have a delightful little museum inside, gives you the whole story!" He waved at an octagonal building behind him.

Relieved that he wasn't necessarily about to be imprisoned by this gregarious oddity of a man, Eric proceeded inside. The fellow disappeared into the kitchen, calling back to Eric "Enjoy yourself! And if you have any questions, you can find me in here."

"Thanks."

It was indeed a little museum, a replica of the Octagonal houses from the 1860s he'd read about while on the train. The exhibit consisted of two walls of old photos, a long explanatory text, and a small glass case filled with artifacts. Russ Gardens had originally been in this same spot back in the 1850s, when the area was surrounded by sand dunes, and the shallow waters of Mission Bay hadn't yet been filled. It had been one of early San Francisco's first recreational "escapes." It didn't last long though, and by the 1860s was already gone, the sand dunes leveled by steam shovels and the sand and other debris dumped into the wetlands to "make land." The land thus formed was quite unstable, of course, especially when earthquakes hit. As the sign told it:

"In the 1906 temblor, the entire area, by then heavily built over by small factories and housing, was leveled. No one ever learned if the structures had been destroyed by the quake because two days later the firestorm passed over and turned everything to ashes. In 1989, the quake killed less than a dozen people in San Francisco but ultimately led to dozens of buildings being destroyed after seismic damage rendered them irreparable. The building boom that followed littered the area with cheap lofts and light industrial facilities, but city officials failed to enforce seismic safety standards, so the whole neighborhood once again was flattened in the big quake of 2044. That earthquake also led to a dramatic sinking across the landfill parts of the city. Rising waters then reclaimed the "made lands." In the South of Market, waters rushed in as far as Howard Street between 4th and 7th Streets.

"In 2103 a new seawall was erected (today's Kyoto Causeway) in conjunction with the rebuilding of the entire sewer system to recycle wastes as fertilizer and gray water. The new fertilizer was perfect to help stabilize the reclaimed lands of the neighborhood. After three years of pumping and soil stabilizing, San Francisco started to rebuild in the area.

"One of the first was Russell Faigenbaum, who, when he learned about Russ Gardens, took the name for his new resort. The eccentric Faigenbaum designed his facility to be a taste of old Europe in the new San Francisco, and attracted others to help him. Greeted with derision and scorned as out of touch, he persisted. Eventually the city accepted the friendly and fun public resort where you are now standing."

Eric turned from the display and proceeded past the carousel that noisily turned without passengers. Eric didn't spend much time in the Gardens, partly because it was a chilly morning and he wanted to keep moving. He went through the gates into the city and walked up 5th Street to Folsom. A velome beckoned across the street, adjacent to a scenic tree-lined veloway. He waited for a streetcar to pass then jogged across, through a small pack of bikes and into the shack. It was the storefront of a fairly large bicycle factory, buzzing with activity.

A tall ebony-skinned man greeted him. He wore a small bike cap, a racing jersey and shocking pink stretch pants to his mid-calf. "Hey James!" came a yell from back in the factory, and he clattered away, mumbling "Scuse me a moment."

Eric admired the gleaming bikes lining the walls. Most of the bikes were made of bamboo. Metal fittings still predominated, but Eric was drawn to one that seemed to be entirely of wood, down to the pedals. The wheels of course were rubber, although instead of spokes the inside of the wheel had a solid disk of some kind of bark or paper or stiffened fabric. Squatting before it, he touched the mysterious material, in awe of the craftsmanship. He didn't notice James on his noisy cleats amid all the factory noise.

"Pretty nice, eh?" commented James proudly.

Eric stood up and whistled appreciatively. "What is that made of, anyway?" he asked, pointing to the wheel's interior.

"That's our own invention. Our chief technologist came up with that while he was messing around over at UC Mission Bay. It's a lab-dish process he calls 'bark extrusion.' They grow it to size and shape right here in our building. It's super strong, too. I've never seen one break yet."

"Do you guys give tours?" asked Eric.

"Oh sure, every Friday morning, but you can just wander around if you keep out of the way."

"I think I'll come back for the tour. Can I take a Bambu out for a day?"

"Please do! That's what they're here for. And actually you'd be helping us out because we're not getting the orders we thought we would. Take your pick." He pointed to a small fleet on racks, "and take some of these too." He handed over a small stack of bamboo cards engraved with a drawing of "Our First Bike."

Eric shoved the cards in his pack. He slapped hands with James, and chose his steed for the day, a tall bike with upright handlebars, handles carved right into the ends. The wicker seat worried him. Maybe it would be too hard on his out-of-shape butt. He swung his leg over and settled in, and it gave nicely. He dropped his bag into the basket conveniently hanging from the handlebars, and with a wave, steered himself out the front and into the passing flow of traffic.

After a few hundred yards he glanced back and had to stop. A rooftop bamboo garden framed a monumental bicycle wheel. *How come I didn't see that before? Got to remember to get my eyes off the ground.* His father used to bug him about that all the time. His enthusiasm waned abruptly as he spiraled into his tried-and-true self-loathing. Pedaling slower he felt very tired.

"Shit!" He slapped his thigh, trying to fight off the dark thoughts closing in. He couldn't hold the anger, and slowed even more, other cyclists now passing steadily as he meandered disconsolately. Seized by an unshakeable aching, he could only pull off the veloway. Once stopped, self-pity gave way again to anger. "Ching, ching, Chingado!" He ground his fist into his palm. Finally he took a deep breath, disgusted with himself.

"Hell!" and he got onto the bike and pushed off, focusing on pedaling and riding straight and steady. Crossing 7th Street he was immersed in dense traffic, primarily freight bicycles of all shapes and sizes. The neighborhood was full of small shops and factories: "Dim Bulb Lamps," "Open and Shut Windows (and Doors)," "Peggy's Pegleg Furniture," "Soft Landing Upholstery," and so on. Eric followed a cluster of bikes ahead of him and turned right on 9th Street towards the Civic Green and the Central Freestore, or so said the signs at the intersection. Streetcar lines also crossed at 9th and Folsom, disgorging passengers into the throngs filling the streets and nearby cafes. Silently and wirelessly aglide on magnetic tracks, the centuries-old streetcars still looked antique.

Eric approached the Civic Green along 9th Street. On the other side of the street, as he crossed Mission's wooden boardwalk, he observed a half dozen workers in overalls with big orange and yellow embroidered suns on their backs doing something to the solar panels on an ornately detailed, block-long apartment building.

"Hey, pay attention, wouldja," spat a guy trying to pass on Eric's left while pulling a heavily-loaded double trailer.

"Sorry!" he muttered and pulled over while slowing.

When the trailer guy turned off to make a delivery to the Freestore's loading docks, Eric rode out of the greenway into a large tree-lined plaza, each of its several sections with its own stage or open air restaurant or fountain. Elegant old buildings—including the famous City Hall, nearly 250 years old a survivor of innumerable quakes and fires—surrounded thousands of people in the Green. Eric dismounted and walked his bike into the central bowl near the imposing fountain. He found a good perch from which to take in the scene. His stomach announced its intention to be fed with a series of loud rumblings. Eric moved to obey.

8.

Squinting through the dim light, Nwin couldn't see anyone's features. He counted five people in the room, including Nance. Her rippling shoulders and arms caught the eerie blue light, throwing shadows that exaggerated her already impressive build. Her hair was pulled back, giving her regal features a hawk-like severity. He couldn't see her eyes within their dark sockets.

"Nwin," she said sharply.

He squirmed and straightened automatically.

"Tell us why you like to set fires," she demanded.

"What are you talking about?"

"Nwin," Nance repeated in a seductive deep voice, "we know about your little adventures, so you can just stop bullshitting us."

He looked at her silently, impassive.

"I like you. I told my associates about you, and they want to like you too. For that to happen, you're going to have show some enthusiasm here, Nwin."

He protested, "There must be some mistake—"

"Nance!" came another woman's voice from the shadows, "can I have a word with you?" Nwin recognized a British accent, or maybe Australian, he could never tell. Either way, she didn't sound happy.

Nance disappeared into the murk where inaudible murmurs were exchanged. After a brief back and forth, Nance returned and looked at Nwin, hard.

"I guess I was wrong about you. You may go." She spun and walked back through the half-light to a door that opened onto darkness. Amid scraping chairs and clearing throats, the others followed her. Nwin had not gotten a real look at any of them.

Exhaling deeply, he puzzled over the inexplicable strangeness of what had just happened. After all that, here he was, alone, in a strange blue-neon-lit room in the back of a bar. "What the hell?" he exclaimed under his breath. Rising from his seat, he started to make his way through the bar, but after a split-second hesitation, reversed himself and exited through the same back door as the others.

He found himself in a yard heavily perfumed by a large Datura just to his left. Ornamental lights strung along rear stairways gave off a warm, festive atmosphere. There was no sign of Nance and her gang.

He strolled aimlessly across a garden, looking for a corridor out to the street. A small carriage house behind an apartment building looked promising. Quietly he walked towards it, but stopped suddenly when a loud gasp pierced the silence. Shadows fluttered in the carriage house windows, as candles back-lit a woman astride her lover, her breasts and long mane of hair perfectly outlined against the window shade. The gasping became rhythmic cries of pleasure as she rose and fell in an accelerating ride to climax.

Nwin was transfixed. His heart pounded and his pants were suddenly too tight. In the window the woman threw her head back, and gave a long shuddering cry of pleasure, and then collapsed on her man's chest. Nwin, suddenly self-conscious, quickly looked around. Seeing no one, he nervously walked away around the carriage house and as expected, found a passageway to the street.

Emerging on Larkin, he walked to California Street, and then circled back around to Polk. Cable cars jammed the intersection but Nwin squeezed by the traffic jam and through the human tide spilling from bars and cafes along the street. Polk Street had a red brick lane along one side, streetcar tracks in the middle, and a curvy veloway on the other. Nwin wove in and out of little curbside tables lining the red brick lane, dodging the occasional streetcar. Racing along, he saw an endless stream of hairy men in black leather. Some of them smiled and reached for him as he scurried by. This was not where he wanted to be. He found his way to the little lot where he'd left his bike, and minutes later was coasting down Polk to the Civic Green, letting gravity do the work.

Gliding into the Green at 11 p.m. on a Friday was always fun. Tonight, the comfortable moonlit air hinting at the promise of a heatwave had kept the fog away. Nwin stood twitching at the corner and glancing from side to side but without registering anything. Twinkling lights and the buzz of conversation filled the plaza. Nearest to him was a sprawling café. Espresso jockeys and bartenders were jumping, barely keeping up with long lines of thirsty people. A screaming blues guitar solo suddenly pierced the buzz. Nwin couldn't see the stage, which pointed away from his vantage point, but applause erupted from the tables around it. Conversations rose in volume to compete with the amplified music. He parked his bike and got in line for a beer.

"I support MacMillan," said a short-haired woman ahead of Nwin to her companion, a lanky slouching guy, completely disheveled.

"Look, he's bent over backwards to answer the objections of the Garden Party and the Integritistas, and I for one am very excited about new research on inter-species communication. Why *shouldn't* we?" she implored with noticeable exasperation.

"First off, MacMillan is an egomaniac. Second, since the Die-off this line of inquiry has been prohibited for good reason," argued her companion. "Humans still aren't capable of making intelligent decisions about the boundaries between species… the fact that a charismatic egomaniac can convince lots of people that he's capable is MORE reason to worry, not less!"

"I don't know why you think MacMillan is such an egomaniac. Have you ever sat down and talked to him?"

"No, and I wouldn't want to. The guy gives me the creeps!"

The woman crossed her arms while stiffening her shoulders, and became silent, obviously frustrated.

The lanky guy ran a hand through his tangled hair, cleaned his glasses, and fidgeted uncomfortably. "Don't be mad, Alison. Can't we just let this go for now?"

She sighed, looking away into the throng. "It seems like we are always letting it go. Makes me wonder what we're doing together in the first place!"

"Okay folks, what'll it be?" offered a sweaty, garrulous bartender who was clearly enjoying himself.

"Coupla pints of Angkor Steam," the lanky guy ordered up.

"Comin'atcha," said the bartender, turning just in time to bump into a tray of glasses behind him. "Hey!" called out the dishwasher, as several glasses smashed to the floor. "Chingado man, watch OUT!" he continued in dismay, adjusting to the lighter load and pushing on to the other end of the bar. "You can clean that up, too!" he yelled back at the bartender.

The bartender smiled sheepishly at Nwin and the couple in front of him, shaking his head as he reached for the broom and dustpan. He soon placed two sculpted, frosted glasses of beer on the counter and gave the customary greeting: "*Salud y anarchia!*" The woman rolled her eyes as they clutched the frosty mugs and vanished into the sprawling audience. "Next?"

"The same, thanks," said Nwin. After a short pull of the spigot, his beer was delivered.

"And there you are, *salud y anarchia!*" repeated the bartender, already turning his attention to a couple behind Nwin.

Nwin pivoted, his Angkor Steam's icy glass shaped like a tall thin Cambodian temple, with the word Angkor in script along the bottom. He took a quick gulp before he began hunting for a seat.

"Hey Nwin, over here!" called Marco and Stefania, friends from the Rice Bowl. Relieved, Nwin joined them.

"What's twirlin'?"

"Hi Nwin, what brings you out here tonight?" asked Stefania.

"Oh, I was just crossing town and thought I'd drop in, see what's new, maybe catch some music if it's any good. Do you know who's playing?"

"DeeDee King and her Blues Allstars I think," said Marco.

"Really?".

"I'm not sure, but I think that's who I saw on the marquee. Why don't you go check it out? We'll hold your seat for you," Marco encouraged.

"Okay, thanks, I'll be right back." Nwin threaded his way past the fountain to the side of the stage. It didn't look like DeeDee King, though there was some pretty mean guitar playing. He leaned forward to see the marquee, and it read "Big Bertha's Power Players" in small type at the top, along with "Tonight." In larger type below DeeDee King was listed, but her show was next week. Just then, Nwin felt a perfumed current of air and a rustle of clothes behind him, and turned to see Big Bertha herself climbing the stairs to the stage. On stage her bandmate announced "And let's have a big San Francisco welcome for the voice that keeps New Orleans above water. . . Big BERTHA!!" The audience clapped and stomped enthusiastically. Bertha was already drenched in sweat, wiping her forehead, and all she'd done was climb up to the stage! Her deep soulful phrasings soon filled the air, the band picking up behind her. Nwin watched for a minute, and then headed back to his table.

Slumping into the chair he told them who was who on stage.

"So Nwin, what about these trampled plantings? You don't know who's doing it, do you?" asked Marco.

"Thanks for asking! Angus seems to think I'm organizing it or something. What an asshole!… No, I have no idea."

"I knew it. Of course you don't know, I don't even know why anyone would think you did," said Stefania supportively. She was only about 20 herself.

"We do have to stop it," continued Marco. "We've lost a lot of workdays over it, and the plantings won't yield as much now, regardless. I cannot understand why anyone would wreck someone else's work! I mean, how DARE they?"

Nwin said nothing. Stefania clucked affirmatively, but also said nothing. After a few minutes, Nwin fixed on Marco and said, "Do you want to catch the culprits or just protect the plantings?"

"Uuhhh—"

"Because we could fence off that area without much effort. And I doubt if anyone is so interested in messing us up that they'll go to the trouble of breaking through a simple fence."

"That would solve it I suppose. What kind of fence?" asked Marco.

"I hate chicken wire fences, they're SO ugly!" interjected Stefania.

"I saw some bamboo fences, assembled into sections, that would be easy to install—and not easy to jump over."

"Let's propose it next week at the Monday meeting," suggested Marco.

Nwin took a long last pull of beer before rising. "I think you should propose it, because if I do Angus will be against it."

"I don't think Angus has it in for you THAT much," protested Stefania.

"You should see how he looks at me, how he talks to me when no one is around," continued Nwin. "The guy is an asshole, and I'll probably have to quit because of him." Angus seemed like an insurmountable obstacle to him, best handled by quitting and going on to something else.

"Well, I hope not," said Stefania grumpily.

Nwin said bye to his friends, and after hand slaps, he departed, buzzed by his beer and anticipating the cool ride home. He pedaled uneventfully to Rincon Towers where he retrieved his skiff for the last leg over water to the Pyramid. Tying up at the residential dock he scrambled up the ladder and into the back lobby, and before long he was in his little room on the 33rd floor. Drowsy after a long day, he was out cold as soon as he hit the bed.

9.

He sat down with a heaping plate of Pad Thai noodles, fresh and spicy just how he liked 'em. The plaza bustled. He had grabbed a strategic corner by a monument to Librarians, tossing his pack down next to stacks of bronze books at the foot of the statue. From here he commanded a view of the Central Freestore and half the plaza sloping down, not far above the stage where poets were reading aloud.

He finished his plate and relaxed, letting the warm sun bathe him. Chattering children ran by, chased by an elderly woman good-naturedly struggling to keep up. Easing down from his perch, Eric threw his pack over his shoulders and strolled towards the fountain. A large message board under a small copse of trees caught his attention. It was divided into Same Day Messages, Upcoming Events, and Announcements. A half dozen personal messages were pinned up plus posters for a Blues Festival at the bandshell, a lecture series on Chinese Art History, another on Maritime History to be held on a historic ship. The only announcement said that the Bart-Mart had moved to the Hayes Valley Commons, a few blocks west but was still open everyday.

Bart-Mart? He walked on, anonymous among the mass of humanity, the plaza's tables all occupied. Others picnicked on the lawn, kids cavorted in the fountain. He climbed up out of the plaza's sunken area towards the majestic old City Hall. In he went, through the ornate iron doors and the marble lobby. A huge sweeping staircase beckoned from the building's brightly lit main courtyard. He lifted his eyes to take in a soaring rotunda. A string quartet on a higher floor filled the air with music as he started up the long staircase. He realized they were accompanying a marriage ceremony when a bride and groom appeared on the top landing. A host of wellwishers poured down the stairs, taking pictures in an excited clamor, laughing and talking excitedly.

Eric withdrew to the side of the rotunda and found a spot next to a thin, dark man. "Beautiful, aren't they?" the man offered.

"You know them?" asked Eric.

"No, I was just here to visit my daughter. She works in the transportation library just over there.

"So what all goes on here?"

"Councils and boards have offices here and hold public meetings on the second floor, in the chambers. The Neighborhood Council meets here, the Transit Board, the Garden Council, the Education Council, the Energy Board, the Water Board."

Eric watched the newlyweds descend the staircase, the bride in a traditional flowing white gown trailed by two small girls in light green dresses, giggling as they carried the train. The proud and happy groom slowly descended with his new wife on his arm. Somehow this left Eric cold. Rituals always seemed lifeless to him. There was no denying the spirit of these people, but something rankled him anyway. At least the music sounded great in the resonant chamber.

Eric nodded to his informant and whispered, "Thanks! Good Luck!" and walked briskly away from the swelling wedding party.

Next to the rotunda was a very big room with hundreds of people milling about inside. The sign over the door read "Hiring Hall." **"Nobody Wants to, So We All Have to! Do Your Annuals!"** blared a big banner at the far end of the room. Tables lined the walls, covered with brochures, photographs and booklets. Larger than usual vyne displays hung along the long wall where he had entered, listing hundreds of jobs. A big sign over the vyne nearest him said **"Try Outs."** Another one across the room said **"Apprenticeships."** A big window in the near wall opened into a kitchen. People took sandwiches and coffee to small square tables scattered throughout the hall. Near Eric sat three old guys, two of them immersed in a chess match. A nearby shelf was loaded down with games and reference books. "Why don't you sit down and get your bearings young man?" called the odd man out in the chess match.

"Thanks," said Eric, and pulled up a chair.

"So how exactly does this work?" he asked the old guy after settling in.

"You never been to a Hiring Hall?" Eyebrows raised in disbelief.

"Well, not here. I used the Hiring Hall by vyne in Chicago."

The old guy nodded. "It's pretty straightforward. Not much different than Chicago, I'll bet. There's the usual categories: Annuals, Tryouts and Apprenticeships. New here?"

"Yeah, just got in a few days ago."

"You can do Annuals to test the waters," he gestured toward the **"Do Your Annuals!"** sign. "Say, you're not looking to make a serious commitment right away, are you?"

"No. I plan to Tryout. Annuals are frustrating. You're always doing mindless stuff and the regulars give you the worst shitwork they have."

"It's a handy way to see a lot of the city though. And it's not always the worst jobs.

I do a day every week, just to keep myself in circulation. I always meet good people."

Eric smiled and nodded. He still felt more traveler than resident, and the drive to pull his own weight hadn't kicked in yet.

"Can you watch my bag?"

"Sure, no problem. We're not going anywhere!" laughed the old guy.

Eric headed to the Annuals wall. Two huge vyne leaves displayed hundreds of jobs, the listings updating themselves before his eyes. What wasn't on that list? Kitchen help, street cleaning, sewer maintenance, dishwasher, waiter, shelf stocker, community tool-shop attendant, espresso jockey, window washer, deliveries, farming, veloway maintenance, gardening, shoe repair, residential building, hospital orderly, hotel service, solar and wind systems, bicycle manufacturing, on and on and on.

Eric picked up a brochure about the Bambu Bicycle Factory where he'd picked out his bike that morning and read about their system of manufacturing from natural materials. The pamphlet invited you to come and take a shift as Annuals, or to sign up for a Tryout prior to an Apprenticeship. Another brochure described the Shit System and laid out jobs available for Annuals, among them household preventive maintenance and ongoing system overhaul.

Next to the Annuals were Educational listings. Again the list was endless and seemed to encompass every human activity. **"Learning Counts!"** said the sign above, a reminder that enhanced knowledge and skills benefited everyone and counted towards your 60-hour a year Annuals obligation. Across the tables, dozens of brochures offered alluring opportunities in enterprises all over the city.

Eric wandered over to the Tryouts wall where he found recruiting calls from artisans, small factories, skilled technical teams, and even the Hiring Hall itself, all hoping to attract those looking to make a commitment. It was generally understood that a short stint of Annuals should precede a Tryout, and that a 90-180 day Tryout was necessary prior to embarking on a 2-5 year Apprenticeship. Eric tucked the brochures into his bag and sat down again.

"Find anything?" queried the oldster.

"Maybe. But I want to see the city and get to know where everything is before I start working," Eric replied.

"No better way to see the city than by working the veloways or the streetcars."

"No doubt, but I'll wander on my own, thank you." This guy was a little too intent on putting him to work. Of course, that was typical of older people—work and responsibility. His parents were like that, but his grandparents had been really bad. You couldn't have a conversation with them without major pressure to pick a profession and get into an Apprenticeship.

The men playing chess looked up at Eric, then at each other and the third fellow. Returning to their match, one of them started smacking his tongue into the roof his mouth, a sound that could have been disapproval, or maybe not.

Eric had used up whatever hospitality these guys had for him. The man he'd been talking to was now riffling through a newspaper. Eric got up.

"Thanks for watching my bag," he said, and they all grunted. The guy half-looked up from his newspaper and said "Don't forget! *We all have to!*"

Eric scowled and quickly departed, relieved to get away. He was glad to get out of the Hiring Hall, too. His self-loathing did not extend to doubting his ability to pull his weight. He knew he could do most any work, when he wanted to.

Bursting onto the Civic Green, he threaded his way through the swirling masses back to his bamboo bike. Taking a deep breath inthe warm afternoon, he determined to explore on his own. *I'll find a good gig wandering around… like those publishers yesterday… that was the dew.*

He spent a few minutes moving and reparking various other bikes piled on top of his. He noticed a little sticker with a red bridge on most all of them. Around the logo it read "Made in San Francisco."

He pedaled to the south side of the plaza, across from the open-doored bustle of the Central Freestore. Glancing inside, he almost ran over a woman trying to maneuver her freight trike onto the path ahead of him. At the last second he saw her and hit the brakes.

"Whoa!" he called involuntarily.

The small blonde was struggling to get the trike moving at a manageable speed. He could only see her head poking out above the boxes and packages lashed to the freight bed. He swung out after letting a few faster riders speed by, and came around. She stood on the pedals trying to get them going but the weight was too much for her.

"Can I help you?" he asked gallantly.

"I don't know. Can you?" she replied, exasperated.

He dismounted and moved to the edge of the veloway. She was already half off to the side. She pulled out a bandana and wiped her face.

"What are you doing with all this stuff?"

"I guess I got a little carried away at the Freestore," she admitted.

"Can you take anything back? It's only right there," he nodded, waving at the front doors a mere half block behind them.

"I guess I'll have to," she conceded.

"Wait. Here's an idea. I could ride your trike and you could ride mine. Is it far?"

"You'll laugh."

"What do you mean?"

She rubbed her neck and looked at her feet. "I have to get to the Haight."

"So? That's not far is it?"

"You don't know the city?"

"No, I just got here."

"The Haight is actually not so far, but it's uphill."

"Oh," he surveyed the load again. "What were you thinking?"

"Listen, can you wait here while I take some things back?"

"Let me try to ride it first. Maybe I can pedal this home for you."

"Are you sure?"

"I was going to there anyway. Let me try. But first," and he grabbed the seat adjuster and raised the seat a few inches. Bearing down on the pedals he got the load moving. Once you got going it kept itself rolling. "How steep are those hills?" he called over his shoulder.

She darted past him on his bike. "Oh not so bad!" she said happily. She'd lowered his seat to her height, which wasn't much over five feet.

"How is that for you? The handlebars too high?"

"It's easier than that thing," she said, wrinkling her nose and pointing at her trike.

Grunting as he got the sizeable load to speed, he was soon enjoying his view. She had a slender waist that merged into a sweet, round butt, which shifted back and forth in a tantalizing rhythm as she pedaled.

"Hey," Eric called, louder than necessary, "what's your name, anyway?"

"Tanya, and yours?"

"Eric, Eric Johanson."

"Great to meet you Eric!" She shot him a winning smile.

He wondered, *Am I a dupe?* Dark thoughts for such a sunny day.

"This is so nice of you," she called over her shoulder. Then she slowed and fell back to his side. "I expect you to come for dinner tonight, and I won't take 'no' for an answer!"

He brightened. "Sure—glad to!" he puffed.

Dozens of streetcars glided through the major intersection at Abundance and Van Ness. Eric followed Tanya through hundreds of bikes and walkers to avoid losing his way. Bells tinkled, streetcars clanged, and voices gave off warnings, epithets and jokes, a well-understood choreography.

He glimpsed a huge sign **"Bart-Mart"** down an alley. "What's over there?" he asked, pointing.

"That's the Barter Market where people trade stuff. Some people just *love* it. The haggling part is so awful, I don't see why anyone would *like* that!"

Now the traffic split between a hard left turn onto Valencia, Abundance Street Hill straight ahead, and a sweeping right turn onto the Octavia Parkway. Across the street at Valencia there was a spiraling wooden tower on-ramp to a rooftop express veloway, a diagonal shortcut across the Mission District to the Precita Levee. Everyone called it "Camino."

Eric and Tanya reached the top where he felt the strain of the load in a rush. Below them lay a bucolic pond surrounded by café tables on one side and a gazebo with stage on the other. Abundance Street disappeared into the water, resuming again on the other side.

Tanya rolled to the right through an sculptured iron portal. Large wobbly letters spelled out "The Wiggle." Eric followed, but gazing back at the pond, he observed a streetcar come gliding down Abundance from the west side of the pond. Now what? To his amazement, the streetcar just rolled right onto the surface of the lake. "Hey Tanya! How does that work?!"

"Huh?" Oh the streetcar? Magnetic tracks are just below the surface, you can't quite see them. The streetcar hovers an inch above the tracks. We're so used to it, we don't even notice anymore. Pretty weird, eh?"

"Well . . . yeah!"

They came to a fruit and juice stand with the usual bunch of tables and chairs scattered about. Bicyclists lounged over drinks and Eric called ahead to Tanya, "Hey, I need a break!"

She pulled over immediately. "Sorry, I forgot, you're working a lot harder than I am! What would you like?"

"A cranberry and passionfruit blend."

Off she went while he plopped into a chair. Minutes later she returned with a tall bloody-orange drink for him, and a fizzy water for herself. "Can I have a taste? I've never tried that combination before."

"Of course." He pushed the drink across to her. "Mmmmm! I'm going to get one of those next time."

A steady stream of cyclists passed by. Eric wiped his forehead with a napkin, and enjoyed the cool drink. A welcome breeze cooled him further.

"So is that the Market Pond?"

"Yep. How do you know about that?"

"Oh I heard about it from some people staying at the hostel. Seems like an odd name for a pond."

"It's named after the street—Oh! Abundance street was called Market Street before the revolution."

"Aaah."

"So, where are you staying?"

"Tweezer Towers."

"Must be a great view. I haven't been down there in years, but I used to hang out in the Pyramid. I had a boyfriend living there, a long time ago."

"Uh-huh," he commented absently. "So, uh, what do you do?"

"Lately I've been writing a lot. Last year I was in a band, playing drums. Years ago I did a Tryout with the Shitsys, but I didn't like it. I can help when I need to, but it takes care of itself. I still do Annuals on the Shitsys every year, to keep up my training. I've been gardening in the Panhandle a bunch lately. I also work at the neighborhood radio station."

"I haven't listened to any radio yet. What do you have on your station?"

"Mostly it's different kinds of music, but we do public interest shows and call-ins too. I produced a half hour last month on clam and shrimp harvesting in the Bay."

"I'll check it out. What's the number?"

"We're 94.9 FM, JIVE 95. One of the DJ's says it used to be called that a long time ago."

Eric laughed. "Well, I guess I'm as refreshed as I'm gonna be. Shall we push on? How much further?"

"About the same distance we've covered, but much easier and no steep slopes at all. This is the Wiggle, it's the way bicyclists have always gone east to west here. See that crumbling wall?" she pointed ahead a short distance where an old wall was held up by beams and piles of rocks, crowning a long slope down to Market Pond. Across the bottom a little ring road connected the two parts of Abundance Street. A small bridge on the road crossed a creek bubbling down from somewhere behind the wall in the distance.

"That's one of the oldest surviving murals in the City. It was first painted in the 1990s and restored about 50 years ago, but the upper section has been lost forever. It's the Wiggle, showing the Hayes River, the Panhandle and the old downtown long before the seas rose. . . You'll see, come on!" and she bounced to her feet.

"Hey, I'm starting to like these high handlebars. It's the dew to sit upright like this!" she grinned, whizzing ahead.

Eric was barely rolling. He'd hiked up Telegraph Hill yesterday, and pedaled up Nob Hill, so his legs were already smarting. At least, he hoped, he had gotten past the hill climbing on this ride.

At the end of the wall, a pastoral creek bubbled down to the Pond below. Tanya approached a bridge, packed with bicyclists and walkers, and he followed. She warned him, "It's steep, so try to gain some momentum. I'll warn people you're coming." With that, she bolted ahead, yelling like a banshee, "WATCH OUT! BIG LOAD COMING! CLEAR THE WAY! BIG LOAD COMING!"

All eyes turned to Eric as he pedaled onto the bridge. It was a nasty quick rise to clear the creek, and he hit it as fast as he could. Halfway up he was straining to keep it moving. Several people rushed to help. He hit the brakes, realizing he was about to fall backwards. "Whoa, whoa!" called several voices. "Hey, lend a hand!" "Everyone PUSH!" Laughing and joking, five or six people soon bunched up behind the freight bike, teasing each other and Eric.

"Whatcha got in there? Dead bodies?"

"I think he dug up a bank and stole all the gold!"

"What is this, the whole library?"

Tanya was at the summit of the bridge, blushing deeply. Eric felt panicky, but when the trike began inching upward he pedaled as hard as he could. He always avoided this kind of attention, but he had no time to worry and certainly couldn't get away. He rolled down the other side to cheers behind him, a few folks scattering at the bottom as Tanya raced ahead, yelling warnings, .

On the riverside veloway Eric focused on maintaining a steady pace. Tanya fell back alongside him. "Are you okay? I'm sorry about this. It's way worse than I thought it would be."

Eric waved her off. As they reached a narrow park, they intersected with another veloway angling in from a dense forest between houses. A steady stream of cyclists merged into the path. "Hey Tanya, where'd you get that cute bike?" called a woman of indeterminate age with short black hair and glasses. She sat upright on an old English bicycle, in black slacks and boots under a long gray sweater, a leather briefcase slung over her back. "Oh, hi Marge," said Tanya, moving over immediately in front of Eric. "It's not mine, it's his," she gestured over her shoulder. Marge swiveled her neck. "Hi." To Tanya she said, "Who's he?"

"Eric, uh, . . . Johnson? He saved me outside the Freestore."

"Oh no! Don't tell me that's all your stuff?!" Marge was immediately aggravated. "Didn't you promise to stop?"

"But—"

Marge sped away, leaving sparks of anger in her wake.

"Shit!" Tanya sank into the bike, her cheeriness gone.

"What's twirlin' with that?" Eric called ahead.

Morosely, Tanya confessed, "Marge is in my household. Actually, we were lovers, but that was a while ago. Anyway, we've been fighting about storage space and clutter. She thinks I'm the worst packrat, at least that's what she called me at the meeting."

"And? . . ."

"Yeah, I probably am."

"What about this load we're bringing?"

"No, no, this isn't junk! It's stuff our house needs. . . Two ceramic tubs for the garden... And I grabbed a few books... Some cases of fruit juice, a few bottles of table wine, a couple of frozen chickens. I can't believe how heavy it all is! I'm truly sorry. You've been so sweet. Hey I know, after dinner maybe my housemate can give you a massage. She owes me a favor and told me I could have one. I'll give it to you!"

Lumbering along Eric nodded, sweat dripping from his chin.

They passed a busy corner with a velome and an "old fashioned" ice cream parlor. Another bridge loomed ahead, again a climb, but not as steep as the previous one. They were at Haight and Rexroth. He looked around but couldn't find anything he'd seen in pictures. Again, Tanya went ahead, bellowing warnings. *What a set of pipes!* He surprised himself, making it up and over without help.

Now it wasn't much farther to Tanya's place. Past another iron green gateway, like the one at the east end of the Wiggle, they entered the Panhandle. Elegant ancient trees towered all around, raised vegetable gardens clustered along the edges near the—

"Wow!" Every house was a delight, huge turrets, curving Bay windows, ornate moldings, wood designs. Some were painted wild colors, others more modestly. It was an outdoor architectural museum, framed by lush green park and farmland.

An ocean breeze rolled in. Late afternoon sunlight fell through the trees. The breeze felt great.

"We turn here," Tanya called, leading off the Panhandle onto Ashbury Street. They turned into a backyard under a huge drooping Eucalyptus. "Here we are," she announced.

"And not a minute too soon, where's your bathroom?"

He dismounted and bolted through the door as she called after him, "First door on the right."

10.

Nwin was thinking about Nance. Then her face changed and she was Valentina. She was the woman he'd seen through the shade in the carriage house, then she wasn't. Tossing and turning, he pulled the pillow over his head. He should have gone to work today, but he didn't feel like it.

*Angus is such a bastard! He wants me out and **he's** the chingin' lifer!* Nwin was nearing the end of his 120-day commitment. Farming and gardening were okay, but he couldn't see working with Angus.

He lay there, running the previous day through his head, proud not to have been trapped into any admissions. At that, he remembered what he'd been looking for at his parents'. He'd have to return to the Library to get the manual again.

He sat on the edge of his bed and blearily looked at sunshine bouncing off the Bay. Scratching his armpit, he padded over and caught his own reflection in the window. *Weird. Really weird!* His eyes, without eyebrows and the bleached blonde hair. Below him, hundreds of small watercraft were streaming at cross-purposes, like ants on the water. Further out a big cargo ship was churning toward an anchorage in the Bay, itself a penetrating blue in the morning sun. Treasure Island rose in the middle distance, the rollercoaster already whipping around the island. Further still, the lush greenery of the East Bay carpeted the hills. Homes and buildings occasionally emerged from the verdant forest, which had long ago taken over the quake-devastated area.

Nwin moved slowly. He stretched, turning first left then right with hands outstretched to the ceiling. He bent down to touch his toes, and a sharp pain shot through his lower back. "Aaagh!" He reached out to the nearby window ledge to catch himself.

What the hell!? He slowly worked his way back up to an upright position, holding his back. The pain subsided, leaving a dull ache to remind him that all was not right with his back. He headed to the bathroom, and adjusted the shower, as hot as he could stand it. In the shower he brushed his teeth, and leaned forward carefully, hands on thighs, letting the jet of hot water attack the aching spot.

Back problems already?! I'm only 17! He got out, dried off, dressed, and grabbed a small pack, making sure to shove his pipe and some reefer into it. He clattered down to the 31st floor and went into the dining room. At the buffet he grabbed pastries and waved his hand at the espresso guy, holding up two fingers. After taking a window seat, he headed back for his double latté.

"Mornin', how's it twirlin' today?"

"Morning Franklin. It's all a ruin! Or it's all the dew! Just depends." He smirked and took his drink. "Thanks," he called over his shoulder. He slumped into his window seat, and bit into a bear claw, strangely comforted by the sugary rush. Washing it down with strong coffee, he looked around.

Across the room Lupe and her friends were chattering. One woman was modeling her Carnival costume. Like hens or something, they picked and pecked, pointing, gesturing, laughing and carrying on. Nwin got up and moved to the other side of his table, turning his back on the scene.

He opened his notebook, and wrote one word: "inscrutable." Sipping his coffee, he thought about how good that word sounded. He wanted to be inscrutable. He fancied himself quite philosophically developed. He could not yet know his own adolescent self-delusion. He straddled East and West with his all-knowing detachment and rigorous analytical framework. In his mind he had already transcended the paralysis that he imagined to have held back his predecessors. He was taking action. In action, he would forge a new synthesis, and single-handedly challenge the hypocrisy of a society grown easy and self-satisfied.

His reverie was broken when someone slipped into the chair next to him. "Hey, how come you're not at work?"

It was Johnny Templer who worked as a cook in the Pyramid's kitchen. He knew Nwin's parents, and tried to keep an eye on him.

"Hi Johnny." Nwin took a drink of coffee. "Needed a day off." He shook his head as if to emphasize the point.

"Oh?"

"This guy Angus. Thinks I know who's been trampling his new plantings."

"And do you?"

"I wouldn't be surprised if it was some kids on Potrero Hill, but I've never seen 'em there, and wouldn't finger them anyway."

"Ah." Johnny nursed his own coffee and glanced toward the distant Golden Gate. He took his long brown hair out of the hairnet and let it fall, running his fingers through it. "Gorgeous day, idn't it?"

"Sure is."

They sat quietly. Sailboats skittered around Alcatraz, a phalanx of windmills turning furiously on its windward side, the ruins of huge legs jutting pointlessly from the forest. The rest of the island was a tropical paradise, palm trees and dense foliage. Deep under the trees, Nwin knew (from his aunt), ran a wonderful series of hot and cold baths, a spa with all kinds of massage and hydrotherapies. Johnny wound his hair back up into his hairnet, stood up, put his hand on Nwin's shoulder. "Well, don't step in any holes."

"Thanks, Johnny," he responded simply, grateful that Johnny never lectured or cross-examined him.

His ruminations on inscrutability broken with Johnny gone, he thought about Valentina and felt stupid all over again not to have approached her at Dolores Park. He vowed next time to be ready.

He shoved his journal into a small pack and departed. Nwin walked around the hall and entered the door marked "Poles," one of the features that attracted a lot of younger people to the Pyramid. He squinted as a body went hurtling past on the express, followed seconds later by another. Grabbing one of the local poles, he wrapped his legs around it and slid down a floor. It could take a while getting down this way, but it was fun. Hopping to the next pole, Nwin started getting his rhythm, sliding down faster, hopping over, grabbing a pole and sliding along. His hands and legs were starting to burn from the friction. He paused to put on his gloves, but remembered he didn't have them anymore. He took an express pole, shooting down three floors at once, always a dizzying trip. Now it hurt. He took a break from the poles and ran down a few flights of stairs, perfecting his flying 5 steps-at-a-time leap.

"Whoa! Watch out!," complained two women vacuuming the elegant rugs that graced the stairway. He danced through them, unconcerned, and resumed his leaping descent. At the 6th floor, he grabbed an express pole to plunge the last three floors to the lobby. He hit the bottom with a thud as the padded floor absorbed his shock. "COMING DOWN!" sent him scurrying to the side just in time, as a wild-eyed fellow came plummeting to earth, roly-poly in overalls and a panama hat held on by string under his neck. He leaped to the side as a carbon copy came ripping down behind him, obviously his twin. They laughed, breathing hard, wringing their hands. "Hi, man, sorry if I scared you," said the first to Nwin.

"Goes with the territory," he smiled, and walked out to the warming morning sun. Negotiating a catwalk around the building he came to the residential docks, found his skiff *Hot 1* and jumped in. Passing the entry, he remembered to stop by the supply shack for fuel discs for his skiff. From the cabinet conveniently attached to the outside of the shack he pulled out two mottled green chlorophyll and sugar discs and inserted them into the fuel slot in the skiff's wall.

Pushing the depression in the back of the craft's center (*its forehead*), he felt the rear fins begin to flap steadily. He nudged the nodule at his feet leftward. Some people rigged long handles onto the steering nodules, but Nwin was a purist and liked *Hot 1* unadorned with mechanical (*artificial*) attachments. Besides he steered smoothly with his feet. Arms extended on the boat's edge he sat back, the sun fully on him now, and steadily moved through the dense traffic in the watery canyons of downtown. Skybridges soared overhead between buildings, as gondolas, water taxis, regular ferry lines and skiffs all danced in and out of the canals. Nwin crossed Sansome, shooting behind the ruins where the sea lions had settled. He paused, noticing a thickening growth of bright green water plants along the edge of a pool inside the crumpled building. It stunk of salt and sea lions. He bobbed in the water, watching skeeter bugs streak across the semi-protected pool, hearing the bubbles of fish popping in and out of the seaweed and underwater ruins. A big fish—*bass? salmon? carp?*—Nwin never could identify fish—surfaced just long enough to grab one of the skeeter bugs in his ugly lips. Seagulls screeched above as they sailed through the warm air in search of breakfasts of their own.

The Tweezer Towers soared to his south, but he continued to make his way towards the open Bay. A long, narrow barge laden with produce was crossing ahead, so Nwin waited behind a clot of other watercraft. Just ahead a blue peapod ferry and several freight taxis clogged his immediate path. Nwin was looking for a seam to sneak through when behind his right shoulder came "What's your hurry? We're not going anywhere for a few minutes at least!"

Nwin wheeled around, impatient and irritated at the unsolicited advice. A long-legged blond man crouched in his own skiff and chuckled. He had an unusually big handlebar moustache and a reddish beard, meticulously sculpted. Nwin knew he was right, but he scowled at him anyway.

"Well, don't blame me!" he chortled, and turning his attention elsewhere, was immediately caught up in last night's game. "You saw that last inning? He had 'im, he had 'im right where he wants him, and he let it get away!"

Two guys sitting on crates of tomatoes atop a small barge were the recipients of his remarks. Dangling their feet, they passed a joint . "'Let it,' what do you mean 'let it'?" said one. His partner, warming to the discussion, ventured "Deford's the best in the division. You can't let him swing with runners in scoring position, and not expect some damage. The guy can flat-out HIT!"

The blond guy unfolded his long legs and stood up to face the men above him, and leaned forward like a tall tree battered by strong wind. "Miller has been fantastic all season. The Seals wouldn't even be in contention if it hadn't been for his relief pitching. But that fat, floating curveball to Deford was a gift from the gods. He hasn't thrown a pitch that sad all year! My grandmother could have hit THAT one!"

The first guy offered him the joint, which he accepted while adjusting his weight to avoid falling into the crates of tomatoes. He took a long pull. The second continued, "that's baseball, man! No one can make the perfect pitch every time, and the good hitters jump on mistakes. So," he accepted the joint's return, "who do you like to make the playoffs?"

The blonde shook his head. "Obviously I'd like to say the Seals, but not if they can't get some hitting. And their defense has lost a few too many, too. The Oaks are a lock for first place." The other two grinned and slapped hands. One pulled out his Oakland Oaks hat and put it on. "Whoo-whoo, you can't beat the mighty Oaks!"

"But the wild card is up for grabs. I guess I like the Slugs. Santa Cruz has just been getting better and better, and they're only 5 games behind the Gamblers. Reno just doesn't have the pitching. Hitting can only carry you so far, especially when you get them out of the thin air and bring 'em down to sea level."

"Santa Cruz! How could a team called the Banana Slugs *win* anything!?!" said the Oaks fan derisively. "If Reno fades, it'll be Sonoma. The Farmers have Morris and Gutierrez pitching, and . . .— "

Nwin's attention shifted back to the traffic jam. He saw his opening and shot through it, tearing around several ferries and freight taxis, narrowly avoiding another oncoming barge.

Soon he had cleared the mess in the California canal and sped around Rincon Hill. He looped down to the ballpark and around it, darted under the railroad bridge and ripped along parallel to the Kyoto Causeway, the seawall's official name. At the weirdly squared corner of 7th and Kyoto, he berthed *Hot 1* at the public dock, ran up the gangplank and over the wall. It was a busy morning. Heavy traffic filled the veloways in all directions. He threaded his way across the intersection to the velome at the Crossroads. The farm's table a short distance to the side of the velome had two buckets full of fresh flowers and a small sign saying, "Our rice harvest starts in six weeks. Training commences on August 1. Leave your name here, or sign up over the vyne."

Nwin barely glanced at it, thinking he might not be around for the harvest himself. He stepped in to the velome, looking around for his favorite. Not seeing anything he wanted, impulsively he thought to jump a streetcar, catching one as it pulled away. For a minute he hung on to the upright handles above the running board, old-fashioned style. He shoved his sunglasses into his pocket and ran his hand through his unnatural-feeling short stiff hair, trying to catch the breeze.

Shortly he went in to take the spiral staircase to the roof. Up top and fully in the sun, he was surprised to find himself alone. He picked up a crumpled newspaper and shook out the wrinkles. Yesterday's *Dock of the Bay*. Since it was the San Mateo section, he wasn't interested except for one item which caught his attention and sent his heart racing.

Mysterious Fires Plague Flooded Neighborhoods

SAN BRUNO—Investigators are seeking help from any eyewitnesses who might have seen anyone near the South San Francisco houses that burned last week. Early indicators are that the fires were deliberate, but investigators haven't named any suspects. Uphill residents with views of the submerged neighborhoods are urged to keep watch. If you see any suspicious activity among the drowned houses, please contact Emergency Services immediately.

Nwin read the short item several times. He put the paper aside and slouched back with his arms folded across his chest. He kicked the chair in front of him, trying to gain leg room, but it didn't budge, so he put his feet on the seat. *Why do they care about those houses? They're ruined anyway. Hell, they've been under water forever.* His thoughts raced. *They should have gotten rid of 'em a long time ago! Sitting there, clogging the Bay, ugly stupid houses. Why would anyone want to protect them?!* The waters had risen decades ago and there was no sign they were going to recede. People were shirking responsibility for huge shoreline areas where old urban development continued to pollute the waters.

Nwin sped down the stairs to the exit, jumping off as it slowed at Abundance Street. He ran crazily across the street, weaving in and out of bicycles, streetcars, big wagons, a few of the old solar-powered trucks. Down into the Library's basement he clattered, straight to the archival desk. He grabbed a slip of paper, and wrote down what he wanted: Documents of the Earth Liberation Front. He turned to the counter and handed his request to a pleasant young woman, who disappeared for about 10 minutes, Nwin was nervously pacing, wondering if she'd gone on break when she returned, smiling, carrying a bulging box.

"Early 21st century stuff, eh? Doing a research project?"

"Uh, yeah, that's right," said Nwin. He took the box and slipped into a nearby booth where he could sift through the contents in private. It didn't take long to find what he'd come for. He'd been through this before. In fact, he was probably the only one to have gone through this material in decades. He pulled out the booklet called "Setting Fires With Electrical Timers" and headed toward the copying machine.

"Found what you wanted already?!" called out the enthusiastic page. Nwin nodded dully, hoping to discourage any further interest. In a few minutes he had his own copies, and returned the box after burying the pamphlet in the pile..

"Earth Liberation. . . wasn't there some kind of uprising?. . ."

"In 2032, but they were massacred. Infected 'em with biological weapons."

"Eeew," she wrinkled her nose, far removed from the meaning of the words.

He smiled stiffly and thanked her again. A few minutes later he was huffing uphill. It was such a fine day, he decided to vist his favorite park at the top of Russian Hill.

II.

Emerging from the bathroom, Eric found a hairy dog who licked his hand. Grimacing, he shoved both hands into his pockets while the slobbering beast nudged his leg with its sopping wet nose.

"Sorry, Benjie's such a pain!" Tanya pulled him away, but looked puzzled at Eric's discomfort. "Hey, are you allergic or something?"

"No, I just don't like big wet hairy dogs. They have a way of filling up space, you know what I mean?"

She grunted as she pushed Benjie through a door and slammed it behind him. At the sink she washed her hands, gesturing to Eric to do the same if he desired. After such a sweaty ride, he was delighted to rinse off.

"Would you like to take a shower?" Tanya offered graciously.

"Man," he slapped his forehead in a comic overstatement, "I don't have anything to change into."

"We have at least three guys in this household, someone's clothes will fit you."

"In that case!" he grinned, and she bundled him off to the shower with a thick, soft towel.

"I'll be back in a sec with some clothes."

When he was scrubbed and dried, he found the pile of clothes she'd quietly slipped into the bathroom. He felt kind of goofy as he emerged. The shirt flopped over his shoulders, the pants were too big in the waist and too short.

Tanya sat at the kitchen table, nursing a cup of tea, reading a magazine. Late afternoon sun gave the room a rosy glow. "Tea?"

"No thanks."

She smiled, and snickered playfully, looking him up and down. "Those really fit, don't they?"

"At least they're clean," he said, far more embarrassed than he let on.

"I put your clothes into the solar oven in back. It's really for baking bread, but it's great for drying clothes in a hurry."

"Care for a tour of our house?"

"Lead the way."

Off the hallway from the kitchen were several rooms. The first was small and dark, a music studio. Then came a big dining room with polished wainscoting, topped by old-fashioned Edwardian wallpaper. Several elegant rooms completed the ground floor. As they reached the second story a woman rushed past in a bathrobe with a towel around her head. She barely acknowledged them, and Tanya said to her back, "That's Monica. I think she has a date." She knocked on the door opposite the stairs and getting no response, slowly opened it, calling out a soft "hello?" She flipped the switch to illuminate the bedroom. An eastern window gave some light, but the room was shadowed in the late afternoon. A deep blue wall surrounded the door, and two small pastoral lithographs hung in gilded frames to their left, next to a tall mirror.

"Jane's room," said Tanya without further comment. Opposite the bed the vyne crossed along the molding and disappeared through a small hole in the corner. They continued along the hall, darting in and out of two other bedrooms, before reaching the second living room overlooking the backyard.

"Let's take the back stairs up to the third floor," suggested Tanya, and Eric dutifully followed. Here the ceilings were lower and the back room was a porch used for storage. Glumly, Tanya admitted, "This is all my stuff. I've got to sort through it and take some to the Bart-Mart or give it away, but I just never get around to it."

Eric read the boxes—dishes, kitchen, books (several of these), clothes, shoes (two large boxes!), costume materials, art supplies, bike parts—all piled on some old wooden dressers and a desk tipped on its side.

"All this is yours?" Eric asked incredulously.

"Yeah, hard to believe isn't it?"

Sharp steps approached from inside. The door flung open and Marge glowered at Tanya. "Where are you going to put all that crap you just got?!" She crossed her arms while Tanya stood before her mutely, unable to offer a response. Disgusted, Marge waved in exasperated dismissal, turned and noisily disappeared, her elegant black boots punctuating every step across the linoleum floor. A door slammed a moment later.

"Oh brother!" moaned Tanya. Pulling herself up as tall as she could, she gently pushed Eric into the upstairs kitchen. "This is for tea, coffee, and snacks. But it's not used much. We prefer the big downstairs kitchen. Sometimes I like to sit here and write in my journal," she said, pointing to a pretty round table, granite-topped, by the window. Eric observed the tilting Dominoes and the Tweezer Towers, the orange Pyramid and the rest of downtown. "What a view!"

Marge's telltale footsteps echoed down the hall and the main stairs. "Oh good, she left!" said Tanya. "C'mon."

On the right they passed the split bathroom. On the left was Tanya's bedroom, a cheerful, zany cluttered space, walls jammed with pictures, paintings, posters, and hung above the bed were a pair of menacing spears. Her bed was disheveled, clothes lay about on the floor. The closet door was half open, clothes bulging from the rack over piles of shoes. Her window looked out on the same view as the little kitchen, the brilliant orange sunset lighting fires in distant windows. Tanya began straightening the bed and pitching clothes into a laundry hamper. "Sorry about this, I'm usually pretty neat," she claimed against all evidence.

"Vyne!" she called, and the green vyne on the top of the wall began unfurling its big display leaf. "Messages?" she asked, and a list of new messages appeared along the right side. Since she didn't seem to mind, Eric scanned the list. "Mom, Jane, Sue, Phil, Garden Party meeting, Radio Ignatius schedule change, house agenda. . ."

"I can't believe it! Phil went off to Brazil three years ago, and hasn't sent me a message or anything. I figured he hated me," she said ruefully.

"Why?" asked Eric.

"Well, I think he was in love with me. He found me in bed with Marge, and it broke his heart."

"Hmmm." Eric didn't know what to say. Tanya sat on her bed now, looking sad. Then she bounded to her closet to pull out a blue dress and matching shoes. "Give me a sec, okay?" she said. Eric returned to the kitchen where the early evening light accented the orange hue over downtown.

Tanya emerged to break the spell, taking his arm. "C'mon, there's still lots more to see!"

They walked down the hall, taking a quick look into Marge's room, austere with a dark single bed against the window, one blue-framed black-and-white portrait of Marge herself on the wall facing a tall thin mirror on the opposite wall. "That was taken by Vivian West. Do you know her work?"

"Isn't she in New York or something?"

"London. Great shot, isn't it?" He could only agree. A small dresser with a few items sat in one corner, and an old rolltop desk stood imposingly against the wall under the vyne.

They looked quickly into two more bedrooms, one for guests, before coming upon a beautiful circular room at the front of the building. "This is our writing studio," she announced proudly. The room wasn't completely round, but the cupola with its big curving Bay windows under a turret gave that feeling. A spiraling polished wooden staircase ascended through a floor into the turret. "You've got to see this," Tanya enthused. Up the stairs they squeezed into a small spherical room, with narrow windows facing each of the cardinal directions and thin skylight windows cut into the roof. An ancient typewriter and a computer nearly as old sat on two shallow work tables. On the opposite side of the turret a small couch with a footstool beckoned the writer lost in thought. Two of the small windows had been left open and wind rushed through the little room.

"This is the best spot yet! I'd love to hang out here."

"Maybe you'll get to," said Tanya hopefully, which surprised him.

Tanya closed one window, remarking that the turret tended to get stuffy without ventilation. After taking a few minutes to admire the peach-colored clouds against the sea of blues at sunset, they returned to the room below. A microphone/headphone setup lined one wall, and several sturdy tables sat in the room's center. A huge blue Persian rug dominated the floor beneath. There was a small library too, with books covering the walls. "I come here to work on my radio scripts. Two of my housemates are pretty serious writers and use this room."

She led him to a hallway door. A blast of evening air greeted them as they stepped on a narrow skybridge. "You've only seen one of the buildings," she announced as they stopped in the middle of the bridge, pausing to lean over the ornate railings. "Our house is one of seven of the larger cluster, called 'Page Mews.' I'd like a more artistic or abstract name but no one ever asked me."

Eric gazed down at the garden, partly visible between the buildings. "How many people live in Page Mews, anyway?"

"About fifty. All seven buildings are connected by skybridges and basement hallways. Of course the garden is an unbroken expanse—vegetables, flowers, play areas. We share the gardening, though there are private plots, too. I found that strange when I got here, but I guess there had been bad arguments about who used which vegetables, so. . ."

"It's not like there isn't plenty to eat!" Eric exclaimed, offended by the idea of private plots.

"True enough, but it was more about the farmer's pride I think. If you've nursed along a certain tomato patch, or planted something special, then discovered someone picking all your beans or peppers—."

"Seems like you could work that out without going all the way to *private plots!*" Eric said, truly bothered.

"Well, like I said, it happened before I got here, and there haven't been any problems since I arrived."

"How long have you been here?"

"Almost three years now. . . Luckily we don't meet as a whole group too much, only four times a year, around the solstices and equinoxes. Mostly, it's each building for itself, sometimes each floor."

This, too, surprised Eric. In Chicago he'd lived in a huge apartment building with over 200 units, and there was no way to handle the place without a building-wide system of self-management. Dividing it up by floor seemed crazy to him.

"How does it work when you need a new roof, or have to replace solar panels, or rewire part of one building and not the others?"

"We don't have problems with stuff like that. Everyone pitches in, and the skilled electricians manage. Actually, our electricians are always getting called to fix other people's places—Oh shit! Your clothes!"

Tanya bolted into the neighboring house, confusing Eric who assumed they should be going the other way. Tanya plunged down a two-story stairway going to the backyard. Eric almost ran over her trying to keep up when she suddenly stopped to take off her shoes. Clutching them to her chest with her left arm, she held the banister with her right as she began leaping down two and three stairs at a time. "Man, I hope we get there before it's too late," she said over her shoulder. They made a beeline for the solar oven. Tanya threw open the door and a little wisp of smoke emerged. She grabbed the clothes from the top rack—"OW!"—and threw them on a nearby table top, where they sizzled, brittle and slightly smoking. She bent over and sniffed.

"Chingo! I'm afraid we might have ruined your clothes—or *I* might have."

Eric touched his shirt, stiff and slightly singed. He sniffed it. Sure enough, it had burned. He delicately flipped it over and saw the black lines etched into the shirt from the grill.

"I'm SO sorry," wailed Tanya.

"It's not a big deal," he reassured her. He was actually glad because he had been feeling out of place and confused by her generous spirit. Even though he'd driven her load up here, during the tour of the house he began to feel like he was receiving unanswered gifts. Now at least he could forgive her small transgression. "Really," he touched her shoulder, "they were nothing special. There's plenty more where they came from."

"Yeah, I know," she said in a low voice. She slumped disconsolately, but in the late dusk light she looked alluring.

"What about that dinner you promised me?" he said, feeling strangely comfortable with this cute, smart, charming woman.

She brightened immediately. "Let's go! There's always something good at Trixie's. She's the best chef in the Mews." She took his hand, which pleased him, and pulled him along through the gardens, through the little playground and into the back of the last house in the row.

12.

Silver moonlight fell over the predawn water of Mission Bay. The campus buildings were well-lit as always, and already busy with bright-eyed students. A clear, fogless day lay ahead.

In his skiff Nwin zipped along towards the 7th and Kyoto docks on his way to the Rice Bowl. The muddy wetlands to the west of Mission Bay were an ideal place to grow the experimental rice from the labs at the UC campus out in the Bay. Restored creeks around town were channeled through Mission Creek's delta, continually flushing fresh water through and keeping the brackish tides on the east side of the 7th street causeway.

Nwin shivered in the pre-dawn coolness as he climbed from the docks over the Kyoto Causeway. Jumping down the stairs, he jogged slowly past the Crossroads, past the farm's table and the shacks along the road to the barn. Arriving, he saw signs of life and greeted Rikky, a farm veteran who had befriended him three months ago at the beginning of his Tryout.

"Hey Rikky," he called, tossing his jacket and backpack into a locker.

Sliding into overalls, Rikky shot back, "How's it twirlin'?"

Nwin did not respond while he pulled his overalls on, but looked over at Rikky absent-mindedly, as though he were already saying the words racing through his mind.

"What is it man? You look like there's an egg trying to get out of your throat!"

"Huh?.. oh, sorry. Just thinkin',... Well, to tell the truth, I'm worried about Angus."

"Yeah, he's been harsh hasn't he?"

"I think he's after me."

"Oooh, no way," scoffed Rikky. "He treats everyone the same."

"I don't know...," Nwin trailed off, discouraged.

Rikky headed for the door. "See you at the circle," she said evenly.

"Yeah, see ya."

Minutes later, he was outside. Dawn had broken and he ambled into a brightly lit circle of trees and found a seat on a wooden box in the back of the group.

"Mornin'," he greeted no one in particular.

To the side of the long picnic table, several farmers were well into their morning Tai Chi, others threw a disc in the field, and still others shared an early morning toke. The frisbee clattered into the breakfast table, knocking several coffee cups to the ground.

"Damn, man, you *have* to do that every pinchay morning?!?" Barry was grumpy. Liza, too. She yelled at the culprits, "You guys are shovelling shit for that!" not that she could actually enforce that "suggestion," but she probably could carry a vote if they resisted.

The sky brightened as everyone slowly gathered around the tables.

"OK, okay enough small talk! Let's get on with it."

As usual it was the staff curmudgeon Angus Kingston who insisted on "starting." Plenty of useful information about the farming was already in the air—observations, lessons learned, and so on—but the process did have its own demands to impose.

"Oh Angus! Pull your weeds, wouldja?" came the chorus response.

Rikky, a veteran of past Rice Bowl disasters as well as the current success, jumped in. "OK, well first off, who's new? OK, you guys (actually two women and a man standing uncertainly at the end of the table) check in with Vicky, our official greeter this month." Vicky smiled and waved.

"News and views?"

Nwin drifted off into his thoughts. He was still groggy from the night before. He sucked absent-mindedly a nasty blister on his finger. He looked forward to getting to work, wanting to look in on the fox lair.

"Hey do you guys *mind?*" carped Liza to a small quartet off to the side plunking on their guitars. They weren't playing loudly, but it did impair the main conversation. The regulars often had this problem with those doing their Annuals. The latter just didn't have much to contribute to the morning round-robin. The regulars needed the morning to make real plans and because it was the only time to check in. It was the rare volunteer who could sit through the morning session every day.

Liza turned back to the meeting. "The weather department says we won't get any rain until October at the earliest, so we should check up on the various pump stations. Barry, will you get on the vyne and send out inquiries?"

"Sure, I'll do it today."

"We need our trailers cleaned and oiled. Angus, will you take Fred and Elaine and our three newbies and set them up?"

"Yup, and I agree that Danny and Helen and Susie should shovel shit!"

"OK, OK, *sorry!* I can't believe you guys can get so bent over a harmless accident!" Helen led Danny and Susie away, making it a point to pick up the polished bamboo disc and toss it as they left.

Angus continued to hold the floor. "Our plantings have been trampled three times now in the southwest corner. We have to find the culprits—"

"Or we have to fence the area," Marco chimed in.

Nwin added quickly, "There's a light-weight, strong fence we can get in sections from the Bambu Factory." Angus looked at him, stunned.

"Isn't that a bicycle factory?" called a woman in the front.

"Yeah, but I have friends over there, and told 'em what was happening here. My pal Jerome told me about their new modular fences."

"Fences!!" roared Angus, slamming his shovel against the back wall. Liza intervened before Angus took over. "I propose that we send Nwin to get a prototype that we can check out. Any objections?"

Angus was enraged, muttering to himself about fences and closing common lands, but everyone else was open to it. "OK, it's agreed. Nwin, will you take care of it?"

"Sure," he smiled, wondering if it could be that easy.

"Nwin, you're on the flower beds, right? Marco and Sylvio, you're out in the fields, weeding, along with me, Bob, Jerry, Rikky, and Stefania."

"Hold up. I've got an announcement," said Stefania. "I got an appeal from my cousins in Chile. They've been raided twice in the past month, the last time three people were killed. Another one of these throwback groups homesick for the Money Era."

"Kill 'em !" said Angus with relish. "Bastards like that should be destroyed!"

"What's twirlin' with the folks nearby? Can't they get help from their neighbors?"

"Seems to me they should handle it locally, but since I got the message I thought I should at least share it. Any other suggestions off the tops of your heads? I'd send 'em Angus's advice, but they've probably considered it or rejected it by now," Stefania said.

"Let's wait and see. I'm for gettin' to work!" said Jerry. That broke up the meeting.

Nwin grabbed a rake, a hoe, his work gloves, and headed up the road to the marshes. He skirted along the causeway, following a small path through blue-flowered bushes. Whistling to himself in the early morning sunlight, he wondered if he might run into Valentina at the café where he'd seen her the other day.

He came to a California buckeye sprawled out over the marsh from the causeway's banks. Potrero Hill rose up a short distance ahead. Behind the tree trunk he'd discovered a fox lair. He didn't want to intrude or cause a panic, so he moved very slowly. He spotted a large outcropping at the edge of the marsh a few meters away. He climbed up and settled on the lookout. Soon he observed the grass rustling in a steady approach to the lair. He stood up quietly and peered as best he could at the tree's base, where he could make out a reddish-brown blob enter the lair and heard a cat-like mewing. He took out his field glasses and had a good look at the mama fox as she dropped a dead field mouse into the nest for her babies.

A red-tailed hawk circled overhead and Nwin realized he wasn't the only outsider to have discovered the lair. But the hawk wouldn't be able to get at the babies in the nest. Nwin sat impassively, enjoying the dance of nature.

He generally worked four days a week from before dawn until about noon, doing whatever was needed around the Rice Bowl. He'd taken it upon himself to prune the rose bushes and apply the skills he'd picked up as a child with his "Auntie" on the Harrison rose jungle.

The old-timers, over five years, seemed to have an intuitive connection with the job. Nwin wasn't sure he'd ever get that, but he enjoyed the marshes and the creatures in their natural element. It was fresh air and good honest work—he knew he was doing something worthwhile, even if his father didn't see it that way. And he still had plenty of time to dabble in watercolors, metal sculpture, and go to cafés, bars and parties.

Nwin settled into his routine, weeding flower beds, cutting dahlias and lilies, roses and geraniums, making beautiful bouquets to put out on the road. He also cut a few datura blossoms for their amazing smell, quickly dropping the cuttings into a water bucket he had stashed a few days earlier. The hours passed quickly and as the sun grew hot and reached its midday zenith, Nwin moseyed back to the yard, carrying his tools and bucket. He waved to the others still working in the rice fields.

He cut and trimmed his bouquets, wrapping them with twine and newspaper, and arranged them in a bucket. He wrapped the datura blossoms in a wet towel and placed them into a waterproof pouch in his shoulder bag to take home. He took the bouquets on a farm bike to the Crossroads where he set them on a table that had a small display about the Rice Bowl and other agricultural zones citywide. He zipped back to the barn, leaving the farm bike aside and changed out of his overalls.

Back at the Crossroads, he caught a streetcar heading up 7th to the Central Freestore. He jumped off at Abundance for the short stroll to the Civic Green.

A forest of colors filled the plaza where hundreds of people enjoyed orchestra music from the bandshell. People were hanging out listening, talking in small groups, reading, sampling new foods, playing chess and checkers, tossing discs. Kids made hoops roll by keeping them up with a stick, and a few splashed in the fountain. In the far corner a small group surrounded a dais from which a lanky blond fellow was urgently addressing them.

Nwin headed into the old Civic Auditorium, a gray classic, built in 1915 for a World's Fair. He had to dodge a steady stream of people leaving, clutching their bags full of household goods, clothing, and whatnot from the Freestore. This was the largest and best stocked one, so you could always find a pair of pants that fit, pens in the right color, a radio or a freight cart, pretty much anything "basic." What you couldn't find would either arrive the next week, or was genuinely scarce. You had to go to Treasure Island to get rare items.

Nwin didn't need much. He had plenty of clothes (his mother loved making him clothes), and his apartment had a built-in radio along with the Vyne. But he needed new sheets. The last set had been badly singed one night while he smoked a bowl in bed and it tipped over. So, new sheets, his favorite mint gum, and a notebook. Food shopping he didn't do, since he could always eat at a communal kitchen in the building, or at a café. He was lucky that a dozen good cooks lived in his building, and they were always looking for more mouths to feed.

He darted among the bustling "shoppers" (the word persisted, even though no "transaction" took place anymore). He leaned away from a woman carrying a box of new curtains down the aisle.

He found a set of sheets, black ones like he'd read about in an old spy novel, and grabbed an extra set in pastel yellow. In the "office" department, he settled on a handmade intricately bound notebook with short aphorisms in elegant calligraphy on every tenth page or so. ("Sometimes paper is the only thing that will listen to you," "There is mystery in the universe, but what is it? —Renee Magritte" "Never make forecasts, especially about the future. –Sam Golden".)

Boxes of gum and candy stood near the food department, and he chose his gum and freeze-dried salted peas and a jar of lemon curd, too. He went through the exit aisles, running his goods through a scanner, which noted the items to track demand.

"Hey Nwin, whatcha doin'?" Nwin turned around and met his cousin Tho, son of his mother's sister.

"Just picking up some stuff. What's twirlin' with you?"

"Doin' some Annuals stockin' shelves. There's foods I never knew about, stuff from Brazil, China, all over! Have you ever heard of 'cupua-çû'? (he pronounced it *koo-pwa-soo*) It's this crazy fruit, here, knock on this."

He held out a strange brown fuzzy cylinder to Nwin, who dutifully knocked his knuckles on it. It felt like metal.

"What is it?"

"Fruit! Ain't it the dew? This one is being grown in a tropical hothouse in San Mateo. Next time you go to the Real Ice Cream Parlor up on Rexroth, try some Cupua-çû ice cream, it's great!"

He shoved everything into his shoulder bag and headed back outside.

The music was full of soaring strings and pounding drums, so he wandered over to the plaza and glided onto the grass, taking out a piece of gum. He laid back and closed his eyes in the midday sun. Before long he was dozing.

* * *

"**H**ey, wake up!"

A shoe poked him in the ribs, and he rolled away, putting his hands over his head instinctively.

"Nwin, wake up!"

He looked up and observed three girls standing over him, hands on hips.

"Wha—?" he mumbled.

Valentina and two friends gazed down as Nwin unfurled from a near fetal position, at their easy prodding. He sat up suddenly, brushing his clothes, embarrassed as he looked around the Civic Green. He'd been asleep for a while, judging by the sun.

The girls giggled and whispered to each other.

He struggled to his feet, dumbfounded that Valentina was here, waking him up on the Civic Green. *Am I dreaming?*

"I knew it was you," said Valentina, "What on earth did you do to your hair?"

Her friends tittered, while Nwin unconsciously ran his hand through his hair, struggling against the weight of the deep sleep from which he had barely emerged.

He squinted at her friends uncomprehendingly.

"Oh yeah, sorry. Nwin, this is Harmony," and she gestured to the short, thin girl in black shorts and an orange sports jersey, "and Shelley." Nwin recognized Shelley as the girl he'd seen with Valentina at the Dolores Park Café. She had long black braids behind her round cherubic face. She offered a winning grin, clutching her elbow with her opposite hand, and absent-mindedly fidgeting with her pocket.

"We were walking through the Green, and I spotted you lying there. We came over, and even though you look pretty weird, I could tell…"

"Yeah, she knew it was you from over there," Harmony added, pointing to the fountain.

"Good eyes," said Nwin appreciatively. "Man, I need a coffee. Feel like getting somethin'?"

"Sure," said the girls in unison. They had been kicking around aimlessly. Getting a drink was what people do.

Nwin and Valentina fell in side by side, Shelley and Harmony behind. Nwin looked sidelong at Valentina. "So, what'cha been doin' since you quit the farm?" he asked.

Thankful for the icebreaker, Valentina bubbled, "Oh, I've been doing Annuals all over.

Let's see… the farm was at least a month ago. What have I done since? Hmmm… my favorite was the transbay ferry. I worked the coffee bar on the Vallejo run, I crewed for a Sacramento overnighter, and I was last mate to Oakland, Hayward, and Redwood City."

"You like the water, huh?"

"It's great! The dolphins leaping around, the fish, the birds, the sky, the smell of the water and the sun, and all the different people. And the ferry crews are fun too… jokers!"

"My dad used to captain an ocean tug."

"Really? I'd love to try that. You think he'd take me on a trip?" she asked eagerly.

"He's retired," Nwin confided softly. "He got badly hurt. He hasn't been on a tug for years." He looked away, frustrated that he brought up his father.

"Sorry."

He shrugged and jammed his hands into his pockets, looking at the ground as they continued in silence. Peeling laughter broke the spell.

Harmony sprawled on the lawn behind them and Shelley laughed uproariously. "She… she…" pointing at Harmony. "She tripped," and she doubled over laughing. Harmony was gathering herself, grinning and scowling, then reaching to re-tie her shoe. She blushed deeply and shot a wicked look at Shelley. "It's not THAT funny," she said sourly.

"Just like that clown we saw last week," Shelley explained mirthfully, "you should'a seen her!" and she burst out laughing again, as she offered her hand to Harmony. Harmony smiled now. She accepted the boost up, and soon they were sitting at the café while Nwin went to order his cappuccino and iced teas for the girls.

"He's cuuute," Shelley whispered conspiratorially and Valentina glared, kicking her under the table. "Owww." Nwin returned with a tray full of drinks and sat next to Valentina. "So, where else did you work?"

"A dentist's office, a bakery, a signmaker's shop. And a few days of velome too, with basic repair lessons."

"Wow, that's a lot in a month!" He still couldn't believe that she had recognized him sleeping, and now here they were. He wished her friends would leave.

"Still at the Rice Bowl?" Valentina asked.

"Yeah, for now. I'm coming to the end of my Tryout. I liked it okay at first, but the cranky old lifer has been giving me a lot of shit. I don't think I'll be able to stay unless he gets off my case."

"What's his problem?"

"He blames me for everything. His plantings got trampled a few times, and he thinks I know who's doing it."

Valentina raised her eyebrows, urging Nwin on.

"Do you know those kids on Potrero Hill, the Russians? Aleksy and Vlad and all them?"

She shook her head.

"They're a tough bunch, they like to break things. We planted a patch of swamp near their territory, and that's the place that keeps getting hit. I wouldn't be surprised if it was them but I've never seen 'em , and I would never turn them in, no matter what!"

"Not even if you saw them?" asked Harmony, incredulous. She was several years younger than the others.

Nwin glanced at her with silent condescension, and shook his head. He looked into his coffee, and turned back to Valentina.

"My pal Calvin works at the Bambu Bike Factory down on 5th. He showed me this modular fence they came up with, so I proposed we fence in that patch." He paused, "This morning seems like a long time ago."

Valentina smiled sympathetically, and asked "Were you sleeping a long time?"

He returned her smile, and shrugged. "Maybe an hour or two."

Harmony announced that it was time to head home. "C'mon Shelley, Mom said we had to be back by 5:30."

Shelley scowled at her little sister, blushing. The resemblance was now obvious to Nwin. Shelley was not going to be dragged off by her younger sister, at least not right away.

Inserting herself into the conversation, she turned to Nwin. "Where is it you work exactly?"

"At the Mission Bay Rice Bowl, off the 7th Street causeway."

"Really? I go by there a lot. I'm taking classes at UC Mission Bay, so we have to catch the launch at 7th and Kyoto."

Nwin looked at her in surprise. "What are you studying?"

"I'm just starting," she admitted hesitantly, "it's basic stuff. I'm hoping to go into biomorphology or maybe I'll be a doctor."

"Biomorphology?"

"Yeah, where you design new biodevices—skiffs, shellfones... even the vyne."

"I didn't know it was called that. I've got a bioskiff."

"Dew! Can we take it out for a flip sometime?" Valentina asked, excited.

Nwin straightened up, marveling at how everything seemed to be falling into place. "Sure, I'd love to."

Harmony leaned forward with excitement, "Oooh, can I come too?"

Shelley elbowed her, shaking her head like big sisters do. "There's not room for more than two, Harmony."

Harmony fell back, disappointment taking over.

Nwin saw it, too, and as glad as he was to have a vague plan with Valentina, he felt sorry for Harmony. "Hey, I'll give you a spin some time, too," he said graciously.

"Really? You mean it?" Harmony jumped up, electrified at the prospect. Knowing glances passed between Shelley, Nwin and Valentina, as Nwin nodded without offering any specifics, smiling.

Valentina stood up to usher her friends home. "Hey Nwin, I'm glad we ran into you." She slapped his hand. "Vyne me, ok?"

"What's your last name?" he remembered to ask.

"Rogers, I live in the lower Haight in the Pierce Palace. You can always get me through my grandparents, the Panduccino's."

Nwin looked up at her, surprised and in awe. Everyone knew the name Panduccino. Claudia Panduccino was one of the better known revolutionaries still alive. "Is it... are you...?" he asked unable to form a complete question.

Valentina laughed. "My mom is a direct descendent," she said swelling with pride. "My grandma Francesca is Claudia's daughter. Claudia lives up in Mendocino... She's 114 and going strong!" Turning to Shelley and Harmony, she said, "C'mon you guys!

We're gonna be late!"

"You guys all live in the Palace?" Nwin asked, and they nodded as they said their goodbyes.

"Don't forget your promise, Nwin!" urged Harmony, not fully understanding all that had transpired at the table.

"Don't worry," he reassured her without conviction. They all slapped hands one more time, and as he turned to leave, he and Valentina made eye contact one last time, grinning happily at each other.

He floated across the Green, practically to the other side before he remembered his pack was still at the café. He hurried back, and excused himself to some older women who had just settled at the table. As they squirmed out of his way, he reached under and grabbed his bag, thanked them, and retraced his steps.

He found the usual cluster of streetcars on Abundance, hopped one going down 8th and at Kyoto jumped off again. At the corner was a common utility box with a first-aid kit, water, a fold-up stretcher, and other emergency supplies. He grabbed three flares and dropped them into his bag. He walked a block to the docks at the Crossroads and found his skiff where he'd left it, and cast off. In seconds he was flying along the causeway, flipping toward the open Bay, the evening sun casting an orange glow on the city as the Bay turned a deep aquamarine.

Nwin's heart pounded as he replayed his encounter with Valentina. He dug the heel of his hand into his thigh as he steered the skiff around the ballpark and north toward the Pyramid. Orange sunlight on downtown towers lessened the Pyramid's normal bright contrast and soon he eased into the residential dock and tied up *Hot 1* for the evening.

* * *

The next day was hot, so Nwin left the Rice Bowl before lunch and went for a ride. He leaned back, absent-mindedly steering *Hot 1* in and out of old ruins, ducking under the remnants of a rusting crane. Seagulls screeched overhead and the wind sent a loose piece of metal crashing against a support beam. Nwin ducked instinctively, and quickly sped away.

He looked at the cranes, rooftops, and upper stories of abandoned, semi-submerged buildings with disgust. Impatiently he accelerated around the Potrero Hill cliffs rising out of the water. He had to stop abruptly in the face of a long fence blocking his way. The fence was made of old marine netting, the kind used for aquaculture farming. As he drew up alongside it, he could hear the excited chatter of children not far off.

He peered at a dozen small wooden piers extending from the shore into the Bay. A class of eight-year-olds stood on the boardwalk with three adults, one of whom led the group onto a narrow pier. After herding the kids into place, the leader went around to the next adjacent pier. Reaching into the water he pulled up a pole, mussels thickly clinging to it. Nwin started flipping further out in the Bay. He accelerated, standing to get wind and spray in his face. His boredom gave way when he began to think about the next hit. Two immense freighters loomed ahead, anchored in the Bay. He slowed and began veering to the south when he noticed people descending a ladder into a launch.

It can't be. He didn't want to get too close, but he wanted a better look. He maneuvered in a broad circle, disappearing briefly behind the freighter, dwarfed beneath its rusting, paint-chipped hull. He cut closely to the ship's bow and popped back into view, much nearer the launch. Three men and a woman were in the launch, someone else still on the ladder. He paused and stared, sure the woman on the ladder was Nance. He reversed in haste, hoping to remain unseen, and pulled back behind the bow before anyone spotted him. His heart thumped. "There's not enough hate in this world," came rushing back, from his first encounter with the mysterious Nance.

Who are they? What are they doing? His mind raced with curiosity and fear. He looped in a wide arc away from the ship and its departing passengers. When he could again see the freighter from the west, there was no sign of the launch. Staring towards downtown he couldn't make it out among dozens of small craft. Despite his intense curiosity, he was afraid to go in pursuit of the launch. If they observed him, they might come after him, and then what? A chill went up his spine.

He angled northward anyway, but made for the Precita Levee. At the Levee he docked and scampered up the winding staircase over the Arcobolo and up the slope of Bernal Heights. Driven by a growing sourness, he climbed steadily. He'd sent some messages to Valentina. No response.

Thoughts of Valentina were pushed aside as he reached the crest of the hill with its panoramic view. Far downtown the leaning Dominoes flashed morning sun from their windows. Across the slope below him he could see his parents' backyard. There was his father on his knees, head down, working the soil. His straw hat quivered so slightly as he moved from one row to the next, the red plaid workshirt setting him apart from his prolific garden. Nwin stared, frowning.

That's the whole world to him, that stupid garden! He threw some dirt he'd unconsciously picked up, and wiped his hand on his leg. Suddenly a hand lay on his shoulder! He jumped away automatically, rolling a short distance in the tall yellow grass.

"Nwin, it's just me," laughed Al Robledo.

"Shit Al, what are you tryin' to do, give me a heart attack?"

"What'cha doin' here? Watchin' yer dad?"

"Nah. I came up here for the view, and because . . ."

"Yeah?" Al raised his shoulders and eyebrows in an inquiring pose. "Talked to the old man lately?"

Nwin shook his head, irritated to talk about his father. "It's not about him!" he spat.

"Why don't you talk to him?" Al had known Nwin since he was little, and his dad before the injury. He'd seen him struggle through the convalescence and close down and withdraw, failing to resume his captaincy. Once upon a time Jeffrey was one of the gang at the Dovre Club, drinking, playing pool or poker, arguing baseball, talking about women into the night. Not every night, mind you. He was a responsible seaman and knew better than to tie one on before a day at sea. But he never came out anymore, not for years. His defeated bitterness was bad enough, but when he started blaming Al for turning people against him, well that was too much even for Al. But Al still felt warmly towards Nwin, and tried to offer him guidance, even friendship. Not that Nwin made it easy! When Nwin was thirteen Al had spent most of the summer helping him with his baseball game, going to his games, offering tips. His father had not been interested, and had even grown hostile, yelling at Nwin to "get serious." Al encouraged Nwin to keep playing, stunned that his father could berate a 13-year-old.

Nwin got up stretching, more comfortable with Al now, but still fuming about his father. "I don't want to talk TO him, or ABOUT him!" he declared, closing the topic.

"So what's happening?" asked Al.

Nwin looked over, struggling internally, not sure if he could confide in Al. He looked down at the ground, sending a small rock tumbling down the hill. "Shit!... Nuthin'!"

Al didn't say anything, just sank to his haunches, plucked a piece of grass and began chewing it. He was in no hurry.

Nwin sat back down, too, noticeably agitated.

They sat there staring out at the city together. Precita Creek gurgled far below where pedestrians and bicycles looped over the curving Harrison Street Bridge. Al remembered a few times over the years when he'd run into Nwin on the hill. It didn't help to press him. He held things close. The boy would talk if he wanted to.

"Hey," Al said softly, "didja hear about the plan to bring wolves here?"

Nwin looked over with curiosity. "No, what's that?"

Al told him about the community meeting where his mother and the rest of the neighborhood council had argued about the latest Restoration Council wild corridor plan. Nwin shook his head, vaguely enthused, whistling his amazement. Another ten minutes went by in silence, and then Al clapped his hand on Nwin's back, "Come over if you ever want to, okay?"

"Yeah, sure... thanks," Nwin said noncommittally. They slapped hands and Al began to labor up the hill, his 81 years slowing him down.

Nwin's thoughts flitted about, from the hit he was planning, to Valentina, to Nance and her mysterious associates on that freighter in the Bay. Angus loomed up, blocking his way. *That bastard!* Nwin's hate found free reign on the subject of Angus. *He should never have picked a fight with me! Chingale, I'm gonna let him have it!*

Distracted by his anger, he got up, and stomped back toward the east slope from where he'd come. He did not see his mother on the back porch, her hands on her hips, peering through the bright sunshine, certain that it was her son who now stalked away at the top of the hill.

Sighing, she went inside, opened the vyne with a curt command and sent a short message to Nwin.

"Hi Nwinnie," she said automatically. "I'm heading to Treasure Island today, so I'll try to get your hat. Will you come for dinner next week? Vyne me. I love you."

Meanwhile Nwin threaded his way through the spiral staircases and courtyards of Arcobolo. Cascades of flowering vines wrapped around the railings, intensely perfuming the air. He quickened his pace, making his way through several more labyrinthine corridors before popping out on the levee, not far from the public dock where he'd left *Hot 1*.

Jumping in and casting off, he once again sped into the Bay. He looped around Potrero Hill and made for Treasure Island. He knew he wouldn't be able to land there, but something drew him. He hadn't been to the island for a long time. He slid around to the east side and made out the Pink Palace. Garish lights from a century of red light districts flashed provocatively. The sight of the Palace triggered an unfocused sexual hunger. He began flipping away from the island, heading around the north end. Peering ahead, he ducked suddenly as a skiff sped away from the island just 150 meters from his own trajectory. He peeked out to see the eight-seater turn south and get up to speed.

No mistake, it was Nance and four others.

That must be the same group that was at the Hurricane. The eight-seater had considerably more power than his little skiff, and quickly disappeared in the distance, heading towards the freighter he had seen them leave from earlier. He wracked his brain. *What were they up to?* They'd been interested in him because of the fires. *How did they know about him? And who else knew? How did Nance find him on Bernal that time? How did they get on to Treasure Island in their own boat?* It was more than Nwin could digest.

He pointed towards the Pyramid, now straight ahead of his position north of Treasure Island. Dolphins leaped through the waves, but easily stayed out of his way. He tried to remember the name of the freighter they came from... *Leopold Tanzania*, that was it! He headed home to do some research.

13.

Trixie's dining room did not disappoint. Eric and Tanya sat back, stuffed with ratatouille over Mission Bay wild rice, steamed Bay clams and garden salad. Conversation buzzed around the huge regal table, ebbing during the serious business of chewing and lip-smacking, but now boisterously rising anew with argument. Candles flickered in chandeliers, shedding a warm glow onto cracked, peeling walls, a faded yellow outlined with dark wooden beams. Two feet from the ceiling on a matching Victorian ledge tiny sculptures gazed impassively at the crowded room.

"Wolves?! You can't be serious!" shrilled a thin, mousy man at the end of the table.

A big woman across from him laughed. "You're just afraid you'll get eaten!"

Angrily, the little man leaned forward jabbing his finger in the air. "That's just stupid! Look, there's a reason cities evolved how they did. There's not room for big wild mammals. Sorry!"

"Oh come on, Vinnie, we can learn new ways to co-exist," said the man next to him in a casual green pullover.

Irritation all over his face, Vinnie glared. "I have enough trouble co-existing with your damn dog!" to which the table guffawed approvingly.

"Hey have you heard about the MacMillan proposal?" asked a round-faced woman, wearing a doctor's lab coat.

"The guy must be nuts!" answered the dog-owner emphatically.

"So you don't think there should be any research on inter-species communication at all?"

"Don't put words in my mouth! I didn't say that," he snapped. Eric thought people knew each other's positions already, given the quick responses and rising emotions.

The dog owner continued: "Research is one thing, but MacMillan goes way beyond that! He wants to break down *all* boundaries of species integrity. I'm with the Integritistas on this one."

The round-faced woman looked around waiting for reinforcement. Next to her a man leaned on his hand, his long brown hair hanging down, walling off his face from Eric's view. He stirred and sat back, whipping his hair out of his face. His sharply edged jaw clenched and his mouth opened and closed as if words were trying to escape.

Against his black sweater his pink face seemed almost luminescent.

"I think this is a hard one," he finally said with a deep mellifluous voice. Side conversation ceased as he took the floor. "I am curious. MacMillan's proposal, in itself, is very specific and I can't say I find it that threatening. I've always wondered what the dolphins would tell us if they could. Imagine if they had an oral history of the last 500 years or even some new jokes! Maybe Angie's on to something here."

"Science is not a dirty word!" said round-faced Angie, defiant. "Research, under social control, is vital. I'm not entirely convinced about MacMillan's proposal, but on principle I support a new openness toward scientific inquiry. We've been held back by fear and self-hatred for too damn long!" Her eyes blazed, a personal edge creeping into her voice.

"Oh come on!" came the rebuke from the dog owner and others chimed in behind him. Geri, a picture framer and mother of three small children who she had just sent out to play, offered, "Self-hating? Do you think the Die-off just fell in from the sky?!? Science had to be locked up for a *reason*."

"Do we have to go there? Science is not to blame, I'm sorry. It was an insane world. Any madman could throw up a lab and the only control was a government that didn't care and the invisible hand of the market. Any businessman could hijack the gene pool. Business held the reigns but science got the blame!!" Angie slumped back in her seat, frustrated at her endless need to defend Science against a false understanding of history.

The man who had wanted to hear dolphin jokes was named Gerald. He put his arm over her shoulder and stroked her neck lightly. Angie reflexively dropped her head onto his shoulder before apparently deciding to resist the mood, and straightened back up.

Tanya whispered to Eric, "You OK?" and he nodded enthusiastically. He hadn't been in this kind of discussion for ages. Chicago cafés and philosophical salons had been far more competitive and pretentious. Tanya sat back, bored. She wanted to go back to her room, but didn't feel it would be okay to leave him here alone, at least not yet. Maybe if he started talking to someone else, she could take off. She unfolded her arms and tried to look interested.

Now the focus moved to the other end of the table, where Trixie the cook was holding court. "But Emmy, you *don't* have to. You've been working more than anyone here for months, and you don't even have a career! C'mon, how many Annuals do you think you've done since January?"

A young woman slouched very low, her head, covered in a red bandana, barely reaching the top of the chair. Her eyes and white teeth flashed from deep black skin as she spoke. "Hell, I don't know... must be hundreds by now."

"But why? Why do you work so much? Don't you have any projects of your own?" Trixie pressed her. "Haven't you heard about the campaign to lower Annuals to 30 hours a *year*?"

Feeling attacked suddenly, Emmy sat upright to reveal herself as one of the taller people around the table. "I know most people are trying to find their calling. I suppose I am, too. But you know, I get up in the morning, and I like finding new things to try, I like the variety. It usually doesn't feel like work to me, it's more like a puzzle or a game. Besides, the appreciation I get is really gratifying," she said in a transparent complaint about household relations.

Trixie shook her head knowingly, and patted Emmy on the arm. "Hey, I guess you're the person the system was designed for…wake up and decide what to do. Farm in the morning, manufacture in the middle of the day, play Lady Macbeth at night…the New Woman!," she declared supportively.

Emmy snorted, and fell back into her slouch. "I don't know about no New Woman," she said, crossing her incredibly long, slender arms. Looking defiantly around the table, she added, "It's boring to do the same thing every day. I don't know why anyone would want to!" Eric watched her from mid-table, fascinated by the mechanics of her movements, which were dramatically heightened by the contrast between her white stretch tanktop, her round curving shoulders, and her almost purplish skin.

A Danish woman across from her piped up, "What is duh problem wit' 60 hours a year? Or having a career? I read in *Free Radical* dat we have to fight de Work Et'ic. Dis is crazy! People like to work, dey want to do dere share. What's duh problem if someone wants to do a lot of tings… we must work to eat, to have homes. I tink we work enough, not too much, not too little. I tink Emmy is great."

"Annika, I hate to say it, but you come from northern Europe, the home of the Work Ethic!" laughed the dog owner down the table. A small chorus chuckled along with him.

"Aaah!" Annika got up, disgusted, giving him the back of her hand. Glaring at him she said, "You! You let your dog run all over the yard, and we have to mind him, pick up his shit! You are a mess. Who cleans your bat'room?" she demanded, and without waiting for an answer, "NOT YOU!!," and stalked out of the room.

An uneasy silence fell over the table. William, muttering and shaking his head, started clearing, noisily stacking dishes. This seemed to be a signal and people started carrying dishes back to the kitchen. On the kitchen radio a rollicking zydeco tune filled the air. Dishes clattered as Tanya grabbed Eric's arm, motioning towards the back door.

"Uh, shouldn't we help?" he insisted.

"Nah, you're a guest, and it's not my week. C'mon!" she urged. She pulled him out the door as he waved back at Trixie, calling "Thanks… it was great, especially those clams!" Trixie smiled back as if to say it was nothing special, and returned to her conversation with Emmy.

"That was really dew," declared Eric.

"Yeah?" Tanya answered skeptically. "I think if you were here all the time you might not think so."

"Why not?"

"These fights go on for years. Ever since I got here it's been like that. William and his dog against Vinnie and his nerves; Angie the doctor acting like Science is an untouchable religion, with Gerald in his shining armor rushing to defend her… it's disgusting, an endless loop!"

He remained silent as they walked through the long backyard in the cool evening. The silence grew awkward, each of them at a loss.

"Uh, well, listen Tanya. Thanks for showing me everything. The dinner was—"

"Oh no, thank YOU, for gallantly saving me from that ridiculous load."

They both laughed at their sudden formality.

"I think I'll take off now," Eric announced.

"Tell me again where you're staying?"

"The Tweezer Towers Hostel, on California Canal."

"Oh yeah…" They came to the bike parking area "Well, here we are."

"My clothes!"

"Oh shit, I practically forgot. Listen, I've got to get you some replacements."

"No, forget about it. I've got too many anyway. But maybe we can find a pair of pants that fits me better?" he suggested as he looked at his bare ankles, clutching the waist to hold it up.

"Man, those don't fit at all! Why didn't you say something?" she admonished, forgetting that he had. "Follow me."

On the 2nd floor of her building she opened a big closet filled with clothes. "Take anything you want."

He thumbed through a couple of stacks.

"The bigger ones are on the left, the smaller on the right, at least that's the idea." On the third try he found one that seemed promising. She stood there looking at him as he pondered where he might go and change.

"Oh, I'm sorry! I always forget that not everyone wants to strip down in front of strangers! Here," she strode down the hall, "you can change in here," opening the door to a small room.

"Thanks," he said sheepishly. A few minutes later he was promising to keep in touch as he wheeled through the gate and tried to remember how to get home. "This way, right?" he called, pointing down towards the Panhandle.

"Yep, just get into the Panhandle and follow the Wiggle to Abundance. You can find your way from there, right?"

"I thiiiink sooooo" he yelled as he rolled away, waving.

14.

From his perch among the branches of his favorite climbing tree atop Russian Hill, the city stretched out to the west. A flock of parrots crossed the sky towards a luscious afternoon snack in the flowering gardens near Fillmore. A massive ship stacked with metal containers chugged through the Golden Gate. The towers of the old bridge still stood at the door of the Bay but the closer tower leaned precariously, windmills spinning from its green frame. Nwin lowered his gaze and tried to find where he'd left off reading in *Free Radical* before he'd started staring into space.

"We Don't Have To!" was a column by Cameron Floyd. Floyd was one of the proponents of cutting Annuals down to 30 hours a year, and was campaigning against the "we all have to" notion.

> You would never know that we've been living in a post-Economic world for 75 years. Incessant propaganda to "do our share" tyrannizes us, promoting a culture of endless toil for its own sake. Why do so many people get up and go to work every day? The world our parents and grandparents created after the Die-off is intelligently designed. They left us a brilliantly efficient and durable system of locally self-sufficient production, for which we all can be thankful. Unfortunately, they also left us

with a work ethic that has long ago become obsolete.

If anyone actually paid attention, we'd have some revealing numbers on how many people have already opted out of the treadmill of careers *and* Annuals. Then maybe the rest of us who still head off to work everyday, just so we can do more of what we did the day before, would realize how often our work is actually unnecessary.

Let us leave behind for once and for all this pernicious Work Ethic. It wrecked the world before, and still has us in its grips. There's more to life than work! Is there a budding Ginsberg or Picasso who has been too busy working to smell the sea air and just while away the day, until creative lightning strikes?

His father, Jeffrey Robertson, tall but stooped, prematurely aged, the wrinkles in his dark black skin clotted with dust from the yard, loomed large in his imagination. *The same boring lectures night after night, on and on, pull your own weight, the pleasure of work well done. . .*

Whether gardening or fixing stuff, he could never meet his father's standards. Nwin grimaced, the memories pursuing him, his father's incessant pressure: do it this way, not that, choose a career, specialize. "Better to choose than have it chosen for you. Words to the wise!"

His father had been a great tugboat captain before he'd been badly injured in an accident at work, when Nwin was young. They'd amputated his foot, and his left hand was unable to grip anything. It took 14 months to grow a new foot and more months to get his strength back. By then he'd been away from the tugboat for almost two years. When he tried to go back, he just couldn't do it anymore. His passion for the work was gone, and the old crew had scattered. He grew deeply depressed, and retired to his garden. As Nwin reached puberty, his father, always around, had become increasingly controlling. Nwin chafed under the lectures, the pressure, the bitterness his father took out on him.

Jennifer, his mother, watched helplessly as father and son grew estranged. She'd tried to act like everything was fine, but by the time Nwin was 14, neither he nor his father could relax around the other. Jennifer was on the Bernal Heights Neighborhood Council and the local water committee. She'd been a Shitsys installer in the Great Conversion during her early adulthood, so she knew how to repair and replace household modules. She was one of eight neighborhood technicians on call although the system needed little active maintenance. (Each house had its own solar collectors, gray water system, methane gas to supplement hot water heating, and a steady output of fertilizer blocks that were redistributed to local farms.)

The Bernal Commons across the top of the hill flourished with native plants, butterflies, small mammals and deer, while along the residential perimeter were gardens and orchards, all enriched by neighborhood fertilizer. Burrowing gophers had destroyed many gardens until a concerted trapping effort had removed them to the hills of the East Bay. A demographic explosion of deer had pushed animals from McLaren Park into the Islais Creek greenway and eventually they'd found their way up the Folsom greenway, past Holly Park and to the top of Bernal for grazing. Now neighbors debated the idea of introducing wolves to control the deer population. Studies indicated that restoring large predators did wonders for species balance in reclaimed habitats.

"But we can't have wolves roaming around our backyards!" a middle-aged mom insisted. "Do I have to lock my kids indoors?" She expected her neighborhood council to nip this one in the bud. Jennifer had looked at her, thinking about Nwin, climbing out of the garden, chasing butterflies up the hill, rolling through the tall grass. With his friends, he had played Ecologists-and-Ranchers, built miniature veloways, scratched in the mud during rainy days, channeling rivulets into little ponds shaped by sticks, rocks and mud. The grass fire he'd started when he was only seven flitted uneasily across her mind, a momentary intrusion.

She wanted to continue studying the question. A restoration expert testified that wolves co-existed with humans without much conflict as long as they had sufficient prey. Others pointed out that there was a limited supply of deer, fox, possum, skunks, and other small mammals in the wild corridors and hilltops. The population explosion was real, but it could be quickly reversed. Finding a stable state in the small range and artificially constricted terrain would be difficult. If wolves were to be introduced, they argued, Animal Control would have to be ready to intervene. So the debate was continued, to be taken up again after further reports from the Wild Corridors Commission and the Restoration subcommittee.

"I don't see how we can make a meaningful decision about this in Bernal Heights. We need to consult with our neighboring councils, probably the entire city. Wolves are not going to stay in one neighborhood, just like the coyotes and foxes haven't," concluded the Council chair, Rhonda Delacorte, a wizened veteran of previous restoration debates.

Jennifer Robertson continued to believe in community and family, even though her son had moved out at sixteen and visited infrequently. She assumed he was separating like a normal adolescent. *He will come back and be part of the family again when he is ready. Nwin and Jeffrey will find a new respect for each other.*

His mother's wishes were far from his thoughts as he sat in the tree, fondling the magnifying glass in his pocket. He had finished reading and felt jumpy. He clambered down the tree and began walking downhill to the west. The street wound down, swinging back and forth across dense gardens. A delivery bike struggled uphill, laden with groceries. At Polk he hopped a passing streetcar, bounding off after three blocks when he spied a velome at Union and Van Ness across from a fuel dispensary, its gleaming metal silo standing amidst dense trees on the southwest corner. He skipped downhill, strangely energized.

At the velome he grabbed a Red Fury, a big cruiser with a high gear ratio, suitable for speed, with a deep basket built on to the back rack. The mechanic on duty waved his wrench at him as he pushed it outside. His choice of wheels made climbing the Van Ness hill to Clay daunting. The high gears were twice as hard to pedal as another bike. But soon he crested the hill, and found a major jam of people ahead, bikes and streetcars, not unusual for mid-afternoon. Overhead the transparent 'Velobrij' carried bicyclists between Cathedral Hill and the upper reaches of Nob Hill. He darted through the Sacramento Greenway to Polk, slid into a stream of bikes heading south in the veloway, and accelerated with gravity's assistance.

At Eddy Street he veered off towards downtown. The tree-lined sidewalks shaded the veloway twisting down the middle. A noisy mob was parading across Eddy at

Leavenworth, clapping and chanting, "Recall Duvall! Rat Abatement Now!" Drummers brought up the rear, pounding out a wild rhythm. Inevitably dancers followed, spinning and gyrating wildly.

Duvall?... Nwin tried to remember who he was. The call for rat abatement sounded like a throwback to the bad old days. Why not just bring in cats, even though it had only been a few years since the cat problem had been resolved. *Humans and animals, what a mess!* He watched the last dancers spinning through the intersection.

A block and a half later he angled past dense bushes at the corner of Tailor, and ducking under a low-hanging tree, stopped in front of a dingy shopfront, dirty windows behind metal grating. Chipped gold letters arching in the window spelled out "ABC Locks and Safes". He leaned his bike against the front of the building and reached for the grimy door handle. It opened without resistance and Nwin entered the strange world of Pius Lee Wong.

Wong sat behind a long wooden counter, immersed in a game of Go with another aged Chinese man, who sat with his back to Nwin, a long black braid hanging down his back. Old locks and chains hung on the wall. Nwin approached the counter. Dusty board games lay in a pile on a table behind the counter. Ancient dishes caked in dust filled a glassed-in cabinet. The air felt thick with dust.

Wong stared at his next move, ignoring Nwin. His companion glanced sidelong, his stringy uncombed goatee twitching as he chewed on a toothpick. A young woman swept through the bead curtain separating the shop's front from the apartment behind. She was not much older than Nwin, and wore a customary pale blue embroidered coat with white needlepoint trees, birds and flowers. She glided behind Wong and greeted Nwin with a slight silent bow of her head. Her face was stark white with pancake makeup, her mouth ruby red. The sharp colors were set off by jet black hair arranged in a traditional round bob, chopsticks sticking out the sides.

"Hi Sue."

"Nwin," she replied, noncommittally. "The same?"

He nodded, "just one this time, okay?" His hands fumbled with his backpack. She smoothly wafted off through the bead curtain, and Nwin thought about what she must have on her feet to move so noiselessly. Moments later she re-emerged, the two men still impassive, concentrating on their game.

"Here." She swung the big can around the end of the counter where it landed on the floor with a thud. "For cleaning purposes only right?" she said without emotion.

"Uh, yeah, yeah, that's all… of course, cleaning. We need it for the tiller at the farm." He spoke while looking down at the can, glancing in her direction as he retreated through the clutter to the door. Outside, he was hit by a wave of perfumed air. Looking up, he identified the magnolia tree, its blossoms emitting its sensuous odor, seducer of bee, bird and human—carriers of its genes to fresh locations. He took a deep breath, relieved to be out of the dust and darkness. He swung the can into the big basket on the Red Fury.

Carefully he slid through the bushes to Eddy. He took the bikepath to Abundance, jogged left a short distance and turned south on 5th Street. At Russ Gardens he circled around to the Kyoto Causeway on his way to the Crossroads, where he entered the garden gates to the Rice Bowl. Two storage sheds were near the entrance, far from the crew's barn. Seeing no one in the hot afternoon, he carefully placed the can inside the first shed, rearranging a few tools to obscure it. On a shelf he found a box of gloves, which reminded him he needed a new pair. He stuffed one into his backpack, and returned to the gate. He headed west along Mission Creek until he came to Harrison Street and crossed the bridge.

Dense rose bushes created an arresting climate of humid sweetness. Yellow, white, red and pink blossoms lay rotting across the veloway, a thorny bush protruding to snag the unwary. Nwin wove and ducked through the rose jungle, breathing deeply, already thinking about what he needed at the workshop.

At 22nd Street an old railroad right of way had been converted into a curving parkway connected to Niños Juntos Park. To the right of the parkway stood a strange turreted structure, the "Atlas Stair Building." An immense woman sat on the porch, smoking a cigar, wrapped in a bright orange and magenta floral print.

"Hey Nwin," she called gruffly, waving her thick hand and pausing to inhale deeply, "where you been?" she wheezed. "I haven't seen you in—hell, what's it been? A year? More?"

"Hi Auntie," Nwin smiled to the gray-haired mountain on the porch. "I moved to the Pyramid."

"Why? You lef' your house 'n Bernal? Wha'didj 'er mother think? She mus' be sad," she shook her head, peering down at Nwin over her heaving chest.

"Nah, Auntie, she's dew—Mom's behind me all the way...really!"

"You bring her flowers?" she squinted, leaning forward.

"Uh, sure, sometimes. I'm workin' at the Rice Bowl," he brightened, "I've been doin' the roses down there," he declared proudly.

Auntie took a long puff, held it, and slowly let the smoke billow out of the sides of her mouth. She grinned through the smoke. "Aaah... tha's good." She seemed satisfied by his response.

"I'm heading to the shop. You think Jimmy's gonna be there?"

"He alla the time is at the shop, y'know." With that, she shoved the cigar into her mouth, and tried to drop her hands on to her padded knees, but by the time they settled over her they barely reached her upper thighs.

Nwin gave her a parting smile as he mounted up, waving. At the corner an old Victorian stood, windows open, the sounds of sawing, sanding and hammering ringing out. A rustic sign at an odd angle in the main window bragged, "Shotwell Community Workshop: If You Can't Make It Here, You Don't Need It!" Nwin rolled the Red Fury along the side and leaned it on the wall. He noticed some particularly ripe blood oranges in the tree behind the building, so he went and picked a few, stuffing them into his bag. He entered the old kitchen, now converted to a snack room and lounge. Going down the hall, the first door on the left opened onto spools of wire, surplus circuit boards, speakers, baskets of old chips, cables, connectors. All the useful parts to fix any appliance or device of the past two hundred years were tidily organized into tall shelves along walls. A big workbench spanned the wall ahead. On it were carefully arranged diagnostic tools including an oscilloscope, voltage meters and magnetic media readers. Dozens of tiny mid-21st century computers sat piled in a box. The left wall next to the window was covered with tools, each outlined in ink so whoever pulled one down would know the proper place to return it.

The vyne was open on the wall, its curving leaf display filling half of the wall and hanging down a good five feet from the knobby, twisting stem that crossed the upper reaches of the room. It displayed a schematic drawing the previous user had been consulting. Nwin looked at it and recognized some basic electrical circuits. A familiar tightness gripped his throat and chest, as he nervously contemplated trying to make something in the workshop. At least he didn't have to worry about his father showing up!

He sat and pulled out the papers he'd copied at the library. He spread out the pages of "Setting Fires with Electrical Timers: An Earth Liberation Front Guide" published 150 years earlier. Finding an instruction entitled "The Bucket-Igniter Connection," he skimmed down to

Option 2: Position the igniter to burn through the lid of a 5-gallon bucket

Advantages: It is extremely fast to set up. Only one container of accelerant is required for each incendiary device.

Disadvantages: The flame starts off small and grows slowly.

Set the 5-gallon bucket at the desired location. Leave the lid on. Lay the timer and the igniter on top of the lid. The flare must point down slightly, allowing the flame that shoots out the top to contact the plastic. To get the flare pointing down, set the non-burning end of the flare on the raised edge of the lid. If the non-burning end needs to be raised even more, set a block of wood under it. Instead of a block of wood, you could tape matchbooks together, setting one on top of another until the necessary height is achieved. When the flare ignites, it will burn a hole in the lid and ignite the gasoline vapors. The hole in the lid will gradually increase in size.

This was what he needed, a step-by-step plan to create a small timer with wire, solder, tape, a clock and a 9-volt battery. Nine volt batteries no longer existed, but he could substitute a small solar cell, easily set to the desired voltage. He pushed the papers together, keeping the timer instructions on the top, put his backpack over the pile, and paused to listen. Next door was the woodshop where he heard sawing and hammering. The roar of a planer started, and soon the whine of cut wood filled the house as a board shed layers. Nwin cautiously stepped into the hallway, looking both ways, seeing no one.

He shut the door to the electrical workshop, and quickly set about his work. The open window let some orange-scented air into the stuffy, chemical-smelling room. The dexterity developed under his father's stern direction served him well. In 20 minutes he made several small timers from available parts. A bin of discarded clocks and watches yielded crucial parts, the rest was generic.

A gust of wind rushed through the room and scattered his instructions. He dropped the clocks and quickly ran around gathering the papers on the floor, and under shelves. One sheet had fallen behind the workbench, the very one describing how to wire the timer.

He carefully wrapped his handiwork and placed the three timers in an empty box he found on a shelf. He taped the box shut, laid it into his pack, shuffled and straight-ened his papers and added them too. All the tools he returned to their places, parts to their bins. Work surface cleaned, workshop as he'd found it, his pack over his shoulder, he went next door to the woodshop. There, as expected, he found Jimmy, his cousin, along with two others, a man and a woman Nwin did not recognize.

"Hey Jimmy!" he called out.

"Nwin, man, where you been?!?" Jimmy grinned broadly. After wiping his hands on his sawdust-caked apron, he slapped Nwin's hand and then grabbed him in a bearhug.

"Whoa!" Nwin gasped. "Man, you are a chingin' brute!" He stepped back after Jimmy released him, brushing sawdust from his clothes.

"Oh, sorry 'bout that, here let me help you."

"No, no," Nwin backed away. "You're covered in sawdust. I can do it. It's nothing."

Jimmy, equal parts muscle and fat, amply filled the corner where he stood over a wild-ly ornate column laying sideways on a workbench. His big hands were chafed and cal-loused, but nevertheless he had a delicate touch, beautifully visible in his work. At its head the column had a fierce hawk's face, the beak hooking out under blazing eyes. The ener-gy was palpable, and spread down the column in fox, bear, possum, squirrel and rat faces, arranged along twisting, turning vines carved into the gorgeous grain of the redwood. Once coated in soylent the faces would leap from the wood grain with even more power.

"That looks great!" he said. "Where's it going?"

"It's for the new gazebo in Precita Park. It's from the redwood that fell last month in the Panhandle, that weird 20-minute windstorm, remember?"

Nwin admired Jimmy's work enormously.

"So, what brings you here after all this time? Didn't I hear you moved downtown somewhere?"

Nwin filled him in—living at the Pyramid, working at the Rice Bowl, a little about his parents. "

"You're looking good, but your hair?! Blonde?! What's that about??" Jimmy teased.

"Oh, nothin'. I was just goofin' and decided to give it a try. Pretty stupid, huh?"

"Hey, man, YOU said stupid, not me!" Jimmy laughed. "Come and hang out with me some time man. Right now I've got to finish this," he said, turning to his column.

"Jimmy, I'll see you around, okay?"

"Don't be such a stranger!" he scolded good-naturedly, and waved goodbye. "Nice haircut!"

It was late afternoon now, and Nwin was hungry. Buzzing with a sense of accom-plishment, he rode on 22nd Street to Valencia, avoiding the permanent game of soccer that had turned patches of the parkway into open dirt. "Centro, Centro!" yelled a swarthy, short guy in the Royal Blue jersey of the Excelsior "Shovels" (or *Excavators* as their jer-seys read) as he streaked towards the goal. His teammate shot a high arcing ball towards him, and he lunged for it, just beyond his reach, and tumbled in a tangle of arms and legs as the ball bounced into the waiting arms of the goalie. Nwin paused while the attack failed, and now proceeded up the sidelines from Mission to Valencia, waving to some pals out on the field.

At Valencia he joined hundreds of cyclists on the broad veloway, darting in and out, lost in the anonymous rush from here to there.

15.

The water taxi darted through an opening to an old archway. They came out on Abundance, or so Eric assumed when he saw a long stairway climbing Twin Peaks in the distance. Gondolas and skiffs plied the waters, maneuvering between freight barges, ferries and taxis. He held on for dear life, certain that a collision was unavoidable. But the skippers knew the rhythm of traffic. A well-developed cooperative ethic turned what could have been a chaotic nightmare into a beautiful self-choreographing dance. Eric grimaced, relieved every time they barely dodged an approaching vessel.

Turning up Stockton, they made the Union Square docks, where he hopped off. It was still mid-morning on a fogless, warm day. Parrots squawked soaring from palm to palm in the park. A huge golden globe topped a tall column in the plaza's center. Out of it gushed water, split into multiple streams and loudly falling 40 meters into the surrounding pool. Eric strode quickly to the other side of the plaza to avoid the wet spray. He sat down to let the sun dry him out.

The sun did its job and he left the sunny greensward, crossed Powell with its ancient cable cars and headed west on Geary past a row of theatres. Wide sidewalks hosted an endless string of outdoor cafés, all jammed with people sipping espressos, munching croissants, muffins and piles of fruit. He breathed deeply under lemon trees scattered among bushes, flower boxes, benches and small booths offering crepes made to order. People spilled from a café several blocks up near Tailor Street, where a contagious energy pulled Eric in.

He slid into an empty seat on the perimeter, relieved when no one paid him any particular attention. He stared at a menu, fidgeting with its corner. He'd eaten only an hour earlier, but the buzz of the place seized his curiosity.

"Yes?" called a server from the other side of the table. Eric looked up, momentarily frozen. He finally blurted "double espresso and a bran muffin!" just as the man was about to go on to the next person. The server flashed the two-finger V, and disappeared into the throng. Silent patrons sat around the table that Eric had instinctually chosen. He was removed from the buzzing intimacy and boisterous sociability that had drawn him in.

Knots of people clustered nearby. Three middle-aged men, pot-bellied with long hair and big beards, stood facing each other near a small hedge to his right, deep in conversation. Just past them a laughing group of more than a dozen sprawled around one of the big tables. Several of them wore leotards. *Probably a dance class*, he surmised. Across the café two smaller tables were occupied by white-haired old ladies, boisterously playing what looked like Bridge. Just to his left was a prominent bulletin board full of handwritten notes and one dominating poster: "Inventors' Corner at 7 p.m. every Thursday night at Café Thimble." Slogans scrawled on it shouted "Innovate or Die!" "To Change is Human" and such.

"SLAP!" The thin man to his left had discarded a magazine and departed abruptly. Eric reached for the magazine: *Free Radical, A Journal of Opinion.* The vibrant cover was a wild image of a kite racer soaring over a desert scene amidst thousands of Monarch butterflies. The racer wore an old-fashioned leather helmet and goggles, but was covered in butterflies; the sky around him was thick with them, too. The wings of his kite were an exact inverse of the Monarch orange and black pattern.

Eric flipped it open. "We Don't Have To!" was the lead editorial, followed by a piece in favor of closing 20% of the city's remaining streets and converting them to farms. "I Refuse to Care About Refuseniks" came next, then "Personal Speed and Freedom of Choice." A featured debate pitted a proponent of "The Self-Provisioning Aquifer" against "Our Mountain Fresh Legacy."

A small item caught his attention: "Cows and Chickens Duke it out in the Dunes" that was about a small cattle ranch in the far western dunes that had challenged a neighboring chicken ranch to see which could feed more San Franciscans during the year. The ranchers and chicken farmers were pictured shaking on the bet. At stake was bragging rights, a trip as San Francisco's entry to the Regional Protein Championships, and a banquet thrown by the loser at the winner's ranch, including a full clean-up of the animals' quarters. Eric marveled at the oddity of it.

* * *

After a wearying day-long ride across the western neighborhoods perched on undulating sand dunes over which the city had spread two centuries earlier, he had made it to Golden Gate Park. Entering an old cement portal from the 19th Avenue Greenway, he'd had a magical ride through streaming evening park light. Ancient stumps gave evidence of trees that had once stood majestically facing the Pacific three miles to the west. The forest had thinned considerably as dunes reclaimed most of the western end of the park. But here at this entrance, a healthy forest of eucalyptus, cypress, acacia and n'oak still held firm at the park's edge.

He slowed on the journey eastward, wandering from sight to sight, passing small ponds and wooded groves, encountering the occasional small herd of deer, taking pains not to antagonize the skunks scuttling across his path. Finally he rolled into a plaza with an ancient bandshell in its center. On the far side stood a low, curving, green glass museum with a high wooden tower. It looked like a kid had built a Lincoln log observatory and stuck it upright into a fallen glass box. The plaza was full of chairs, a beautiful old fountain gushing behind them, with an odd assortment of sculptures and statues strewn about. On the near side stood an anachronistic structure that looked like nothing so much as a fallen gantry to a 20th century space rocket. Behind it rose another structure, tall and egg-shaped, with various ramps jutting out connecting to a series of grass-covered mounds. The sign announced it as the Academy of Sciences, a Planetarium and an Aquarium. Eric sailed through the plaza, making a mental note to return.

He swerved along a twisting path through a dense forest, emerging into a tunnel of floral arches which in turn dropped him at the foot of "Hippie Hill," a rather unprepossessing mound of grass with a timeless band of longhaired youth smoking pot and playing drums. The sun had gone below the horizon. Dusk fell on a warm gift of an evening. Eventually, Eric's path took him to Haight Street, a sprawling pedestrian mall dotted with dozens of booths offering food, pot, crafts, handmade books, sheafs of poetry, and a sea of old recorded music. He found a velome in a small park across the Stanyan veloway, where he deposited the Silver Fox he'd ridden all day.

In the Haight Eric felt like he'd stepped off a time machine. He wandered aimlessly through dancers and small audiences before stages that seemed to pop up every block or so. He accepted offers to smoke, and was soon buzzing like he hadn't for a long time. He giggled as a sweet, heavyset woman in a full-length paisley dress, her matted hair tangled with feathers, swept him into her arms and swirled him around to the beat of a reggae band. After a few minutes she released him, and off he bounced through the multitude, until he was sitting on a bench at the edge of busy café. He'd reached the Haight Ashbury.

Just then a procession filled the street, turning the corner from Clayton in white, orange and pink robes. Most had necklaces of brown beads, and they all wore little wire rim glasses beneath small triangular hats and wooden sandals. They played small drums, finger cymbals, and chanted as they spun like dervishes. Eric sat back and watched.

"Hey, weren't you at our house last night?" came a question. Startled, he looked up into the face of Emmy, the intense black woman who had been defending her pleasure in working Annuals at the dinner table.

"Yeah… hi!" he said, aware of how tired and stoned he was. He held out his hand for a slap, which she returned. "I'm Eric, Eric Johanson."

"Hi. I'm Emmy Ndbele Hodges." She was with some of the others he'd met at her house. "This is Angie and Gerald, Annika," she gestured, and each waved perfunctorily, engrossed in a conversation of their own. "You wanna join us?" she chuckled. "I wouldn't want you to get swept away in the religious fervor out there."

Eric turned back toward the frenzied procession, recoiling as another female acolyte reached for him. He noticed that a few others had been drawn into the celebration or whatever it was. He hopped a small hedge into the café, where he sat down next to Emmy.

"I don't think they'd *want* me," he disclosed, "and of course, I don't want them!"

"Oh?" she raised her eyebrows. He was again struck by her amazing visage, white teeth flashing, luminous round eyes glowing in a long, thin face. Her hair frizzed out in an Afro, which softened her angularity even as it added to her unusual height. He smiled at her, not noticing that he was for once at ease, and confided, "I am NOT a religious person, in fact I HATE all those stupid rituals."

"Hmmm," Emmy looked thoughtful.

"Oh shit!" he caught himself. "Sorry if I offended you. Nothing personal!" His mood teetered on the edge of an abyss.

She smiled, lighting up the place, and especially Eric's sinking spirits. "Don't worry about it! I'm not one of *them* either," she explained, "but I try not to make an issue of it. I mean, I can respect someone else's beliefs even if I'm not looking for some guiding spirit myself, y'know?"

He nodded, unsatisfied. Mentally he kicked himself. "I respect people, not stupid ideas!"

Emmy laughed. She was completely relaxed, leaning back in a chair beneath an umbrella decorated with figures wrestling in a forest. Her long body somehow found a way to fit, comfortably sprawled on the small café chair, perched between two others at the little round table. She put her long fingers on Eric's upper back, and stroked him familiarly, sending a powerful surge down his spine to his groin. "Would you like a drink?"

Grateful, he looked at her with a spreading smile, and nodded, "I could use an iced tea, or maybe something stronger…," thinking she might suggest something. She pushed her drink over. "Try this." It had alcohol alright, a tropical juice mix with rum and vodka he guessed. "Wow!" His stoned palate immediately latched onto the strong flavor of the drink. Emmy raised her glass to the passing waiter, who flipped her the V sign. When she called "Two, please," he nodded.

They leaned into each other and rushed to fill in the blanks of her story and his. Laughing, they caught themselves as words exploded, piling up correspondence and coincidence. She was from Oakland originally, he had lived on the South Side of Chicago. They both loved the blues and Dostoevsky. Rituals, prayers and ceremonies made each of them uncomfortable, though she was more open, he more intolerant. Neither was a Gaiaist, but both were sympathetic to Integritism, which argued for species specificity and the integrity of diverse habitats, human and non-human. Neither was pointed at a career, and both wondered if specialization would ever come.

They were on their third drinks, knees pressing together under the table, chattering away, when Annika, Gerald and Angie got up. "Uh, if we could just cut in for a second," Gerald smiled, his pink skin glowing in the evening reflections. Angie, with both arms around one of his, grinned at them conspiratorially, her straight black hair hanging down over her shoulders. Annika was looking away at the street scene. "We're heading home," he said, "you staying?"

She put her arm around Eric. "Yeah, but we'll be along in a bit," which sent a wave of excitement and anxiety shooting through Eric.

He drunkenly grinned, nodding goodbye. Annika nodded back, not warmly, irritated perhaps that Emmy had abandoned her for Eric. Maybe she somehow felt like the odd one out with Gerald and Angie. She gave Emmy a curt smile before turning to follow Gerald and Angie.

After they were gone, Emmy gave him a mischievous smile, dropped her arm to his thigh, and began stroking him. His head was spinning and his pants grew tight as Emmy's warm hand worked up his thigh. Emmy whispered in his ear, "Let's go back to my place," to which he offered no objection.

Stumbling down Haight Street, avoiding the street furniture and clusters of animated humanity, Emmy did her best to keep Eric from losing his balance. "Let's stop for a second, okay?" he urged, so they sat on the edge of a flower box. "You alright?" She peered into his eyes with concern.

"Well," he slurred, "I been goin' all day, rode all the way back…"

"So you don't want to come over?"

"NO! No, it's not that!" Even in his stupor he was anxious. He didn't want to miss out on a chance to go to bed with this beautiful, brilliant woman.

"I don't think you're in any condition to make it back to your hostel," she said sensibly. She didn't seem drunk at all. "Look, Eric, come home with me. We'll wake up together tomorrow and see what the world looks like." She clutched his arm, pulling him back to his feet. "It's not much further." He gave himself over to her, letting the intoxicated fog swallow him whole while she led him along. He barely noticed entering the Page Mews, or anything else about the evening.

When he woke up it was morning and it took a minute to get his bearings. Morning sun streamed into the unfamiliar room, adorned with delicate miniature paintings. A fake marble dresser with a mirror sat opposite the bed. He rose, noticing that he was in a single bed, and observed himself in the mirror. "Oh man." Soiled and disheveled, he looked like he'd crawled here. About that moment he noticed a major drum roll in his head, his hands involuntarily grabbing for it but only coming up with his ears. He threw back the covers and sat on the bed's edge, realizing he was naked and his clothes were neatly piled on a chair in the corner. *Did I take off my clothes? I don't fold them, so I guess not.* Rising embarrassment seized him.

The door opened. Reflexively he pulled the cover over his nakedness. Ducking slightly through the doorway, Emmy straightened up before him, hands on hips, her narrow wrists flowing into impossibly long and delicate arms. Her bare black midriff was the tallest, tiniest waist Eric had ever seen. Her white teeth beamed at him like a spotlight. She started to laugh, and threw her head back, her chest caving as her shoulders shook, and she clutched her elbows in a helpless attempt to contain her easy mirth. A contagious chortle came from Eric before his pounding headache stopped him cold. Clutching at his throbbing head sent her even further into hysterical laughter, which was starting to seem less funny to Eric.

"I'm… I'm…" She just couldn't stop laughing. Gasping, she finally got out a weak "sorry!" as she doubled over trying to stop.

"Guess I was pretty ridiculous," Eric mumbled through his haze. He was feeling deeply embarrassed now. She finally managed to stop howling, wiping away tears. "I don't know why you look SO funny this morning, but…," and she came over and put both hands on his head, working her thumbs directly into his temples, relieving the pressure, ". . . you do!" She chuckled again, as he began to purr at her reassuring, relieving touch. After a short while, she stopped the massage and sat down next to him.

"You should come and have a plate of eggs and some coffee. It's the best hangover remedy I know."

"Mmmphf." He nuzzled her shoulder.

She got up and he nearly fell over as she moved away. He didn't know where he stood with her. He certainly couldn't remember last night after the blurry walk home. "Come on, get dressed," she said with a tinge of impatience. "I'll go and get your breakfast ready. You want to take a shower?"

"That would be great."

"Two doors down. There're clean towels on the shelf. Breakfast is two floors down, just head to the back once you get downstairs, okay?"

He nodded, and admiringly watched her leave. "She must be nearly 7 feet tall!" he marveled after seeing her duck to clear the doorway. He wasn't short at 6' 3", but Emmy had a few inches on him easily, packed into incredibly long limbs. He couldn't stop thinking about her endless legs extending out of her shorts as he gathered himself and went for the shower.

After a wet blast in which he brutally scrubbed himself head to toe, attacking his face in a futile attempt to expunge the hangover, he dressed and found his way to the dining room. It turned out to be the same room where he'd had dinner with Tanya, Trixie's place. Annika was at the table nursing a steaming mug of coffee, reading a newspaper. Through the kitchen door Emmy bustled in bearing plates laden with eggs, sliced cantalope and peaches, and fresh bread dripping with butter.

"Thanks!" he enthused, wet hair brushed back, his face resuming its normal youthful countenance. She sat next to him, and together they dug into the hearty fare.

Annika glanced over, a knowing smile on her face. "Hey, says it's going to be a heat wave for a few days." They grunted through full mouths. Warming to the task of imparting the news, Annika continued. "Let's see, terrorists attack Chilean farms, drought ravages east Africa, T'ousands gather around Alpine Glacier's last days." Nothing much penetrated Eric's immediate focus on chewing. She rattled the paper as she turned to local news. "Integritistas To Hold Convention in September, Mercx Diagonal Repairs Completed, Wolf Debate Howling."

"Uh," Emmy finished chewing a mouthful of the luscious bread. "Annika, thanks, but I'd actually rather read it myself later, okay?" Annika looked stung, her brow knit with consternation. "Sorry." In a minute she folded the paper and took her coffee mug and left.

"She is driving me crazy!" Emmy admitted. "I know she means well, and she can be engaging and—"

Emmy shook off her frustration. "Hey, how did you meet Tanya, anyway?"

Eric told how he had nearly run Tanya over and then had pedaled her unwieldy load home for her.

Emmy shook her head. "That's Tanya!"

"What do you mean?"

"She's the Page Mews hoarder. A pack rat. Collects all kinds of weird objects, old dishes, pictures, clothes, furniture, you name it! Did you see her room?"

"Yeah, but it wasn't *that* bad," Eric claimed, half-heartedly.

"You must be kidding, right?"

He raised his eyebrows and shrugged.

"Well, look, anyway, I've got a job to get to."

"Really? What are you doing today?" Eric asked with genuine interest.

"Canal maintenance. The Hiring Hall says there's been a shortage of workers there lately, so I volunteered. Today is my shift."

"Hmmm," Eric said with barely concealed disappointment. "So…"

She shot him a look that said "forget it," so he stopped.

"I'll vyne you, okay?" She got up, gathering her dishes on the way to the kitchen. He mumbled his assent, but could hardly speak, the depression and confusion momentarily crushing him. He stared at his fruit, and took a desultory bite. She came back through the dining room like a whirlwind. "So I'm outta here." Tenderly, she put her hand on his neck, and leaned over. He quickly swallowed his fruit, just in time to receive the juicy kiss she laid on him. Her tongue darted in after the cool fruit juice, and as she pulled back, exhilarated, squeezing his neck with surprising strength, she flashed that dazzling smile and said "Mmmm, peaches! You ARE sweet!" Laughing at his reaction, she clapped him and said, "I'll see you soon. I like you!" With that she spun around and disappeared.

He sat in a daze, feeling like he'd been on a seesaw. He carried his dishes into the kitchen, rinsed them and set them in a dishwashqer. No one was around as he wiped the counter and turned to go. Gerald padded in to the kitchen just then with a bleary greeting. He headed straight for the coffee, and with a fresh cup in hand, turned to Eric. "Hey, I guess you'll be around, eh?"

"Um, well, I don't know… I hope so!"

Gerald's head turned in an unconsciously inquisitive gesture. But Eric didn't feel like elaborating. He said goodbye and headed out toward the morning heat. It was going to be a scorcher, he thought, as he turned towards the Panhandle.

16.

he vyne display showed four dozen ships flying the flag of Tanzania. The *Leopold Tanzania* was a 70-ton container hauler, captained by Alfredo Lopez-Carrillo. "Display Captain Alfredo Lopez-Carillo" ordered Nwin.

> Born November 8, 2119 in Valparaiso, Chile.
> Schooled at the Chilean Marine College, graduating January 2144 with license to captain all classes of ships. Authorized for entry by Harbor Masters in . . .

According to the list that scrolled up Nwin's vyne: Valparaiso, Tokyo, San Francisco, Lisbon, Manila, Djakarta, Mombasa, Genoa, Istanbul, Tunis, Cadiz, Melbourne, Port Elizabeth, Dar Es Salaam—almost anywhere he'd heard of and plenty more.

Hmm, he thought, trying to figure out an angle on the ship and its crew. *The crew!* "Display crew registered to Leopold Tanzania," he declared.

> Jose Serra, John Anderson, Sven Nilsson, Margaret Wong, Melilah Absour Nardz, Charlotte Bellinger, Ricardo Donatello, Jaime Suarez-Ochoa.

Nothing familiar. He had another idea, "Display passengers registered to *Leopold Tanzania.*"

> Josephine Grigeirevich, Elliot Simpson, Jane Simpson, Anna N. Kzcyzcynski, William Morales, Carlos Gonzalez.

Except for the unlikely chance that the initial 'N' in one name might be Nance, he hadn't figured out anything. Last thought, "Display cargo manifest delivered by the *Leopold Tanzania* to San Francisco."

> Peru: 2 containers: hats, recycled silver, wooden furniture and kitchen utensils, dried botanicals; Ecuador: 6 containers: coffee, aquatic plants in suspended animation, dyed cotton, finished women's clothing, bicycle tires, mobile wind converters.
> Colombia: 12 containers: cocaine, coffee, hearts of palm, musical instruments.
> Mexico: 4 containers: coffee, sporting goods, men's clothing, shoes, solar lighting systems, hemp rope.

He studied the list but could not make any connections. Discouraged, he sighed, "Nwin Robertson, over," and the vyne display leaf rolled up. He drummed his fingers on the table, staring out of his window at the *Leopold Tanzania* in the distant Bay. His thoughts drifted aimlessly until he glanced through downtown's neighboring buildings towards the Rice Bowl, west of the semi-submerged Mission Bay campus. At first he felt his irritation rise at the thought of Angus and his plantings. "You'd think I was out there at night trampling all over 'em !" he said aloud with exasperation.

"SHIT!" He involuntarily hit himself in the forehead, thunderstruck at an unlikely but vague possibility that might help unravel his mystery. "Stefania, Stefania… what were you saying? Something about attacks… in Chile!!" The captain of the *Leopold Tanzania* was from Chile.

"Vyne!" It immediately started unfurling its display. "Message to Stefania Listero, working at the Rice Bowl in San Francisco. Stefania, I need to meet with you and talk about a coincidence I'm exploring. Let's have lunch on Friday at work okay? Nwin Robertson over." The vyne rolled back up.

He walked over to a closet and pulled out the Earth Liberation Front papers again. In another sack he had the three timers he built the other day. And he'd brought home the flares he needed. He spread it all out on the floor and began to assemble the pieces.

* * *

Meanwhile, earlier that morning, his mother had gone back inside after seeing her son in the distance on Bernal Hill.

"Hey Jeff, do you have that list?" she hollered out the back door.

Her husband was on hands and knees, digging weeds in the backyard. He paused and reached to his back pocket. "Nope. Check on the fridge!"

"Damn. Where's that stupid list? The boat leaves in twenty minutes!" If she missed today's chance Jen knew she'd have to wait another full week.

"I can't find it! You wanted some red wine and what else?"

Jeff got up, straightening against the stiffness in his knees and lower back. He dropped his trowel and gloves by the screen door as he went in to the kitchen. He was 79 and although he took his daily supplement, was feeling his body in new and discouraging ways.

"Yeah, a case of the best Sonoma Chianti, and a case of a good Alexander Valley Merlot, too, ok? And see if there's anything new in the pharmaceuticals for stiff joints."

"There's tons of herbal stuff at the freestore. Have you tried any of it?"

"I want some real drugs! Those herbal teas aren't bad, but I get stiffer by the day. Hmmm, oh yeah, see if you can find one of those new sprinkler heads I read about from Australia. Didn't Nwin ask you to look for one of those funny hats from Peru or Tibet or something?… and don't forget we need a new freezer for the block…"

God, how could I have forgotten that?!? She wondered whether she was losing her mind. First she couldn't find the list, then she couldn't remember anything on it, even though some of the items were for herself. She had been taking memory enhancers, but as far as she could tell, they didn't do a thing. Just then she saw the list, poking out from under the composting can.

How the hell did it get there? She stuffed it into her pocket, glancing it over to remind herself what to get. "Gotta go, hon', I'll see you when I get back, probably about 4 or so. You gonna make dinner?"

"I thought you had another meeting?"

"Oh yeah. Well, if you make something I can eat it later, okay?" With that, she gave him a peck on the cheek and was out the door.

Jeffrey stared after her. He loved Jennifer, he told himself, but he didn't feel much beyond his stiff joints. He could smell her apricot lip balm where she'd brushed his cheek. Back to the garden, where lettuce, tomatoes, beans and peppers all were coming up nicely. Theirs was actually part of a continuous band of vegetable gardens around the upper slopes of the hill. He gazed beyond them at the native grasses and a profusion of wildflowers that held together the windswept landscape.

Jennifer leaped on to her three-wheeler, her long black braids dancing behind her as she hurtled down the hill to the Precita Creek levee. The docks protruded from under the old roadway. It was covered with dense multi-story apartment buildings, one of the major communities in town, maybe 1,500 residents in the "Arcobolo." As she reached the bottom of the hill the levee came into view. A small knot of people slowly moved towards the dock, boarding the Treasure Island shuttle, so she relaxed and pedaled along, knowing she had time.

She flashed into the velome, dropped her trike and called to Serge, "Hi, would you mind giving me a minor lube this afternoon?" running out before he could answer.

She got into the queue for TI, seeing a few familiar faces.

"Franklin, how are you? I heard your lovely daughter was heading off to Vietnam to study?"

"Yes, she's going to live on the Mekong River, studying their rice farming and improving her Vietnamese. Her grandparents have been teaching her, but you can't beat immersion," Franklin beamed proudly.

"Yeah I wish I'd done that. I hardly know any Vietnamese anymore. I never read or talk to people in it. I should, I suppose." But she knew she wouldn't.

Upon seeing her neighbor Mariko she called out, "I'm putting in for the new freezer, remember?"

"Sure, no problem. I'm going for a new solar pump which the freestore couldn't get enough of. And Julian wanted me to look for new art."

Jennifer thought about her own house full of Nwin's dark charcoal drawings from years past. "Hmmm, maybe I'll get a painting, too."

They shuffled onto the double-decked ferry and took seats. After it eased away from the shore the zany sound effects and calliope music started. The steward passed through the passengers distributing order forms and shots. Jennifer downed a shot of tequila, as did most of the others. The whole experience was so wacky that getting tipsy only made it that much better.

Jennifer filled out her form, checking off a freezer and adding "Australian sprinkler" and "Peruvian Mountain Hat" in the miscellaneous area. On the wine list she checked off Jeff's requests, adding three bottles of rare champagne for herself. She perused recent arrivals, and noticed the section "Specialties from Eastern Europe." Crystal glasses, a bottle of Becherovka, a case of Bohemian Pilsner, and a set of Rumanian table linen rounded out her order. Just for going today she'd receive a box of Mexican papayas, a pair of Chinese binoculars, and a choice of Indonesian batik scarves.

"Treasure Island, indeed!" she laughed, the tequila loosening up her funny bone.

"Hey Mariko, what are we gonna do with all those papayas?" she giggled.

"Somebody'll want 'em, I'm sure." Mariko answered in a tone rather more serious than the question warranted.

Pelicans and seagulls swirled about the ferry, seals and sea lions barked in the distance. Dolphins gracefully leaped out of the water a hundred feet to the starboard. As usual, the San Francisco Bay teemed with life.

Jennifer moved up front and leaned over the rail, watching the ship cut through frothing water, schools of fish and various sea creatures darting out of its way on either side. Breathing deeply Jennifer exhaled slowly. The sun warmed her cheek even as a bracing breeze bit the other side of her face. It was always a pleasure to get out on the water, and humbling too.

Treasure Island loomed ahead. The name had been given to a flat expanse of land-fill, home to a 20th century world's fair. In those days, this island had been called "Yerba Buena," but after the original Treasure Island was inundated the name stuck to its rocky neighbor. After the revolution had altered ideas of scarcity and need it became the place to go to for "treasure."

They pulled up to the dock and disembarked, handing in their forms in exchange for a numbered receipt. The steward took forms and scanned them to link the orders to receipts. The revelers thronged off in various directions, seeking their favorite games and activities.

Mechanical laughter echoed around the hill, a huge ferris wheel spun at the peak, and a soaring roller coaster circled the island. Booths were everywhere. Barkers exhorted the visitors to take a spin, take a tumble, try your luck, see what you can win today. A Pleasure Palace with flashing pink lights beckoned anyone in want of anonymous sexual fun. The men and women within were usually doing their Annuals, a way to experiment with their own sexual proclivities. (A relatively small percentage of people preferred being sexual playthings for random strangers to other kinds of work.)

Jennifer and Mariko each gulped another shot of tequila on the way off the ship, and woozily headed up the hill.

"C'mon, let's take the roller coaster first," Jennifer urged.

Off it went, plunging immediately into a steep descent that stretched their faces into preposterous grins.

"Eeeeeeeeee" they screamed with the other passengers. After circling the island the ride careened into a tunnel where it sharply spun around several times in the pitch black and suddenly spit them out into a nice straightaway facing across the water at San Francisco. They returned to the station, gasping and slightly queasy.

At the exit, they were accosted by a young man in a straw hat and bowtie. He put his arm over Mariko's shoulder and invited them to play his game. They offered no resistance and he led them to his baseball toss.

"Three balls. Knock down all fifteen milk bottles for a prize TODAY. Twelve down and you cut in half your waiting time on two items. Ten down and one item is yours within a week. Less than ten, well, a small token of our appreciation." He gestured to a glass case full of odd art objects.

"Wish me luck!" Jennifer grabbed the first ball, and calling upon her years on the softball mound, let it fly. She hit the bottles hard at the second row and nine of the top ten all tumbled down.

"Okay, now *get it*!" rooted Mariko.

The second ball brought down another three, but she missed with her final throw.

"Damn!" she exhaled.

"Congratulations! You can pick two items from your list to get in half the time."

"I'll put the Chianti and the freezer on that." She waved her receipt under the scanner and made her selection.

"This is fun! Hey look—" she pointed to a skiff out in the Bay. "I think that's Nwin!"

Mariko remained impassive, eyeing the skiff and shrugging, turning away without comment. Jennifer stood for a minute staring out at the skiff until it disappeared around the edge of the island. She caught up with Mariko.

They came upon a jumping frog contest. A dusty corridor was marked off with a starting line, midpoint and finishing line, a low wooden fence on either side. The game conductor and her assistants were dressed in Old West cowboy garb.

"Ladies and Gentlemen! Please select your frog and place your bets."

Mariko picked Strawberry and Jennifer took Avocado. Each put her chit into the bet corner and found a spot along the course. The frogs were color-coordinated with their fruit or vegetable names, as were the racing lanes.

A bell rang, followed by a small 'pop' and the gates sprang open. The frogs leaped forward, Banana forging ahead as though fleas nipped at its heels. About 50 people gathered around the course cheering and slapping the sides. Banana lost its lead early but eventually surged ahead and won.

"Ohhhh damn!" Mariko slammed her hand into the wooden wall, disappointed. But second place had won her one item in a week, so she put in for the solar pump.

They bet the frog races twice more, but picked losers each time. They took a stab at holo-mimicry, where you had to closely imitate a dance and pose routine performed by a hologram of yourself.

Throughout the island were small galleries, with paintings, photographs, sculptures, holographic displays, and wild sonic environments. They both were hunting for art, and poked around a wooden cabin buried in shrubs on a low hillside. The proprietor was an elderly, white-haired man who greeted them like old friends, introducing himself as Davinciano.

They strolled to the back alcove where the walls were covered with a crazy hodgepodge of paintings. One container alone had a hundred or more prints, which Mariko immediately began to flip through. Jennifer was drawn to a painting on the back wall, only about 18 inches wide, maybe 14 inches tall, a seascape, or a huge tidal wave cresting into a night sky. In the wave were dozens of buildings, bridges, ships, some identifiably San Francisco. The wave was leaping into space from Earth, and carrying the manmade world in it… "Hey Mariko, check this out."

"Hmmm, interesting," she said without interest. "You know, I think I'm going to take off. "I'm going to the Palace!" Mariko declared defiantly.

Jennifer did a doubletake, never suspecting that her neighbor would go for anonymous sex on the Island. She tried to act nonchalant, but was disturbed nonetheless.

"I'll see you on the ferry." And with that Mariko pulled a print from the bin, walked to the counter and handed it to Davinciano, gave him her registration, and quickly strode out.

Jennifer took the wave painting off the wall, and on her way to the counter an alluring bronze sculpture, rather abstract, caught her eye. It made her think of a tree hollow with a child playing hide-and-seek inside. She grabbed it too.

Davinciano inspected the items. "Ah, a Giselle Carrerra—she's remarkable, no? Let's see, who is this sculptor?" He looked at the bottom, and found no marking. To his vyne he said "Sculpture listing please." The big leaf displayed a column of titles. He touched the scroll down node and eventually came to "Tree Stump" by Axel Pedersen, Denmark. "Well, he's not even local!" To make sure, he had the vyne show an image of it, and confirmed that it was indeed the same piece. "I'll have these wrapped up for you and on the boat, okay?" Davinciano promised.

"Yeah, thanks," said Jen, but her mind was elsewhere.

She left the gallery, pleased with her acquisitions, but distracted by the thought of Mariko having sex on the other side of the island. She came to another contest, a single elimination tournament of staring. It required eight people, and there were five already, so she sat down, joined immediately by a swarthy man in a white t-shirt, whose smile made her strangely uneasy. A few minutes later an elderly coffee-colored woman arrived and they started in. Jennifer was eliminated in the first round.

Her day unfolded slowly: After a leisurely lunch of Portobello mushroom sandwich, organic pears and cheesecake, she was ready to head back but decided to try one final game—shuffleboard—and won first prize. She chose to get Nwin's hat right away.

As she re-boarded the shuttle she exchanged her receipt for a new printout. On it were listed the items she had signed up for.

Jennifer's list:

ORDER DATE: JUNE 18, 2157

a freezer, 2 months, ~~August 20, 2157~~ double speed, I month, delivery July 20
Australian sprinkler, 3 weeks, delivery July 11, 2157
Peruvian Mountain Hat, 2 weeks, ~~July 2, 2157~~ TODAY
1 Case Sonoma Chianti, I week, ~~June 25, 2157~~ double speed, 3 days, delivery June 21
1 Case Alexander Valley Merlot, 2 weeks, delivery July 2, 2157
3 bottles Chateau Clicquot champagne, 2 months, delivery August 20, 2157
A case of crystal glasses, 2 days, ~~June 20, 2157~~ TODAY
a bottle of Beckerovka 2 days, ~~June 20~~ TODAY
a case of Bohemian Pilsner , 2 days, ~~June 20~~ TODAY
a set of Rumanian linen tablecloth and napkins, 2 days, ~~June 20~~ TODAY
a box of Mexican papayas, TODAY
a pair of Chinese binoculars, TODAY
Indonesian batik scarf, TODAY

Mariko showed up on the shuttle, disheveled. On board, their take-home items were boxed up and labeled. They were both spent after all the commotion and drinking. Jennifer looked at Mariko with sidelong glances, the fantasies of her visit to the Palace racing through her mind.

Get over it! she thought to herself. *What's the big deal, anyway?* But there was no denying that it made her think about sex more than she had in a while, her arousal making her uneasy.

"So, how was it?" she asked.

"What, the Palace? It was great! I never had a bald, pot-bellied guy before. Something about him, I don't know what, but I picked him. It was strange, but I got off and had fun. You know, you should try it."

"Oh, it's not for me," Jennifer said, "Jeff and I are fine. I never think about sleeping with anyone else."

"Really?!?" Mariko was truly surprised. "Whatever twirls you, I guess."

The shuttle lurched along on choppy waves. When they got back, they pulled their boxes onto the dock, and helped each other haul them to the velome, where they loaded up their trikes and headed home.

It was a steep climb. After laboring mightily halfway up Bernal Hill they dismounted next to the tow rope that came down to that point. It was a continuous loop with grab holds along the rope. They attached their trikes to the rope, and then clipped their belts to the extenders. Jennifer pushed the red button and the fat rope started taking them upward. They walked and held the trikes steady on course. At the top they slapped the stop switch, and got off.

Jennifer pedaled home after a perfunctory "goodbye."

No one was about, and Jeff hadn't made dinner. She hitched the trike to a post under her porch, and carried in the goods. She absent-mindedly made herself a meal, reheating yesterday's soup and slicing papaya to go with it.

Sad piano music drifted from a neighboring apartment so she opened her kitchen window to let it in. A few neighbors were hanging around a picnic table outside the gardens three houses down. But she didn't feel like socializing, and slurped her soup, worrying about her son.

17.

A week had gone by and Eric had covered most of the City. The heat wave over, the morning was gray, overcast skies concealed the sun. Being the visitor was getting old. *Maybe it's time to start doing some Annuals*, he thought, like Emmy and the others he'd met kept suggesting. Plus, he only had a few more days left at the Tweezer before he had to find new accommodations.

Emmy was on his mind a lot. She had vyned him to meet her a couple of times, but each "date" (what else was it, he thought) ended with them retiring to their respective beds. So far, in spite of all his self-deprecation and urge to withdraw, he was having fun. *She's articulate, witty, irreverent, and stunningly beautiful,* he marveled. And she touched him with an easy familiarity and relaxed sexiness that made him melt. He struggled with his own awkward physicality but she didn't seem to notice or care. Kissing Emmy was already a peak sexual experience in his life!

Flushed with excitement he surged out of bed and went for a quick shower. After breakfast he passed the front desk.

"Any messages for me?"

"Yeah, one I think…" Jack swiveled around to check the vyne. A small dot glowed next to Eric's name on the guest register. "Yup, why don't you take it over there?" He gestured to a small lounge with three comfy chairs against a wall and smaller vyne displays for guests. Eric hurried over and opened a vyne with his name, falling back into a chair. The leaf unrolled and up came two messages, the first from his parents, the second from Emmy. He felt a twang of guilt, remembering that he hadn't checked in with his folks since he'd arrived. But first he had to see the latest from sweet Emmy.

"Hiii EerrrrrIC!" she started playfully. "Whaddya say to dinner, drinks, maybe a moonlight Bay ride… tonight?!" She twirled her hair and leaned forward on the leaf's display. "I'll still be working on the Minna Canal behind Rincon Towers. Swing by in the morning before you get going and let me know if we're on." Her big white teeth shimmered with a greenish tint as she smiled seductively and blew him a goodbye kiss.

He sighed, a deep shuddering tension rolling down his spine. Eric squirmed and his muscles tightened.

His parents were next.

"Hi honey," his mother chirped, "we don't want to bother you, but we are a little worried. Would you just send us a message so we can see that you're doing okay?" Her small tanned face wrinkled earnestly with a plaintive beseeching look. She slid over and his father came into view. "Eric, hello! Everything around here is pretty much the same…" He looked to his left, his jaw twitching, then turned back with a rather grim expression. "Guess that's why you're there," followed by a tight-lipped half smile, half grimace that Eric didn't recognize as his own expression of moments earlier. "We hope you find what you left for," and a more obvious scowl. "Anyway, leaf us, ok?" and he slid aside, poorly concealing his discomfort. The message ended.

Eric sunk back, empty, guilty, resentful, and he put his hands to his head. "Gotta send an upbeat message, something light!" he instructed himself. Then he sank further into the chair and groaned. "No work, no home, no friends… well, there's Emmy, but…" He got up and walked to the window, this one facing north towards Alcatraz and Angel Island, the Golden Gate off to his left. Finally he returned to the vyne.

"Message to Stan and Sharon Johanson of New Haven, Connecticut. Hi Mom and Dad." He forced a smile which he knew wouldn't look good on the vyne. "I've been in San Francisco a little over a week. What a place! I've been walking, boating, bicycling and riding streetcars all over the place. Met lots of people. Having a great time, really." Lack of conviction rang loudly in his ears. "Gonna start doing some Annuals soon, and find a room of my own too. This hostel has been a great place to start, though. You wouldn't believe the view from the 29th floor!" That rang true. A good place to leave it. "So I'll check in when I'm settled, but don't worry about me. I'm fine. San Francisco is an easy place to live."

"Eric Johanson, over."

Relieved as much as agitated, he hurried back to his room to grab his bag. It wasn't long before he was striding through the glass doors to the busy dock. He jumped a peapod ferry heading south and grabbed a spot near the rear so he could get some choice photos as they floated away. He stood next to the ferry pilot, a typical peapod skipper, loud, heavy and female.

"SOUTHbound: Domino 2, Rincon Towers, Bay Bridge, Rincon South, Panduccino Station,…"

What? Eric was framing a picture when she called the train station by that unfamiliar name. He took some shots of the Tweezer and the Pyramid while she finished her route call.

"What was that you called the Central Train Station?" he asked her.

She was lighting a cigar while effortlessly steering the peapod through treacherous traffic. Puffing furiously she looked over at him through a cloud of smoke which he batted away, trying to look casual as he did so, blinking rapidly. "'Panduccino'," she replied, turning her assertion into a challenge.

"Is it a name I should know?" he offered innocently.

She grunted and let out a long hoot, which Eric took at first as a comment on his stupidity, but then realized she'd been hailing a passing northbound ferry. More smoke and some delicate maneuvering through an Abundance Street traffic jam preceded her terse explanation.

"Claudia Panduccino, a hero of the revolution, especially to women. ESPECIAL-LY to women *skippers*," she emphasized.

They came to a halt and she bellowed "Rincon Towers!" Eric jumped off and made a mental note. *Claudia Panduccino*. Facing the ancient murals along the dock he took a few more photos before proceeding through the building's lobby to the west side where he found the Minna Canal. A stretch down the waterway a work crew bobbed on a compact maintenance barge, Emmy towering over the others.

Eric stood on the catwalk and waited for her to look his way. When she did he waved frantically, yelling her name. But he was too far away to be heard above the boat traffic and she seemed completely absorbed in ripping out dense pockets of stationery seaweed that narrowed the canal and impeded passage. He sat down where he could see her. He pulled out a tiny mirror he carried for no particular reason. Now he would finally find a use for it—but only if the sun could be coaxed to clear the top of the tower behind him. The sun fell a good six meters out in the water. Still mid-morning, it wouldn't hit his spot for another three hours, he realized dejectedly. He resumed his waving, trying to holler through brief pockets in the ambient noise.

Finally one of Emmy's barge-mates saw him waving and pointed. Emmy quickly put her long arms up, flapping in recognition. Eric imagined her as a Great Black Heron ris-ing into the air to soar to his side. He relaxed, relieved, and waited. In minutes the barge pulled up, the crew working the long canal poles expertly, Emmy in the middle, Queen of the Minna Canal, her languid but erect posture giving off an unmistakeably regal air. Spreading her arms to their full 7 foot span, she delivered an electrifying smile.

"Hey sweetheart! Are we on?"

"Hell yes we're on!"

"Aaah, you are a darling," she gave him her most flirtatious and mischievous look, sending him into a palpable swoon. "The Union Square docks, pier 4, at 7, ok?" He nodded helplessly, grinning like a fool. "Tonight," she added, "sharp." The crew looked on in silence but with great interest. Emmy gave the signal to shove off and they all broke into appreciative banter.

"Got yourself a live one there, Emmy. When you're done, pass him on to me," teased a young stocky man in overalls. "Where'd you find him?"

And then they were out of earshot, Eric waving to Emmy who stood looking at him for a long time.

He decided to check out work listings. The Hiring Hall in City Hall was probably the best place, but something put him off, maybe the size, maybe the old guys he'd met when he visited a week ago. On a vyne in the Rincon Towers lobby he found the current listings. He made himself comfortable in a well-padded chair and began to browse.

The vyne instantly displayed three columns: Annuals, Tryouts, Apprenticeships. The list of Annuals left him uninspired. He did not want to wash dishes, stock shelves, wait tables or clean canals. The offshore windmill farm had potential, but it was described as manual work and required staying on an ocean-based platform for at least two days and one night at a time. *Nah*. He didn't think he could handle that long at sea. A bicycle tire factory at a dump full of centuries-old discarded tires sounded dirty and he hated the smell of burning rubber. Bakeries need help, but they start at 3 a.m.—*forget that!* Roofing. Outdoors and it took you around town and you get to see lots of people's homes. Maybe worth a try. He took down the address on Goodlett Street in the Fillmore.

Recycled Manufacturing to Order. He wondered what exactly that could be, and wrote it down too, an address out to the south at Parnell and Geneva. Hospital aide, delivery service, aquifer monitor, beach patrol, coast guard, longshoreman. He waited to see words that promised excitement, stimulation, something to tap into his natural analytical bent.

He glanced over the Tryout list looking for more intellectual substance, but the possibilities were much the same. A quick scan of the available Apprenticeships showed promise: feature writer, radio news editor, greenway and wild corridor designer, architect, jazz trumpet, blues guitar (*I wish!*), periodontal technician (*ack!*), underwater construction. They all required multi-year commitments he wasn't ready for, and he would have to arrange a Tryout first anyway. *If I had the talent, he sighed, I would be a Bluesman. In a heartbeat!*

He glanced at offers he'd written down and decided to check out the roofer job first. He needed to get to the Union Square docks and catch a streetcar out to Goodlett. He stuffed the notes into his sweater pocket where he discovered a card already there. "Public Investigators Office, 15 Civic Center Plaza." He remembered he'd gotten it at his first meal at the Tweezer.

The guy had hinted that they were not the religious types… "Not many of us around," he had told Eric guardedly. *It's practically on the way. Might as well stop in and see if they have anything. I wonder what they investigate around here?* He foresaw himself hunting down dangerous and violent people, but he dismissed it quickly, certain that the job would be far more mundane and safe than that.

A half hour later he entered the Public Investigators Office. A bookish young man pointed him to the waiting area. Shortly, Ron O'Hair, the man from the Tweezer dining room, appeared at the little swinging gate that opened onto the rest of the office. He was even more wrinkled than Eric remembered, his thick white hair and beard almost comical. A green velvet vest over a burgundy and scarlet plaid lumberjack shirt gave him an unmistakable St. Nick glow. "Yeah?" He obviously did not remember or recognize Eric.

Eric cringed. "I… you…" he stammered, blushing brightly, "you gave me your card at the Tweezer," he finally blurted out.

O'Hair gave an inquisitive twist with his head and then put one hand on his hip as he snapped his fingers with the other. "Sure, okay," he lit up, "the prayer, you didn't like the prayer." Friendly now, he said, "Come on in. You gotta meet Kathy—I mean Katherine Fairly, the P-I."

"P-I?"

"Public Investigator—… Man, you're going to take some work!"

Eric smiled and followed, but that last line had stung. *What a start! Anyone could have figured that out—so chingin' obvious! SHIT!!* Outwardly he looked calm as he tailed O'Hair into Kathy the P-I's office.

"Anyway, emphasis on 'public' around here. We kind of watchdog public safety and well-being. We investigate people who are dangerously violent to themselves and others. We also expose and explain anti-social behavior like hoarding, exploiting others' work for personal advantage, using social resources without approval of a public body, that sort of thing."

Fairly rose as they entered while her associate finished his explanation. "Nicely said… that'll be our new manifesto—er, ah, I mean mission statement." She laughed, eyes focused on Eric.

"Kathy, meet Eric Johanson. The guy who grumbled over the Food Prayer?"

"Oh yeah!" After looking him up and down like a prize heifer she reached over for a slap and beamed. "Pops here told me about you, and we hoped you'd stop by." A salt-and-pepper gray cardigan matched her closely styled short hair. She was nearing 70 but felt the same as she'd felt for decades, and was in excellent condition. As Eric would soon discover, Kathy carried a portable desk in the many pockets of her big black cotton shorts, her everyday work clothes. Soft but tough, flat-sole leather boots left her muscular, trunk-like calves for all to see.

"Have a drink?"

It was only lunchtime. "Bit early for me," Eric pleaded.

"Fine! I always like to celebrate, but we should wait, I agree!"

"I could come back after lunch?"

"Oh, no, not at all… Let's have lunch. I'd like to chat, check out our chemistry—"

"OK, sure, why not?"

"Pops, where will we take him?" the P-I asked with a mischievous glint. O'Hair shrugged dramatically. "I suppose we could take him to,.. but nooo, no, let's go to. . . nooo that's no good either. Oh!" snapping his fingers in his face, "Spec's!"

Kathy started to object, putting up her hands, but then he said, "New Spec's. Only six blocks over on Fulton and Octavia," and she nodded her consent.

They strolled across the Civic Green, cut through City Hall's block long lobby, and over the Goodwill Bridge to cross Van Ness's permanent traffic jam. West of the Civic Center they walked a few blocks through the plum orchards that filled Fulton from City Hall well past Octavia. Their destination proved a suitably seedy bar on a less flourishing corner. As they pushed inside, Eric adjusted to the darkness. The walls were covered with strange objects of San Franciscana. Turned out it wasn't a place to eat either. It was a bar—"With snacks!" they assured Eric.

They sat down and in a few minutes they had pretzels, a small cheeseboard, two gin & tonics and a fizzy water.

"What a place," said Eric, impressed.

"It's all about nostalgia, a false nostalgia," Kathy started. "As long as there's San

Francisco, people here will believe in a golden era of some dim romantic past. Souvenirs of events, clubs, games, you name it! Why?" she rolled along, "It feeds a comfy, reassuringly simple view of the past."

"Oh let 'em have their *tshotskes*, the little gew-gaws and packaged memories, where's the harm?" argued Pops.

Kathy took a deep breath and then trained a knowing smile on Eric. He smiled back, a nervous mirror. O'Hair looked back and forth and snorted. "You guys havin' some kind of love fest?" jolting Eric into an embarrassed blink. "Oh, come ON man! You're gonna be fine—just relax!" He drained his drink and waved for another.

Eric sat up straighter and looked across at the P-I. "What exactly are we discussing? I mean, I stopped by to have a look and I'm getting the feeling I'm already committed to something?"

"Not at all. No pressure," reassured Fairly. "You sure you're from Chicago? You are SO San Francisco—don't like commitments."

He laughed along and tried to relax. "The first question is still on the table. Just what is it do you do and what would I do—if I *did* sign on?"

"Yes, well, fair enough. First, obviously we can't take anyone here working Annuals. The minimum is a three-month Tryout," she spread her thick hands before her, "because I don't have the time to spend on anyone who won't stick around." She shot him a look that made him not want to get on her bad side.

He nodded.

"I'm looking for someone to work closely with, to examine crime scenes, conduct interviews, write reports and publish summaries for the public record," she peered at Eric, looking for a reaction. "That's why," she finished off her drink and waved for a third, "chemistry comes into it, make sense?"

He nodded. "Uh… what about dangerous people, violent types? Do we have to catch them?"

She looked at him archly. "Cops and robbers?? No, definitely not! We are not police! There are no police, remember?" Actually he'd never thought about it until now. "When someone is acting crazy, hurting people, there's no time to wait for someone else to take care of it... Didn't you get the public safety training when you were 12?" she asked, suddenly surprised. He nodded but the expression on his face conveyed doubt. "Anyway, when someone needs to be "caught" they are usually subdued by people at hand. Our job is getting the facts and making them public." She leaned back, crossing her arms, scrutinizing Eric.

"Don't get me wrong! We do take risks... not mostly from direct violence, but we go places where assaults have happened, or into buildings that have burned or collapsed." She could see Eric wrapping his mind around this warning. She smiled after a pause, "But I've never had an injury in 27 years! And I've only been hit twice!"

Eric's eyes widened, "What happened?"

Pops leaned in, grabbed Eric by the shoulder, and stage-whispered, "This woman has a black belt, and she's twice as strong as anyone I've ever met... Don't make her mad!" He fell back laughing at his own preposterous theatricality.

"Seriously Eric," continued Kathy. "It helps if you can handle yourself in a dust-up... If someone's had too much to drink, or there's a domestic conflict, or they're plain crazy...

you may have to convince them to behave differently," she said ominously. "P-I's don't often get pulled in to lovers quarrels or violently jealous fights. But when it's your neighbor, you better be ready to intervene." She smacked her palm into the table.

"I'm not sure," Eric balked. He'd never been in any kind of fight, and the few times a fight had broken out near him, other people had handled it.

"Your training will cover this. Conflict resolution, advanced First Aid, and self-defense. I'll even give you a few pointers myself."

"How many P-I's are there?"

"Anywhere from two to five in each watershed. Right now we have four lifers, three Apprentices and two Tryouts… you would be the third."

He nibbled cheese and crackers, and then drained his water glass. "Can I have a few days to decide? It's a three-month deal, right?"

"Yup, three months," Kathy affirmed. "Not much of a lunch here, eh?" she said as Eric picked at the corner of the cheese without interest. He wondered if they drank their lunch routinely.

"Well," she said with an air of finality, pushing her chair back forcefully. Eric followed suit, and they stood up in unison. "We've got to get back to work."

"Before Friday," Fairly urged, "drop by and let us know."

He nodded, then followed them into the plum orchard outside the bar. They walked together as far as City Hall, making small talk. When they entered the venerable building, Kathy and Pops clapped Eric on both shoulders, and enthusiastically repeated that the job was his for the taking. He watched them recede down the corridor, Fairly erect and crisp next to the waddling hunch of Pops. Eric beamed, a man with an offer on the table.

Kathy Fairly returned to her cluttered desk to study another case of domestic violence, an alcoholic who denied everything—no drinking problem, no explanation for the bruises on his wife and kids. The family was not helping, afraid of losing their father and husband, or afraid of his wrath. Kathy hated these cases the most. The neighbors had denounced the guy, Lars Tyving, four times in two months. Once it came to blows with the neighbor, who lodged the complaint.

Sighing deeply she put it aside, staring out her window at a kite dancing in the wind over the Civic Green to the strains of a bluegrass band. She pursed her lips, drumming her fingers on the chair's arm. Publishing the facts wouldn't be enough. The neighbors were already involved, and given the ugly personal tone of it, weren't going to solve this on their own. The Community Boards could do nothing without Tyving's cooperation. Public pressure from a P-I notice on the vyne usually brought the parties to mediation, to clear their names if nothing else. But this looked like one of too many exceptions. The Tyvings might just leave, solving the problem for the neighbors. But the wife and kids. . . She sighed deeply again. Protection vs. autonomy, intervention vs. independence. It was precisely these kinds of cases that made her doubt the social tilt towards letting people solve their own problems. *That poor woman and her kids are completely terrified. How are they supposed to be responsible for saving themselves?* She wanted to go and drag the man out of the house and put him in a situation where he could feel the kind of isolated fear that he was causing. But she couldn't do that. Vigilantes, she knew where that led.

"Shit!" she got up, frustrated and unsettled and glad she'd had a third drink.

18.

Standing in muddy water to mid-calf, chilled in spite of warm rubber boots and insulated gloves, Nwin looked towards the sun fighting to break through the fog. *Can't take more than another half hour*, he thought, and turned back to his work, anticipating that the heat would soon bake away his chill. He and several others were slowly working their way down the rows, planting new seedlings in the fresh water. Frogs croaked all around, nursed and loved by all the Rice Bowl workers as their best ally against the mosquitoes.

His back ached. He squatted on his haunches just above the water, and did some stretching and bending, trying to unkink his lower back. When he bent down to his work, he knew he better stop.

"Hey, Marco, Jerry," he called ahead. They stood up and looked back at him, shading their eyes against the bright sky. "My back is killing me! I'm going in."

Marco waved.

Nwin entered the barn where he found Angus, Rikky and Stefania arguing at the table. They paid no attention to his entrance.

"A fence! What's next? Barbed wire?!?" Angus roared. Rikky looked like she was going to explode. Stefania sat between them, frantically trying to calm things.

"Angus, hold on there!" she urged, and turning to Rikky, "Can we calm down and have a civilized discussion?"

"Don't ask me!" she spat. Then, slamming her fist into the table, she pointed a finger at Angus, "HE'S the one who turns every problem into a huge fight. HE'S the one who keeps blaming people"—

"CH—FUCK YOU!" Angus roared in his oldtimer slang as he stood up, both hands on the table. "I've been here for 52 years. I STARTED this farm, goddammit! I will not let all this work be destroyed by people who can't do their jobs, and I will NOT stand for the return of private plots!"

"AAARRGH! YOU ASSHOLE! NO ONE WANTS PRIVATE PLOTS!!!" Rikky screamed. Stefania sank helplessly into her seat, putting her hands on the top of her head and closing her eyes. Angus lifted his end of the table and let it crash down, jarring Stefania back into action. She leaped on the table, standing between Angus and Rikky.

"STOP IT! STOP IT!" she yelled. Angus and Rikky, who had been near to attacking each other, now stood back, stunned that the mild-mannered Stefania was standing on the table yelling. A small blonde woman with square shoulders and thick thighs, Stefania, looked about ready to burst out of her jeans. She stomped her foot, first at Angus, and then at Rikky. "OK, OK, will you behave?!?" Rikky sat back down, folding her arms, tight-lipped. Angus put his hands up in surrender and also sat down, grudgingly biting his tongue.

Silence settled over the room, and Nwin shuffled to his locker across the back wall. They all noticed him now. "Nwin, what do you have to say about all this?" asked Rikky. Angus jumped in without a moment's hesitation, "We already KNOW what he thinks! The fence is HIS IDEA!!" He glowered menacingly at Nwin. Nwin looked back impassively. His back hurt and he was going to take a hot shower. At his locker he waved his arm at them dismissively and said, "You guys figure it out. I don't care, I really don't..." and then with a glint of malice he turned back. "Take the chingin' fence down, Angus. You can stand guard out there night and day. *Then* you'll catch your culprits!" He slammed his locker shut, threw his towel over his shoulder and headed for the showers without waiting to hear any rejoinder.

Hot water poured over him, the noise and steam drowning out everything else. He scrubbed his body, spending the adrenaline coursing through him on the mundane task of cleaning. He grew calmer under the comforting warmth of the shower, finally ridding himself of the bone chill that had tightened his back and led to the spasms that drove him in from the field.

When he returned to his locker, Angus was gone. Rikky and Stefania were talking quietly at the table. Once he'd dressed he poured a cup of coffee and sat down. "So, what's going to happen?" he asked.

"Angus is on a rampage," said Rikky, stating the obvious.

"Well, he does have an argument," Stefania reminded her.

"OK, I admit it, but I'm not convinced."

"He wants to take down the fence, right?" asked Nwin.

"Yeah, but he's the only one who feels so strongly about it. You heard him. He thinks it's the beginning of a scheme to reintroduce private plots! What an absurdity!" Rikky's green eyes blazed beneath her tousled amber hair. Dried mud caked her arms down to her wrists, where her hands' clean whiteness looked like gloves.

"We'll have to talk about this more formally at the meeting next Monday," said Stefania.

"That's gonna be fun," Nwin commented sarcastically.

"So Nwin, you wanted to have lunch today, right?" Stefania changed the subject, much to everyone's relief.

"You ready to eat?"

"I guess so. I'm not that hungry, but maybe by the time we get to the food I will be."

"Gwen's? The taqueria? The noodle bar?" he suggested.

"Let's do Gwen's," she agreed, the prospect of a fresh seafood salad already starting to sound good.

Gwen's was pretty close, a three story curving wooden building overlooking Mission Bay just behind the Kyoto Causeway. They were early, beating the lunchtime rush from the campus across the water. Just as the food hit the table they could see a small flotilla of skiffs and taxis heading towards the 7th Street docks from the UC dock. Moments later an ancient steam whistle sounded in Russ Gardens, the official sound of noon in that part of town.

"Remind me what you were announcing about Chile at last week's meeting."

She crunched contentedly on a big crispy shrimp, had a drink of water and cleared her throat. "Terrorists! My family's farm has been attacked twice."

Slurping down a mussel, Nwin let the idea roll around for a second. "People getting killed?!?"

She nodded with a worried expression. "Yup, three people died last time."

"Why? What do they think they are trying to do?"

"It's crazy," she finished another bite. "They think they are fighting for a better way of life. They left some kind of manifesto claiming that things were better in the old days of the Money System. No waiting, no shortages, and hard work for everyone… can you believe it?!"

Nwin compared this account to his brief encounter with Nance at the Café Hurricane. There were no obvious connections.

"Why did you want to know about that?" Stefania asked.

"Oh, I'm trying to figure out something about these people I met. They seem kind of weird, and I think one is a Chilean, so I thought…" he trailed off, not wanting to talk about it in more detail, afraid of where it would lead.

Luckily Stefania wasn't that inquisitive. "I can't imagine having to defend against an armed attack! My poor great-grandmother! It's worse for her I'm sure. She went through it all during the Revolution."

"How old is she?"

"Let's see, I saw her on her 115th six years ago, so I guess she's 121 by now."

"Is she in good shape?"

"I'll say! She's stronger than my grandmother, and still the most active elder in her town. Plus she's on the Chilean Council of Elders, like our California Council of Elders, revolutionary guardians."

"Dessert?" Nwin proposed.

"Nah, thanks, I'm full. I can't do desserts anymore, they're making me too fat!" she wailed.

Nwin laughed softly, thinking Stefania didn't have to worry about being fat. They got up and slapped a thanks with the waiter, sending their compliments in to Gwen. Outside, the warm sun had finally overcome the fog and San Francisco was awash in bright sun under blue skies—at least until later when fluffy cotton fog would envelop the city.

Nwin said 'bye' to Stefania as they passed the 7th Street docks. Hundreds of people streamed through the transit crossroads. He found *Hot 1* where he'd left it and cast off, quickly heading across Mission Bay towards the campus. The lunchtime exodus was still underway as he tied up at the school's docks. "No good food out here I guess," he thought, puzzled that no culinary artists had set up shop among all the scientists and students.

He jumped off *Hot 1* and headed up a spiral stairway on the outside of the Botanical Studies building. He took a skybridge across to the Institute of BioManufactury and cut across the roof garden, careful to avoid stepping on any of the student projects that squeaked and buzzed across his path. He stopped to marvel at a thick green log with stubby legs (about the size of a small dog) growling over and over, "Call Me Ishmael." At a small gate he made sure to hold back the small creatures who tried to sneak through behind him, and ran down a flight of stairs. Here was the indoor student lounge full of small groups in conversation and individuals buried in deep chairs intently studying. In the far corner, facing the Bay's blue waters, he found him right where he always found him.

"Joseph," he said as he sat down next to the white-haired, frail fellow, "how are you doin'?"

The old guy looked at him, blinking repeatedly as if to focus on an apparition that had appeared out of the sea. "Oh," startled, "Nwin, is that you?"

"Yeah, Joseph, who else?"

"I hardly recognized you," he croaked, "with your hair like that."

Nwin put his hand up to his head, having forgotten again his blond hair.

"Joseph, do you know anything about terrorists who want to restore the Money System?"

The old man looked at Nwin without expression. He stared at him for a long time without speaking. Nwin knew he just had to wait.

Eventually Joseph looked back at the Bay, his hands comfortably resting on the chair's arms. He shook his head slowly, making soft 'tsk tsk' sounds almost under his breath.

"Where'd you hear *that*?" he finally asked.

Nwin filled him in on what he'd just heard from Stefania, neglecting to say anything about his investigation of the *Leopold Tanzania* and its captain.

Joseph took up his walking stick, an ancient polished piece of wood that practically vibrated with the accumulated wisdom of ages. He leaned forward with both hands on the knob, the staff planted between his feet. "It's a lot more complicated than that. I don't know where to begin," he said, almost a hint of apology in his voice.

"Well, you don't have to explain all of world history, if that's what you're thinking," said Nwin, knowing that Joseph would start his story long ago and far away.

Joseph gave him a look that told Nwin he didn't appreciate the last comment. He fell silent again. "Sorry, uncle," Nwin used his familiar nickname, even though Joseph was old enough to be his great-grandfather and was not a direct relation.

"Remember what I told you about keeping an open mind?" scolded Joseph. Nwin nodded, subdued. "Restoring the Money System… I don't know what terrorist attacks could have to do with that…" he shook his head. "Maybe they think?…" and he stopped. He sighed deeply, remembering a little too vividly the death and mayhem that followed the Great Die-off and the revolution that followed.

"Nwin I don't know about any Chilean terrorists. I do remember the Money System," he struggled with his memories. "It's about fear. They want to make people frightened and insecure. That was the key to the Money System."

Nwin was clueless. This didn't help at all. "Killing some people tending vineyards?…" he started.

Joseph shrugged. "Kind of hard to imagine isn't it?" he smiled. "Seems like a bad dream to me. It was an awfully long time ago," he sank deeper into his chair. "Did you bring me a little something?" he asked hopefully.

"Of course, uncle, here," and Nwin pulled out a small folded up newspaper, which emitted a strong perfumed smell as he opened it. Joseph sat back in his chair smiling and breathing deeply, "Aaaaaaaah. Now that's a sweeet smell!" The dense green buds of San Francisco's finest marijuana passed from Nwin to Joseph. "You're a good boy, Nwin."

Nwin rose, giving Joseph a small kiss on the top of his head. "Thanks uncle. I'll see you soon, ok?"

Joseph waved one hand while pulling out his pipe with the other. As a Die-off survivor he had a special appreciation for smoking marijuana. The virus that had swept the world back in 2074, killing nearly 3 billion people in a month, didn't affect anyone who had at least traces of THC delta-9 in their blood. Before Nwin was out of the lounge, the sweet smell of marijuana caught up with him as Joseph puffed enthusiastically behind him. "Oh shit, where's the nonsmoking lounge?" asked one girl of another near the door that Nwin walked through. He went down the corridor to a public vyne and sat down to check messages.

Finally Valentina had responded! He brought up her message. There she was, reddish brown hair falling over her forehead. She smiled warmly through the green display. "Hi Nwin. Sorry for not getting back sooner. I was on a trip up to Reno with my brother, and then I worked a bunch when I got back. Thanks for vyning me!" She seemed earnest. Nwin's heart was beating furiously. "Listen, my grandma is doing this performance tonight at Duboce Park at 7. Do you want to meet me there? Leaf me a message," she giggled and faded away. He quickly responded that he would be there. He ignored a message from his mother, figuring he'd get it later. He headed back to the docks, barely noticing anything along the way.

19.

Hurrying through the lobby, Eric remembered to comb his wet hair. He'd just showered and put on a nice pair of canvas pants, his best boots, and a brown linen shirt. On the shirt's breast pocket was embroidered an intricate rising sun over a gnarly forest. He had his favorite black leather jacket slung over one arm.

A loud wolf whistle followed him towards the door. He turned and was embarrassed to see Jack, the Hostel's front desk guy, leaning on the information desk with two lobby staffers, smiling broadly, flashing a thumbs up to Eric. Grinning sheepishly, Eric rushed out to find a taxi at the dock. He urged the cabbie to get him to Union Square as soon as possible. The cabbie was a gray old man wearing a blue sailor's hat and a thick blue peacoat. He looked like he might have stepped out of the 19th century. He didn't pay much attention to Eric after he boarded and gave instructions. He hummed to himself as he steered through dense traffic.

Just two blocks west they were stuck waiting to turn into the Kearny Canal when suddenly blaring sirens filled the amber-tinted skies. "What's that?" Eric asked, startled. "Mus' be some kind of accident," said the cabbie, as he sat back and fired up a joint. Seeing this, Eric's jaw pulsed involuntarily. He looked back and forth but he could only see dozens of boats jammed together, waiting. The cabbie offered him a toke, but he declined, asking, "Isn't there some way we can go around? I'm supposed to meet someone in three minutes!"

The cabbie spread his hands wide and shrugged. "We're kinda stuck, y'know?" Eric couldn't dispute that. They were wedged among more boats than he could count, with no visible means of escape. Then the emergency boats appeared ahead on Kearny. First two small skiffs, red lights flashing, followed by a small red peapod, an old siren blaring from its stern along with another flashing red light. An emergency crew strained forward to reach the site of the accident, somewhere south of California where Eric was stuck. He was still a half dozen blocks from the north side of the Union Square docks. He thought about climbing out of the taxi and making his way across the boats to the nearest building, rushing up and finding skybridges until he made his way to Union Square. Not knowing the way dissuaded him. He might take three times as long wandering through all those unfamiliar buildings. Frantically worrying, he sat and fidgeted. The cabbie watched him, unimpressed. He wasn't used to anyone being in such a hurry.

Finally the traffic began to move. They slowly followed those ahead of them, turning left in a great wave of boat traffic onto Kearny. After a short stretch of open water, ahead on the left they could see one of the emergency skiffs still on the scene. As they drew alongside, everyone slowed to see what had happened. A skiff and a barge had apparently collided, the skiff ending up smashed into the corner of Sutter, the barge bobbing a short distance out in the Sutter Canal, crew members disconsolately poling it away. The emergency skiff was tying the broken skiff to a towline, making ready to drag it to a repair lab where it would be reshaped and given nutritional supplements until it had the tensile strength to resume its boating functions.

Traffic finally cleared and the cabbie accelerated through a small opening, whipping around onto Geary and ahead to the docks. In the distance, standing near the top of the pier silhouetted against the peach and ruby sunset, unmistakably, it was Emmy. She was not one to minimize her remarkable size. As they drew near, Eric smiled up to her, and she returned his gaze from beneath a very broad, swooping white hat that must have been over two feet in diameter, the brim dipping on the right and rising on the left. A large red carnation adorned it, matching the lipstick she'd applied for this romantic occasion. Her two meter frame gracefully swayed in a long white cotton dress that followed the classic curves of her body wherever they wanted to go. A fringed bottom tickled the calves of her ebony legs, which in turn disappeared into small white boots with good-sized heels, increasing her dominating height even further.

Eric was breathless and somewhat numb as he disembarked. He had trouble feeling his legs as he fought his way through to Emmy, walking forward automatically, trying to calm his beating heart and remember to breathe.

"You look amazing!"

She gave him an incredibly bright smile, spread her arms and embraced him, making sure to get his head up under her wide hat brim where she could give him a long lingering kiss. The delicate touch of their meeting lips just about stopped his heart and it *did* stop his breathing. He recoiled a short step involuntarily, gasping for breath. They looked at each other and burst out laughing, falling back into each other's arms and squeezed and kissed again. Finally they slowly separated, turning to enjoy the waning moments of the sunset's deep blues and purples.

"Now what?" Eric said, his anxiety falling away like an old skin.

"I have a surprise in store for you!" she said conspiratorially. "Come with me," and with that she took his arm in her own. They made quite a striking couple and everyone stopped to admire their passage. An old black couple sitting on a bench called over, "Emmy, you are the queen of the night!" to which she waved, smiling, and then dragged Eric over. "Auntie, Uncle, this is Eric Johanson," she said proudly. He touched hands with each of them, and gave a small bow, inspired by the moment and Emmy's elegance, which won them over completely. "My, my," said her aunt, "what a fine young man!"

"Got a real gennelman, there, Emmy," complimented her uncle. They wished each other a good evening as Emmy and Eric continued on across the plaza.

Eric was feeling absolutely giddy as she led him up to a beautiful horse-drawn carriage with tiny kerosene lamplights hanging on each of the four corners. As they approached the driver put out a small stepladder. Eric looked at Emmy, disbelieving. She smiled and extended her arm, urging him in to the carriage. He accepted her gracious offer and once in, turned to help her follow him into the velvet-lined, gold-trimmed bit of history. They fell together into the back seat, their arms around each other. Sitting they were nearly the same height. He turned his face into her neck, kissing her behind the ear while she giggled and half-heartedly pushed him away. He gave up after a second, feeling the jolt of the carriage's start. She called forward to the driver, "Sous les Pavés, OK?" to which the driver turned, tipping her black top hat and answered "Bien sûr!"

Eric didn't know any French so this all sounded mysterious and exciting to him. Emmy moved her arm from his shoulders to his thigh where her long fingers slowly made their presence felt. Eric fought his urge to grope Emmy's gorgeous body, sitting as still as he could under her sweet probing touch, admiring the old buildings that still stood along their route, rising above the dark trees that lined the path. Hot breath filled his ear, sending electrifying chills down his spine where they met her hand under his bulging pants. He squirmed uncontrollably, but just then she pulled back, straightening her dress, and looking at him with a sidelong glance, coquettish and provocative.

"Ah, here we are!" she announced. The carriage pulled up in front of the ruins of an old apartment building. The façade still stood in places, and at the head of a small staircase disappearing down into the basement was a sign that said "Sous les Pavés". She got up, leaning forward to plant a kiss on the cheek of the driver, "Thanks Linda!" Linda put out the small stepladder, offering her hand to Emmy as she elegantly stepped down. Eric following.

After blowing a goodbye kiss to Linda, she pulled Eric down the stone steps into a subterranean passageway. It was a long corridor, dark except for an occasional candle on the wall. Down it went, deeper into the ground, loose stones lying about on the dimly-lit floor. The hall turned and ahead glowed a faint yellow sign "C'est la Plage!" They went through the door and entered a restaurant that didn't look like anything Eric had ever seen before.

The floor was covered with smooth white sand. The walls were incongruously stained dark wood, with large grainy black and white photos of some kind of street demonstrations or riots, apparently in Paris, though Eric wasn't sure, having never been there. Small wooden tables were covered in white linen tablecloths and simple candles, heavy silver, and multiple wine glasses. There were two historic wooden surfboards, each some 10 feet tall, separating a waiting area with small palm huts, one of which had a group of friends wrapped in towels imbibing piña coladas. The place was a little more than half full.

The maitre'd came up to Emmy, whom he seemed to know. He was dressed in a formal suit, a small bowtie echoing his little moustache, his hair greased and parted in the middle. "Bon soir mes amis!" he said jovially. "Dinner?" he asked without waiting and led them to a table. Eric was confused by the place's mixed metaphors, a confusion that worsened when one of the waitresses came out of the kitchen bearing a tray laden with sumptuous meals. She was wearing only a skimpy bikini. Seconds later another waiter burst out from the kitchen, wearing his own tiny bathing suit.

They sat down, Emmy beaming at Eric as he looked around in amazement. "So…" he started, not sure where to begin. She was loving it. "OK, I give up!" he laughed. "Explain please?"

"Explain?" she said innocently, her big eyes dancing, "What's to explain?"

He let his eyes fall on the swaying hips of a waitress as she served the next table. He tipped his head towards the cute ass. Emmy reached over and made as if to give it a feel, pulling her hand back before the woman noticed, laughing.

"You don't know any French, huh?" she asked. He shook his head. "Well, first the name of the place. It means 'Beneath the Cobblestones,' and then the second sign at the door says 'There is the Beach!' Ring any bells?" Eric looked blank. "How about these photos?" gesturing to the poster-sized pictures of old demonstrations. "You're not a student of history, eh?" she smiled. Again he shook his head, his self-confidence draining away as his terrible ignorance was being revealed. "Don't feel bad!" she laughed, seeing him shrinking across the table.

Another waiter appeared, a gorgeous Adonis, rippling muscles gleaming in the romantic candlelight of the restaurant. Emmy and Eric looked up from his washboard stomach to his friendly, rather effeminate face, made more so by his very long black hair arranged into two braids and coiled up over his ears. "Tonight's specials are" and he rattled off a bunch of French things that Eric didn't recognize. Emmy observed his bewildered look and just ordered for the two of them. She also requested a bottle of Chateau Clicquot, one of the best local champagnes. Eric relaxed when he saw that she didn't mind taking charge of the ordering. If anything she seemed to expect it.

"You're having Bay scallops in a light lemon-garlic sauce, and I'm having roast chicken with vegetables prepared in red wine. I think you get some steamed vegetables with the scallops."

"I love scallops! How did you know?"

She just smiled and tilted her head. The waiter returned with the champagne and after the ceremonial POP they were toasting each other, laughing, delighted to be in the first blush of romance.

"So, back to history," she said seriously, after draining her first glass of champagne. "The restaurant's name, *Sous les pavés, c'est la plage* ('Beneath the Cobblestones... is the Beach') was a graffiti on the walls of Paris way back in May 1968, nearly 200 years ago. It was one of the biggest general strikes and uprisings in history before the Die-off. Here, take a close look at this photo," and she stood up and led him to a photo a few tables away. "Excuse us," she said when they stopped in front of a table with three people who were nearing the end of their desserts and coffee. They nodded tolerantly. She pointed to a wall in the back of a mob of students at a barricade, and sure enough there it was, "sous la pavés, c'est la plage" scribbled prominently on the mottled surface.

She explained more about the course of events in that long ago time, pointing out another graffiti on the photo over their table, "Pouvoir a l'imagination!" (All Power to the Imagination).

"I read some books that argued that this was the real turning point, even though it was more than a hundred years before the Economy was finally overthrown, and then only because of the Die-off. No one had articulated the idea that material prosperity was an empty accomplishment. Uprisings happened around the world in 1968, and although they were each quite specific to their countries, somehow they all spoke to something deeper." She paused.

"I never knew about that. I guess my sense of history doesn't go much further back than the Revolution and the Die-off," he admitted.

"Well, honey," she said in a surprising southern twang, "don't you worry your pretty li'l head, cuz I'm heah to hep you sort it ahhhll out!" she laughed.

"Thanks," he said as he refilled their glasses, both of them enjoying the tipsiness brought on by the delicious champagne. The food came, and they ate, sharing bites, letting the delicate cuisine fill their senses. She told him some more history, and he told her about his family background, sheepishly admitting that he came from a long line of sullen New Englanders who had ducked during the Revolution, he being the first to venture out of Connecticut in generations.

The talk turned to his afternoon at the P-I's office and his doubt about signing up for a three-month Tryout.

"I went to the roofing place after the P-I's, but I don't think that's for me. I took a look around the yard where they grow the roofs, and I watched them harvested for installation, but it just looked like it would be awfully dull after one or two jobs." She nodded, savoring a last bite of the wonderful baby green salad with tangerine slices.

"So I think I should take it. It's the kind of work where I have to use my brain, and hell, it's probably a great way to see the underbelly of life here, don'tcha think?"

"Yeah, I suppose..." she said through her chewing.

He leaned forward slightly, downing his fifth glass of champagne as she held up the second bottle to see if there was any left. There was just enough for them each to have a last drop. "I'll tell you the truth. I'm scared of having to deal with violence. I also feel a bit weird because... well, what if I have to enforce the rules on resource use? I mean, if they send me to investigate something that turns out to be a case of wrongful use, I don't know if I could do it."

"Why?" she asked, surprised.

"My uncle is an inventor. He came up with a great way to resurface the veloways, but nobody thought it worth the trouble."

"Didn't get approved by the Resource Review Board?"

"Right. So he got some friends together and did an area anyway. Well, it led to a huge scandal, and he was banned from using community resources for three years. And that made it impossible for him to do any of the work he cared about. He was bitter, so angry with his neighbors who hadn't supported him. I was only about six when it happened, but I remember it."

"Hmmm. So you think that kind of investigation would be hard for you to do?"

"I don't know, maybe not. Now that I told you about it, it sounds kind of trivial." He tailed off, and realized he had taken the conversation far from the romantic buzz it had held for most of the evening. Chagrined he excused himself and went to the bathroom. He was drunk, and the evening was going great, but he had to do something to get back on track. He splashed water in his face, thinking he didn't look so bad in his beautiful shirt. When he got back to the table, Emmy was there, chin on her hands looking kind of dreamy. He reached over and stroked her cheek, which made her purr appreciatively. "You want dessert?" she asked.

"I'm really full, and," he grinned ruefully, "pretty drunk!"

She laughed. "You're not drunk! I've seen drunk and it's a whole 'nother ball o' wax!" which made him think she had some dark stories he hadn't heard yet. She continued, "Shall we head out?" and he nodded. They spent a minute piling their dishes in neat piles, brushing crumbs into the sand at their feet, and arranging themselves.

Popping into the cool evening air, they hugged close together against the surprisingly biting wind. "I thought we might have a boat ride," she started, "but it's too damn cold!" She looked across at him, eyes glowing. They stopped and turned toward each other. The kiss lasted a long time, each of them submerging into the tender exchange of sweet lips. Finally they pulled apart, gasping and laughing softly, holding hands and walking gaily up the street. It was a magical moment, and neither wanted it to end. "Eric," she started hesitantly.

"Hmmm?" he responded encouragingly.

"Ready to come over to my place?"

"I thought you'd never ask!" he said sincerely. Heart beating rapidly, his spirits soaring to heights they'd rarely reached in his life, they found a streetcar and started the half hour journey to Page Mews and Emmy's warm, welcoming bed.

20.

Past seven, way past! Nwin sped over the Sans Souci Bridge on the Wiggle at Church leaning into the rising wind. Valentina said the show started at 7, and he was nearly forty minutes late! At the park he dropped the bike at the corner velome. At least 200 people spread over the grassy slope surrounding two women hanging from a flower-covered trapeze. Nwin circled around the side, searching for Valentina. He spotted her sitting near the center in the front row, so he hunched over as far as he could and ran in front of the audience to a place near her.

"Nwin!" she whispered theatrically, "Shhhhh!"

He slid to a halt in front of her and, lying on his side, he turned to face the show, propping his head on an elbow. She gave him a petulant slap in the back of the head that he ignored. Two elaborately costumed women assumed poses and held them for 10-15 seconds. He noticed that the women both had gray hair, although from where he sat they didn't look very old.

* * *

The world turned 90 degrees and everything was suddenly on its side. Francesca observed her granddaughter sitting in the front row with some friends, but from this angle it was hard to see their faces. A young man ran and jumped into a slide, coming to a stop right in front of Valentina. She seems to know him, Francesca thought before her attention was drawn back to her next pose. The lights at the back of the audience twinkled as people "oohed" and "aahhed" at the seemingly effortless grace that Francesca and Bridget brought to the stationary trapeze.

Blossoms twisted around the uprights. Their feet grazed the sides, extending perpendicularly out from the rope swing from which they each extended. Their remarkable strength hid in smooth passages from one pose to another, sideways one moment, then a slow symmetrical air dance into a new position, legs extended at right angles in front of each of them, one facing the audience, one facing backwards.

At each completed pose the audience erupted in applause. A small five-piece ensemble consisting of an accordian, a clarinet, a trumpet, a violin, and a small drum, played an accompaniment, but without amplification the sound rose and fell in the evening air.

Francesca and Bridget finished with a swirling, perfectly timed drop to the ground and a sweeping bow. The two grandmothers looked a lot younger than their 68 years, but then no one looked old unless they stopped taking age-blockers.

"Do you think we should take this down now?" asked Bridget, after the applause subsided and the audience broke up.

"No, let's leave it. I'd love to do another show, either tonight or tomorrow," said Francesca. She hailed Valentina, "Hey Val, c'm'ere!"

"Grandma, you are the dew! That was so *rich*," Valentina ran up enthusing. "You know Shelley and Harmony. . ."

"Sure. Hey, you guys wanna go with me and Bridget and get some ice-cream? I've got a shift tonight starting in a couple of hours anyway." Francesca still loved working the ice cream parlor. She did at least three shifts a week, closing up at 1 a.m. There was an adjacent velome that ensured a steady stream of patrons. She got to see all the kids falling in love, the little ones coming in with big eyes stammering out the flavor they wanted to try, and plenty of other people too.

"This is Nwin Robertson. I worked with him at the Rice Bowl, remember? Nwin, my grandmother Francesca Panduccino."

Francesca smiled, realizing immediately the look of a suitor, and gave Nwin a warm slap, "Glad to meet you Nwin."

"Me too... uh..."

"Call her Francesca!" urged Valentina.

Nwin flashed her a grateful glance before continuing, "—Francesca! Nice to meet you!" He didn't know what else to say. *That she is very famous? That her name is well known? Nah. Everything sounds stupid. Better to remain silent he thought, be "inscrutable."*

They left Duboce Park and walked up the hill along the Hayes River, winding along the shoreline between shrubs and trees. On Haight Street, at the corner of Rexroth, the Real Authentic Organic Ice Cream Parlor buzzed brightly. Bicycles came down the Haight Street hill and disappeared on Rexroth behind the parlor. Other cyclists crossed Haight on Rexroth, north and west.

Nwin and Valentina walked together just ahead of Shelley and Harmony, as they had at the Civic Green a week earlier. Francesca and Bridget were a little bit ahead of them, speaking quietly.

"You were so late! Too bad," said Valentina.

"Yeah, sorry. Lost track of the time and hit some bad traffic on the way over," he pleaded, and quickly continued, "Are they going to do another show?"

"Hey grandma, you gonna do another show?"

Francesca turned around at the call of her granddaughter. Nwin looked expectantly at her. "Yeah, I think we're going to do it again." She raised her eyebrows questioningly at Bridget, who mouthed "tomorrow" at her. Francesca called "Tomorrow, I guess at 7 p.m. again. But we might do a lunch time show in the warm sun at 1 p.m."

Bridget cringed playfully and patted Francesca's shoulder. "You're going to do a lunchtime show!" she teased, "I'll watch!"

Francesca returned a playful punch to Bridget's shoulder. Nwin asked Valentina "You wanna come and see it again?" but she was too irritated to agree. "Nah… well, maybe."

Nwin felt awkward, defensive about being late and Valentina not being very nice. He struggled to think of something clever to say, but came up blank. Valentina walked along with her arms crossed, her lips knit into a tight line.

Harmony squealed behind them, "SHELLEY!" and was flailing at her sister. Shelley was laughing and holding out a dead parakeet towards her. "Get it away!" she demanded. Valentina saw the bird and turned to have a better look. "Let's see," she said.

Shelley handed it over. Valentina took it by the feet, hanging upside down. The gray-white feathers clung stiffly to the corpse. A small yellow beak and beady, lifeless black eyes. "Sad," Valentina pronounced.

"Why sad?" asked Nwin. "What's the big deal if a bird dies?"

She glared at him. They came to the Ice Cream Parlor before the conversation could continue. They lined up, carefully examining the day's flavors.

"So, what'll it be? Chocolate and peanut butter? Spumoni? Asian strawpear? Or our latest, lemelon?"

"Chocolate chocolate chip, please" said Shelley.

"Vanilla bean with sprinkles for me, please" said Harmony.

Nwin pointed at a pale yellow ice cream and said "I'll try that Koopwasoo. Isn't that Brazilian?"

Francesca looked at him again, surprised that he'd know that. "Well, yes, that's where the fruit comes from, but we get ours from a hot house in—"

"San Mateo County!" Nwin cut in, triumphantly.

"Have you worked there?" Francesca asked pleasantly.

Nwin shook his head, enjoying his little victory. "Nope. My cousin works at the Central Freestore and he told me about it."

"Ah."

"I'll try lemelon, plus a scoop of chipotle cookie dough," said Valentina.

Francesca and Bridget both wrinkled their noses at the idea of eating chipotle cookie dough. People their age just couldn't get used to that smoky hot flavor as a sweet, but the kids *these* days, well they'd eat *anything*!

Francesca went to the counter, donned her crazy quilt apron and began scooping. "Hey if you're coming in early, can I leave?" asked Arnie, a kid doing his Annuals. "What's the hurry? I'm not *really* here for another hour and a half," said Francesca.

Arnie scowled and went back to the next patron, while Francesca calmly scooped out the orders she'd just taken. She put the cups on a tray, poured a few glasses of water, and headed back to their table.

"Harmony you are such a jerk!" Valentina scolded. "Grandma, don't you think it's stupid to be thinking of permanent work already?"

"Well, Valentina, the only thing I know, is nobody knows what's best for anyone else. If Harmony feels that excited about something, why shouldn't she consider committing to it? She can always change her mind and do something else later if she wants to."

"Yeah, but she'll hardly try *anything* out before she locks into one job. That can't be a good idea."

"Hey, I can do whatever I want!" said Harmony indignantly. "You've got a lot of nerve trying to tell me what I should or shouldn't do, considering that you don't have any idea what you're going to do… You're just jealous that I already know I want to go into aqua-culture. Water farming is the dew! And I'll be outdoors all the time!"

Nwin chimed in, "Aquaculture? We're doin' that at the Rice Bowl … remember Valentina?"

Valentina didn't appreciate Nwin defending Harmony the brat. She turned back to Harmony, "Didn't you say you were going to go to UCSF at Mission Bay? That place is a factory—you wanna be a workaholic? You'll end up a lab jockey, you'll see," Valentina snorted derisively.

"Jeez, Valentina, what's your problem?" Shelley rushed to Harmony's defense.

"Uuh, Valentina can you come over here for a second?" asked Francesca.

Valentina glared at first Harmony, then Nwin as she got up and walked to the other side of the café with her grandmother.

"What?"

Francesca looked at her granddaughter with intense blue eyes. "What?! I'll tell you what. You are out of line! That's what. I don't know Harmony very well, but I can tell you what I just saw, and that was you being rude and self-righteous. I think you owe her an apology. And you should ask yourself why you are so worked up."

Valentina crossed her arms and glowered. She didn't like being talked to like she was a little kid. "That's ridiculous!" she snapped back. "It's obvious that a 12-year-old girl should not be making plans for permanent work yet. I can't believe that you'd take *her* side of this!"

"That's not the point. I'm *not* taking her side. I'm just telling you—you were act-ing creepy, and I didn't like it." Francesca turned her back to Valentina and strode back to the table to rejoin the others.

Valentina couldn't believe her ears. She slammed a hand into the wall in rage, and then spun around and stormed out. Nwin rose to follow, barely saying goodbye to Shelley, Harmony and the grandmothers. Francesca shook her head as she watched him disappear. But inwardly she had to smile. She looked at Bridget archly, "A little romance in the making?"

"We'll see," replied Bridget skeptically.

Blindly Valentina stomped to the bridge at Walker Street and went to the middle of it. She stopped and leaned over the railing, staring down at the little fish swimming in the creek and listening to the chorus of bullfrogs in the shoreline grasses. She started crying, out of frustration at first, but then the torrents came as all her pent-up anxiety and anger overwhelmed her.

She sobbed uncontrollably. Then she thought of Shelley and Harmony, from the sup-posedly *happy* family—god, she *hated* their little planned lives. It was like they were already middle-aged! But she knew her grandmother had been right, too. Why did she hang out with Shelley and Harmony, when they bugged her so much? She thought darkly that it was because she didn't have any other friends. But that wasn't true.

"Hey, Valentina…" said Nwin from a short distance behind her. She wiped her face and looked at him as she swallowed her tears.

"What do *you* want?" she sobbed involuntarily.

"Shit… I dunno," he said looking at the ground. "Thought maybe you needed someone to talk to?"

"You wouldn't understand… *that's* obvious!" she spun back to the railing, turning her back to Nwin.

He was stung but he tried again. "I might surprise you."

A minute went by. Then another, and another. He stood there patiently while Valentina sobbed quietly at the railing.

Finally he went over and put his hand on her shoulder. This was the first time that a boy had tried to console her. Valentina jerked at his touch, so he pulled back and stood near. Then she cried some more, finally turning to him. "I'm sorry. It's not your fault," choking back the last sobs. She wiped her eyes again and then blew her nose.

He smirked towards the creek, "I can't believe a 12-year-old would already be talking about being a *Lifer!*"

She looked at him gratefully, but immediately sprung to Harmony's defense. "She's just talking! What's wrong with being excited about something? I'm an asshole!"

He put his hands up, "Hey, whoa, lighten up!" He smiled.

She laughed, relieved to let some of it out without more tears.

"Shall we go and have noodle soup?" he asked, remembering Niggle Woodles he'd discovered a block down.

She smiled through tear-stained cheeks. "I guess so. I'm not hungry, but…" He took her arm and they walked down the path to the bridge in silence. In a minute they were sitting in a window seat, the Hayes River gurgling below them.

The proprietress approached them almost immediately, and recognized Nwin. "Hi, nice to see you again! Brought your girlfriend, eh?" she said turning to Valentina. "Aren't you Francesca's granddaughter?" She nodded, blushing brightly at being called Nwin's girlfriend.

"Glad to meet you," and they slapped hands. "While we're at it, I'm Carolina Fasonara, and you?" she asked Nwin.

"Nwin Robertson. Hey, Carolina, you don't know my mother do you? Jennifer Robertson? You look just like her!"

"Ahem!" she cleared her throat in an exaggerated manner. "I think maybe she looks just like *me!*" and she laughed. "Yes, I have met your mother. I've seen her at the Water Council Committee. We talked briefly afterwards, and had a chuckle over our resemblance. Weird, huh?"

Nwin nodded, amazed. He spoke to Valentina, "This soup is *really* good!"

Valentina suddenly felt very hungry. Looking at her menu, she picked the Soba noodles with seaweed. Nwin wrinkled his nose, and then stifled himself, picking the same Noodles and Mushrooms that he'd ordered the last time. Carolina took their orders and disappeared.

"I never saw this place!" she marveled. "Been here for years and never noticed!"

"I'm not sure, but I think they only started pretty recently," he offered, and realized as he did that he didn't know anything about it. Hey, I have a favorite place that I'd love to show you."

"Yeah, where?" she answered, suspiciously.

"Over on Russian Hill… I have a tree that you're gonna love!"

"I do like climbing trees," she admitted, warming up. "My fave is in our backyard."

"Where's that?... oh yeah, you told me, the Pierce Palace, right?"

"Yeah, good memory," she looked at him, pleased that he had paid attention.

"What kind of tree is it?"

"It's a big ol' n'oak, must be 200 years old. It was one of the first New Oak strains that could resist the blight that wiped out most of the forests in the early 21st century. It was invented here in San Francisco," she explained. "My grandma told me people used to call 'em Not Oaks, so eventually it turned into n'oak. They're all over the East Bay."

"Dew! I'd love to climb it!" he said, eyebrows raised hopefully.

Their soup arrived along with another wave of Carolina's high energy. "Soup's on! Thanks for coming and say hello to your relations." They both grinned in assent, already starting on their steaming bowls of soup.

They slurped quickly, each pleased and relieved to have survived the conversation thus far. No sooner had they finished, than Valentina, hoping to prevent any further awkwardness, announced she'd better get back to her grandma, that she was expected.

Nwin was surprised at the abruptness. "Really? I thought maybe we could take a walk." She demurred. He thought it could go sour again quickly if he said the wrong thing. They called their last "thanks" in to Carolina and her husband Norman while leaving their dishes in the doorside bin.

Outside, Nwin followed Valentina and caught up with her, as she walked briskly back to the bridge. "Hey, hey, what's the hurry?"

Her brow was furrowed, and she said nothing.

"Did I say something wrong?"

"No." She shook her head emphatically, the dark cloud in her mind had nothing to do with Nwin. "Vyne me another time, ok?"

"Sure, but are you OK?"

She shook her head, and gave him a dark glare that just said "get lost."

Nwin started to feel angry.

She stopped and faced him, very serious. "Forgive my mood. This happens to me sometimes."

He tilted his head, not understanding but realizing he'd better get out of the way.

And he went straight ahead over the bridge, while she turned back to the Real Authentic Organic Ice Cream Parlor, calling soft goodbyes over their shoulders.

21.

It was hard to focus on the papers on his desk. A tall stack of folders stood to the side, full of reports with which he was supposed to familiarize himself. But he couldn't concentrate. He stared out the window at the Civic Green. Emmy danced in his thoughts. He could hardly think about anything else. And his third-floor view of the Civic Green itself was quite a distraction.

How am I going to work? he thought as he stood up and leaned on the wall next to the window, unable to take his eyes off the swarming people below. He ran his hand over his face, rubbing his eye that had been itching off and on for several days. The smell of Emmy filled his senses, a whiff of her having lingered on his hand since earlier that morning. He'd been sleeping with her every night since he left the Tweezer, but he had to find his own room soon.

"Shit!" He sat, trying to buckle down. He wasn't going to find a place to live while working, so better to forget about that for now. He pulled over a folder labeled "Hoarding 2150-2156," and stared at the first report without comprehension. Something about an old guy who lived in Sutro Forest. There was a picture when they found him in a lean-to he'd built amidst the Eucalyptus trees to hold his collection of clothes, appliances, books, furniture… Staring at the photo it was hard to understand why this grizzled old man carried all this stuff into the forest. He read the report for a minute, glancing over the psychological profile of the man: a loner, advanced age, isolation, frightened.

Already feeling kind of sleepy, he reached over and switched on a small radio on the shelf.

"—call-ins in about 20 minutes, when we start the Mid-day Muddle, our daily live discussion program. This is David Ramirez, El Loco da la Mañana, finishing up the last half hour of The Late Risers' Club here on the Jive 95. The last piece you heard was the classic "Barbarians in the Genome," by Crystal Baker taking us back almost 100 years. Now, we're going live across the planet to Timbuktu in Mali, where it's just starting to heat up at the Club Caravan… can you hear me Françoise?"

"Oui, oui, mais bien sûr… Dahveed?

"Yeah, how's it twirlin' in the music capital of the Sahara?"

"Eet's a HOT party here. Ze dahncing ees just beginning… Ecoutez! "Le Lion de Plumage."

As the bluesy guitars started and the syncopated rhythms of west Africa jumped out of the radio, Eric daydreamed about traveling with Emmy, perhaps doing a caravan across the Sahara from West Africa's pounding urban rhythms to the east African highlands where her distant ancestors came from.

"Eric! How's it going?" Pops clapped him on the shoulder, breaking his reverie.

"Oh, well…" he looked sheepishly at the pile of folders he hadn't yet cracked. "I've been reading about hoarding cases," he said vaguely.

"Good. Good. Listen, don't worry too much about all this. We just want you to have some idea of the reports we develop. By the way," he dropped his voice to a near whisper, "have you ever been in therapy?"

"No, no I haven't," Eric said, startled at the question. "Is that a prerequisite?"

"Of course not!" chortled Pops. "It sometimes helps if you know the lingo. As you may have noticed, a large percentage of our reports are stories about people who are… how shall I say it?… psychologically damaged?"

"Hmmm, yeah, I noticed some of that," he offered, failing to mention that he'd hardly read much at all, so distracted by his new love, the view, the radio, and anything else he could lean on to rationalize his lack of focus. He felt a sinking sensation that he would be found out, that he was a fake, and they would realize it any minute.

"Doesn't that music make it hard to concentrate?" Pops frowned.

"Actually it helps," he claimed. "I usually read to music."

"I don't know how you can do that!" he humphed, and disappeared into the office.

I've got to get through this! He flipped through a few more reports of sad, lonely people with secret stashes of goods. *What happens to them after they are discovered and publicly reported?* He put aside the Hoarding folder and took up one labeled "Exploitation 2155." The first report, dated June 4, 2155, was an account of a woman in the Building Trades, a Lifer, who had fooled three Apprentices into working on her house, putting in a skylight and a new bathroom. As the report had it, the Apprentices had not noticed at first that the house they had been sent to improve was the Lifer's. But after two weeks of hard work, they figured it out. After a little more investigation, they learned that they had been taken out of the normal public service work flow. The Lifer, a Jeri Syracelli, had a defense motion attached to the report, claiming innocence of any wrongdoing, but the complaint was sustained. She was given a choice between a six-month stint in a Fire Lookout in the mountains, or a one-year retreat to an organic farm in the northern San Joaquin Valley, her apartment to be made available as a temporary home on the public Housing List.

Hmm, that's an idea! I can find a temporary room or apartment on the Housing List. He turned to the vyne, and asked it to display the Housing List. There were several dozen listings, everything from hilltop apartments with a view to single hotel rooms in the center of the city. There were even a few apartments listed in the Pyramid, that bizarre orange landmark. Empty apartments were few, and those seemed to be temporary deals. *That would suit me fine. I don't know where I'm going to be in a few months.*

The audience in far-off Timbuktu erupted into applause as the tune wound down. The San Francisco dj cut in as he faded the live sounds, "That's the hot sounds of the Well-Read Lion, the newest stars to burst on the world scene from the desert of Africa, with their tune, hmmm... well I forgot to ask Françoise what the title of that great number was..." Sounds of rustling papers momentarily filled the airwaves, then "Okay, we have time for two more tunes before Cameron Floyd starts taking your calls. Today's topic is—what's that Cameron? ... Oh. Okay. Cameron says it's open mic today, no particular topic, just call in with whatever's on your mind. He's wearing his Oakland Oaks hat, so you baseball fans..." he tailed off as the music came up, a rollicking Norteña from the Gigantes de Sonora. Its infectious rhythm got Eric tapping his toe, as his stomach start rumbling.

A young man came by his desk, "Hi, you're the new guy?"

"I'm Andy Steinway," said the thin, pinched-face fellow, his stringy brown hair hanging over his collar. He was wearing a leather vest that hung down a little too long over loose jeans, billowing over his small pelvis. "I'm on a Tryout, been here a month now," he looked at Eric with guarded hope—would he be a rival or a friend?

Eric smiled at him, relieved to find someone besides Pops or the P-I who he could ask for help. "Hey, me too, just started this morning. Say, did you read all these reports when you started?"

Andy glanced at the pile, and laughed. "They gave those to you, too, huh? Don't worry, none of it is essential. It does help," he reached over to flip through a folder, "to get a sense of what this office does. When I started, I wasn't sure what a Public Investigator actually does."

"So, now you know?"

"Well, sure! I've been working on some cases this past week. Nothing big, mind you, but interesting. Neighborhood complaints over here," he pointed to the Richmond District on a big city map on the wall, near the edge of the Presidio, "about screaming in the night. At first they thought it was some kind of kinky sexual thing. But then it kept happening. One neighbor here on 21st Avenue, right where it ends at Lobos Creek, reported hearing doors slamming, things getting smashed, and crying and whimpering. No victim has come forward, but the neighbors are convinced something terrible is going on. I went door to door a few days ago, on 21st, 22nd and 20th, even Lake Street here." Andy stood at the map confidently describing his investigation. "But I haven't had a break yet. The mystery continues. I did find some broken plates and a smashed table down in the creek, but it could have been put there by anyone." Andy stared at the map, rubbing his chin. Then he turned back to Eric. "My other case is from the Arguello Community Workshop. A sudden depletion of materials and a number of tools missing. I looked all over and didn't find any clues at all. The P-I said I should go back and try again, interview the regulars, walk around the neighborhood and see what I can find. So I guess I will."

"Hey, you wanna get lunch? I'm starvin'!" Eric stood up.

"Uh, well sure, I guess. I brought my lunch today. My sister made it for me," he admitted, blushing lightly.

"Lucky you! I have to find something, what do you recommend out there in the plaza?"

"I actually bring my lunch every day," he looked at the floor. "I'm allergic to a lot of foods," embarrassed now.

Eric assured Andy that it didn't matter to him. As they walked silently to Andy's desk on the other end of the office, Eric felt vaguely encouraged. Andy was obviously a serious nerd, so he wouldn't seem that bad by comparison. "So do you like it here?" he asked Andy.

"Yeah. It's my third Tryout, and so far it's the best."

"Where else have you been?"

They were heading out into the sunlight now, and Andy was glad to talk about his work experiences.

"I did a Tryout at General Hospital in the Information Center."

"And?"

"It was good work. People definitely appreciated my help. But I hated the two Lifers that were in charge there." They walked up to a booth selling roast chicken and burritos. "They didn't like me either, I guess."

After Eric grabbed a burrito with extra salsa, they sat in the grass. The sun was hot, and the lunchtime concert was just beginning on the other side of the plaza. "What was your other Tryout?"

"Fishing. Everyone told me to do Annuals first, but I was sure I was going to love being on the ocean." He inspected his sandwich for suspicious ingredients, concluded it was safe, slapped the bread back together and took a big bite. When he'd gotten it down, he looked at Eric.

Eric tried to read the look on Andy's face. Andy continued, shuddering as he said, "I got SO seasick! I couldn't stand it. They said it would get better after a few days, but it didn't. So that was the end of my fishing life," his mouth twitched with the rumor of a smile, but he fell silent, focused on his lunch.

Between bites of his burrito, Eric told Andy about coming to San Francisco and his adventures during the first days. Andy chuckled at his story about Tanya and the overloaded trike.

"Do you think she's a hoarder?" he asked, sitting up a bit straighter.

"I guess you'd have to say she has 'hoarding tendencies'," he laughed. "But she's not harming anyone, except maybe her housemates!" Andy joined his laughter. "I toured her whole house that first day, and I've been staying there for the past week and a half." He explained briefly about Emmy, the Page Mews, and his certainty that nothing untoward was going on there.

"Wow, you got a girlfriend already!" Andy was impressed, which in turn gave Eric a surge of happiness. He could hardly believe it himself, and when he thought about Emmy, it seemed even more unbelievable.

After lunch he returned to his desk and the pile of folders. The radio was still on, some kind of argument raging. He paused to listen.

"—don't like the wild corridors?"

"No! Cameron, what is the point of filling a city of people up with wild animals? It's not safe! It's not sanitary! It's just plain stupid!"

"Thanks for your thoughts, Bob. Let's go to Sue in the Mission. Sue?"

"Hi Cameron, thanks for taking my call."

"Thanks for calling. What do you think about this wild animal debate, especially the latest, bringing in wolves?"

"That's a tough one. I have small children. Do you know any numbers on wolf attacks? That's my main worry."

"Yes, I've got a report right here from the Western Regional Bureau of Social Statistics. Let's see... under Urban Centers, animal attacks, 2156, so these are last year's numbers. In the whole western North America there were 1,351 incidents reported. One hundred sixty-one bear attacks, three hundred forty-one snake bites, fifty-two rat bites, 743 raccoon attacks—Whoa! Watch out for raccoons people!—seventeen possum cases, 26 coyotes, and only 11 wolf cases."

"That's interesting. So wolf attacks are the fewest on the whole list?"

"Yes, but you can't tell from this what the population is, nor does it distinguish between big cities like San Francisco and smaller, more rural places like Garberville for example."

"I don't know Cameron. I'll be awfully worried about my children."

"Yes, who wouldn't? Well, thanks for your call. Next is Roger down in Brisbane. Roger?"

"Hi Cameron. Great show, as always."

"Thank you."

"Hey I wanted to discuss this campaign you're part of to reduce the Annuals."

"Great, LOVE to talk about it," glowed Cameron in his smooth, deep voice.

"It seems to me that we've already got a problem with waiting times. I don't think we're doing *enough* work. I think the Annuals are not enough!"

"Roger, Roger... what's the hurry? What are you waiting for that you can't do without?"

"That's not the point! It's the *idea* of having to wait for something you want!"

"Well, I'd say it IS the point. But let's have it your way, and talk about the idea. As I understand it, the Annuals system is designed to share the work we all agree should be done, but that nobody wants to do all the time, right?"

"So they say. But that's not how it works! Really a few Lifers and their Apprentices do all the real work! People doing Annuals make things worse as often as they help!"

"So Roger, can I ask, are you a Lifer?"

"Damn straight I am! You can thank me and my mates here at the Brisbane Lagoon for your Bay Clams. We started this aquafarm ten years ago and—"

"OK, so you and yours brought back the Bay Clam. I LOVE those tender morsels. I thank you and I'm sure everyone listening does too. But it seems to me that your argument might actually back me up on this. I think too many people are working too much. I think the system we have is actually pretty well designed. We could work less, maybe a lot less, and still enjoy the same lives we have now. Let's face it, it's not the Annuals workers who—"

"Eric," Pops called as he walked up behind him. Eric turned the radio down so he could concentrate on Pops.

"Here's something Kathy wants you to do. It's tonight, can you make it?"

"What is it?" he asked.

"Here." He dropped a flyer on Eric's desk. "Inventors' Corner, Thursday 7 p.m. at Café Thimble."

"What am I supposed to do there?" he asked, feeling as though he'd been punched in the gut.

"Just go and listen. We try to keep an eye on this forum because people there are always plotting ways to get around the Resource Review Board."

"But…" what could he say? He didn't want to tell about his uncle. "Um… OK. I think I can. I have to check with my girlfriend," he mumbled.

"Great, I'll tell Kathy that you're on it," and he shuffled off.

"Shit!" he cursed. Just what he didn't want to do! And on his first day! He turned to the vyne and called "Message to Emmy Ndbele Hodges, Page Mews… Hi sweetie," he peered into the vyne trying not to look too glum. "So here I am at work on my first day, and guess what? They are sending me to a meeting tonight." He paused and ran his hand through his hair. "I should've known! I have to go to Inventors' Corner to see if anyone is plotting to get around the Resource Review Board… can you believe my luck?!?" He shook his head, already feeling defeated by the mountain of folders he hadn't read, and now this. "So I'll be home late, probably after 9 or maybe even 10. Or," he suddenly brightened, "you could meet me there. It's at Café Thimble on 9th Avenue, not far from home. I'll be there in any case, so if I don't see you there, I'll see you later in the evening, OK? Eric Johanson over."

He turned the radio back up, but the talk show was over. He turned to his folders again, pulling out the one titled Resource Violations, 2155-56. Inside was a list of cases with the quantity and type of resources that had been misused. He scanned down through a number of mundane items, mostly very small and local like a batch of lumber or a shipment of bike parts that had been diverted. One listing caught his eye, "Satellite Time Misappropriation." He read a story about a couple who had applied for satellite telescope time to conduct some astronomical experiments, but had been rejected by their peer review board. They had then built a software patch that overrode the main controller, which they then used to carry out their experiments.

"We sought to prove that space mirrors would prolong the growing season in the northern hemisphere and increase food production by 30% in the higher latitudes. This in turn would promote local self-sufficiency in areas where it had been particularly difficult to achieve," they argued in their brief. The premise of their effort had already been rejected as misdirected and the experiment was deemed poorly designed in their original Peer Review. This was before they even got to the Resource Review Board. Convinced it was a matter of professional jealousy and scientific rivalry, they had chosen to go ahead, pirating the telescope over the outraged efforts of the satellite staff to control it. They were quickly exposed, after which they lost all credibility and were suspended from lab work for one year.

Eric thought again about his uncle and the anger that he must've carried to his workbench day after day. He vividly remembered sitting in the corner of his uncle's garage when suddenly there'd been a terrible crash. His uncle roared like a wounded bear, blood dripping as he struggled to wrap a towel around his wound.

"Hi, are you Eric?" asked a cute young woman.

"I'm Robin. Just thought I'd say hello. I'm a first-year Apprentice."

"So you did the Tryout already?"

"Yep. Loved it. Kathy took me under her wing, but now they want me to go indy," she grinned proudly.

"You must be good," Eric offered.

"Aaah. They're desperate!" she laughed.

"Hey, have you been to Inventors' Corner?" he asked suddenly.

"Sure! It's great fun. A bunch of zany people."

"Did you overhear any resource theft when you were there?"

"Oh no!" she laughed. "Is that what they told you to look out for? Don't worry about it. There's nothing going on there to investigate!"

He wondered what made her so sure, especially after reading the folder on his desk. "So are you assigned to a type of investigation?"

"Yeah, I'm on Arson and Vandalism."

"Is there a lot of it?"

"A fair amount of petty stuff. I've got a complaint I'm looking into right now from the Rice Bowl farm about someone who's been destroying a field. Well, I've got to get back to work. Nice to meet you Eric!" and she spun around, whipping her black hair behind her, tucking a hand into her snug back pocket.

"You too," he called to her retreating back. *I'd rather do Arson and Vandalism*, dreading the Inventors' Corner in spite of Robin's assurances.

He turned back to study his files. A message came vyning in, with the telltale twanging sound. He called for it, and there was Emmy, her dark face beaming with a sunny smile. "Hi cutie. Just got your message. Sure, I'll come. Sounds like fun. Do you want to meet for dinner before? We could eat at the Thimble before the meeting I suppose? Leaf me, ok?"

He replied immediately, suggesting a 6 p.m. meeting at the Café Thimble, signing off, and taking a deep breath, reached for his cup of coffee and focused on reading.

22.

Stars streaked through the pre-dawn sky on August 12, the Perseiades Meteor Shower. The sky over the Bay—outside the fog—was completely clear. Nwin steered *Hot 1* around the Rincon Towers in the darkness. The air was very cool, so he pulled his hat down over his ears. Peruvian wool was very warm.

He grinned, thinking it funny that the hat his mom got him was finding its first use on this little "errand." He had stopped by some days earlier after work in the mid-afternoon.

"Nwin!" his mom had rushed to him, giving him a big hug. "Why didn't you answer my message? We were worried!"

He mumbled something about being busy, waving off the routine guilt that seemed to always accompany visits home now. "Where's dad?"

"Your father has been feeling bad, Nwin. He's gone to the hospital," tears welling.

"What's wrong?" Nwin asked cautiously.

"We think it's his heart. He's been having chest pains. Last week I found him in the garden unconscious. The doctors think he had a small heart attack," she shook her head, turning away as she choked on the words.

"But he's not that old!" Nwin protested.

"They say his heart is in bad shape. Might be genetic, might be some old infection never properly treated."

"Whoa," he slowly slid into a chair at the kitchen table. "Have you been staying at the hospital with him? Where is he, at General? St. Luke's?"

"General. I've been there every day. I was there this morning very early, but I came home when he fell asleep. I've been letting things slip with the neighborhood work."

"The Shitsys?"

"No, the Neighborhood Council. We've been working on the housing plan for the coming year. The big debate is over tearing down a block of houses on the south side to give the architect, Lloyd Lu Fei, a chance to build a new structure for 1,000 residents."

Nwin listened blankly. He felt nothing. He flashed through a kaleidoscope of memories: dad coming through the door when he was very little, impossibly big and dark, wearing giant black rubber boots, smelling of salt water and fish, a frightening monster who was as likely to scold him as not. Later, his father sitting depressed in the corner of the kitchen after he got home from field trips with his classmates.

Nwin learned not to tell his father stories with a lot of animation. It was almost like the more excited he was, the more he'd enjoyed his day at the bike factory, on the beach, on a ship, making clothes, cleaning City Hall, or any of the dozens of things his class did around the city, the angrier his father would get. He learned to keep it short and simple when he was about seven, after a story about helping in a chair factory where they let him and his friends actually work on a lathe. As he told the story about working the tools and bringing the chair leg to life, his father's breathing had grown louder until he bellowed "GODDAMMIT!!" slamming his fist into the table, knocking a plate and their iced teas to the floor. Nwin had sat in stunned silence while his father had struggled up and out into the garden and his mom cleaned up the mess.

"Nwin? Nwin?" his mother's voice broke through the memories.

"Huh?"

"Here's the hat I promised to get you at Treasure Island."

"Oh, yeah!" He held it up, twirling around the orange, purple and brown pattern on his hand, quickly mesmerized. "Thanks, Mom."

She gave him a kiss on the cheek as she put her arm on his shoulder. "I'm going back to the hospital later. Do you want to come?"

"I'll try to stop by, but I can't today," he lied.

She sat down across from him. "Nwin, what's happening at work? You're coming to the end of your Tryout, aren't you? I saw Auntie the other day, and she said you told her you were handling the roses."

He was scowling at the mention of work, but when she said 'roses,' he smiled. "You should see these rose bushes, Mom, down near the 7th Street Causeway," he said proudly. "I think they just needed someone who knows how to talk to 'em. In fact—!" He slid noisily back from the table, and went to his pack near the door. He pulled out a small bouquet and presented it to his mother.

"Nwin! How beautiful! Thank you!" she said happily.

He had dropped the hat into his bag, and after vaguely telling her work was going fine, he refused a meal and went on his way.

"Don't forget to visit your father. It's room 2214 at General, OK?"

He waved and nodded, but he hadn't gone to see his father.

* * *

He pulled up to the 7th St. dock, fog blotting out the star show above. In the bottom of his skiff he already had the timers, the flares and three small buckets in a box. In the quiet time before day he found it easy to skirt across the big intersection. A half dozen streetcars sat quietly parked at the terminal across Kyoto. Streetcar conductors talked to each other a block away. At the velome lot he grabbed a Red Fury. The repair room was closed this early, but a fleet of 40 bicycles stood ready. He sped through the Crossroads and into the Rice Bowl gate. Some early bird was starting to get the coffee going at the barn. But Nwin wasn't going that far, stopping at the little shack a short way from the front gate.

He leaned his bike against the side and opened the door. It was dark inside and stank of gasoline. When he flipped on the small light several large moths flew towards his head, giving him a start. He moved a few tools aside to get to the five-gallon can, right where he'd left it. He struggled to lift it into the basket on the back of the Red

Fury, feeling an ominous twinge in his lower back. With the can planted in the basket, he started riding back towards the dock.

OK, no one is going to come by NOW, he wished, counting on his co-workers' arrival after dawn. The darkness was still complete when he passed through the Crossroads a minute later, yellow fog lights casting a fuzzy glow beneath the poles where they stood. A couple was walking arm in arm from the docks, but they were lost in each other. He carefully put the can down at the head of the pier where he'd tied up *Hot 1*, using his legs to move the bulky weight off the bike. He returned the bike to the shack's lot, noticing a few more pedestrians around the sprawling intersection that would be jammed in a few hours.

He awkwardly carried the big can to his skiff, hoping his back would cooperate. He realized he would have to find a place to stop to make the transfer from the large bucket to the three smaller ones. Seals barked in the distance. Larger waves washed into the dock, apparently stirred up by the wake of a ship passing out on the Bay. He rose and fell a half dozen times as the wake crashed into the cement wall along the causeway. When it calmed, he cast off and began a slow ride out towards the Bay. A peapod ferry was pulling in just as he cleared the dock's breakwater, so he maneuvered out of its way.

Potrero Hill loomed on his right as he aimed at the starry night over the open water. The fog disappeared over his head. It was 4:45 a.m. so he still had about an hour. Moving southward again he sat back startled when a threesome of dolphins leaped across his bow before bounding away into the murky Bay. He accelerated by stepping quickly on the directional node.

Lights twinkled on several ships in the Bay, presumably the *Leopold Tanzania* among them. Out of the darkness loomed a skiff not far off his course, but it redirected itself to pass well behind him. Breathing deeply he leaned forward into the skiff, balancing as it bounded along. He swung out around Hunter's Point and then abruptly slowed, turning back to have a closer look. The old shipyard cranes made an obstacle course in the shallow waters, surrounding the remaining hilltop island. A sprawling compound occupied most of it. Concentric circles of rooms spiraled around, interspersed with gardens, converging at the top around a small grove of n'oak trees. An observation tower rose out of the trees and commanded the top of the hill, but it looked unoccupied, silhouetted against the night sky.

Nwin bobbed silently in front of the residential dock where a big sign said "The Lodge," noting a dozen skiffs tied up in the darkness. He didn't like it, too much chance of someone showing up. In fact, there was someone now—an old woman slowly walking down a long staircase towards the dock. He quietly pulled around the back side to the Portola Canal, where the fog's edge hung over the cement walls of the canal. Once there had been a freeway through this gully, but now only the ruins of it were visible along the walls. A 15-foot eyeball in the center of a mural stared at him as he flipped by. At the sound of a door opening he glimpsed a young man holding a baby on the balcony above, light pouring from the room behind them. The man pointed to Nwin in his boat, as though his baby could see him in the dark far below.

"Too many people around here," he muttered. The canal's straight banks suddenly opened into a muddy plain, the channel connecting to Yosemite Creek. He steered through the narrow waterway and in moments popped back out into the Bay, Double Rock and Bay View Hill looming to his right, the backside of the The Lodge still commanding the heights to his left. Lights were starting to wink on in various apartments.

Early risers here, bakers or fishermen.

He moved around Bay View Hill and into Brisbane Lagoon. San Bruno Mountain towered ahead. He ducked to the west, into a long watery fjord. Roofs rose out of the water, large warehouses long ago submerged. Houses lined the ridges above on both sides. Down in the darkness it was quiet but for the occasional seagull and waves softly lapping on roofs and hillsides.

He pulled alongside a long flat-top building, just a foot above the waterline. Leaning over the lip of the roof, he couldn't tell how intact the roof was, but it looked just right for his task. Water pooled in the roof's sagging middle. *Must be water just below… could be waterlogged… might not hold me.* He found a place to tie up his skiff and then strained to lift the big can in the bobbing boat. He felt his back complaining as he heaved it up and got it trapped against the ledge, feeling his boat sliding away under him. "SHIT! Unnnnhhhhh" and a mighty last heave sent it crashing on to the roof, where he could hear it moving as he fell backwards into the boat. His back throbbed as he got up, reaching for the roof and hauling himself onto the edge. His 5-gallon can had stopped a meter and a half away, after rolling across the sloping roof before coming to a halt. The lid remained sealed.

He went back into the boat and took the smaller cans, placing them over the edge on the roof. He climbed up, stopping to feel it sag beneath his feet, cracking and creaking with each step. He inched forward towards the big can. Each step sagged, water appearing around his feet. *Shit, this chingin' roof ain't gonna hold me,* panic rising. He got on his knees and reached forward, just able to grab the handle. He pulled. His back screamed in pain, freezing him in breathless agony. He tried to breathe, shallow at first, then more deeply. Breathing helped. He slowly adjusted his back over his knees. It hurt, but he could move. He looked at the can lying on the dangerously weak roof. He stood up very slowly, water pooling at his feet. A louder crack beneath his feet! He moved one foot back, clutching his back, and the first foot started to give way as he pulled it back, too. He reached the roof's edge looking wide-eyed at his can sitting on the other side of a new hole that had just opened where he'd been standing. Water lapped in plain view.

He climbed into his boat, wobbling against the waves and his back pain. He took the long pole in the bottom of the skiff, kept on board for emergencies. One end had a small hook that he opened. With one arm leaning over the roof lip, he reached the bucket with his hook. He stood back to maximize his stability and leverage. With one arm stiffly holding the building he pulled the can towards the edge, a meter to the side of the new hole. Slowly it came closer, until he could reach it with his hands. He managed to stand it on the most solid bit of roof left.

Things were not going to plan, which had been vague anyway. Now the can was on the roof, and his back was too hurt to think about getting it back into the skiff. He observed a taller warehouse further back in the dark fjord. "Okay, let's do it!" he said to no one. He pried off the lid and carefully tipped the bucket towards a smaller one, spilling the smelly petrol into the hole he'd just made. But most of it filled his bucket. He repeated the process for the other two small buckets.

He closed each one and brought them back on board. Now he took a small stack of matches and blocks of wood and attached the bottom of a flare to each of three similar piles. After winding the tape around the flare and angling it downward, he taped it to the bucket and set the timer to 15 minutes. He repeated it two more times. The skiff shot across the black water to the taller warehouse. This one had sloping eaves hanging over the edge, at least two meters above the water line. The glass was smashed out of the windows. Nwin peered into the darkness and found nothing, ducking reflexively as a bat sailed out of the window. He lit a match and held it in the window. Inside was a long concrete room, broken furniture here and there amidst puddles and even some weeds sprouting along the edges.

Light was just appearing in the east as he set two buckets in the window, and slid over to put the third in a window around the corner. He double-checked his timers: still six minutes to go. He took another look at the roof and liked what he saw. *This ruin'll burn!* He quickly got his skiff up to maximum speed heading across Brisbane Lagoon in the dawn light. A ferry was plowing northward on the peninsula run, but he paid it no attention.

* * *

One of the passengers in the ferry, a young thin-faced man clutching a bag lunch and staring out absent-mindedly, saw him out of the corner of his eye. He may have made nothing of it, but just then an explosion rocked the darkness beneath the hills. The young man, along with the rest of the passengers, all leaped up and pointed to the shooting flames, shouting and calling to each other. The skiff that he'd just seen dashing out from the shore had passed behind them. He darted to the other side of the ferry and got a look at the skiff as it bounced through the ferry's wake. It was two-seater, he couldn't see the name on the back, and there was one person lying in the boat. He turned back to the conflagration near the shore.

* * *

Nwin lay back in Hot 1, admiring his handiwork. He hadn't imagined the fire would be so explosive. He'd resigned himself to failure this time, assuming the roof over the wet, concrete structure would burn, but not much. He could not resist masturbating to the shooting flames, but as before, it took only seconds for him to climax, so turned on was he by the site of the fire. Mopping himself clean, his bad back once again clamored for attention. He couldn't get comfortable, so he stopped to reorganize.

The flames were still leaping in the gulley. He stood now, gazing at the distant fire. Noticing that several boats were headed his way on their paths to San Francisco, he thought he'd better get moving. He turned northward and began his own journey home, the pink sky in the east promising a beautiful day.

23.

Eric squinted into the 5 o'clock sun. He had stayed at work longer than planned. The reports they expected him to read were overwhelming. *No wonder they need new people*, he thought, exasperated. It better not be like this all the time, or he'd never want to stay. His breathing grew labored as he pedaled up Abundance Street with traffic. The fog wasn't rolling in, and Eric already had grown appreciative of rare summer days that stayed warm into the evening.

Two young men sped by him, one handing the other a joint as they effortlessly pedaled up the hill. At the top Eric veered through Wiggle Gate to Sans Souci Bridge. Soon he was crossing another bridge at Rexroth and Haight, wondering if it too had a name.

"Excuse me," he asked a woman next to him, "does this bridge have a name?"

Her gray eyes flashed as she looked at Eric, making him wonder if he had offended her. "Depends!" she was smiling now, so Eric stopped worrying. "I think it's officially called Rexroth Bridge, but a lot of people call it Ice Cream Bridge because of that," she pointed back at the Real Authentic Organic Ice Cream Parlor behind the creek where they'd just come from.

"You new here?" she continued.

"Yeah, been in town about a month now."

"How are you finding it?" she asked warmly.

"I like it! Definitely! I really like it!"

They were turning into the N'oak Greenway, wiggling towards the Panhandle. Eric glanced at the time and realized that he could stop at home before the 6 o'clock dinner with Emmy at the Thimble.

"All settled?" the woman asked him, eyebrows raised expectantly.

"Sort of," he nodded. "I started a Tryout today at the Public Investigators'. And I've been staying at the Page Mews, just off Ashbury."

"I know it well. Trixie is an old friend of mine," her eyes twinkled. "What's your name?"

"Eric Johanson," and he awkwardly offered his right hand for a slap. She took it in her left, and squeezed it warmly. "I'm Bridget O'Reilly." She was a striking older woman with a face that could still melt hearts, gray braids held together over her long blue coat by an orange velvet ribbon. He noticed her long delicate fingers on the bicycle handlebars, her right hand bearing a twinkling diamond ring. They came to a stop at the Panhandle's Wiggle Gate as merging traffic poured in from Baker and opposing traffic came at them, clogging the gate.

"This is where I turn anyway," Bridget said. "I'll be seeing you Eric!"

He watched her disappear up Baker. San Franciscans are so friendly. It surprised him. When the traffic cleared he was pushed through the gate by the backed-up throng. *Home or café?* It was only 5:25, so he decided to drop his stuff and change clothes.

He rode through the same gate he'd entered on his first visit with Tanya. And there she was, pulling some bread from the solar oven. "Hi Eric! How's it twirlin'?" she called cheerfully.

"Great!" he returned her good cheer. They hadn't talked much since he'd hooked up with Emmy. He was sure Tanya hadn't been interested in him anyway. "Whatcha makin'?" he asked.

"Olive bread. Here, smell," and she held a loaf to his nose.

"Wow, amazing!" Warm bread, in this case mixed with the smell of delicious olives from their backyard, filled his nose. "When can I eat some?" he demanded.

"Hold your horses!" she laughed, "There'll be some at dinner."

"I'm not going to be here tonight," he told her, "Emmy and I are going to Café

Thimble."

"You better go early or late!"

"Why?"

"Tonight is Inventors' Corner"

"That's a pretty big deal, huh?" She nodded, concentrating on moving her loaves in the oven. "I have to go for work, actually."

Tanya looked puzzled. "What work is that?"

"I started a Tryout at the Public Investigators' Office today."

"Why would you go to Inventors' Corner as an investigator?" she asked innocently.

"I'm not sure. They just told me to go and listen. Another woman who works there told me it is more of a party. It's only my first day, so I'm doing what they ask me to for now."

"Hmmm, yeah, I suppose…" she trailed off.

"How do you know about it?"

She shook her head. "Doesn't everyone?"

He shrugged and walked across the small lawn, down the dirt path through raised vegetable beds. A thick hedge surrounded the picnic area, adjacent to the hot tubs and outdoor showers. He waved to Gerald sitting in one hot tub and William and a woman he'd not met sitting in the other.

He ran up the stairs to Emmy's room, two at a time. No one was around as his wake sent papers flying off a table. He knocked and went in without pausing.

"Oh… sorry," he mumbled, when he saw Emmy pulling covers up, obviously frightened by his sudden entry. He stroked her face and neck, kissing her lightly. She began purring and released the covers to wrap her arms around him. Her long black nakedness starkly contrasted with the white sheets and blankets. Eric kicked off his shoes, while she starting working on his shirt. He fumbled out of his clothes, utterly aroused, and once clear of the annoying encumbrance of clothing, merged his body with hers, warm skin delicately grazing one another as he slowly moved in and out of her.

It was past six when they lay spent in each other's arms, sweat trickling from their bodies. Emmy giggled, "good thing you came along or you'd be sitting all alone in that café and I'd still be fast asleep!"

"Wha?" Eric feigned horror. "You would have stood me up?!?" but he laughed too, unable to sustain even a pretense of discomfort in a moment so incredibly comfortable. Then he remembered the Inventors' Corner.

"Shit!"

"What?"

"I do have to go to this thing."

"Really? We can't just stay in bed the rest of the night?" she asked coyly.

"Well, you don't have to go, but I do. It's the first thing they asked me to do." He groaned, "It already feels like work!"

She jumped up, energized. "Don't worry, sweetheart, it'll be fun. Inventors' Corner is supposed to be quite a scene, and I've never been." She was getting dressed rapidly. "C'mon," she urged, "or we won't have time to eat before it starts. We may not even get a seat!"

"Okay, okay," and he got up and started getting dressed as fast as he could, regretting putting his day's clothes over his sweating body, but more concerned with hurrying up.

In twenty minutes they were walking into Café Thimble. A huge thimble hung over the door and all the stools in the café were large thimbles, too. The place was packed, only a few empty tables near the back patio.

"Let's grab one of those," said Emmy, pointing, and pulling Eric along behind her.

"Emmy! Hey Emmy!" came a call out of the middle of the restaurant. The frantically waving arm of a blonde woman in a deep green velvet suit caught their eyes.

"Hi Lorelei!" Out of the side of her mouth, "she's a friend I met working at the hospital... I think she's a doctor."

"C'mere! There's room!" Lorelei insisted they join her.

"Suits me," Eric assured Emmy as she hesitated, glancing once more at the empty table in back. They squeezed through the densely packed tables and joined Lorelei's table, where there were already three others.

"Eric, Emmy, this is my beau... Beauregard, better known as 'Bo'," she giggled. Bo was a rugged, handsome man, flowing brown locks and a trim beard, broad shouldered and big chested. When he stood up he was taller even than Emmy. "This is Lou and this is Zette," Lorelei finished, sitting back down. Lou and Zette were an older couple. His black hair had almost vanished except for a few wispy clumps holding on above his ears. He wore gray-rimmed glasses and a white button up shirt. His wife Zette wore her thin brown hair long like most San Franciscans, flowing down over a lemon-colored cardigan stretched tightly across her large bosom. She wore a lot of makeup, Eric noticed, giving her an artificiality that seemed out of place the more he looked at her. They exchanged taps and smiles as they all sat down.

"Try the ratatouille," urged Lorelei, "it was great." They had finished dinner and were contemplating dessert as Eric and Emmy joined them.

A waiter appeared, a short dark man in an orange apron decorated with a big silver thimble. "Dessert?" he asked pleasantly, and then did a doubletake as he noticed Emmy and Eric. "Emmy!"

"Abdul!" She jumped up and gave him a hug. "What are you doing here?" she asked astonished.

"Y'know, I love the Inventors, and this way I get to hear..." he looked around from side to side in mock concern, then whispered very loudly, "ev-er-y-theeng!" They all laughed. "So what'll it be?" and he took their dessert and dinner orders and effortlessly bounded through the densely seated patrons.

"Abdul and I go *way* back," Emmy told Eric. "Remind me to tell you about him some day."

Eric looked around the room, enjoying Emmy's warm fingers playing on the back of his neck. On the walls hung dozens of portraits with honorific titles. Nearest to his seat was one with a guy and a child sitting on a bicycle, another with a woman in a corn field, yet another with two men holding some kind of device between them. Above the portraits was a small sign "Inventors Corner Hall of Fame" next to an oversized golden hammer.

"Did you come for the show, or are you looking for something in particular?" Emmy asked Lorelei. Eric looked at Lorelei, her rosy skin glowing against the green velvet choker that matched her suit. She had bright green eyes that shimmered in harmony with the green velvet pillbox hat over her nearly white blonde hair. She was stunning, no doubt about it. Her wide smile revealed perfect teeth. "I'm here as a hospital delegate. We're always looking for creative ideas to make hospitalization better, easier, more pleasant… you know."

Lou and Bo conversed softly. Zette craned her neck to see if the desserts were on the way. Sure enough Abdul appeared with a big tray, and soon they were all eating. Across the room near the window a small stage was being set up, tables pushed back and a corridor being opened.

A strange humming sound grew louder, distracting Eric and the others from their plates. Overhead a series of crisscrossing wires seemed to be vibrating. Three different toy gondolas appeared on the wires, slowly traversing the room on complicated routes. Just then the front door burst open and a huge, disheveled mountain of a man clumped in. The patrons buzzed as the man maneuvered towards the stage, putting a dufflebag he'd dragged in against the wall, and tossing his overcoat on it. He stood up straight, hands on his hips, staring at various people, nodding "hello" here and there, looking for someone.

"That's Brian O'Bannon," Lorelei muttered to Emmy and Eric. "He's one of the giants of our time. His lightbulb…" and they knew immediately who he must be. The biobulbs had completely replaced the electrical bulbs that had been the source of indoor light since kerosene was supplanted. The biobulb drew its sustenance from the vyne, could be placed anywhere, and used the firefly's luminescence genes to produce light. Except where somebody had actually crushed one or dropped it from a great height, they were so far indestructible. Moreover, they had been an essential part of the transition from the old electrical grid to the vyne.

People were steadily streaming in now, squeezing along the walls and sitting on the floor. At least ten different people were moving slowly from table to table, introducing themselves and handing out brochures or samples. A woman appeared between Zette and Lou wearing an eye-grabbing snakeskin suit that she was a little too big for. Her chest heaved with a deep breath before launching into her rap.

"Have you seen anything like this?" She thrust a piece of fabric onto the table amidst their plates and glasses. "Touch it, go on!" so they all quickly touched the material.

"What *is* that?" asked Zette with genuine interest, "it's so soft and delicate."

"My sister and I have a small shop in North Beach. We've been playing with different materials, trying to make a truly adjustable blanket. This is our first success," she said proudly.

"So it's a blanket?" asked Lorelei.

"That's what we were working on. But this could be used for so many things. Notice how sheer it is," and she held it up in front of her, demonstrating its translucence. "Now watch this," and she squeezed a small button at the bottom, and then held it out in front of her again. The fabric became completely opaque in seconds, and even its texture seemed to change. She threw it on the table again. "Touch it now!"

It was transformed. Now it was thick, warm and furry.

"Let me have your brochure," Lorelei piped up. "I'm from General Hospital, and we may be quite interested in this."

"Great!" enthused the snakeskin-clad woman, "give me your card, too." They traded and she went to the next table.

No sooner had the snakeskin lady left than up clattered a tall black man wearing tight-fitting bicycling pants and a racing jersey, a small cap jauntily perched on the back of his small head. "Hey," Eric started, "aren't you from the Big Bambu Bike Factory?"

The fellow grinned, "Yeah, that's me! James Sullivan's the name, and bamboo is my game." Emmy groaned at his tired introductory line. "Have you been to our place?" he asked Eric.

"Last week. I think you were the guy who helped me, actually."

James glanced downward, apologetically, "Sorry, I meet so many people…" He smoothly shifted from apology to pitch. "Here's a list of our new bikes, all made of at least 80% solid bamboo. We're also branching out into new products, like this adjustable modular fence," and he showed a miniature model. "Our latest invention is this bark extrusion technique," and he held up a bike wheel that had been between his legs. "No spokes, no plastic, and sturdy as they come," he bragged, punching the wheel.

Lou sat up and asked to have a closer look at the bark wheel. "Can you shape the bark to any configuration?" James had reached the limit of his knowledge, so he gave Lou a card and invited him to come to the factory and talk to the chief technologist.

The front door opened again, and a hush fell over the place. A tall, striking man with long blonde hair and a short, sharp red beard entered. He wore his trademark blue tunic, silver studs along his sleeves glittering in the café's lights. Thick eyebrows bobbed as he smiled and looked around for familiar faces. "Hey Sharon," he called, and made his way to a table not far from the door as the audible hush soon returned to the normal buzz.

"That's Sam MacMillan," announced Bo to the table. He looked at Eric and Emmy, "You know about his proposal, right?"

Eric remembered hearing the name somewhere, but he didn't know why. He was too embarrassed to admit it, though, and was very relieved when Emmy asked Bo to explain it again.

"MacMillan has become a lightning rod. Mixing species is forbidden, and he wants an exception. His plan is to grow a dolphin embryo in which he will plant human vocal cords, mouth, and tongue. His goal is to talk to the dolphins!" he laughed.

"Or really, to have the dolphins talk to us!" said Lorelei. "He's using our affection for dolphins as a wedge to break the prohibition," she shook her head with obvious disapproval.

Lou looked at her. "You're an Integritista, right?"

Lorelei nodded.

"Would you explain your position on biodevices? I've been confused. I don't understand where you draw the line."

"Our position is pretty simple. We are against creating new species as combinations of existing ones. We are for the Integrity of existing species on earth… Hell, we've lost so many already!"

"Yes, but what about all the new devices, are they not species?"

"We don't object to biodevices. Our party's position is that it is okay to invent new biological devices using genes from different species, but only if the resulting organism has no brain, can feel no pain, and cannot reproduce itself. We are 100% in support of the current state of ethical limits. And no, they are *not* new species, they are *devices* of human design. That's a crucial difference."

Emmy asked, "What do you think about the argument I've heard that says biodevices have cellular memory? All the research on hearts and other primary organs show that memory is not limited to the brain, no?"

Bo jumped in. "That's an interesting theory, but there's no evidence for it. I think it's a matter of faith for its proponents. No brain, no pain, and no memory either!" he said emphatically.

"Won't you be in a tight spot if someone proves that cellular memory does exist?" asked Lou, an edge creeping into his tone, "since your lab is one of the biggest producers of biodevices."

Bo's nostrils flared as he sent a stabbing glare at Lou. Lou sat back, arms folded over his paunch, smirking.

Before Bo could launch into a defense, the lights went down and the stage was hit with a bright spotlight. A large woman stood at the microphone, a red sequined turban perched on her head, totally inconsistent with the work clothes and leather apron she wore. She was laughing and pointing to different people at tables nearby. "Okay, okay, folks, it's time to start the evening's presentation. Tonight Inventors' Corner is honored to have Genevieve Bamfield, one of the pre-eminent thinkers working in the field of tidal technology, presenting her latest invention, the Integrated Solar/Tide Conversion Engine. Please welcome Genevieve Bamfield."

Hooting and hollering and much foot stomping accompanied the small, aged woman's ascent to the stage. She turned, looking kind of frail, and pulled the microphone down to her face. Waving off the applause, she smiled. "Yah, yah, you are very nice, thank you." The audience hushed, anxious to hear her talk. The first slide was projected on a big screen that covered the far wall. It was a complicated series of mathematical formulas, with a drawing of a patterned grid below.

Eric stared at the image and tried to focus on the old woman's explanation. Her talk was extremely theoretical and over his head. He marveled at the quiet attention the woman commanded, and wondered if was possible that everyone in the Café Thimble actually understood what was being presented. He leaned over and whispered to Emmy, "do you get it?"

She shook her head ruefully, smiling sympathetically. She put her finger to her lips in the 'sshhh' sign, so he sat back, trying to understand what he was seeing.

"When this material covers the bottom of a ship, it can pull through each cell minute amounts of energy from the sea. The regulator on the bridge stores this energy in the onboard batteries, along with what's brought in from solar collectors. Oceangoing vessels have always depended on some kind of wind power or fossil fuels to supplement the solar propulsion engines. We think this will solve the problem of navigating through prolonged storms, and eliminates the need for further fossil fuel burning at sea."

Applause rose in the back, and quickly spread to the entire place. Bamfield waved her hands, grateful but embarrassed. She was used to working things out in the privacy of her laboratory, not presenting her ideas to the public like this.

Assuming the audience had correctly perceived the end of the presentation, the woman in her red sequined turban returned to the stage. She clapped Bamfield on the back, which almost sent the poor woman sprawling, but nearby patrons caught her before she fell. "Sorry, I'm so sorry!" said the slightly drunk hostess, who quickly recovered and threw open the floor to questions.

Once again Eric was completely lost. The technical jargon, challenges and counter-arguments all went completely over his head. But he could see the old woman knew her stuff, because eventually she had conquered every objection, and people once again burst into applause. Meanwhile, the café was buzzing again, conversations percolating through the place. Eric got up to go the bathroom, where a line of people was already waiting.

"She's awesome," exclaimed the woman in front of him to her companion, to which he nodded his assent. "Do you think MacMillan is going to speak?"

"No, he's going to save his ammo for later, I'm sure."

The woman looked back at Eric, flashing him a nervous smile when she saw he was listening. She turned back to her companion speaking in a voice too low for Eric to hear over the roar of the place. He looked around. At a table nearby a group of people argued over a drawing, gesturing wildly, one guy throwing his hands up in disgust and falling back in his chair. All around the room, knots of people talked intensely, some leaning against the walls, others in huddles over tables.

Am I supposed to eavesdrop on all these people? he thought with dismay. *I'm not a spy!* He folded his arms, wishing the line would hurry up. He looked back at his table where Emmy and Lorelei were sharing a laugh while Bo was gesticulating at Lou and Zette with unmistakable fury. Another well-dressed woman walked by with a basket on her arm, giving out samples of a new soap. Behind her a fellow was soliciting signatures in support of clinical trials of a new anti-itch cream he invented.

Finally it was his turn for the bathroom. Some kind of salsa was playing. He discovered two small dolls swirling around a shelf on the back wall emitting the music while they danced. He stood peeing into a long looping tube that vaguely resembled a miniature tuba, looking at the strange yet familiar accoutrements of the little restroom. The sink was shaped like a big lily, the mirror was a three-dimensional mosaic of mirror pieces that somehow allowed you to see your entire head at once. The porcelain throne was just that, with a tall red velvet back and a ruby-studded scepter that one pulled to flush. He washed his hands in the lily sink and walked back to his table, noting that many were leaving.

"Everything okay?" asked Emmy cheerfully.

"There was a long line," he explained. "Are you ready to go?"

"Sure, if you are. Did you get whatever it was you were supposed to get?"

He sagged, shrugging his shoulders, "I guess so… I mean, *I* didn't hear anything that seemed like it would interest a public investigator, did you?" She shook her head.

Lou and Zette had departed while Eric was in the restroom. Lorelei was trying to calm Bo down after he and Lou had gotten pretty vicious with each other. "You just have to let it roll off you… I think Lou wants to provoke you."

"But why?"

"I don't know. Did you tell him any more about what you're doing at work? Maybe he's fishing for ideas…"

"SHIT!" Bo slapped his forehead. "I should have known!"

"What? What did you let out?"

"I was so mad at him. He kept egging me on about the cellular memory thing, and how we would be in trouble if it proved true. So I started talking about our process, and I think I mentioned it." He looked crestfallen.

"It?" Eric asked.

"He can't say," Lorelei explained. "They haven't finished it yet, and they're neck and neck with some other groups working on the same problem."

"But didn't—?"

Emmy put her hand on his arm. "C'mon, let's go."

Eric didn't understand why they couldn't tell him, someone clearly not involved in whatever technology they were talking about, but Emmy understood not to push it. They slapped goodbyes with Lorelei and Bo, Emmy promising to come back to the hospital soon for another Annuals stint.

They retrieved their bicycles and pedaled home, Eric pondering what the mystery of Bo's work was.

"I'm sure it's some new biodevice, or maybe it's an enhancement that will improve whole categories of them... Who knows?" Emmy speculated. "But you shouldn't be resentful. Technologists are crazy competitive. They all want to be the first or the best with something important. You know that don't you?"

Eric nodded, but he didn't get it. He'd never been friends with an inventor, and his uncle's story wasn't one of wanting to be first or best. He reminded Emmy about his uncle. "He believed it was better. Why wouldn't people embrace something that was simply better than what it replaced?"

"I don't know. Did it require lots of resources? Was it going to drastically change how people did things? Undermine certain workplace practices? There are so many questions that affect these things."

"I guess so." They were gliding through the Panhandle, the stars twinkling in a fog-free sky. "There's a lot of stuff I just haven't thought about much," he admitted.

Emmy smiled, enjoying Eric's lack of pretension. Within a few minutes they rolled into the backyard of Page Mews, where a small bonfire roared a short distance from the hot tubs. Residents were standing near the fire, or jumping in and out of the hot tubs. Tanya was laughing in one of the hot tubs with another woman. Gerald was sitting in the exact same place Eric had seen him at 5:30. "Have you moved at all?" Eric teased.

"Well," Gerald sighed deeply, lost in a haze of intoxication and hot water, "yes. I got out to eat, and then I cleaned the kitchen. After that, there was nothing to do but come back here."

"Wanna?" Emmy looked at Eric mischievously.

"Let's!"

They tore off their clothes, still sweating from their ride. The night air felt cool but not painfully cold. "Watch out Gerald, here we come!" and they splashed into the steaming tub as he recoiled. "Okay, okay, I can take a hint!" he laughed, and got out, leaving them alone to frolic in the deliciously hot water.

24.

"Good morning. It's Thursday August 12, 2157. This is the 6:45 news on Radio Ignatius in San Francisco, the Jive 95 at 94.9 FM, Don McQueen reporting.

"Folks, we've got a major fire burning out of control on San Bruno Mountain. It's five alarms, all fire teams south of Islais Creek are being called out. I repeat, a major fire is burning out of control on San Bruno Mountain. All fire teams south of Islais Creek are requested to report to the staging area at Guadalupe Parkway. No casualties are reported as yet, but at least two buildings have burned, and the fire is moving fast towards Oak Canyon."

"In other news, the San Francisco Water Council met yesterday at City Hall and determined that repairs to the rain collection and gray water system would take another year. Therefore, discussions to acquire fresh water for the Hetch Hetchy viaduct will be re-opened with the Council of Mid-Sierra Foothill Communities.

"A two-boat crash stopped traffic in downtown San Francisco yesterday. Traffic reports say that a private skiff was speeding south in the Kearny Canal when it smashed into a barge crossing at Sutter, sending it into the Jameson Building on the corner. One person is still hospitalized with contusions.

"Revelers in the Indian city of Mumbai paralyzed the city yesterday. Calm is returning after Mumbai's victory in the cricket finals over rival Peshawar, 99-21.

"Scientists in Hanoi report a breakthrough in age-blocker enzymes. They predict lifespans reaching 150 years will soon be common. Pharmaceutical workers in Hanoi promise to expand production within six months. Data on the molecular structure of the enzyme is available on the vyne. Bay Area drug factories in Fremont and Santa Rosa immediately announced plans to produce local supplies, but estimate it will take at least three months to get it into local freestores.

"A neighborhood fair will be held this weekend on Potrero Hill, featuring bake-offs in pies, roasts, cakes, and puddings, winners to advance to the citywide fair in September. (I'll tell you folks, I was there last year and those bakers on Potrero Hill are among the city's best!). Food, dance, live music, luge racing, skatepede races, triathlon and—this is one of the great things on Potrero Hill—disc tosses into the Mission.

"Last night the Oaks extended their winning streak to seven games at the expense of those sad sacks we call the home team, the Seals. Billy Bonds, the Seals shortstop, extended his league-leading strikeout total to 154, and his season-long hitting streak to 32 games, in what must be one of the strangest combo streaks in baseball history. The Farmers beat the Slugs 8-2, and the Gamblers lost in extra innings to the Grizzlies 2-1, in last night's only other scheduled games.

"Today's weather: The sun is out, the fog is not! Temperatures will reach 28° in San Francisco, up to 37° inland. Thunderstorms are predicted for the weekend—You know, David, I still find it strange to have thunderstorms around here."

"Oh, you're such an old fart!"

"Thanks, I love you too! This is Don McQueen with the 6:45 Jive 95 news. Once again, fire crews south of Islais Creek are called to Guadalupe Parkway to help on a five-alarm fire burning out of control on San Bruno Mountain. El Loco?"

"Thanks Don. This goes out to the brave women and men fighting the fire. 'Rain, rain, rain' by The Rhythmaholichaliacs.

ull! PUUULLL!" They slid in the mud, grappling with the huge hose they were dragging from the cliff's edge. Below, the fire tug *Giant Josea* was bobbing in the waves next to the smoking hulk where the fire had started. The scorched hillside had already been soaked during the past hour of firefighting. Everything was turning to thick mud. William Grayson had never faced anything like this.

I'm not even supposed to be here! he thought with exasperation. He looked ahead where the girl he'd gone to bed with the previous night was pulling the hose. At just before 6 a.m. almost an hour ago, they had been startled awake by the jarring sound of the fire alarm. Frieda was a volunteer, like about a third of the city's population. She, too, was covered in soot and mud, assigned as they were to the job of hauling up the fire hoses from the fire tug to bring Bay water to the fire.

William shivered in the water and mud, dwarfed by the billowing gray smoke ahead, flames just visible in the distance amid dozens of tiny yellow ants, firefighters at the front lines. This was the fifth hose they had run up from the Bay since they'd arrived a half hour earlier, rushing to support the 300 or so firefighters who had converged on the blaze within 15 minutes of the alarm's clanging. Crews ahead of them attached smaller hoses to the ends of these, and so on, up to the fire lines.

He had prepared for a much smaller version of this plenty of times during the routine weekly drills. It was shocking to be here on a muddy slope far from the cityscape he'd trained for. He was miles from his home in the Page Mews, and right now, he wished he'd stayed there last night with Frieda instead of accepting her invitation to go back south to her place on McLaren Ridge. They were only ten minutes from the fire at her house, and well within the alarm's reach.

"Hey! We need ten more at the second stage," called the marshall, screaming back and forth into his shellfone… More and more firefighters arrived, rushing to get their bright yellow slickers on, most of them having pulled on their thick boots before leaving home.

People scrambled back and forth with no apparent rhyme or reason. Yelling and pointing, people running. William and his crew gave another big heave to get the fifth hose into position adjacent to the firetrucks. They labored to attach it to the pump truck and once it was done, they bent over, hands on knees, gasping for breath after the tremendous effort. After a moment William straightened up, looking for Frieda. "Oh man," he said unconsciously, disappointed to see her running with a squad of others into the distance. Before he thought about it, the marshall sent him to help douse any remaining hot spots to their south. Wispy smoke still rose along the perimeter of the burned zone. No time to hesitate, he ran off, the boots he borrowed from Frieda's vacationing housemate rattling loosely on his small feet.

* * *

Andy Steinway ran back and forth several times in the dim pre-dawn. He gazed at the flames, and then moved back across the ferry to peer into the slowly fading darkness. The explosion and fire was bigger than anything he'd ever seen. This wasn't a monster fireworks show. The peapod steadily flapped through the dark Bay waters, shimmering with distant flames. He was trying to remember something recognizable about the skiff. He was sure it was connected to the explosion. It had been moving quickly on a line directly into the Bay from the place where the fire erupted. There was one person in it, he was sure of that. The person had been laying down… maybe hurt? Hiding?

He trembled with excitement. *Looks like a huge fire,* he thought. *I wonder if Robin's gonna get this one?* The P-I's office would surely have to investigate. He may already have important evidence! When he started to write down his observations, he realized that he hadn't seen enough. The sky was lightening behind the East Bay hills, casting a grayish glow onto the Bay. *There—there!* The skiff was out there, and whoever it was, he— yes it looked like a he—was standing up now, looking back at the fire. He wrote "tall, thin, male, standing and watching" to complement his first note about a skiff speeding on a line from the scene of the fire.

* * *

"Es el muchacho, Capitán," reported First Mate Suarez-Ochoa, peering through infrared binoculars on the bridge of the *Leopold Tanzania.*

"Bring her," he said quietly to another mate standing behind them.

"You want me to wake her up?" he asked, surprised, noting that the dawn light was just beginning to illuminate the Bay, the bright flames dancing on the distant hills. The captain nodded, glaring because he had to ask twice.

The mate quickly moved through the ship to the passenger deck. Down a long wooden corridor he knocked at Room 311. There was no answer. He knocked a second time, a little louder and longer.

"Yes?!" came the woman's voice with a note of alarm.

"Madame. The captain requests your presence on the bridge."

"What?! At this hour?"

"Madame, there is something you should see."

"Very well. I'll be there in 5 minutes. Please tell the captain."

"Yes, m'am," and he returned to the bridge.

When she walked onto the bridge, the room was warm and the control panels glowed green. A pink dawn was breaking over the Bay. The captain took her by the elbow and directed her to the binoculars that the First Mate had been using. He pointed towards San Francisco where a half dozen ships were moving northward on typical morning commutes.

"So?" she asked.

"Look," he said, tight-lipped and tense, directing her view to a small skiff bounding through the water, nearing Treasure Island, maybe half a klick away.

"It's him, isn't it?"

"Yes, and look there, his latest work," pointing to San Bruno Mountain where billowing smoke filled the sky.

She took it all in. She shook her long mane of black hair, pulled it back and tied it into a quick knot. Her sharp profile cut the morning grayness, enervated by the unfolding picture before her. "Let's have some radio!" she demanded. "Track him," she pointed to Nwin in the distance.

"Do you still think we can use him?" the Captain asked drily.

She looked at him without flinching, well aware that her previous claim had been overridden. "I don't know. But this can't hurt."

* * *

Hot 1 flipped through the dawn light. Nwin looked back from time to time at the growing cloud of gray smoke, slowly filling the sky over San Bruno Mountain. *That's a helluva lot of smoke for one lousy roof!* he thought. *What was in that pinchay place? It couldn't'a burned that long, it was practically falling into the water.* But his back hurt so much he couldn't stay focused on his exploit. He lay down in the bottom of the boat, setting a course between Treasure Island and the downtown area. He maneuvered his life preserver and some old sweaters under him for extra padding. The skiff, being a bioboat, was also a lot softer than a wooden or plastic boat. He used his feet, one on the accelerator button and the other holding the rudder steady.

Every so often he would have to rise up and turn over his shoulder to make sure he wasn't going to run into anything. As he rose but before he turned, he noticed for the first time that the *Leopold Tanzania* was still sitting in the middle of the Bay, where it had been for the past two weeks. "Chingado!" he made a course correction. *Why would it still be here? Waiting for a cargo?* His mind raced.

Soon he approached downtown. He turned towards the Washington Canal that would take him to the Pyramid and his bed. The sun was almost peeking over the east Bay hills now. The sky was bright blue, except for the huge cloud of smoke to the south. He looked back, feeling a rush of excitement and a sense of foreboding and confusion too.

Struggling to an upright position he approached the canal. He skirted around a small jam in front of the residential docks at Domino 4.

A woman stood on the dock yelling to a friend, "Fire! Did you hear? A huge blaze on San Bruno Mountain! They think it's arson!"

Nwin's head whipped around at the word "fire" and whipped right back again when he heard "arson." He sank slowly on his knees, his back throbbing, trying to breathe through the stabbing pain. Slowly he maneuvered into the docks at the Pyramid, past the little supply house. He opened the panel in the bioboat. The last fuel pellets were almost gone, so he reached in and grabbed two more 'phylls and dropped them in. After docking he left behind his gloves, failing to notice in his pain the rather strong smell of gasoline that still lingered.

He was exhausted, very sore and a little dizzy. His head spun as he climbed on the 'vator, and by the time he got to floor 33, he was clutching his head with one hand and his stomach with the other.

"Hi Nwin, what's twirlin'?" Lupe called automatically as he practically fell out of the pod. She gave a little gasp when he staggered out in obvious pain, totally disheveled and stinking of gasoline. "Are you okay? Do you want me to call a doctor? Hey, Bobby!" she called to another guy walking towards them. Nwin fell against the wall and began sinking.

* * *

"Nwin, Nwin are you there? Can you hear me?" Jennifer Luoc-Don Robertson couldn't stop crying. She sobbed uncontrollably as her son lay silent in the hospital bed. "What have I done? Jeffrey dies—before I can go home, my son is brought in unconscious." She cried. Finally, after leaning over and wiping Nwin's brow, utterly exhausted she fell back into the big soft chair and into a fitful sleep.

25.

Eric wiggled through the city on his bicycle towards his Tryout as a Public Investigator. It was a bright sunny day, and he felt a light cheerfulness that was completely new. Chicago memories were losing their hold on him as his new life was taking their place.

What a contrast to his former life back east, either with his parents, or his first attempt to live on his own in Chicago. It had been so difficult to find friends, to make his way. The year he spent doing Annuals in Chicago had made him feel more isolated rather than less. Wherever he went, intact communities seemed impenetrable. He had made casual friends here and there, but never had he felt so included as he felt here, after just a month.

Cynthia back in Chicago finally stopped haunting his daydreams. She had ended her relationship with him so abruptly. A familiar ache appeared, like a relative you wished would go away. He pushed the ache back, chagrined by its familiarity and surprised by its sudden alienness. Chicago had been a disaster, but maybe it wasn't all his fault after all. San Francisco was so completely different... but maybe he was different, too, after spending fifteen months in a pit of despair and loneliness.

Velo traffic streamed out of the Wiggle, past the Octavia Greenway and over the Abundance streetcar tracks. He passed the cross-Mission *Camino* Elevated with its handsome wooden three-story spiraling entry, bicycles plunging out of it while others sped into it for the climb. The morning sun felt so good that he couldn't resist the temptation to delay at a sprawling outdoor café on Abundance just east of Valencia. Eric parked the bike and went for a double cappuccino and a croissant. Carrying his snack to an empty table, he worried slightly about eating again after just having a big bowl of cereal and fruit to start the day an hour earlier. But sitting in the sun with coffee and a rich, buttery croissant was close to perfect, and anyway, he'd already gotten them.

"They think it's arson! Who would do such a thing?!?" said a fellow at the next table in a loud voice. His companion, a middle-aged man with long brown hair and a long scar on his gaunt cheek, shook his head. The first guy, wider than his friend and wearing a Seals baseball cap, his hands folded over his paunch under his overalls, continued "I heard the fire alarms this morning. My place on Bernal is north of the response area. You could hear the bells ringing all over the valley. I got up, but when I saw the smoke south of McLaren, I went back to bed. I couldn't sleep so I put on the radio and heard the report from the scene. Man, what a mess!"

"It's over by now, isn't it?" asked his friend, glancing at the clock in the café. It was nearly 10 o'clock.

"Hell'if I know!"

Eric listened, recalling a conversation at the breakfast table along similar lines. But it was all very far from his world or his thoughts. A fire in an unknown place south of the city didn't seem particularly important, although the fact that there was a suspicion of arson did catch his attention. He polished off his second breakfast, and soon after arrived at work.

The office was abuzz with talk of the fire. "Hey Eric, didja hear?" asked Anita, the other Tryout in addition to Andy Steinway, who was hurrying past the entry when he came in. "We're having a staff meeting right now! Good thing you got here!" she urged him to follow.

In the meeting room Katherine Fairly and Pops O'Hair sat on one side, their counterparts, Bill Mooney and Stella Brooks across the table. The three Apprentices, Robin, Leigh, and Luis, and the three Tryouts, Andy, Anita and Eric scattered around the table. The big window on the Civic Green was open to the endless murmur of the plaza, falling water mixing with thousands of voices, the quiet weight of streetcars, the whir of gears and spokes on countless passing bicycles. The day's heat was rising, but the room's stuffiness demanded fresh air regardless of its temperature.

Kathy started the meeting. "Okay, we have our normal staff meeting, but obviously everyone is thinking about the big fire on San Bruno Mountain. Is there anyone here who needs a basic report?"

Everyone shook their head, including Eric even though he actually would have liked one. It was too embarrassing to be the one person who didn't know what was happening, so he went along.

"The last report I got said the fire was almost completely contained. No one was killed, thank goodness. Three houses were destroyed, and at least 135 acres of the mountain have burned, most of it rare habitat."

"The Mountain Committee has already put out a call for volunteers to help defend the burn area from invasive exotics," said Stella, a P-I lifer with 19 years experience. Her territory covered the southern part of the city, but she was also the P-I most involved in Garden Party politics and the factional disputes among gardeners.

"Yeah, okay, but that's not our concern at this point," said Kathy curtly. "Robin, you've been running Arson and Vandalism, but I don't think you've actually investigated any arsons yet, have you?"

"No," she explained, visibly upset. "The past four months have been all about trampled gardens, broken windows, and that one case of an illegal dam on Precita Creek."

Pops entered the discussion, "This is going to take our best effort. Stella, you're going to be on this because it's your part of town," to which Stella nodded, putting a pencil in her mouth. "Robin's got to be on it, since arson is her beat. And I think Eric should be assigned to it, too."

Andy was practically jumping out of his seat. "But I was there! I saw... I saw the explosion and fire, and I saw a skiff!" He was beside himself, urgently wanting to be assigned to the investigation.

Bill Mooney, a big broad African-American man, conservatively dressed with a quiet, no-nonsense demeanor, peered through his spectacles at Andy. He reached over and touched him on the arm, and said in a quietly confident voice that instantly demonstrated his long experience, "You are a witness. You can't investigate a crime in which you are a witness." He looked around before continuing for all to hear, "Besides I need you to help me with the report on Canal Maintenance. The Transportation Council has requested a Public Investigation into the deteriorating canals, and we have a lot of research to do, including on-site inspections and interviews."

Pops waited for Mooney to finish, noting that Andy was not particularly satisfied by having a big public works investigation instead of the temporarily glamorous fire to work on. "Kathy and I are both going to work with the arson team, in addition to our three ongoing resource diversion investigations," to which Kathy nodded vigorously.

Kathy gave quick summaries of their progress on the resource diversion jobs. She assigned Anita to making some visits around the city to gather eyewitness accounts. For the sake of Eric and Anita, both still quite new, she ran down the procedures for taking statements, emphasizing the importance of doing background work on the context, knowing the history of community approaches to controlling or punishing different transgressions, and making good use of audio recordings.

Bill Mooney gave a brief account of the role of the P-I in protecting the public interest vis-à-vis public infrastructure, telling a story about an unauthorized veloway extension through a midtown orchard. "My lifer colleagues will remember this, but you newbies don't. A few years back, we had to intervene when bicyclists took it upon themselves to plow a veloway right through the Webster Commons. The neighbors were divided. We learned that some of them had helped. We were investigating in response to a legitimate public concern, but we were accused of taking sides. Complaints by Garden Party activists had started the investigation, and truth be told, they had a case. But we have to stay out of factional fights. This was one of the early explosions in the Garden/Transit fight."

"You better tell them how we solved it, too, Bill," urged Kathy.

"It was a good chance to fall back on our mandate: to expose and explain. Remember that! We do not accuse anyone, and far be it from us to propose or carry out any remedies. Our job is to expose and explain. Then the public can argue it out, decide what's to be done."

"So if we find out the name of someone who has broken a window, say," Robin asked, "don't we make that public?"

"Yes, if we can find solid evidence linking someone to an event or problem, our job is to publish that on the vyne for all to see. Invariably the neighborhood committee decides to act on such reports if the "crime" is deemed enough of a problem to require a social response. Plenty of times it's enough just to publish the information. The perpetrator is embarrassed, can't refute the evidence, and is dissuaded from further similar behavior."

"What about when it's something dangerous or destructive, like this fire?" asked Eric.

Pops took it up. "Still, our mission is to expose and explain. If we can identify the culprit, the people who live with that person will certainly feel responsible to hold a hearing in which their neighbor or friend can clear their name. Often enough the person who is identified by our investigation will insist on a public hearing to refute our work."

"And then?"

"At the hearing, you have the right to a jury, and the right to confront the witnesses and evidence in public. You can have an advocate if you want. And you can testify or not as you prefer."

"What happens if someone is found guilty by a jury, say of arson, since that's what's up today?" Robin asked.

Stella put her pencil down and grabbed a handful of peanuts from the bowl in the middle of the table. Tossing one into her mouth, she continued the explanation, "it hasn't happened very often, to tell the truth. We just don't have too much of this kind of thing. Much more common is violence between domestic partners or housemates. But in a case like this one, assuming it IS arson, if we find a person or persons responsible, and then they're found guilty by a jury, the remedy will be negotiated between the jury and the guilty party. Same as we do with violent offenders. Usually people are offered several choices of going away. It is rare that anyone who has gone through the whole process and is found guilty is allowed to stay. Sometimes they leave forever, but usually it's anywhere from six months to several years."

"Where do they go?" asked Eric.

"Depends. There's lots of rural places that'll take 'em in. There's isolated places on fire lookouts, sheep ranching, farming of all types, wilderness stewardship. Some people just go on long journeys around the world..."

"Don't they just go and get in to the same trouble all over again?"

"Practically unheard of. Taken out of the context in which they behaved badly, and after a drawn-out confrontation with witnesses and evidence, few people remain defiant and in denial about their own actions. Sometimes they remain bitter, feeling they were forced by circumstances in some way. But when they make their case to a jury, if circumstances are indeed a legitimate part of the explanation, the remedy is invariably adjusted to reflect that. That helps reduce anyone's sense of being treated unfairly."

"Uh, if we're done with this Civics Lesson, I have an announcement," said Robin, blushing.

Kathy looked around, hands spread out inquiringly with her eyebrows raised, and seeing that no one had any more questions, she nodded to Robin.

"I'm getting married!"

Smiling and laughing, everyone offered congratulations and various sarcastic comments. "Did you have to use drugs?" laughed Stella. "Who's the victim?" hooted Pops. "Tied up at home?" teased Mooney. The lifers responded as one, full of derisive good cheer.

"I'd like you all to come to the wedding," Robin continued, cheerfully ignoring all the sarcasm. She started distributing handmade invitations prepared in elegant calligraphy. "My love's father is a Calligrapher—"

"Hey, does he work at Worth While Books by any chance?" asked Eric, remembering the beautiful letterpress and calligraphy work he'd seen there.

"How did you know that?" asked Robin, surprised that a guy who had only been in town a month could have known such an obscure place.

Eric smiled, proud of his lucky guess, "I came across it when I first got here, just wandering around one day."

"So who is the lucky...?" asked Kathy, trailing off.

"OK," Robin was beaming now. "She's the love of my life. Her name is Trish, Trish Wadsworth."

Kathy, feeling a surge of sisterly solidarity, went and gave her a big hug. "So where is this shindig, anyway?"

"It's near a little town in Sonoma called Valley Ford. Trish's family has an old farm up there. A ferry leaves North Beach that morning. It will drop you in Old Petaluma, the walled town."

"Dew! I always wanted to see Petaluma," said Anita excitedly.

"After a shuttle to the shoreline, you'll be brought to the farm by horse-drawn wagon. It's about 25 kilometers. You'll be traveling about three and a half hours altogether, so we expect you all to spend the night, okay?" Robin euphorically explained the details. All thought of the fire on San Bruno or the other investigations before them had evaporated in the communal pleasure of Robin's plans.

Walking back to their desks a few minutes later, admiring the invitations a last time before putting them away, Eric turned to Leigh, one of the Apprentices. "Do you know what happens to hoarders?"

She laughed, "Sure!... Nothing!"

"What? I don't understand. I thought this was one of the things we investigate?"

"It is. But it's not much of a problem is it? And the people doing it are hardly a threat to anyone. I've done hoarding cases."

"So what happens after you expose and explain?"

"It's sad, really. Usually hoarders are humiliated. I mean, what does it say about you if you are hoarding stuff? You can go and get whatever you want whenever you want it..." she shook her head in puzzlement. "What I've noticed though, is that the embarrassment doesn't last, and before long they are back collecting things again."

"Are they sent away?"

"Oh no! Goodness, that would be harsh! No, often the neighbors are exasperated, seeing a hoarder dragging so many things in. But everyone is embarrassed to confront the individual. Practically all the hoarders I've seen are lonely and quiet people. Faced with nosy neighbors they withdraw. Normally hoarders are asked to redistribute their surplus goods. If they refuse to allow a community reallocation, a jury is convened. Assuming the charge is sustained, the hoarder chooses a selection of things they want to keep—way more shit than I'd ever want in my house, I'll tell ya—Then the rest of it goes back to the freestores. But like I say, it's usually not long before the hoarder is at it again."

"Why bother?" asked Eric.

"I suppose it's a gradual process. I read some studies on hoarding, and the consensus is that it is less and less common. One study suggested that the public embarrassment was an important means of discouraging it. On the other hand, some lonely hoarders only get attention by getting caught." She shook her head again. "I don't think it's worth as much effort as we spend on it, but what do I know?"

"I have to read up on Arson, since they just put me on that fire case," Eric changed the subject.

"It's pretty rare, but you can find some psychological studies of arsonists in our library down the hall," Leigh recommended. "So far, we don't know if this is an arson or not, even though everyone thinks it probably is."

"Don't you believe Andy? He seemed pretty convinced that the guy he observed had started it."

"Andy was on a ferry in the dark. He is free to believe whatever he wants, but he does not have any real evidence, that much I know!" she said, her black curls bouncing emphatically.

Eric put up his hands, not wanting to get pulled into an argument on Andy's veracity or the nature of evidence. He headed down the hall, happily digesting the meeting. Reminded suddenly by Leigh about the rigorousness required to actually claim something as evidence, he thought *I knew I was going to like this work.* He entered the musty library, walls jammed with ancient books on jurisprudence, rules of law, investigative techniques, and the accumulated knowledge of several generations of Public Investigations.

26.

Entering the 4th floor hospital room, she threw open the curtains, surprised the food service helper hadn't done so. "How are you feeling today?... Nwin?" she was examining his chart. "It's important that we get you out of bed and start moving as soon as possible." "I'm Dr. Sung, but call me Angie."

Nwin lay in bed, surprised to wake from a dream where he was flying down a sun-soaked hillside on a bicycle that he'd never seen. "Uh, um," he tried to turn on his side, and grimaced as the pain shot through his lower back. "Not so good," he gasped.

"You've damaged the discs here," she was holding out a color photo showing his lower spine. "This is L4 and this is L3. Can you see how the disc is pooching out here?" The full color photo was hard to look at, shiny pinks and reds with whitish gray bumps.

His vision was blurry. "What does it mean, doctor? Am I crippled?" he asked with real anxiety.

She gave him a comforting look and put a hand on his shoulder. "Certainly not! You will recover, but it will take time and patience. It will also take work. Once we get the swelling down and you can stand up, you have to start physical therapy."

The door opened and in walked Nwin's mom. She rushed over to Nwin's side, taking his hand, and putting her other hand on his forehead. "Nwin, honey, how are you doing? Do you feel any better?" Then she turned to the doctor. "I'm his mother, Jennifer Robertson. How long do you think he has to stay in the hospital?"

"You can take him home as soon as he can get up. We're giving him medicine to take care of the pain, and reduce the swelling. He might be ready to go later this afternoon or tomorrow at the latest."

"Really? That's great! Nwin, you come home with me, okay? I'm going to arrange a ride."

He looked at his mother without expression. Haggardly she looked at him, her usual buoyancy subdued, her whole body slumped. He remembered now that his father was dead. That he had woken up in the hospital two days ago to his mother crying over him. That he had passed out in the Pyramid after coming home that morning. Did anyone know? It didn't seem like it. He had slept a lot since then. The doctors had taken pictures of his back, and now here was this woman telling him that he was going to be OK.

"Doctor, when can I start physical therapy?"

The doctor looked at him, encouraged that he wanted to face his condition head-on. "If you can make it home today, we can schedule you to come in later this week.

Here's some things you can start right away." She showed him some exercises, just lightly raising his leg and arm on opposite sides as he lay face down. "But don't do it if it hurts. It's better to stay in bed for a few days until it's all calmed down."

"How long will it take to get better?"

"You're very young, so your body will help a lot. If you are careful, and you do the physical therapy every day, you can resume most of your normal life in a few weeks. You won't feel great for at least 3 or 4 months, but you'll be able to get through the day. What kind of work do you do?"

He explained about the Rice Bowl and she immediately vetoed any further stooping in the rice paddies. "But the rose bushes, as long as you don't have to bend to the ground repeatedly, that should be OK."

* * *

Two weeks later, Nwin and his mom walked on to the Harrison Street Bridge over Precita Creek. Boys were fishing from the far side, looking at the elegantly attired couple with curiosity. The tall young black man walked tentatively, like someone much older, holding the arm of a much shorter Asian woman. She wore an elaborately embroidered full length dark blue dress, suede black boots, and clutched a black shawl over her head and shoulders.

Jennifer snuffled as she pulled a small container from under her shawl, and handed it to her son. "Nwin, here," and she began crying more freely. "I can't do it."

Nwin took the urn, and faced the creek. He felt empty. He tried to think of something to say, something that would comfort his mother. But nothing came. Blankness gave way to bitterness and resentment. His mother tried to keep her crying to herself.

Finally, Nwin tipped the urn and his father's ashes swirled downward into the creek, disappearing as soon as they hit the water. A throaty sound followed the ashes, but no words emerged from his tortured memories. He put his arm around his mother's shoulders, squeezing her, his own eyes dry as a bone, feeling neither grief nor relief.

She murmured something in Vietnamese that he couldn't understand. Her sobbing subsided, and soon even the snuffling passed. She blew her nose once, and tucked her black handkerchief into her sleeve. Looking up at him, red-rimmed eyes still full of tears, she said "ready?" to which he nodded. They slowly walked down the bridge and back to the solar cart they were using during his convalescence, and drove home to the top of Bernal Heights.

* * *

From the kitchen door, the yard didn't look so bad. But the month of inattention since his father's death showed in the clumps of weeds crowding the beans, the drooping tomatoes, the debris that had collected along the paths. He thought about working on it, but the memory of his father on his knees out there prevented him. Besides, the doctor said he had to avoid work close to the ground. He went to the Rice Bowl a couple of times, but getting back and forth was much more difficult than working the roses, so he had announced a leave of absence. Now he wondered if he would ever go back.

"Hey Nwin," called his mom, coming through the door, "Look who's here!" He turned to see his cousin Sonia and behind her, wheezing loudly, labored Auntie.

"Nwin! How are you doing?" called Sonia, walking over and giving him a hug. He smiled, surprised to see them. He hadn't seen Sonia for more than a year, not since the family reunion at the Presidio the previous spring. She had grown a lot, practically as tall as he was, and no doubt about it, she was more of a woman now than a girl. Standing awkwardly near the wall, her big black eyes glowed warmly as she played with her long braids.

"Give me a han' Sonia!" called Auntie, groping to the sofa. Sonia and Nwin both went to her side, and holding her hands, helped her sink into the couch, which noticeably gave way, barely hovering over the floor. "I forget how far up it is!" she puffed.

"You come in a cart?" Nwin asked Sonia, and she nodded. "We borrowed the one from Jimmy's workshop."

"What can I get you?" Jennifer asked eagerly.

"Lemonade?" suggested Sonia. "Beer," grunted Auntie.

Jennifer happily headed to the kitchen. Guests were rare, and family even more so. She and Nwin had settled into a pattern that neither noticed as a near duplicate of the routine she had lived with his father for the past 12 years. Now, with the surprise arrival of 'Auntie,' and her niece Sonia, Jennifer bustled in the kitchen, putting together a tray of small sandwiches, cakes, and fruit.

Nwin sat with the visitors, explaining about his back, taking a leave from the Rice Bowl, his physical therapy. Auntie pulled out a cigar and lit it up, taking a liberty that was terribly rude. She puffed away, silently listening to Nwin's story, looking around at the comfortable house. Jennifer came in with the drinks, recoiling at the powerful smell of cigar. But she said nothing, just grabbing a small plate for Auntie to use as an ashtray.

Auntie tried to lean forward through the cloud of smoke to get her glass of beer, but couldn't overcome her own bulk. "Here, Auntie, I'll get it for you," Nwin said helpfully. His back was stiff but not so sore now. After handing Auntie the glass he straightened up. Putting his hands on his lower back he bent backwards as far as he could, which wasn't far.

"Does that help?" Sonia asked.

"Usually." He took a plate and put some sandwiches on it, handing it to Auntie. Then he made another for himself and sat down. She put the cigar out, stubbing it carefully in the temporary ashtray. She took a bite and turned to Nwin, speaking with her mouth full, "y'know, ... de roses on H'rr'son Street..." she finished chewing, "you could come and hep me wit de roses, Nwin."

Jennifer thought it was a great idea. "Yes, Nwin, why don't you? You're so good with them." She'd seen him sinking into a pattern of inactivity that was starting to worry her. She remembered his father, the long slow physical therapy, the depression, the defeat. Nwin wasn't as hurt as Jeffrey had been. She couldn't let him give up like his father had. Returning to the roses with Auntie would get him out. It was close, and he and Auntie had always had a special bond.

"I'll think about it," Nwin said through a mouthful of his own.

Sonia looked at him with a glint of mischievousness. "Hey, Nwin, I know someone you know." He looked at her expressionless, waiting for the punchline. "Valentina Rogers, she told me to say 'hi' to you."

"How do you know her?" he asked, his heart already beating faster, happily surprised to hear this.

"I know her from a chorus we were both in a few years ago. Then I ran into her two weeks ago at that ice cream place in the Wiggle. We were talking and somehow we figured out that we both knew you—Oh yeah! Her friend asked her if she'd talked to you lately while I was there, and then we figured it out."

"How is she?" he asked, trying to contain his excitement.

"Oh fine I guess—"

"You sweet on her?" demanded Auntie, not knowing who this girl was.

Nwin ducked his head sheepishly, and nodded reluctantly. Jennifer watched this with great interest, not remembering any girls since Nwin's first crush two years earlier, but Mimi hadn't lasted more than a couple of weeks.

Nwin asked Sonia, "Are you going to be seeing her again soon?"

She shook her head, "No, I don't expect to. Why?"

"Oh, I thought I'd send a message along with you if you were."

"Why don't you just vyne her? I'm sure she'd like to hear from you."

He nodded, returning to the sandwiches, lost in fantasy about Valentina. The others talked family gossip, Jennifer eventually clearing the tray and the leftover food. Auntie resumed her cigar, and sat contentedly with her second beer.

"Jimmy said you should come and see him," Sonia told Nwin.

"Tell him I will." He looked at Auntie, feeling a sudden lightness. "Auntie, how 'bout I meet you day after tomorrow? We can do some roses together?" She smiled broadly through her cigar smoke, nodding. "You come whenever you want, hon'. If I'm not at home, you can find me in the bushes!" She laughed at the suggestive connotations of her unconscious remark, and they all joined in.

* * *

After Auntie and cousin Sonia were gone, his mom busied herself in the kitchen. Nwin went to the vyne, and called "Message to Valentina Rogers, Pierce Palace, San Francisco. Hi Valentina!" A few words describing his injury, then, "What about that boat ride we were going to take? I haven't been in my skiff for a month. Let me know…" he smiled, feeling like it must look fake, staring into the vyne like an idiot. But better to smile than not, he knew.

"So who is Valentina?" asked his mom, having overheard him send the message.

"Oh, just a friend," he demurred.

"Sounds like more than just a friend," she pressed on.

He looked at his mother, and knew she meant well. "I'd be glad if she was, but she isn't yet," he admitted.

"I hope it works out for you honey," she said sweetly, and came over and gave him a kiss on the top of his head. Neither noticed that this was the exact same gesture of affection she routinely used to make to his father.

27.

'mon!" Emmy stood in the doorway, arms folded, glaring at Eric as he slowly rose from the table where he was trying to finish reading the chapter profiling arsonist psychology.

"Coming..." he said absently, still standing with the open book in his hand, not understanding that she wanted to leave NOW.

Emmy stamped her foot and walked over and grabbed the book out of his hands, snapping it shut and slamming it to the desk. "Jeez! Eric! What're you doin'?!? Let's GO!!"

"Okay, okay, sorry!" he grabbed the book and threw it into his pack. They hit the Panhandle brilliantly illuminated by late afternoon sunshine. Eric felt both humiliated and frustrated, sitting on the back of the tandem recumbent, customized to Emmy's great height. Her lanky torso hid big knobby knees pumping in front, while Eric pedaled in unison, letting his vision stray from side to side while she steered. The place was full of small groups of picnickers, game players, elderly men and women on benches, discs soaring through the air, a folk jam under a big cypress tree. The orange light gave everything a healthy glow.

He looked at the back of Emmy's impossibly long neck. *She's sure crabby! What the hell did I do? I was just reading!* He sunk into a funk of victimization. He was confused by her irritation where previously she'd been tolerant and easy going.

"Can you hear it?" Emmy called over her shoulder.

"What?"

"Listen!"

The strains of the folkies disappeared well behind them as he tuned in to a deep rhythmic throbbing.

"The drums?"

"Yeah! Let's go!"

"You're driving," he said.

She turned left as they entered Golden Gate Park from the Panhandle, bumping over a maze of magnetic streetcar tracks. Swooping through a dense grove of low bushes, they came to a tunnel, a crumbling relic from centuries past. The fake stalactites hung from patches of broken chicken wire in the amber afternoon light. Dust swirled in beams of sunlight, giving the impression of riding into a dense fog of suspended material. They popped out the other side to face the warm orange orb. Blinded momentarily, Emmy slowed and veered to the right, avoiding noisy cyclists obliviously racing with the sun at their backs. The drumming was much louder now. Resuming speed, they made the turn across the meadow, and in full view before them a swirling mass of people whirled around the pounding drums.

They dismounted near a small field of bicycles. Two boys ran up, maybe 12 years old. "Hey, can we take a ride?"

"Sure, but don't be long, because we're heading to the beach, okay?" Emmy admonished.

"We'll stay close," said the tall skinny Chinese-looking kid. His pal grabbed the bike and tried to sit in front, but his feet couldn't reach the pedals, set up for Emmy's two-meter frame. The tall one playfully punched him on the shoulder, "outta my way shorty! You're in back." They laughed as they wobbled away.

Emmy turned towards the drumming circle, less circular than it appeared from the distance. She looked at Eric curiously, trying to gauge his interest. He was already tapping his foot and swaying to the contagious rhythm, so she smiled and began twirling into the middle of the throbbing scene.

Eric stood on the outer edge, not ready to lose himself in public dancing, but entranced by the pounding noise, his backbone vibrating sympathetically. He watched Emmy along with the eyes of dozens of strangers. She was wearing a bright orange, red and yellow dashiki wrapped around her columnar torso. The matching turban wrapped around her head added an extra few inches to her height so she towered over the rest of the dancers and drummers. Her blackness devoured the orange sunlight in contrast to her garment, which almost seemed on fire by comparison. Her luminous eyes and flashing white teeth charismatically lured an extra dozen people into the dance circle, but Eric held back, just too self-conscious. Like the rest, he was transfixed by the inspirational whirling dervish that he tentatively thought of as his girlfriend.

Different drummers were seizing the lead, sometimes competing in hilarious head-on confrontations, one frenzy of intricate rhythms topped by the next and then back again. Many of the best drummers looked to be from the Caribbean, Brazil, or Africa, although it was hard to be sure where anyone was from anymore. As he looked around, Eric was surprised to see three old Chinese ladies pounding their own battery of djembes, a grizzled Filipino elder tapping a discarded metal piece of unknown machinery, a few young white hippie chicks putting down a mean beat, and off to the side, a latin percussion section of snares, timbali, bells, shakers, and all manner of extra sounds. He was grinning like a fool, catching the spirit from the smiling drummers, suffused in the dense pleasure of a house of sound with so many rooms that he could never finish exploring them.

Back in the center of the circular mob, Emmy had attracted a coterie of worshippers, who now danced around her, frothing with sweat, trying to move their bodies to the impossibly fast beat as it reached crescendo. Suddenly, in what always seems like magic to those not attuned to the hidden signals, most of the drummers stopped, leaving two maestros to knit a duet of somber syncopation. The dancers were lost in midair like cartoon characters who had walked off cliffs. Some of them played with the predicament, swirling downward in clever transitions to the newly slowed beat, while others just threw up their hands in resignation, having offered their inner souls to the rhythm and were now left high and dry by the impossibility of actually merging with the noise. Smiles and laughter, hugs and kisses. People moved back to sit down, others stood ready for the next upsurge.

Emmy came over to Eric, through the slapping hands and kisses and hugs of her new acolytes, laughing through the sweat dripping down her beautiful face. She grabbed Eric's shirt before he could say a word and ducked her face into it, turning it in to an impromptu towel.

"Hey! Hey!" he tried half-heartedly to pull back but she silenced him with a big sweaty kiss, her long arms pulling him against her steaming body. His senses filled with the sheer animal magnetism of Emmy's physicality. They merged into a deep hug, squeezing away the irritability of the previous hour, turning eventually to face the setting sun through the trees before it disappeared completely behind the hill. The drumming had surged again while they kissed, he now noticed, realizing that his heart and breathing had aligned with the steady rhythm to the point that it didn't seem outside any more.

They walked arm-in-arm through the friendly but envious glances of many of the men and women towards the bike parking area. Not seeing their recumbent, Emmy walked up Hippie Hill and stood with her hands on her hips, looking around like a hunter in search of prey. "Where are those damn kids?"

"I knew we shouldn't let them take it!" he said, for which she shot a stabbing glance at him.

"That helps!"

He shrugged, looking at the ground as self-loathing automatically rose inside, kicking himself for breaking the moment with yet another stupid comment.

"Here they come!" she announced, pointing to the path emerging from distant bushes. Sure enough the two boys were pedaling furiously as dusk was falling, and as they drew near, the bigger one in front called "We can't stop!" laughing hysterically. Emmy looked at them approaching the hill with maternal disapproval, waiting for their little joke to end. They shot off the path and straight up the hill, scattering several people from comfortable perches. The momentum finally broke and it seemed that they hadn't been joking... they didn't know how to stop. As the tandem vehicle rolled to a stop, they fell over sideways, trying to catch themselves, but instead ending in a tangled pile halfway up the hill. No harm done to boys or bike, everyone had a laugh.

Emmy and Eric remounted, and slid forward onto the path, determined to enjoy the balmy evening at her friends' beach bonfire and cookout. With wine and fresh bread from the Page Mews solar oven in the back basket, they turned towards the fading purple and magenta sky, rolling through Golden Gate Park's thickening darkness.

Behind Hippie Hill they pedaled onto Kennedy Drive, a wide, relatively straight veloway alongside a streetcar track. The Arboretum crew had landscaped the entire area, each successive zone having its own distinctive flora from a different part of the world, somehow all adapted to the often cold and foggy park. The ancient Conservatory of Flowers gleamed luminescently, its delicate wooden frames and old windows still holding the tropical air inside where some plants had thrived for more than two hundred years.

Loud whirring and clicking approached from behind. "Hey, what's twirlin'?" said William Grayson, smiling through the gloom. He wasn't alone. An unfamiliar woman and Gerald and Angie pedaled along. "This is my friend Frieda," he gestured to the curly-haired stocky blonde, who smiled and gave a little wave.

"Gerald, what are you—? Did Angie drag you out here?" Eric teased good-naturedly. He'd come to know that Gerald was pretty lazy and not much of an initiator.

Angie broke in, "I told him he needed the fresh air for his sinusitis," and she winked broadly.

"My doctor!" Gerald sang in mock admiration, followed by a noisy inhalation and a big spit.

"That's disgusting!" Angie slapped him on the back. "You don't have to do that ... it doesn't help, and it's SO gross!"

"You guys heading to the bonfire?" asked William.

"Yup, just took a little detour to the drumming, but we're heading there now," said Emmy.

They all fell in to a steady rhythm, covering the dark miles to the beach. The temperature dropped noticeably as soon as the sun set. William and Frieda regaled them with tales of fighting the San Bruno Mountain fire. Eric strained to hear details, listening for clues that might help his investigation.

"Apparently it started on the roof of a waterbound warehouse, and then leaped to some foliage on the cliff nearby," explained William.

"Leaped?! How does it do that?" asked Gerald.

Frieda elaborated: "I'm not sure. Someone said it may have been some piece of flaming shingle that the wind caught and carried ten meters where it hit the dry bushes. It sure looked like that, 'cause the cliff was black when we got there, and the fire was already racing towards the mountain. My crew was sent to hold the firebreak along the southeast side. We almost lost it," she stopped to catch her breath as they all kept pedaling.

"Was anyone hurt?" asked Angie.

"Nothing serious," answered William, "luckily! Three houses burned, but everyone was out before that happened. I think there were a few minor injuries among firefighters, cuts and bruises. One guy with an oxygen mask was lying on a stretcher, but I was told that he'd just had too much smoke. He looked okay later when I saw him walking around."

"Did you hear how it started?" asked Eric.

"Everyone was saying someone had set it on the roof of that warehouse, but I don't know how they knew."

The cyclists fell silent, and soon spread out, making further conversation difficult. Emmy asked Eric over her shoulder, "aren't you going to go out there and look around?"

"I think Kathy and Robin already went to the site the day after the fire. We're going over evidence tomorrow. I've been assigned to read up on arsonists," he paused, remembering the spat over the book before they got rolling. "I guess there must be reason to suspect the fire was set on purpose."

Emmy ducked down as they suddenly accelerated. "Let's go, man, it's the last hill to the ocean!" They emerged from the park's dark trees into an endless sea of sand. The path curved ahead into the dunes, where the old asphalt was starting to disappear under drifting sand. Before too long they came upon their companions who had reached the end of the road moments earlier.

"Guess this is it!" said Gerald, already dismounted and slinging his pack over his shoulder. He grabbed a small sack of sticks and logs he'd brought along.

"Y'know, that's not going to last more than 15 minutes!" Angie admonished.

"It's better than not bringing anything. I'm sure Mark and Jeff thought about bringing enough wood before they invited us all to come."

"C'mon you guys, give it a rest!" William scolded.

Bright moonlight was already hitting the ocean. A whale breached, visible against the horizon. They all oohed and aahed, suffused in silver light and the distant crash of surf. Everything arranged, they trekked through the dunes towards the beach, still a good half hour west. Small fires twinkled along the shoreline in the distance, but their walk took them into a depression, dunes towering all around. The apparent flatness of the walk proved entirely illusory, as they found themselves ascending and descending, laboring against the loose sand. Finally they could make out dark figures around big bonfires, salt spray and sand hitting them as they left the dunes behind.

"Hey, look who's here!" yelled someone at the bonfire as they approached. A surge of excitement passed through the two dozen faces, happy to have their ranks augmented by six more. Eric only knew the folks he'd arrived with, but Emmy seemed to know everyone. The organizers, Mark and Jeff, lived in the Castro, and at least half the gang were queers. Emmy had gotten to know Mark and Jeff during a stint working together at a tire manufacture in South San Francisco, where Jeff was an Apprentice.

The fire roared, piled high with wood taken from an old deck Mark and Jeff had recently demolished, and also from a tree that had fallen in the backyard of another guy there, Gustavo. A horse-drawn cart had brought it out here, borrowed from the stables in the park. The horse, a huge beast, grazed contentedly on a big basket of hay a short distance away, the trailer parked near it.

"We've never pursued anything like this since *before*, and I think that's the way it should stay!" Gustavo was getting pretty heated. He passed a bottle of tequila along after taking some big gulps. He had a long handlebar mustache and very thick gray eyebrows, long gray-black hair parted in the middle, held in place by a bandana around his head.

"Gustavo, you don't know anything about it!" said his companion, an androgynous, smooth-skinned man with Asian features. "Science has been bottled up for decades by the Die-off. We've got to move forward."

"Francis, you are just parroting the line of the scientific establishment, and you know it!" argued an old round-faced Filipino, eyes flashing through his wrinkles. He shook his head as he reached for the tequila, while people close to him all waited respectfully. After a big gulp, he resumed, "The Die-off happened because science wasn't controlled by society. If you have a good argument about a specific experiment I suggest you stick to that. Because science cannot justify itself. You have to explain what you want to do, why, who benefits. What will it do to our daily lives and local ecology? Without social evaluation, science easily becomes a monster," he wiped his mouth and grunted, "or at least it leads to the creation of monsters!"

Murmurs of agreement rumbled around, with a few notable exceptions. Francis, frowning, tried to organize his response, but before he could rise to the moment, a loud screech erupted outside the fire's ring. William had pulled a burning crate out of the fire, and having attached a long chain to it, he began spinning it around in the air, sparks flying off in every direction. Several people danced in and out of the perimeter of his hazardous game, daringly ducking under the flying fire in a strange impromptu limbo.

The night wore on, conversations and debates ebbing and flowing. Eric and Emmy curled up in each other's arms in front of the fire, mesmerized by the blaze, lost in private thoughts and the warmth of each other's touch. The alcoholic haze of tequila eventually reduced the quality of debate, leaving raging social arguments as unresolved as they'd been at the evening's start.

"Shall we go?" whispered Eric, feeling drowsy, and not at all enthused about the long walk back to the bike, and then the long ride back home.

"Unless you want to sleep here," Emmy mumbled, half-asleep.

"It's too cold," he said, becoming more alert at the prospect of an imminent departure.

"I'm not cold," she answered, curling up a little tighter in his arms. He smiled, enjoying her pleasure at cocooning. He leaned over and whispered in her ear. "I love you," which served as an electric jolt. Her eyes opened, suddenly awake. When she looked at him, he was smiling just enough to make his declaration suspect.

"Really?"

He nodded, and pulled her to his mouth, disappearing into a long, lingering kiss. Her hand covered the back of his head, warming his cold scalp. "Shall we go?" he asked again, and she nodded sweetly, already looking forward to their warm bed waiting at home.

28.

Valentina jumped off the streetcar at Mission and 22nd Street. The Mission was not her territory, so it took a moment to get her bearings, Bernal Heights to the south, Twin Peaks west. A worn grassy field occupied 22nd Street west towards Valencia, where young boys and girls chased a soccer ball. She crossed Mission, hopping over streetcar tracks and weaving in and out of bicycle traffic.

On the corner facing the intersection beckoned Joyce's Nzyme Station, a boisterous neighborhood bar. She elbowed her way to the counter, where a lithe young man with long wavy brown hair and a scruffy beard eventually turned to her. "What'll it be?"

"An orange/papaya smoothie with skincleer and thikhair, okay?"

"Comin' up." He flashed a winning smile, perfect white teeth between his black beard and mustache, his earring catching the light as spun around and set to work.

In the crush Valentina was jostled. "Excuse *me*!" she said irritably, turning to a woman in soiled work clothes, shoving back to keep her place.

"Hey, don't mind me," laughed the woman, dirty blonde hair pouring out from her blue bandana, practically covering her eyes. She squinted at Valentina through hair and sweat. "Aren't you…?" she paused, wagging her finger.

Valentina didn't like the attention this smelly woman was paying her, and felt very claustrophobic.

"I know! You're a *Panduccino*, aren't you?" The woman practically shouted the word.

Valentina winced at the unwanted attention. She looked at her impassively. "Do I know you?"

"Valentina right? Can't place me, huh? Well… I guess I do look sorta different," and with that she burst out again in her big, look-at-me laugh, shaking her dirty hair around. "I'm Evelyn McCauliffe, I lived at the Pierce Palace until about seven years ago—remember?"

Valentina couldn't place this odd woman, medium height, square shoulders, small-ish head, and that cascading mop which she was unsuccessfully trying to control with the bandana.

Evelyn peered at her, waiting for a glimmer of recognition. "Gimme an AgeBlocker Special!" she bellowed at the bartender when he delivered Valentina's smoothie. Wheeling on Valentina, who was sipping her drink, she launched in again. "You were a lot smaller then. Loved the swings—and you were up in that big n'oak a lot, remember?"

Valentina nodded, trying to summon anything about this woman, drawing a blank.

"I know! That time you got stuck in the tree, trying to get your kitty, and you climbed almost to the top. You were, what, maybe 4? We had to rescue you… Don't tell me you've forgotten that?"

Valentina hadn't forgotten. She'd clung to the branches for dear life, crying, furious that getting down was so much less obvious than going up. "Aaaah yeah, now, okay… you're the one who shinnied up and took me down." Now she saw the waif-like teenager at the time.

"I thought you were going to bite me."

Valentina ventured a friendly smile and sipped her drink. Evelyn's AgeBlocker

Special arrived and she began inhaling it through a straw. "Yow! Love that rush! … So," she shuddered as the powder did its trick, "whatcha doin' 'round here?"

"Meeting a friend over on Harrison in the Rose bushes." She blushed at the innuendo, which Evelyn ran with.

"Oohh! In the *rose* bushes," and she winked theatrically, even nudging Valentina with her elbow.

Valentina shot her an arch glance, replacing her embarrassment with diffidence, and emptied her drink. "Well, gotta go. Nice to see ya, Evelyn." She was already on her feet.

"Still at the Palace?"

"Yup," she called over her shoulder, then turned around, backing away, "You?"

"I'm at Creekside Commons on upper Precita Creek."

Back on Mission, a faint shudder escaped Valentina's shoulders as she remembered how creepy Evelyn was. In five minutes she passed through the curving green oasis of Parqué Niños Juntos on the way to Harrison. The park gave way at the Harrison entrance to dense rose bushes lining the old veloway. Staying out of the cyclists' way, she scooted under small trees and among the bushes.

A "Hey" startled her, seeming to come out of nowhere. To her left she observed Nwin leaning against a fence behind a row of roses.

"C'mere," he waved her over. She reached his spot where he now squatted before a cluster of perfect roses, in a stunning pattern of yellow, orange and scarlet. He picked one as he stood up and presented it to her with a flourish. As their eyes met they darted away and down. They couldn't look at each other directly.

"Was it hard to find me here?"

"No, no, it was easy!" she reassured him as they both turned halfway to look at anything but each other. She attached the rose to her lapel.

Nwin looked back at her as she fondled a rose still on the bush. She was tall with wavy reddish brown hair, her waist shaped by a leather tunic with red velvet lapels. Red batik pants hung loosely to mid-calf above brown leather boots, and a red neckerchief set off her electrifying green eyes. He looked at his own clothes, filthy after an afternoon in the garden. "Hey, lemme take a quick shower and change over at my Auntie's." He pointed past the corner.

She frowned and said nothing. He ran ahead, his lanky frame ambling like a giraffe. His huge feet flapped, reminding Valentina of a clown. His torn light blue workshirt was stained with grass and mud, his pockets bulging with tools and materials. Sweat flew from his two-tone hair. It had grown out a few inches since he'd bleached it blonde. She quickened her pace, but he soon vanished into the trees ahead. She turned the corner in time to see him disappear into the curving Atlas Stair Building.

She approached the porch, stopped by the powerful smell of cigar pouring through the door. She leaned against the post at the top of the stairs and waited. After only a minute or so, Auntie emerged from the smoky gloom inside.

"Hmmphf…you da girl?"

Valentina stood up straight at this blunt question.

"You come wit' Nwin?" Auntie persisted.

Valentina nodded, "I'm Valentina, how's it twirlin'?" extending her hand for a slap that didn't come.

Auntie was noticeably put off by such familiarity. But it wasn't her style to respond directly. She shrugged and lowered herself into a porch chair, exhaling loudly as she landed.

"I'm sorry, what was your name?" asked Valentina.

"Jus' call me Auntie." She took a big puff on her cigar.

"So you're Nwin's aunt?"

"Nope... his ma is my cuz..." she wheezed, "but everybody calls me 'Auntie'. ... Where do you live honey?"

"Pierce Palace."

"Oh." Auntie raised her eyebrows, and Valentina braced herself. "You a Panduccino?"

Valentina nodded silently, looking out at the lane in front of the house.

"Tha's a great t'ing! You should be proud!"

She continued nodding, dreading having to say anything on the subject. Thankfully, Nwin reappeared, a towel on his head, his muscled chest and long dark torso exposed to her gaze. Valentina felt a minor earthquake in her chest, a strange queasiness starting in her stomach.

"Hi again!" he said, cheerfully smiling through wet cheeks, "hope I didn't make you wait too long."

"No problem." She let go of her earlier annoyance, relieved to be rescued from the forced conversation with Auntie.

"It's going to be an amazing sunset," said Nwin. "Auntie, we're going out for a little ride on the Bay. I'll see you tomorrow, or maybe day after, okay?" He planted a kiss on her forehead and said "let's go," before Auntie could say a thing.

Nwin took Valentina's hand, grabbed a jacket and blanket he had near the door, and they clattered down the stairs. They made small talk as they walked briskly along Harrison towards The Willows where Nwin had left his skiff.

"Been on the Bay much?" asked Nwin as they made their way to The Willows' small dock on Mission Creek.

"Yeah, some. But mostly on ferries."

"There's some dewy stuff out there, you'll see!"

Valentina looked Nwin over while he stiffly climbed down into his skiff.

"Hey, Nwin," she started as she took his hand, "what do you think about the Garden Party?" She gave him a sidelong glance, but he stared straight ahead.

"I'm a gardener, as you can see." He spread his calloused hands. "But I think the Party types are kind of weird. What about you?"

"Weird? 'Weird' doesn't mean anything. Not to me, anyway."

He pursed his lips, feeling an attack, and retreated into his inscrutable mode for a long couple of minutes. They maneuvered into the water traffic on the wider Mission Creek, leaving behind the colorful lights strung over The Willows dock. He steered through several gondolas, the preferred craft on Mission Creek.

"Like the gondola!" he suddenly blurted.

"Huh?"

"Did you know it used to be impossible to bring a bioskiff on Mission Creek?" She shook her head.

"See, it's the traditional gondoliers, they're like the Garden Party leaders, they all want to impose their version of what's best. I guess I think you have to leave room for new things, for changes. The Gardeners say everyone should have a daily relationship with the land. But not everyone wants to!"

"Exactly!"

"So that's what I mean. They're 'weird' because they think theirs is the only way."

"Or at least the *best* way."

He nodded, relaxing. This kind of conversation was rare enough with anyone, let alone a girl he liked.

He pointed out the earthen berm alongside the Rice Bowl paddies. "Haven't been there lately."

"Really? Because of your back?"

"Yeah, the doc said I had to stop working close to the ground. In the roses I don't have to stoop down all day. It's only a few hours a day and it's easy. Auntie has the whole Harrison Rose Garden under control."

They skimmed along next to the UC campus, its gray and peach colored buildings piled up like blocks in the water. Valentina looked up at a glassy façade and leaned on her elbow. "Been in there?" she asked.

"Yeah, sure, haven't you?"

"I've gone through it once or twice, but I didn't like it."

"Why not?"

"They're all so self-important! And busy! So many people so focused on work!"

"So? Maybe they like being there."

"I bet they do. But they're scientists! Who knows what kind of ruin they're up to?"

Nwin smiled as he steered the skiff out into the open Bay, the train depot to their left, columnar palms marching up Rincon Hill behind it. Treasure Island loomed in the Bay, screams echoing from the roller coaster whipping around the island. "So you think science is bad?"

"Of course not!" she folded her arms with a pout. "But I don't trust those lab jockeys, that's for sure!"

He turned past Potrero Hill's outermost point into Islais Cove. "I'm with you on that. I don't see why they're not spending more time undoing the mess that's still out here."

She looked at him momentarily before shifting her gaze to the cascading terraces on the corner of Potrero Hill. A water slide connected a swimming pool with a lower one, kids squealing in delight as they thundered down. Pot patches filled some of the terraces, coffee trees others, green gardens the rest. Straw hats bobbed among dense foliage all over the hill. At the summit a sprawling compound dominated the horizon, under an elaborate sign of intricately trained vines spelling out P-O-T-H-I-L-L P-L-A-T-Z. A giant shimmering golden glass of beer stood in the middle of the sign, small bits of shiny paper creating the illusion of liquid.

"What mess?"

"You know," he gestured to and fro, "all the crap still sitting in the water. How long has it been since inundation, 40–50-years? And all these buildings still sitting in the Bay."

"Hmm. Never thought about it... What should we do about it?"

"Take 'em down," he said emphatically. "It's not natural, leaving all these buildings half-submerged. It's bad for fish and wildlife. Restore the Bay!"

Valentina had worked with the Baykeepers when she was a little kid. They had shown how partially submerged houses had become refuges for squid and octopus. Roofs had been taken over by breeding seals, the underwater wreckage had become new habitat for species making comebacks.

"Well… it's actually a mixed bag," she ventured cautiously. "Plenty of species have thrived in those ruins."

"Chingale! Those buildings should be destroyed!" His voice shook with defensive anger, and Valentina, hearing it, decided to drop the subject.

Standing now, Nwin steered *Hot 1* through crumbling towers in the old Hunters' Point waters beneath an observation tower rising out of The Lodge. He stayed out in the Bay, avoiding the old canal that snuck behind the hill to Yosemite Creek. "I would expect you to agree," he said matter-of-factly.

"Huh?"

"Because of your background… everyone knows the Panduccinos were big revolutionaries… aren't you carrying on the family tradition?"

"Chingado!" she glared, eyes blazing, nostrils flaring, blushing with rage. "My great-grandmother and my grandma did what they did. They're who they are…" implying her own independence but leaving it unspoken.

"Whoa! okay, okay,… sorry!" he fell silent. The skiff was bounding southward over choppy waters.

"Where are we going? How long until we're back?" she complained, thoroughly aggravated at the turn of events.

"Up there," he pointed, to the blackened cliff in Guadalupe Canyon under San Bruno Mountain, just coming into clear view.

"What's that? Oh," she realized, "that big fire?"

He nodded without comment. They entered the mouth of the canyon, water lapping at the sides about a quarter mile across. Docks bobbed on the waves with staircases leading up to sprawling complexes of interconnected housing and gardens. On the northeast ridge, sun glinted in the glass walls of a shimmering structure split into a dozen levels, a blue-ish glare occasionally blinding Nwin. They fell silent as he glided deeper into the sun-washed canyon, more and more debris floating as they approached the black cliffs ahead. Squawking parrots soared overhead, chased by gulls in search of food.

They flipped up to a broken concrete wall. Valentina stood up for a better view and observed the remains of a large building, concrete wall emerging from the water on two sides. Blackened sticks and small planks floated randomly in the former warehouse's interior. Bits of colored plastic, remains of old bottles and markers bobbed in the same waters.

"This is where it all started," Nwin said authoritatively.

"Yeah? Did you help with the fire crews?"

"Nah. I read about it."

She looked from the waterlogged ruin to the blackened cliff a dozen meters away. "How could the fire have started here and then crossed the water to there?"

"They think burning debris flew over on the heated air."

"Can we go up and have a look?" Now she was curious.

"I s'pose…" He maneuvered *Hot 1* towards a spot where they could ascend the charred slope. Looking around, everything was utterly unfamiliar. Sunshine highlighted small blades of green already emerging from the burned soil. The Bay water was downright grimy, the fire's detritus still littering the shoreline after a month. They scooted past the burned area and found a small dock amid dense bushes. Nwin looked at the remaining unburned warehouses still standing in the water. "See? Why isn't anyone taking this stuff down?"

Valentina didn't respond. Glad to be out of the boat, she bounded onto the dock as soon as they'd tied up. A light breeze rustled her loose red pants as she ran her hands through her hair. She pulled off her neckerchief and held it under a small stream pouring down the hillside. She wiped her face with the cool wet cloth, temporarily relieved from the sun's heat. Nwin stood opposite her on the dock, studying the stairs. Their polished, curving wood railings demonstrated the care of a longtime resident above; such craftsmanship took time and patience. Nwin shot her a cautious glance, nodding his head towards the stairs inquisitively. She shrugged and waved him ahead.

He was stiff after the boat ride. He started up the stairs and automatically reached for his lower back with one hand, and grabbed the railing with the other. His muscles throbbed tensely. Returning to the scene, no matter how alien it seemed now, was making him nervous. Also the ugly expanse of partially submerged warehouses littering the canyon angered him anew. And Valentina was irritated, loud and clear. He paused to look back at her, but she looked away and said nothing.

When they cleared the stairs, a bucolic wooden house appeared amidst a colorful garden of wildflowers, accented by a sprawling live n'oak tree that spread its arms around the rear. A blue hammock swayed, strung between the house's corner and the n'oak, but whoever was in it couldn't see them. They quietly walked towards the expanse of black where the fire had been. Two other ruins stood in the near part of the burn.

"Those must be the houses that were lost," Valentine ventured.

"I guess." Nwin was stunned by the devastating scene before him. Watching the fire as he'd sped away that morning, then reading the papers, he hadn't understood the extent and intensity of the damage. He was seeing it for the first time, weeks later and after nature had already begun tentatively to restore what he'd accidentally destroyed. This was not what he wanted, and a numbness set in as he refused responsibility.

They tiptoed through the first house, a blackened wreckage practically burned to the ground. Remains of the walls still stood, along with the frame of one window. Beyond the charred rubble rose a brick fireplace, black but intact. Nwin walked through it like a zombie, trying to shake a rising sense of guilt, still disbelieving that his fire had led to this. They emerged from the house to tromp through black ash and dried mud, practically a moonscape. He gazed ahead blankly, unable to speak. Valentina, too, was overwhelmed by the desolate landscape, broken only by the occasional green shoot sprouting in the ruins. Bones of small mammals—mice, squirrels, possum, raccoons—were strewn about, already picked clean by scavengers, airborne and roaming the mountain.

Valentina noticed her brown boots were black with ash and mud. They would take a serious cleaning to regain their luster. Nwin suggested they turn back.

"Not much to see here I guess," he said neutrally.

"Whaddya mean?! This is amazing!"

"We're getting covered with this shit. Let's go," he said with more urgency. She offered no further resistance. They got to the stairway where a gravelly voice hailed them.

"Hey! What're you doin'?"

Nwin spun around, a kid with his hand in the cookie jar, which Valentina found odd. "Uhh, we're just having a look... 'zat OK?"

A grizzled fellow with long scraggly blond hair, in blue jeans and jean jacket, approached them briskly. "What a disaster, eh?" he said, in full view.

"We're just leaving," Nwin fidgeted, uncomfortable, but unable to walk away. Valentina just watched.

The old hippie was upon them now. "I'm Jack Weatherly, this is my place. I guess you came up my stairway, eh?"

"Yeah, it's a beaut!" said Valentina, and introduced herself. Nwin followed suit, mumbling, which caused the man to ask for a repeat.

"Nwin Robertson," he said more clearly, head swinging back and forth, avoiding eye contact with Weatherly.

"Were you here during the blaze?" he asked.

"Uhhh," Nwin hesitated, "no... no we weren't."

Valentina felt his discomfort and grabbed him by the arm, pulling and saying, "I gotta get back." She turned to Weatherly, "My parents are expecting me."

"You guys live in the city?" Weatherly squinted at them.

They nodded in unison, Valentina saying "the Haight," to which Weatherly nodded.

"Have a safe trip home," he urged, and they slapped hands, taking leave. In a few minutes they were flipping back past the burned-out warehouse again, Nwin glancing at it and steering his skiff towards the mouth of the canyon.

"What was that all about?" Valentina asked.

"Huh? Whaddya mean?"

"You seemed real nervous. Or maybe I was hallucinating."

"I don't know. I just wanted to leave."

"All of a sudden you seemed uncomfortable."

Nwin started to say something, but nothing came out. They entered Bay traffic, sun still glimmering in the little waves as they pointed north. Laughter peeled in the distance from a hilltop household where a small group enjoyed a late afternoon party. Music grew louder from behind; a peapod ferry loomed on their flank, piping a popular tune over the water. Valentina sat glumly in Hot 1, while Nwin stood over her, busily piloting.

"I can't believe you'd act so weird, and then act like you didn't!" Valentina complained.

"Whaddya mean, 'weird'?" he responded tightly, returning to their earlier theme.

"Chingale! You acted like you'd been caught red-handed by that guy. Until then, you were... If I didn't know better I'd think you knew more about this . . ."

He felt trapped and clenched his jaw. She folded her arms and gazed blankly at the passing ferry, fury rising. His back was throbbing again, and he tried to sit down, sending a sharp pain down his right leg. "Aaagh!"

"Your back?" she asked, without sympathy.

He resumed standing and nodded.

"Look Valentina..." He wanted to tell her but couldn't. "Listen..."

She sat there, immobile, arms folded, staring at him coldly.

"I'm all ears."

"OK, well, I saw the fire."

"Really? You were way out here at—what time?"

He nodded. "Six o'clock. Early."

"What were you doing?"

"Just riding around. I do that a lot, I like cruising in the dark. I'll take you out some time."

She ignored his invitation. "So you happened to be cruising by, and happened to see the fire?"

He nodded.

"And what did you see?"

"Well, there was some kind of explosion in that warehouse and flames leaped from it. I was out on the Bay and didn't see the fire go up the hill."

She watched his eyes flick back and forth as they remained fixed in the distance. His nervousness was palpable. The more she thought about it, the less sense it made. Why would he be cruising by before dawn, so far south, right when a big fire erupted spontaneously in the water?

Nwin repeated himself about seeing the explosion in the distance, elaborating on the colors of the flames casting wild shadows on the canyon walls. After a second time through the same story, with a few more details, he fell silent, noticing that she was no longer asking questions.

"We heading back to the 7th St. dock?" she asked.

"We could. Is that where you want to go?"

"Actually I'd prefer it if you could let me off at Union Square. I'm meeting a friend for dinner downtown.

"Okay." His lips pursed again, in a surge of jealousy. "Who you meeting?" he tossed off, trying to sound indifferent.

"My friend, Francis."

Was that a guy? How could he ask, without being obvious? He stewed in his thoughts, while she took in the traffic filling the canals ahead.

A small parade of wildly decorated boats appeared from the mouth of the Battery Canal, stopping the rest of the traffic. A funeral procession. And in fine San Francisco style, a floating wake. The revelers followed a large portrait of the deceased, an old photo of a young, mustachioed *cholo*, his thick black hair combed into a grand pompadour, a white studded shirt revealing a hairy chest, gold chains around his neck. A brass band played a funeral dirge, incongruously jubilant, while another barge was full of mourners more intent on drinking to the setting sun than on mourning. Colored flags flapped in the late afternoon wind as dozens of watercraft bobbed quietly, waiting for the procession to pass.

Not long after, they maneuvered quietly through the throngs to the Union Square dock. Nwin didn't plan to linger, so he held the skiff alongside the landing while Valentina climbed ashore.

"Thanks for the tour," she said formally. "I enjoyed it."

His heart sank, realizing this was a bad ending.

"I'll vyne you OK? Let's do a tree climb or something?"

"Yeah, sure," she responded perfunctorily. "You know where I am." With that she hurried off, her boots flaking dried mud and her red batik pants pressed against her legs as she walked into the evening breeze. As Nwin watched her disappear he felt confused and defeated. Slamming a fist into his palm, he pointed *Hot 1* towards the Pyramid, forgetting he no longer lived there. After entering the residential dock in a dazed autopilot state, furiously reliving the past few hours with Valentina, he remembered that home was back on Bernal Heights. No one recognized him as he pulled back into traffic, fighting his way through the dinner time bustle into open water.

29.

Robin, Stella and Eric sat around a table in the main conference room. Outside the air was hazy, the afternoon sunshine glaring over the Civic Green's buzz of activity. Bike horns and streetcar bells sounded intermittently, and a string quartet was tuning up for an afternoon recital. Eric was drowsy after a long morning poring over old arson investigations as he had been doing for more than a week.

"So let's go over what we have," Robin led the discussion. "Stella, you have a partially burnt plastic bucket?"

"We found three actually. Two were burnt down to the bottom, more or less black molten plastic. One was slumped over the cement window jam where it apparently had been set. The divers found the others under two meters of water. One must've been knocked into the water by the first explosion. We got the whole bucket with a flare and clock still attached to the top." Stella paused, fiddling with a garland of woven grasses and flowers in her long brown hair. She wore a green denim jacket over an embroidered full length cotton dress, her ample girth minimized by its loose fit.

"Any witnesses?"

"No one who lives in the area saw anything. Kathy and Pops talked to all the neighbors. They got a lot of reports about people coming to see the burn area in the days following the fire. But no one noticed anyone they thought might have been the arsonist."

"What about Andy's account?"

"Sure. Eric, you got that. Anything useful?"

Shaking off the sleepiness hanging around his temples, he sat up and cleared his throat.

"Andy was on the 5:40 peapod out of Oyster Point. He says he was sitting near the aisle when a big explosion erupted at the back of Guadalupe Canyon under San Bruno Mountain. Along with the rest of the passengers, he jumped up to get a better view, but because there were others in front of him, he looped back to the stern to get a better view. As he emerged on the rear deck, he noticed a skiff floating not far from the rear of the ferry."

"How far?"

"He wasn't sure, guessed maybe 100 meters at most. Anyway, it was before dawn when this happened, so visibility was poor. He described looking back and forth from the fire to the skiff. He is certain that the person in the skiff was involved because he'd seen it minutes earlier speeding away from the site of the explosion."

"Pure speculation," scoffed Stella. "He didn't keep eye contact with the skiff throughout, did he?" Eric shook his head. "Well, his 'certainty' is worthless, so let's forget that. Did he get a description of the person on the skiff? That might be helpful."

"Nope. It was dark and he couldn't make out anything distinctly. He reported a large figure standing at one point, but most of the time he couldn't see anyone. He guessed whoever it was had been lying down in the boat."

"That's odd. Why would anyone do that?" questioned Robin.

"I don't think we're going to get anywhere with this," Stella insisted with the authority of her experience. "What do we know? There were three plastic buckets. One of them survived intact, full of gasoline with an electrical timer attached to the top. We have to pursue this evidence. Eric, you go to fuel distributors and see if anyone remembers anything unusual. Robin, the arsonist had to make the timers, probably in a community workshop. Will you vyne the workshops with questions?"

Robin nodded, chewing on her knuckle and jotting some notes down. "This is like looking for a clam in the Bay…" Her black hair glistened in tightly shaped curls, practically a helmet. She looked up suddenly, eyes sparkling behind her blue-rimmed glasses. "Gasoline! Eric—while you're investigating the dispensaries, why don't you also check local hospitals for any admittances that were associated with gasoline, fire burns, that kind of thing? Maybe our culprit got hurt?"

"Good idea, Robin!" admired Stella.

"Can I do it by vyne?" Eric despaired in the face of what seemed an overwhelming job.

"Go ahead and vyne 'em first. If something comes back, you'll probably have to go in person," Stella advised.

"I'm leaving after this weekend for a month," Robin reminded her associates. "So you'll have to finish this up without me. I'll get the workshop inquiry underway by tomorrow, but I doubt anything will come of it immediately. I'll have them answer to you, Eric, okay?" He nodded, not knowing how to say no, but a panicky feeling was rising.

"Ummm, uhh, I… I…"

"What's the problem? You need some help figuring out where to start?" Stella could see Eric starting to wilt under the pressure.

He nodded gratefully, catching himself as he was sinking into his chair. "I've only been in San Francisco—" he paused, sweat beading on his brow, wracked with discomfort. "I don't know… *how or where* gasoline is distributed. Nor do I know where the hospitals are. Is it all on the vyne?"

"Robin," Stella took charge, "before you take off, you've got to help Eric. He's just a Tryout and you're the Apprentice." She reached over to pat Eric's arm. "He's a smart guy, but you can't expect him to suddenly know how to conduct a complicated investigation. The whole idea of his being on our team was to train him, remember?"

"Eric, let's get together first thing tomorrow morning, say 10 a.m., okay?" Robin straightened her papers and stood up, her trim athleticism clear to see through her snug cotton top and jeans. "I've got leave early today to finish up some last minute stuff for the wedding." She grinned, her mind clearly more involved with her imminent betrothal than the investigation before them. The meeting broke up, Robin bolting from the room.

Stella sighed, and then chuckled. "What a love bird!… You see how smart she is. She's a great brainstormer. But she's too distracted now."

Eric smiled grimly. "Are we on a deadline?"

Stella shook her head. "Not really. But frankly, this arsonist could strike again, so we've got to find him or her before another catastrophe. In this dry period everything is more prone to burn."

He nodded glumly and turned to leave.

"Eric?"

He turned back to Stella.

"Don't worry. You'll do fine. Start with the vyne. You can find basic info there: fuel dispensaries, hospitals, all that. But the gasoline story is more complicated. The dispensaries you talk to will not know a thing. There are only a few, and they're very above board and keep good records. The gasoline our arsonist used is very unlikely to have come from them."

"Then where?"

"There's some small shops in town that deal in unregulated supplies... gasoline, fireworks, poisons, solvents, that kind of thing..."

"You think it came from one of them?"

"I'd bet on it. So make your inquiries with the dispensaries and then we'll move on to the remnant dealers."

"Remnant?"

"Yeah, that's what we call 'em. They distribute old supplies that someone has discovered and brought to town... from abandoned gas stations or old farm stores in distant rural areas where everyone died."

Eric shook his head, taken aback anew. He'd never heard about such things. "I'll get started, and then you can point me in the right direction, okay?"

"Sure!" Stella waved. "Robin will give you some leads tomorrow, too."

Back at his desk, he sagged in the face of the tasks before him. He stared at the birds flying across the Civic Green, wishing he could spend his days soaring through the air. His stomach churned as he anxiously contemplated the work before him. But he knew he wouldn't—he couldn't—quit, not now. He wanted to solve the puzzle. There were only a few pieces visible so far, but he felt sure he could find the missing pieces and put it together.

On that surge of enthusiasm, he turned to the wall. "Vyne!" and it unrolled before him, the broad green leaf slowly flattening itself against the wall. A thin line drew a one-meter square box around the surface, and a small question mark appeared in the upper left hand corner. "List fuel distributors in San Francisco." A moment passed and then the dark green veins of the leaf began to pop up, forming letters and the list he sought. He grabbed a pad of paper and jotted down the five locations: three hardware stores, and two internal combustion shops. "Next!" and the leaf cleared, a flashing question mark reappearing. "List hospitals in San Francisco." Several dozen facilities appeared, including numbers of beds and specialty services. He noted the emergency room locations.

Might as well give it a try right now, he thought. "Display emergency room admittances for August 12, 2157." A long list began displaying, organized by time, showing entries to various hospitals from midnight the 12th until the 13th. Each line gave a name, time of admittance, hospital name, and preliminary diagnosis. He read down the list and found seven entries that were admitted with severe burns. He wrote them down. Then he remembered that the fire had taken place at around 5:30 or 6 a.m. so that eliminated the three that had been brought to the hospital between midnight and 2 a.m. The remaining four burn patients had been admitted in mid-morning, so he made plans to check each of them.

His office turned orange as the sun moved lower in the northwestern sky. He made more notes to follow up and decided to call it a day. He tidied his desk and grabbed some reports he still meant to finish reading, stuffed them into his pack and headed out. Walking down the hall he didn't notice anyone still working until he had almost reached the exit. Kathy Fairly was sitting at her desk and hailed him. "Eric, c'mere for a sec?"

"Stella tells me you've been given a very full plate." He nodded without comment. "Just remember, there are no deadlines, and you're learning as you go. No one expects you to make any huge breakthrough all by yourself. You can ask for a staff meeting whenever you want, and you can always come and get my help, too, ok?"

"Sure, thanks."

"On another topic, you coming up to Petaluma this weekend for the wedding?"

"I don't know anyone that well, so I wasn't sure…"

"Hmphf! I thought so. You must come! You want to ride up together?" She leaned back in her leather chair, folding her arms under her large bosom, her western shirt bulging open below her neck. Her wizened eyes stared at Eric expectantly.

Eric was surprised at Kathy's vigorous insistence. Before he could answer, Kathy reached into one of her many pockets and took out an old-fashioned gold watch on a long chain. "It's settled then!" She looked at her watch as though setting an alarm. "Let's meet at the North Beach dock at 10 a.m. Saturday morning, ok? You bringing anyone?"

"Uhhh, well, I think m- m- my girlfriend," he stuttered, still not accustomed to being able to make such a claim publicly.

"Great! What's her name?"

"Emmy, Emmy Ndbele Hodges."

The middle name caught Fairly's attention, and she raised her eyebrows. "African?"

"Huh?"

"That name, Endibeelee, it's an African name, isn't it?"

"Yeah, I'm sure it must be. But she's a San Franciscan."

"Hmm," Kathy made a mental note, "I like that name."

Eric began backing out. "I'll be in tomorrow morning. I'll check it out with Emmy about Saturday, and let you know, ok?"

"You're coming, don't try to get out of it!" Fairly laughed. "See you tomorrow."

* * *

Eric stepped in to the cool breeze rolling off the fog in the west. He went to the velome to grab a bike but before he could get there, he noticed that clusters of people were standing around the edges of the Green, all intently reading the evening headlines. He stepped up behind one group and was shocked to see the headline, "WAR!"

"In Chile!"

"—massacred 700 people…"

"Massive sit-in fired upon by mysterious soldiers."

It took a few minutes to get the gist of the story, but apparently a series of raids that had been plaguing outlying farms in Chile had been a precursor to a more organized effort to take power down there. Passive resistance had been futile when the raiders had shot hundreds, terrorizing the region. A general call-up was underway in larger cities in Chile, Bolivia, and Ecuador. Weapons had been seized by the rebels from two small armories in the Chilean towns of Ovalle and Illapel. Their numbers were estimated at less than 3,000.

"Three thousand soldiers with guns, ready to kill!" exclaimed one young man. "When was the last time something like this happened?" asked another. An old guy stood with his hands on his hips, shaking his head somberly. "'Ssss been a looong time," he whistled through a gap in his teeth. "The last armed rebellion? 50 years ago wasn't it?" he asked another old-timer across the circle. The woman shook her head, "no, it was 43 years ago, in the Philippines, remember the Huk revival?"

Eric stood there numb, uncomprehending. War was something in the history books, something from the barbaric times before the revolution, before the Die-off. He had only the dimmest sense that there had been any organized violence since then, not being a student of history. "W- wha- what do they want?" he asked innocently.

"They want to overthrow the Commons! They call themselves the Pinochet-Reagan Freedom Army!" the man guffawed. "That's going to go over well! I bet the Chileans are dying to go back to a military dictatorship!"

"This army isn't asking anybody what they want," said a woman soberly. "They must assume that no one is ready to fight them."

Eric walked away from the circle towards the velome, reeling with the news. *It just doesn't make sense! How can there be a war? What would make anyone take up arms to kill people? What did they imagine they would do if they succeeded?* And how would people stop them?

He walked into the velome in a daze, said hello to Tina, the regular mechanic there, and grabbed a Silver Fox.

"Hey, can you bring that one back tomorrow? I was just going to give it an overhaul," she called to him. He stopped and wheeled it back in.

He noticed a bamboo bike in the corner. "Can I take that, or is it someone's private bike?"

"Nope, go ahead. It was left here a few weeks ago, so . . ."

Outside, he mounted the wicker seat and began pedaling out of the Civic Green. The veloways were jammed with people in the early evening. The bamboo bike was so light, he felt like he was gliding on air. He wove in and out of traffic, and when he hit a clear patch with the hill ahead, he accelerated unconsciously until he was speeding up the hill faster than he ever had. Cresting the top he turned right through the iron gate to the Wiggle and before he knew it he had crossed Sans Souci Bridge and was passing the ice cream parlor at Rexroth and Haight. *This bike is amazing!* He'd forgotten how great the bamboo bike's ride was. He sped along, not crediting his own adrenaline rush for his remarkable speed, pedaling frantically as if he could escape the disturbing war news.

His mind raced faster than his legs until he surprised himself by arriving in the Page Mews backyard, unable to remember riding the last klick. He left the bike with the rest, walking briskly past the solar oven, the gardens and the hot tubs, spied upon by two boys high in the old n'oak tree, who couldn't stifle their giggles. He looked up just in time to step aside and avoid the acorns the boys were hurling at him. He shook his fist in mock anger, and ran indoors. Upstairs he ran into the room he shared with Emmy, startling her.

She sat by the window writing in her journal. "You look like you've seen a ghost or something!"

"It's war! Did you see the news?"

"Hard to fathom," she concluded. "Listen, Eric, I hope this isn't too terrible in terms of timing, but we need to make a change."

"What?" A raw panic surged up. "What's wrong?!?"

Emmy came over and put her arms around him, and kissed him, first on the forehead, and then tenderly on his lips. "Don't take this the wrong way…"

He could hardly breathe, the fear tasted metallic. Her warm arms around his back holding him close were not comforting but making him squirm.

"I want you to get your own room," she said softly. "There's a new opening two buildings down—the same floor as Tanya. It's Marge's room, she's leaving."

"Bu—but why?" he asked plaintively.

She kissed him again, and then sighed. "Look," she turned away and gazed out the window. "We've been having a good time. But I need my own room, my privacy. You've been living here for a month, but it's a one-person room. You can see that, can't you?"

He nodded, but felt morose.

"This is not a rejection," she said emphatically. "I still want to sleep together… a lot!" she grinned. "But sometimes I need to be alone, and sometimes I'd rather sleep alone."

He looked at her sheepishly, glad for her encouraging words. "You sure it's not me?" he asked timidly.

She came back and hugged him again, pressing his face against her neck. Sweetness, sweat and spice filled his senses. He ran his hands along her back, caressing her long narrow waist and coming to a rest on her tight round butt. They began swaying together, slowly grinding their hips in rhythm, their mutual arousal rising. She pulled him onto the bed.

* * *

"So I'll tell the Resident Committee that you do want the room, okay?" she asked him as he emerged from the shower, toweling off his head.

"Yeah, definitely," feeling vaguely excited about having his own room now that he'd gotten over the fear of rejection that it had first implied.

"I'm going to the dining room, meet you there, okay? I'll save you a seat." She gave him a quick kiss as she sailed past him.

He watched her disappear, reliving the intensity of their lovemaking. Her fondness for wrapping herself around him and pulling him closer and harder as he accelerated always led to such an explosion! He shook his head, feeling like he'd dodged a bullet, amazed that she still liked him. He pulled on his socks, thinking about a room of his own, suddenly worried about finding furniture. Pushing away the anxiety, it was replaced by the war creeping into the corner of his mind again. *What is happening?* He was confused. The fire on San Bruno Mountain blazed across his imagination when the war took no shape in his thoughts. He finished dressing, his mind jumping over his expanding list of worries.

In the dining room the table was full, and the food had been served just moments before. A warm bustle greeted him as Emmy waved him over to the seat next to her. The room's dark wood wainscoting added to the warmth, emphasized by the candles twinkling amidst piles of chicken, potatoes, steamed broccoli and cauliflower and big salads.

Emmy had already served him a heaping plate of hot food when he got to his seat, so he busied himself with eating. The rest of the table was focused on eating, too, small talk here and there about household items, a request to pass the salt or butter. After a few minutes of serious chewing, Vinnie punctured the silence when he cleared his throat. In his squeaky, grating voice, he vocalized what everyone had heard by now. "My gawd, a war! I thought we were done with that kind of thing!" The table immediately buzzed with rumors and comments all around. Eric sat eating thoughtfully, trying to listen to snippets of conversation, but didn't hear anything new.

He turned to Emmy who was listening intently to a conversation between Gerald and William. He waited.

"—would you do?"

"I've never seen a gun, let alone shot one!" said Gerald.

"Yes, but if some group suddenly starting attacking farms in the valley, wouldn't you want to fight?"

"No. Couldn't we negotiate?"

"Of course that's preferable. But what if it's like Chile? The attackers won't negotiate, they want to take power. Don't we have to fight in that situation?" William was less frightened at the prospect, having faced danger plenty of times as a volunteer firefighter.

"Can't we just deny them cooperation? They can't kill everyone!"

"Have you ever been coerced by a bully?"

"No—wait! Yes I have! When I was a small boy, a bigger boy scared me, threatening that he was going to beat me up."

"So? What did you do?"

"I told my parents, who told his parents, and that was the end of it."

"What about now, when there are no parents to turn to? How shall we handle someone who is bent on gaining power through violence?"

Gerald shrugged, a stupid smile crossing his face.

William turned to Emmy, who he'd noticed listening.

"What do you think Emmy?"

"It's hard," she said, putting her chin in her hand. "Seems like you can't just let 'em come in and kill people. Noncompliance and noncooperation is fine, but armed thugs can't terrorize the rest of us."

"Right. So how do we stop them, without our own force?"

"I don't know. What do you think, William?"

"I think we have to be ready to fight. I'd rather not, and I'd certainly rather stop them with barricades, nonviolence, and passive resistance. But I'm not inclined to get killed, nor do I want to see anyone else get killed by an armed minority."

"Call out the militias?" suggested Trixie, catching the drift of their conversation, now dominating the table.

William shrugged. "I think we'd have to. Even though it's been years and everyone's forgotten how to do it, we should practice mobilizing, just in case."

"Oh come on!" squealed Vinnie. "*We're* not at war! That's half a globe away. We don't have to do anything!"

William looked at Vinnie with thinly disguised disdain. "They are us, and we are them. If it happens to them, it *is* happening to us, and we owe it them to offer whatever help we can."

"You don't think we should be going down there, do you?" asked Gerald incredulously.

"Well, maybe... some of us anyway," said William.

The dinner ended and several people were busily bussing the table. The conversation broke up again, people turning to those closest to them.

"Emmy?"

She turned to Eric, expectantly.

"This Saturday there's a wedding I've been invited to, and I can bring a friend. Will you come?" He spoke rapidly, as if expecting a negative response.

She frowned, thinking about her schedule. "Well, I had planned to work in the Arboretum that day," she said. But she felt his vulnerability, and wanted to give him what he wanted. "Where is it?"

"In a place called Petaluma, or near there."

"Oh? That place is the dew, walled in from the Bay. You know about it?"

"I heard a little. Will you come?"

"Sure! Sounds like fun."

He started to tell her the plan, but before he could finish, Trixie came in to the room bearing a big birthday cake with dozens of candles on it, starting up the inevitable "Happy Birthday." It was Angie's birthday. She fidgeted uncomfortably as Gerald beamed at her, producing several wrapped presents and putting them in front of her with a flourish to accompany the arriving cake. "Make a wish!" he commanded.

She paused and blew out the candles, and began cutting up the cake. Soon after devouring the cake, everyone retired for the evening, still buzzing about militias and the unexpected re-emergence of war. Eric and Emmy went back up to her room and crawled into bed, curling up with their respective books.

30.

re you OUT OF YOUR MIND?!??" What about MY BABY?!?"

"Calm down, Ginnie, your baby is safe!" Jennifer stood at her back door, facing her wrathful neighbor. "We are talking about two pairs of wolves in the whole city. They are basically nocturnal, and anyway, they are a lot more afraid of you than you are of them. You'll probably never see them!"

"I CAN'T BELIEVE THIS! How could you vote to bring predators into the city?? Where are our children going to play? I TOLD you this was unacceptable. You're MY representative!"

"Ginnie, I represent the whole neighborhood, and the whole city on the water council. I have a child—"

"He's a grown man! Don't give me that crap!"

Jennifer put up her hands, trying to calm Ginnie. "Will you come in and have a cup of tea?" she asked.

"Don't try to distract me! And NO, I'm not coming in to your house and act like everything is peachy, goddammit!"

Jennifer was running out of patience. "Ginnie, I'm sorry we don't agree about this. I took everything into consideration. Your children will grow up in a wilder and richer place. Yes, there is some risk. But it's no worse than the risks we take every day, just riding around the city in gondolas, on bicycles or streetcars."

Ginnie stood at the foot of the steps, hyperventilating. "You are an ASSHOLE! And you—all of you who voted for this—are INSANE! I'm going to start a recall petition right now!" With that she stomped off down the path through the commons towards her side of the hill.

Jennifer stood at the door, breathing steadily, gathering herself and resisting the anger she felt rising. Turning back into the kitchen, she started some water to boil for tea when Nwin appeared at the foot of the stairs.

"What the hell was that about?" he rubbed his sleepy eyes, having been rousted much earlier than his normal midday rising time. "Wolves?"

Jennifer dreaded having to defend the decision any further, but cautiously she confirmed it to her son. "It's actually a city-wide decision, but the Bernal Council endorsed it. We're going to introduce two pairs of wolves into the wild corridors. All the research indicates that large predators are key to healthy ecosystems, and we're being overrun with small mammals and deer."

Jennifer poured her water into the teapot and offered some to Nwin.

He started rummaging through the cupboard. "No cereal left?"

"We're out I guess." She observed her son, a young man spinning in place. She hated to think about him like that. But suddenly, in the wake of the emotions stirred up by her neighbor, and his bleary appearance in the morning light, she was starkly reminded how directionless, bored and bitter he was. "Do you think you could go to the freestore today?" she asked cautiously.

He looked in another cupboard, convinced that cereal or some reasonable alternative breakfast would appear if he just kept looking. "Do I haaave to?" he whined, still looking half-heartedly through various cabinets.

"I don't ask you very often," she said quietly, a hardness creeping into her voice.

He looked at her, surprised. "I have to work with Auntie today."

She sipped her tea in silence.

"My back is pretty stiff," he started rubbing it, standing stupidly looking into the fridge. "We're out of milk, too, huh?"

Jennifer looked at the weeds that had taken over the backyard. "Weren't you going to put some time into the vegetable garden?"

He fell silent.

"Nwin," she started, fighting her own discomfort, "you can't go on like this. We can't go on like this!"

"I know you're only 18, but there's no reason why you can't be more responsible. Especially with your father gone now, you can help out more around the house. There's laundry, shopping and cooking, gardening, cleaning the house, and since you got hurt, I've been doing it all." She took another long sip of her tea, looking at him over the edge of her cup. He stood sullenly, absent-mindedly rubbing his lower back, his head drooping. "You have to pull your own weight."

His head snapped at that last comment. His own mother! Parroting the official line, "pull your own weight," it was disgusting! He looked at her with undisguised rage and walked out waving his arm behind dismissively. "Fine, I'll move out then!" he yelled as he climbed the stairs.

Jennifer wrapped her arms around herself, and fought the urge to rush after him. Something in her knew that it was best to push this now, and not back off just so they could face it again another day. The situation was intolerable. His reaction confirmed it. She recoiled from the painful clarity of her son's life. Jeffrey—well, he was part of the problem, but now he was gone. She couldn't escape her own responsibility, her coddling of Nwin when he probably needed something else. Jeffrey had never coddled him, so she compensated by always giving her son whatever he wanted. She couldn't hold the tears back any longer and began sobbing quietly, still hugging herself. What a mess!

* * *

Nwin was throwing clothes into his dufflebag. "The nerve!" he fumed. "Tell ME to pull my own weight! Fine! I'll pull it right outta here. Chingale!" He hurled the last of his clothing into the bag, followed by two books and some folders of papers he dug out of the closet. He finished dressing, grabbed his coat and threw everything over his shoulder. Clattering down the stairs, he observed his mother weeping at the table, but felt only anger. He said nothing, going through the front door, slamming it behind him.

His back throbbed as he started down the hill. He stopped to rearrange his bag, realizing that he wasn't going to last long carrying it straight up. Ahead was the Harrison bridge curving over Precita Creek with its usual gathering of people fishing. He took the bag in his hand, bracing himself against further pain. He walked onto the bridge, putting his bag down at the top behind three boys and an old man.

"Nwin!" the old guy turned around. It was Al Robledo, his dad's old friend.

"Hey Al."

"Just showin' these boys here some tricks… same as I used to show you about ten years ago, I think," he smiled, and introduced Nwin to the youngsters. They all looked up at Nwin, seeing a man even though they were much closer to Nwin's age than Nwin was to Al's. "You don't look so hot, man."

"I'm okay. It's my back."

"I bet the boys here would be glad to help you… wouldn't you boys?"

"I'll do it!" volunteered the smallest, a short ten-year-old African-American boy. "Where you goin' man?"

"Uuhhh, well, I uh," Nwin stared down the creek at the sun shining on the shimmering surface. "I'm going to the Shotwell Community Workshop over on 22nd Street."

"That's close. No problem." The boy carried his bag to a nearby bike trailer.

"What's his name again?" Nwin asked Al.

"Melvin, Mel. He's a good kid. You should talk to him. He lives with his mom."

Mel came running back up. "You wanna go now? Or you wanna fish some first?"

"Let's go, okay? I'm not much into fishing these days."

"Sure!" and Mel headed back to the waiting trailer.

"Thanks Al."

"Good luck Nwin. Take care of that back, y'hear?"

He walked delicately off the bridge. Mel was waiting for him, holding the front of the trailer. He would pull it along on foot.

"You know, I can do that myself," Nwin said, when he saw how easy it was to pull the trailer along.

"You wanna?" Mel squinted at him, plainly disappointed. Nwin noticed, and decided to leave good enough alone.

"Nah, that's okay, if you don't mind?..."

Mel smiled broadly, and spurted ahead enthusiastically. Noticing that he was leaving Nwin behind, he slowed. "You hurtin'?"

"Yeah, my chingin' back! I did somethin', not sure what."

Mel tried to imagine his back hurting, but it was an alien thought.

"You workin' yet?" asked Nwin.

"I been in the gardens a lot. My uncle took me with him planting roofs. I did that a few times. I did a Gondola workshop in school..." he trailed off.

"You done some good stuff, sounds like," said Nwin encouragingly. "You been to the Community Workshop before?"

"I been to the one on Holly Court a lot. I live over there. But not to the Shotwell place. You?"

"My cousin is a main guy there."

Mel grunted as the cart bounced over some tracks on 24th Street. The dense greenery along 24th Street hung low, casting deep shadows all around. Parrots squawked noisily in the trees, while a bustling café scene percolated to the right. Bike bells jingled, urging Nwin and Mel out of the veloway. A small historic streetcar approached from the east. Mel got the cart to the opposite corner, Nwin trudging deliberately behind him, as the streetcar slid to a stop.

"Fernando! Fernando!" a young woman called loudly from the corner café. They looked back to see a handsome young man disembarking from the streetcar. The bubbling woman leaped into his arms as he dropped his bag, and they disappeared into a long, passionate embrace. People began clapping after a moment, at first lightly, but as the kiss lasted, the clapping merged into a rhythmic accompaniment, everyone laughing and enjoying the moment. Mel wiped his forehead while he and Nwin stood silently against the wall, watching. Serenaded by a dozen enthusiastic voyeurs, the young couple finally broke apart laughing. They both blushed deeply and waved at everyone to stop.

Mel and Nwin resumed their trek to 22nd Street, and were soon pulling up outside the elegant old Victorian with its boastful sign. Mel read it to himself and snickered. "Tha's the dew, man. Your cuz's place, huh?"

"He's one of the regulars, Jimmy Van. Come on in and I'll introduce you. If you're interested in woodworking, he's the best!" Nwin said proudly.

"Woodworking?" A loud buzz sounded from inside as a table saw ate through a board.

"It's got all the same stuff as your Holly Court workshop, and all the others, of course," Nwin continued, as he started getting his bag off the trailer.

"Hey, that's *my* job!" Mel complained cheerfully.

"Okay, okay," laughed Nwin.

Mel worked the bag to the ground, proudly leaning his cart against the side of the house. Inside sawdust hung in the air. Two people were working at benches near one of the open windows. Jimmy was in a cloud of sawdust at the table saw, partially hidden behind his respirator and hat. Nwin and Mel stood in the door peering in.

"Hey Jimmy!" called Nwin.

"Nwnngh" he mumbled, before pulling the mask off, making sure to put his cut wood against the wall. "Nwin, howzit twirlin'? Who's yer pal?"

"This is Mel," and Mel stood up as tall as he could. Jimmy came over and slapped hands with Mel, then gave Nwin another dusty hug.

"Maaan! Watch out! My back..."

"Sorry, I forgot. What brings you here?"

"My mother... I couldn't take it. I had to go..." He looked at his cousin, who returned the look, expectantly.

"Uuhhh, I, uh, ... was wonderin'," Nwin trailed off.

Jimmy kept his eye on the boy while he said to Nwin, "Hey why don't you come and stay at my place for a few days?"

"Hey Mel, you want to do some woodworking?" The boy nodded eagerly. "Let me set you up. First put this on," and Jimmy threw him an apron. "Come over here. Start by getting a feel for the wood. Here, let's put this on the vise," and he tightened one of his boards into the vise. "Now take this block and sandpaper, and start working it like this... see? Stay with the grain and smooth it while I chat with Nwin, OK?" He watched the boy get started, nodding approvingly, and then patted him on the back. "Just keep doing that, I'll be right back."

Nwin and Jimmy walked to the front porch.

"Nwin, my man, what're you doin' fightin' with yer ma? You gotta take care of her!"

"You know how it is with her, she's on committees and boards and all that—she's never home anyway." He went on explaining the problem that morning, and Jimmy took it in impassively.

"Well, you stay with me for a little while. Your mother needs you. But take a break, stay at my place, and we'll see in a week or so."

Jimmy looked into the distance, a frown crossing his face. Nwin didn't notice, feeling relieved to have finished the awkward family talk. A few minutes passed before Jimmy finally cleared his throat uncomfortably.

"Uuhh, Nwin,..." he pulled out a crumpled piece of paper. "Do you know anything 'bout this?" He thrust the paper to Nwin.

It was the first page of his Earth Liberation Front arson instructions! He fought off the urge to run. He avoided making any strange noises, and he took the paper without trembling, saying only "Huh?" He stared at it briefly before handing it back to Jimmy. "What is this?"

"You've never seen it?"

Nwin shook his head.

"I don't know Nwin. Harriet found it in the electrical shop when she was cleaning up last week. She brought it to me. I didn't do anything with it cuz I didn't know what the hell it was either. But a coupla days ago, we got vyned from the P-I's office. They're looking for clues about that big fire on San Bruno Mountain. Seems they've concluded it was arson. They put out a request to all Community Workshops to respond if there's anything that might be helpful to their investigation." Jimmy paused and looked long and hard at Nwin.

"Why— why do you think *I* would know anything? I haven't used the shop in a long time."

"Yeah, I didn't think so. Forget it, man." He stuffed the paper back in his pocket.

"You— you, uh, you don't think *I* had anything to do with that fire, do you?"

"Nah, forget it," Jimmy waved it off with a dismissive hand. But he remembered Nwin started a big fire on Bernal when he was a little kid. He had had to ask.

"Hey, you heard about the war?" Jimmy suddenly asked.

"War? What war?"

"Down in Chile. It was on the news this morning. Three thousand armed soldiers attacked two towns down there, grabbed the arsenals."

"No shit!" Nwin whistled his surprise. "In Chile you say?"

"Yep. Some kind of crazy thing, they wanna end the Commons!"

"I heard about this at work. But only about small raids on a family farm down there."

"Well, whoever that was is probably with the same group. Sounds pretty bad."

"Chingale!"

They sat on the porch a while longer, the afternoon sun disappeared over the roof bathing them in shade.

"Listen, Nwin, I got—Oh shit! Your friend!" and he rushed back in to find out what mischief Mel might have gotten in to. Mel was near the workbench watching Anne carving a face. When he saw Jimmy and Nwin he came over, grinning.

"Man, that's the dew! I wanna learn how to carve like that! Can you teach me?!?"

Jimmy clapped him on the back. "You bet I can!" Jimmy was always happy when a new kid came in. "Nwin, if you wanna go home, I think Sheila's there, although she might be at the restaurant. Make yourself at home. You can use the couch. Just put your stuff in the corner of the living room…"

Nwin slapped hands with Mel, congratulating him on finding the dewest guy in town to learn woodworking from. Breathing deeply against the anxiety raging inside, he picked up his dufflebag but before he went five steps, he heard the door open behind him, and light steps fall rapidly on the stairway.

"Wait, man! I gotta take your bag for you!" Mel ran to get his trailer to help Nwin get to Jimmy's house.

"Mel,…" he paused. The boy looked up at him expectantly. "Look, I can do this. Tell ya what. Howzabout you loan me your cart, and then after you finish up here you walk home with Jimmy and get it?"

"You sure?" Mel felt obliged to finish helping Nwin.

"Yeah, no problem." He swung his bag onto the cart and took the handle from Mel. "See, it's no strain at all. Don't waste your time with me, go on back in there and have some fun! Besides, Jimmy likes you," he told him with a conspiratorial wink.

"Okay, man, thanks!" Mel dashed back into the Shotwell Community Workshop.

Nwin started walking down Shotwell, smelling the perfumed jasmine bushes that seemed to be in front of all the houses on this block. He felt dizzy, anxiety surging through him. How the ching did that get left behind?!? He stopped and opened his dufflebag, groping for the folders. He picked out one, opened it. "Shit!!!" Sure enough, page one was missing. He quickly stuffed it back in, looking furtively back and forth. No one could possibly link him to the paper, or to the fire.

Jimmy's Folsom Street place was a small house on stilts, all the rooms being on the 2nd and 3rd floors, the ground floor stood open, mostly a storage area. Nwin left the cart in the shade, took his dufflebag and climbed the spiral stairs to the second floor.

"Hello!" he called. No one was home. Sheila was probably at the restaurant down at the Willows where she worked. He went to the kitchen, poured himself cold water and took it to the porch. He tried to lie in the hammock, always a favorite, but his back started to give before he could fully let go. Instead he found a small couch looking northward towards The Willows. He could just make out Mission Creek, and the densely traveled veloway on the other side of it. He grabbed the binoculars laying on a small table, and adjusting them and himself, he sat back to watch the passing traffic.

After a little while, he grew drowsy. The sun was low enough in the sky to cast its bright heat on the porch. Nwin retreated to the kitchen. He opened the fridge to find some leftover rice and beans, which he threw into a pan to reheat. He reached over and flipped on the radio.

"—eporting from Valparaiso, Chile."

"Thanks, Ophelia. So, Hank, what do you know about this group in Chile, the Pinochet/Reagan Brigade?

"Dave, they've been operating for the past couple of years, but this is by far their biggest attack yet. They don't have a lot of popular support. Their operations have so far been confined to smaller towns in the Chilean foothills.

"What do you think they'll be able to do?"

"Obviously, terroristic attacks like today's, killing dozens of passive resisters in cold blood, will test Chilean society, as well as our own. It's been a half century since we have had to deal with any serious armed insurgencies. The end of guerrilla war in the early 22nd century seems like a very long time ago."

"Do you think this will force us to reactivate our militias?"

"I think we will have to seriously consider it. We learned a long time ago that passive resistance is very good at producing martyrs but does not lead to military success."

"By 'success' I assume you mean not just stopping aggression, but also avoiding the militarization of our own lives?"

"Yes, well said. I'm old enough to remember how hard we fought over this issue fifty years ago. Younger folks who were born since 2110 won't remember much about it, so we have a job to do. It's important for younger people to learn that history. Responding militarily implicitly concedes important ground to the aggressors."

Nwin turned off the radio. He couldn't stand all the blather. He sat down to his meal, and after polishing it off, he decided to go out, although he wasn't sure where.

31.

It was a spectacular day. Skies were bright blue and everything looked vibrant and clean. The dense greenery atop the hills cascaded amidst the dwellings scattered across the slopes. Flocks of birds swooped over Parnassus Heights, while hawks circled further above.

"Bridget, honey," Kathy Fairly leaned over, kissing her mate on the brow. "Bridget, we should start moving." She stroked her back while kissing her lightly behind the ear, pushing her thick gray hair out of her face. Bridget stirred, making little groaning sounds as she was rousted from her deep sleep.

"S'mornin' already?" she mumbled, scrunching up the covers more tightly, vainly trying to prolong the comfort of a lost sleep.

Kathy stroked Bridget's back one more time, pulling the covers back to let the cool morning air flow over her lover's shapely back. Bridget's skin showed its age here and there in small wrinkles where her arms joined her shoulders, bumpiness where her thighs met her still firm butt. As far as Kathy was concerned, her mate was a goddess. Bridget was a strong, witty, brilliant, beautiful artist and writer. During their three decades together, much had changed but they'd endured. As Kathy became the Public Investigator, Bridget's writing and performance art had flourished. Somehow the two lives, separate but complementary, had worked to each's advantage.

Kathy was brushing her teeth when Bridget crossed behind her towards the toilet, her sagging morning posture out of sync with her still trim physique. Blearily she sat on the toilet to pee while Kathy finished her teeth, and began humming to herself while she finished her ablutions.

"Why are you so cheerful this morning?"

Kathy looked over at Bridget, sinking into the toilet with a crabby expression. She laughed softly, and walked over to kiss her on the forehead. "My dear. Please don't fall in! You will ruin my good mood if you get stuck in there!"

Bridget wrinkled her face into a snarl, but couldn't hold it and started smiling, infected by Kathy's good spirits.

"You want cereal this morning?" Kathy asked.

"Sure, I guess."

Ten minutes later they were sitting in a big bay window in the turret atop their Queen Anne Victorian. Their southerly view from Fulton and Lyon was bright and sunny: Buena Vista, Twin Peaks, and Parnassus Heights with Sutro Forest behind it—green landmarks filling the panorama. Kathy prepared two heaping bowls of cereal, topped with a medley of raisins, raspberries, peaches and kiwi fruit. Steaming mugs of strong coffee accompanied a small wooden board with bread, honey, butter and several cheeses. Wind poured through the open window and rattled the papers on the shelf behind their table, so Bridget reached over to shut it. "Looks like a great day for a ride on the Bay!" said Kathy.

"Oh yeah, that's why you're so happy. It's Robin's wedding day. So tell me again, what's the plan?"

"We're meeting folks at 10 o'clock at the North Beach dock. A boat takes us to Petaluma. There we get off, walk through the old town, and then shuttle to the shore, where we will be met by a horsedrawn carriage. The wedding is a ways inland, near Valley Ford I think. We will stay overnight at the farm there, assuming we don't have to sleep with the cows."

"Your allergies?" Bridget asked, remembering a number of miserable journeys to the countryside over the years.

"I'm bringing my drugs. If it gets bad, I'll just medicate myself until it's ok."

Bridget said nothing, busily devouring a big mouthful of the delicious fruit and cereal. She was skeptical, all too familiar with Kathy's stubborn refusal to manage her allergies with drugs.

"And what about the ceremony? It's not religious is it?"

Kathy snorted, losing some coffee out of the corner of her mouth. "It better not be!..." After a thoughtful pause, she continued. "Robin has never shown any signs of being particularly religious, but I've never met her sweetheart, Trish. So who knows? Maybe there's going to be some treehugging mumbo-jumbo... Hell, for all I know, maybe Trish is a Buddhist!"

"You going to be able to sit through a ceremony like that?" Bridget was not thrilled about going all the way past Petaluma only to find out that her mate was going to melt down in the face of someone else's choice of ceremonial ritual.

Kathy glared at her. "Look, I may be intolerant at times, but this is a lesbian wedding! I will be on extra good behavior, I promise!"

"So you won't make rude noises, you won't stomp out, and you won't make a scene?" Bridget pushed her.

Kathy put up her hands, "I promise, swear to life, I promise!"

Bridget laughed. "Whoa! Swearing to *life*, now that's serious. You realize that you'll be struck by lightning if you blow it now?"

Kathy laughed along, shaking her head, a little frustrated with her own well-deserved reputation for intolerance. "Hey, my new Tryout Eric Johanson is coming. He's a religio-phobe. Maybe I can watch someone else freak out for a change!"

Bridget was pushing back from the table. "I guess we'd better get going if we're going to make it to North Beach by 10. It's already 9:15."

"Oh shit! My watch stopped again," Kathy wound it up and shoved it back into her shorts pocket.

"You're not going to wear those same shorts are you?" Bridget asked impatiently.

"Why? What's wrong with 'em?"

"You only wear them every day!" Kathy wasn't exactly a fashion horse, but Bridget wished she would sometimes take it upon herself to dress up a little. "Look, we're going to a wedding. You can do better than that! What about those new pants you got for special occasions? Why not today?"

"Okay, okay," Kathy growled. She hated dressing up for any reason. The whole wedding thing was offputting enough, but to have to dress up and endure some stupid ritual, well, that was going above and beyond. But it was Robin, her favorite Apprentice, and it was a lesbian wedding. And Bridget was always prodding her to wear nicer clothes, so she could do it today and kill several birds at once. She went into her closet, grumbling to herself.

"C'mon! We gotta hit it!" called Bridget.

Kathy came out wearing flowing dark green pants and a matching v-necked shirt. She grabbed one of her favorite necklaces, a silver and turquoise miniature star that hung just at the top of her cleavage. When she appeared at the top of the stairs, Bridget gave her a big smile, and an enthusiastic thumbs up.

"You look fantastic!"

As Kathy clattered down the stairs in her special occasion cowboy boots, Bridget gathered her into her arms and gave her a passionate kiss. She whispered "thanks" before they separated, and then in a normal voice, "let's go! We're gonna be late!"

Kathy raced behind her, noticing the casual elegance of Bridget's choice of dress. Knee-high blue suede boots, a pair of wide floppy knickers, and a tight, form-fitting gray knit shirt with a low neckline, emphasizing her magnificent bosom. She also wore a silver and turquoise necklace, hers featuring a small trapeze artist swinging at the bottom. Her gray braids were coiled elegantly on her head. "Where did she find time to do her hair like that?" Kathy wondered, in the same way she'd wondered countless times in years past at her mate's astonishing ability to look great in just a few short minutes.

* * *

"Messages?" Emmy was already out of bed, sitting in a bathrobe, addressing the vyne when Eric woke up. "Shit!" she hissed.

"What's up?" he mumbled through his raspy sleep-filled throat.

"Oh nothing! I forgot that I promised to work over at the Exploratorium today."

"Mmmmm, I toldja..." he trailed off, not wanting to set her off first thing.

"Message to Roy Woolery at the Exploratorium. Roy, I'm really sorry. I completely forgot that I'd promised to come in today. Look, I'm going to a wedding. I promise to make it up to you. Can you let me know when you most need help this coming week? I'll try to make it work. Thanks, Roy, and I am sorry..." She paused the customary five seconds, and then "Send it! From Emmy Hodges, Page Mews."

"Man! I've got to stop booking so many things!" She walked across the room to her closet, muttering to herself, clearly frustrated.

"Hey," Eric called her. "Come here a sec?"

She came out of the closet, hands on her hips. He reached for her and she came over, sighing, and flopped down on the bed.

"Why do I keep doing this?"

"You're just trying to help?"

"That doesn't get it." She kissed him on the forehead. He took the opportunity to hold her close. She stretched out next to him, kicking her slippers off. He kissed her face, stroking her back through the robe. She squirmed appreciatively and pressed against him through the covers.

"Maybe it's time for a Tryout?" she pondered aloud.

"You ready for that?" he asked, propping his head up on an elbow.

"Well, I have to admit, I am getting tired of missing appointments and overbooking myself."

"You don't have to work at so many places you know."

"I know, I know. But I just get intrigued. When somebody wants me I can't say 'no'."

"Maybe you need to learn how to say 'no' before you do a Tryout?"

"Maybe…" she buried her head on his chest and let him stroke her neck.

"Hey, what time is it anyway?" he asked.

"S'round nine, I think."

"Really?" he pushed her away, and sat up abruptly. "I've got to shower—We have to hurry!" He leaped out of bed and ran to the shower. She rolled over and lay with her arms under her head, staring at the ceiling. *This whole wedding trip is just a hassle,* she thought. But she knew she had to go now, especially after asking Eric to move out of her room. Somehow, she needed to make more space and time for herself. *Tomorrow!* she thought. *Starting tomorrow, I'm going to do less working and more… more…. Well, less working!* What would she do? Somehow, she couldn't think of anything and kept turning to the Annuals listings. She wasn't an artist, a writer, a photographer… She did love to dance. *Maybe I'll take a dance class. But that's so frivolous.*

Frustrated, she urged herself up. She went back to selecting her wardrobe for the overnight trip. She was just finishing packing her bag when Eric appeared, toweling his wet hair.

"I can't believe how long my hair is all of a sudden!" he trumpeted. She looked over at his pale skin, firm and muscular without being "built," and smiled at his ragamuffin hair, now falling all over his face. She went over to squeeze his butt, and playfully bit his nipple.

"Ow!" he recoiled automatically, but was happy for the physical attention. She playfully slapped his belly before grabbing her bag.

"I'll get something we can eat on the way."

She disappeared through the door. He chose his nicer clothes for the wedding. He put on green corduroy pants, brown leather shoes, and a deep red button-up western-style shirt with ornate embroidery across the chest and shoulders. For fear of missing the boat, he quickly dressed and finished packing, then bolted with his bag in hand. In the kitchen he found Emmy ready with her own bag and a small container of muffins and two mugs of coffee.

"Let's take a tandem and we can switch off, ok?" she suggested.

"Good idea."

In minutes they were whizzing down the Wiggle, Eric behind Emmy, enjoying his coffee and a muffin while she steered. They had a good thirty-five minutes to make it, so he relaxed. "Good coffee!" he exclaimed.

"I made it strong!" she called into the oncoming wind. "Do you like those lemel-on muffins?"

"Not bad," he mumbled through a mouthful. After devouring a muffin and finishing his coffee, he asked, "you wanna switch so you can eat?"

"I had a half a muffin while I was waiting for the coffee, so I'm ok. I'll just eat on the boat."

They cruised along, having hopped over the Sans Souci bridge and through the iron gate at the east end of the Wiggle, down the Abundance hill and past the spiraling wooden tower to "El Camino Real" on Valencia.

On Polk Street they carefully maneuvered through pedestrians in front of City Hall. In thickening bicycle traffic, they passed a number of other cyclists. Crisscrossing lines above the street held banners and paintings and an occasional sign. One sported a three headed dog and said "It's not a myth! Species Integrity is Essential!" in an exhortation from the Integritista movement. A number of green banners hung displaying various trees and flowers, sometimes including the words "Gardens Grow... Grow Gardens."

"Hey Eric!" Emmy hit the brakes at the salutation, and they slowed next to Kathy Fairly and a beautiful woman with gray braids coiled on her head, blue suede boots pumping the bike as they pedaled side by side. She looked terribly familiar to Eric, but he couldn't place her. He grinned at the P-I.

"Hi boss!" he teased. "This is my sweetie, Emmy Ndbele Hodges."

Emmy gave Kathy a big smile, "Eric told me all about you."

"Oh no!" Kathy expressed mock horror. "Eric, I told you not to tell anyone!" she continued the joke. "This is my partner, Bridget O'Reilly."

Then Eric remembered. "Hey, didn't we meet on the Wiggle?— "

"Yep! I was wondering if you'd recognize me. I remember you! In fact, I realized when we met the first time that you must be the new Tryout that Kathy had told me about." She smiled mischievously, remembering that she hadn't let on when they'd met previously.

Eric was surprised. "How come you didn't say anything?"

Bridget just shrugged. "I knew I'd see you again." She left it at that. They all focused on their progress down Polk Street, as they were reaching the fork in the road where they'd either have to go through the Broadway Tunnel, or continue to Bay Street and the Aquatic causeway along the shoreline back to the North Beach docks.

"Let's take the tunnel, ok?" suggested Kathy, who was now barely ahead.

The dimly lit tunnel was darkened in part by generations of paintings that had piled up on the walls' surfaces. Somewhere in the past muralists had started working on the tunnel, but they had been painted over so many times by so many different artists that now it was a jumble of incomprehensible and overlapping images... everything from jungle scenes to skylines on fire in imaginary wars, underwater scenes to historic views of sailing clipper ships that once filled the Bay. Eric turned back and forth repeatedly as they tore downhill through the tunnel, trying to digest the barrage of conflicting and partial images that whizzed past. Emmy let out a long yell to take advantage of the tunnel's acoustics, and was soon joined by Kathy and Bridget. There weren't many in the tunnel this early, so when they had to jog over to the other tunnel to avoid the decades-old collapse, they barely slowed down. They popped out and made the quick left turn onto Powell.

Reaching Columbus, they turned towards the docks, just a few blocks further. As they parked at the adjacent velome they chattered excitedly about the day ahead.

"Do you know what boat we're supposed to take?" asked Eric.

"Let's see..." and she fumbled with a paper in her pocket. "*Gamle Ole*, at Pier 53, North Beach Docks."

They moved in the direction of the 50s and found 53, and sure enough, there was a small ferry waiting there, called *Gamle Ole*. A red-faced, white-bearded man was laughing heartily as they approached the ship. Had he been wearing red he would have easily passed for Santa Claus, his long white hair and beard in sharp contrast to his beet red skin. His eyes laughed as he greeted them, gesturing to the rear of the ferry with his pipe, "Jus' t'row your t'ings down dere."

They all climbed aboard and went below to stash their bags. Back on deck, more people were coming on board, an elegant older woman in an elaborate white robe and headdress, followed by three young females.

"Francesca!" Bridget gave the woman a big hug. "You going to this wedding, too?"

"Yes, are you?" she asked, surprised. "Hi Kathy," and they hugged too. "How do you know Trish?"

Kathy explained that it was Robin, one of her Apprentices, that had invited them, and they hadn't yet met Trish. "And you?"

"I've been pals with the Wadsworths for as long as I can remember. Back in the day..." she paused, glancing at her granddaughter, who looked at her with undisguised impatience. "I'm sorry. This is my granddaughter Valentina Rogers, and her friends Shelley and Harmony Medina."

They slapped hands while Kathy introduced her companions, "This is my mate, Bridget O'Reilly."

"Hi Bridget!" laughed Valentina and the girls, who knew her well.

"And this is a new Tryout at my office, Eric Johanson and his girlfriend," she paused trying to remember her name exactly, "Emmy Ndbele..." and Emmy cut in, smiling, happy that she got the harder part of her name right, "Hodges."

Valentina warmly smiled as she tapped hands with her. "I've seen you around. Do you live in the Haight?"

"Yes, the Page Mews—know it?"

"Sure, I'm just downhill from you at the Pierce Palace."

"I haven't been there. Is it on Page, too?"

"Yeah, in the middle of the Wiggle, northeast of the creek."

Emmy shook her head. "You know, I almost never get to that side of the creek. Somehow I'm always heading back and forth along the main route. But I kind of know where you mean. I was doing Annuals with a solar crew up near Alamo Square... that's pretty close, isn't it?"

Shelley chimed in, not wanting to be left out, "Yeah, just five blocks!"

They settled on cushioned benches around the back of the ferry while they waited for departure. Eric was glad to see Andy appear at the gangplank, accompanied by a short, wiry dark-haired woman. Luis was right behind him, with a very handsome man with deep olive skin, thick black hair and eyebrows, walking with the self-conscious pleasure of a person used to being looked at. They went below to stash their things too, and then emerged to enter the wedding party.

"This is Eleanor," Andy called to everyone. She waved nervously, and they retreated to a bench by themselves, talking quietly. Luis brought Roy around to each person, glad to be seen with his gorgeous boyfriend.

The captain announced that they would be departing as soon as the last two passengers arrived, which happened less than a minute later when two more women, short and heavyset, huffing and puffing, pulled themselves onto the ferry. They stood gasping for breath on the deck, looking around, and made eye contact with Francesca Panduccino.

"Hey!" gasped the closer one, a bleached blonde in a white muscle t-shirt, an ornate tattoo gracing the bulging bicep of her right arm. She was squarish, thick, and looked like someone who had been in a few barroom brawls in her time. "Francesca! Howzit twirlin'? Goin' to the weddin'?"

"Hi Janet," Francesca walked across the deck to greet her. They exchanged a big hug, laughing as they separated.

"You know it!" gleamed Janet. "This is my honey, Sal." Sal was shorter than Janet, built like a tank, and seemed to sport a permanent scowl. Her black hair was closely cropped, and her diamond stud earrings glinted in the sunlight, softening the controlled fury of her posture. When she smiled, her rows of perfect white teeth dissipated the cloud that seemed to be hovering over her. *Gamle Ole* sounded its siren, and began moving.

Harmony, who had been exploring the boat, came running straight to Francesca, who was already finding herself informally surrounded by the rest of the party. "Didja know that there's a whole 'nother crowd inside going to the wedding too?" she blurted eagerly.

"Really?" and several people started inside to see who else was on board. Peels of laughter erupted from below, and moments later another dozen young women poured onto the deck. Big band music piped over the sound system gave the entourage a joyful vibe as friends found each other and others made new acquaintances.

"Emmy!" a black middle-aged woman happily greeted her.

"Eric, this is Sue Billings," and they tapped hands, "she's a close friend of the family."

"I'm her aunt's best buddy, actually," Sue explained. "And this is my love, Paula Pandit," as she introduced another beautiful woman about her same age, with long black hair framing her perfectly symmetrical face. "How do you do," Paula greeted them both cautiously. Sue smiled and put her arm around Paula, explaining, "I finally convinced her to move to San Francisco a year ago."

"Oh?" Emmy was intrigued. "Where are you from?"

"I'm from England, but my parents were from Mumbai, India."

"I would love to visit India!" Emmy exclaimed. "Wouldn't you Eric?"

"Uhh, yeah, sure, I guess so." He'd never thought about it. While he was trying to stay upbeat and at ease, his normal reticence was taking over. He only knew Kathy and Emmy and his coworkers, and the latter not well. Most of the party were obviously acquainted already, some kind of lesbian scene that he felt disconnected from.

Emmy chatted with Sue and Paula while Eric turned away and walked to the far side of the boat to watch it leave the city. Dozens of colorful flags flapped in the morning breeze from tall apartments on the slopes of Telegraph and Russian Hills. More flags and tall buildings loomed over the hills in the downtown area. Eric slumped on the railing, looking eastward at the hazy hills in the distance. Snippets of conversation swirled behind him, but it was an indecipherable buzz competing with the canned music.

Dolphins leaped out of the water just off the port side, shiny gray skin gleaming in the sunlight. He moved forward to gain a better view, and for the first time he got a good look at Alcatraz. He'd seen photos—*damn! I forgot to bring my camera.*

The largest statue in the middle of the island was in ruins, only the stumps of its legs still stood six meters above the rest of the sprawling sculptures that had proliferated over the years. In old photos of the unveiling of the giant American soldier, standing ready to defend the shores, thousands of small boats had surrounded the island while fireboats had spouted water jets to the skies. It had fallen in the big quake of 2044, and since it was so controversial, it was never rebuilt. Now the island sported hundreds of strange sculptures and installations. As they drew near, Eric could see water streaming down from a central fountain, cascading through the sculpture gardens and cliffs to the

Bay. A huge half head emerged from the western slope, two eyes at least ten meters wide peering at the Golden Gate. As they passed to the west of the island, the eyes eerily followed them.

"Hey, you OK?" Kathy Fairly appeared at his elbow.

"Huh? Oh… sure, I'm fine," he said unconvincingly.

"You get seasick?"

"Nah." He didn't feel comfortable, but it wasn't physical.

"Quite a party back there," Kathy mused.

"Yeah, sure seems like it," he concurred, laughter echoing again.

"I find it a bit much, especially so early in the morning," Kathy confided.

"Really? I thought you were friends with everyone?"

"Not my scene. Bridget is close to Francesca Panduccino, and Francesca is the queen bee of this swarm. I don't know too many of them, just Francesca and the women I've met through Bridget. And all you guys of course!"

"I guess I should try to be more sociable," Eric said grudgingly.

"Not for my sake! You can hide anywhere you want as far as I'm concerned. But don't feel like you're the only one who isn't part of the scene, okay? Everyone from the office—except maybe Luis and Roy—feels out of sorts."

Kathy started to walk away, then turned back to him.

"Hey, have you heard anything from Robin or anyone about what kind of ceremony it's going to be?"

He groaned deeply. "Ooohh shit! We're not going to church are we?"

"I don't think so, but actually I don't know the details. I think we're going to a farm… o'course that doesn't mean there isn't going to be some kind of ritual. I just hope we don't have to all stand in a circle and sing and pray!"

Eric was horrified. "You're kidding, right?"

"Well," she gazed at the partying lesbians dancing on the sun-washed bow, "It totally depends… Robin is a sensible girl. Maybe she'll have a ceremony that is simple and direct," but she didn't believe it herself. "Eric, uhhh, listen, I've been through this a few times before. I'm good at avoiding the worst of it. If it starts to get too squishy, just follow me, okay?"

Eric sighed, his anxieties surging. He was relieved that Kathy offered solidarity, maybe even escape. He smiled weakly, "Thanks. I'll definitely be looking for you at the crucial moment."

She clapped him on the back. "Don't worry! I'll save you! But if we get stuck, it's over eventually, and as far as I know, it doesn't leave any lasting damage." She laughed and went back to the party.

* * *

Valentina sat watching couples spin around the deck. Shelley was at her side, silently watching too. Harmony was running all around the boat, reappearing occasionally with tales of things she'd seen.

"So he took you all the way down to San Bruno Mountain? To where the fire was?" Shelley was still trying to get Valentina to tell her more about her date with Nwin. Val hadn't been very talkative earlier but maybe now she could get the story.

"Yeah..."Valentina got up on her knees and turned to lean over the boat's railing, catching the fresh saltwater spray as the solar ferry plowed through the Bay. Shelley joined her, elbows on the polished wooden railing. Valentina continued, "Such a strange day! First, he's a dirty mess when I find him, not ready at all. So we go to his auntie's place and he takes a shower."

"That's not so bad, is it?"

"No, I guess not, but—"Valentina slipped back into a frustrated silence.

"Well, then what?"

"We were just going for a ride on the Bay. We got into his skiff and started out... It seems like we were arguing the whole time."

"About what?"

"I can't even remember... The Garden Party, science, gondolas." She paused and Shelley waited. "We were passing Hunters Point, you know where there's all those old warehouses and cranes in the water?"

Shelley nodded.

"He went kind of crazy there, talking about the buildings still in the Bay, that it was some kind of ecological problem... He doesn't know what he's talking about!"

Shelley stared at distant brown hills, white puffy clouds filling the deep blue sky above. Birds careened back and forth in thick flocks, casting shadows over the ferry, speedily gliding through the waters of San Pablo Bay.

Valentina continued her story. "Anyway, I didn't want to argue, so I just let him say his piece. After that we came to where the fire was. He steered right up to the place where it started. We walked through the burn area... It was eerie. We checked out a burned house, practically nothing left of it but a few bits of walls and a brick fireplace. There were dead animals, too, poor critters that got caught in the fire."

"Eeewwww!" Shelley wrinkled her nose.

Emmy came up behind them at that moment, after admiring their pert butts waving side to side as they leaned over the Bay. "What's twirlin' with you guys?"

Valentina and Shelley turned around abruptly, surprised to be interrupted. They looked like kids caught doing something wrong.

"Sorry, am I interrupting?"

"No, no! Just jabberin'," Valentina assured her.

Shelley blurted, "Val was just talking about visiting the San Bruno Mountain fire zone."

"Really?" Emmy had been hearing about the investigation for weeks. "Why did you go there?"

Valentina was flattered that Emmy was interested in her. Seeing her around, Valentine had always been fascinated by Emmy's incredible height, slenderness and unusual beauty. Now they were talking. She gave Emmy a quick synopsis of the dysfunctional date with Nwin, the trip to San Bruno Mountain, and then got into some details about what she had seen, the ruins and the death and the bits of green already pushing through the ashes.

"Why do you think this boy took you there?"

"He admitted that he'd been there when the fire started that morning."

"Really?!?"

"Yeah, he claimed that he'd been tooling around in the Bay at dawn... said he does that a lot. He happened to be offshore when the explosion occurred and he saw it start... That's what he told me."

"My boyfriend is working at the P-I's office. You know what that is, right?"

Valentina nodded.

"He's on the team investigating the fire. I'm sure he'd love to talk to this boy... what was his name?"

"Nwin, Nwin Robertson. He used to work at the Rice Bowl, but I think he stopped. Some kind of back injury or something."

"Wow. He might be an important witness. Would you tell your story to my boyfriend? He's on the boat somewhere."

"Sure, I guess so."

Emmy went off to find Eric. Valentina sat down on the bench again, Shelley looking at her.

"You think it'll be a problem, telling them about Nwin?"

"Why? Maybe he can help."

Harmony came running up. "Hey you guys! There's great food downstairs. And I got to sit in the Captain's chair too!" She was flushed with excitement. She pointed over their heads, "Look! That must be Petaluma."

They all turned to see the faux castle walls looming out of the water, still a good distance away. Small skiffs dotted the surrounding waters. Other people crowded around the bow, getting a look at the approaching town.

"Looks like an old Italian town or something," exclaimed one of the young women.

"When did they build those walls? There weren't any renaissance cities here!" Paula said loudly in her proper British accent.

"They had problems with flooding even before the deluge," explained a wiry man with brown hair falling into his face. He was older than he looked, because as he continued they realized that he'd known the place in the times before the oceans rose. "Those walls were started over 100 years ago, around 2035 I think it was." He scratched his chin, suddenly lost in memories. "Yep, they were fake in their time, but I guess after a century, you'd have to say they're pretty real!" he laughed.

The solar ferry glided to a halt at an ornate dock, resembling a drawbridge hanging from the wall of the town. People surged to and fro from dozens of watercraft. A wide golden staircase gleamed in the bright sunshine, rising up and over the wall at the back of the dock.

"Petaluma!" boomed the captain's voice as the mate tied to the dock and got the gangplank arranged. Amidst happy murmuring and laughter, the wedding party filed off *Gamle Ole*.

A whistle sounded and everyone gathered around a young athletic woman who was taking the lead. "Hi folks, I'm Barbara. I've got the plan here. We're going to take a short walk across the town to the western dock, then take a shuttle to the shore where horse-drawn carriages are waiting for us." She looked at her wristwatch. "It's 11 o'clock now. We should get across to the western dock by 11:25 for an 11:30 departure. The carriage ride will last about an hour and a half, so assuming we don't lose anyone, we should get to Rolling Oaks Ranch in plenty of time for the 3 o'clock ceremony. Follow me!" and she started up the golden staircase.

Harmony ran ahead, giddy with pleasure. The rest proceeded in small groups. Emmy and Eric sought out Valentina and found her with Shelley and her grandmother Francesca at the top of the stairs, just in front of Sue and Paula and several young women from the Wadsworth side of the affair.

Francesca was talking when they caught up, and they walked in a group down the stairs into the old town. "… held out here for two months before the insurgents convinced them to stop. They thought they were besieged! I remember how surprised people were when they came out waving white flags, and we all applauded and threw flowers at them. A lot of folks didn't understand what the revolution was all about. So they were afraid."

"You were here then?" asked Shelley, wide-eyed.

"Sure. I was wasn't even your age then, but I remember it clearly."

Emmy touched Valentina on the shoulder, "um, Valentina, this is Eric."

"Hi, yeah, we met on the boat."

Eric wanted to plunge in to the fire investigation, happy to have something purposeful before him. But it was loud and everyone was busy going into the old town. "Let's talk about it later? We have all day and probably tomorrow, too, right?"

Valentina nodded noncommittally.

Shelley pulled her along, and Eric and Emmy fell behind, as the group meandered through the streets. Petaluma was less dense than its walled perimeter would have suggested. As they walked down the Grand Staircase they came into a public square facing a modern glass structure that was City Hall. An office building was on one side, and a big public swimming pool filled the other, full of splashing children on this hot Saturday in late August. They followed along herd-like as Barbara and her friends led the way past the perimeter of the swimming pool. A translucent material hung in four canopies over the pool. One of the canopies was opaque and shadowed its corner, where a lot of the smallest children were gathered with their young moms and dads. Eric pointed at it, noting that the material looked the same even though it wasn't letting the sun through like the rest.

Sue Billings was behind them. Noticing Eric's interest she leaned forward, "Pretty great stuff, eh? That's a new sun textile… comes right out of UCSF y'know."

Paula proudly announced, "She's too modest to admit it, but she had a hand in developing it… Sue is a bio-engineer there."

Emmy poked Sue in the ribs, laughing. "So those sunburns people are getting walking around in sunshirts… that's your trick?"

Sue smiled sheepishly. "It's adjustable and extremely flexible. You can make it translucent, or opaque letting ultraviolet rays through, or it can block sun completely. I am surprised it's been so popular for clothing. We designed it for window shades, and maybe this," gesturing to the pool's overhang, "over outdoor places that need occasional shade."

They entered a narrow street leading away from the plaza. Three- and four-story buildings abutted both sides, stucco and plaster facades, occasional wooden slats, mostly residential apartments. At street level were small artisanal workshops and stores. Paula's eye was caught by a jewelry display and she dragged Sue over for a look. Other members of their party were scattered along the street, stopping to ogle sculptures, paintings, jewelry, and textiles.

"Is this an artists' colony?" asked Eric.

"I don't know. All I know about Petaluma is that it sits in the water protected by walls," Emmy answered. "Look at that!" She broke away from Eric's embrace and walked over to examine an ornate elongated mask, carved from a dark wood. It had no eyes, just empty holes in the wood. She picked it up and turned to Eric as he followed her to the small shop, her eyes peeking through the openings.

"Creepy!"

"I love this!" Her muffled voice came from behind the mask. "It's perfect for Halloween. And I like the piece."

She turned to the artist, a man of indeterminate age, slightly graying hair around his temples, but ruddy dark skin and a mischievous smile. "You like that one?" he asked, and Emmy nodded, obviously delighted with it. "Will you hang it where it will be seen when you're not using it for Halloween?"

"I live in a big household. I'll put it up near the dining room, where upwards of 50 people will see it regularly," she promised.

"Take it and enjoy!" he urged.

She wrote down her address and invited him to dinner when he was next in San Francisco. She explained about the wedding, and he told them about his world travels and fascination with mask-making. They slapped hands and promised to meet again.

They weren't keeping up, but luckily it was a straight shot to the western dock. Besides, several others were still lingering at different workshops, picking out treasures, making connections with the locals. No doubt Trish and Robin had planned for this detour knowing their friends would enjoy visiting local artists.

Emmy and Eric caught up with Sue and Paula. "Are we going the right way?" asked Paula anxiously.

"I haven't seen any turns yet, have you?" Emmy asked Sue, who shook her head. Just ahead, Barbara was briskly heading back towards them, her whistle bobbing on her chest as she jogged.

"Okay, you guys. Let's go! Ten minutes till departure." She ran past them, trying to catch other dawdlers. They soon emerged onto a long greenway that skirted the edge of the town, next to a big gray wall. They didn't see much of Petaluma after all, just a small touristy street off the main plaza. They found a sign pointing to the Western Dock where their party was gathering. Once again they approached a big stairway up the wall, but this one eschewed the tacky golden glamour of the dock where they'd arrived. They walked down the iron steps to floating docks.

"Look, there…" Eric pointed to a peapod ferry where Kathy and Bridget and the others were already on board, the women waving to get their attention. They hurried over and boarded, followed a few minutes later by Barbara and the last stragglers, clutching their hats, scarves, paintings and sculptures.

As they started off, Barbara stood up at the front of the boat and held up her hands for attention. The peapod captain stood at the rear, yelling "Next stop, Petaluma West!" Barbara took the whistle from around her neck and held it up.

"Just want to announce that my job is now done," and everyone laughed and applauded. One girl near the front yelled, "Barbara! What a great leader!" which got another round of laughter.

"I'd like to introduce Lily, who will get you from this ferry to the carriages." Up jumped one of the many young women in the group. She wore an orange tunic which functioned like a minidress over her bare legs, which in turn disappeared into brown work boots. Her hair was dirty blonde with green highlights, and stood straight up on the top of her head. She had an electric look, and as she began to speak it was obvious that her looks were matched by her personality.

"I never thought I'd be going to Trish's wedding," she started, and everyone began laughing. "and there's a few of us wondering if we shouldn't be saving her from this infamous fate!" She carried on in the style of a roast at the expense of Trish and her friends.

Eric withdrew into his thoughts. The bantering was already wearing him out, partly because he didn't know anyone, but partly because such insider joking always left him outside. He looked sidelong at Emmy but she was enjoying the jokes, so he looked away. They weren't crossing a wide body of water now, more like a big river, even though it was part of the Bay that surrounded Petaluma. Golden hills rose ahead, dotted with beautiful n'oak trees. A long cut in the distant hill seemed to be a roadway, he could make out various trucks and vehicles laboring up the slope, ant-like in the distance. His thoughts were interrupted when Emmy pressed a green number 3 into his hand.

"What's this?"

"They're giving numbers to everyone of the carriage you're supposed to take."

"But you're a different number!" he said with undisguised anxiety, noting the 2 she was clutching.

"Eric, relax! You know a few people here, and if you just let go, you'll make new friends… really!" She was getting tired of Eric's whining. "Get over it!" she snapped with finality, and turned towards the approaching dock.

Eric was nervous, irritated, and now he felt nauseous. He wanted Emmy to console him, to promise to stay close, but had enough sense to realize that he'd better keep his mouth shut. So he sat there, holding himself back, feeling a rising anger with Emmy's lack of sympathy.

* * *

Harmony was straining forward, impatient to get off the ferry and find her carriage. She clutched her number 3, eyes darting around at the people around her, trying to see who else had one. Bridget did, but her sister and Valentina were 1 and 2. She didn't care much, since everyone was indulging her.

"Keep an eye on her, okay?" Francesca nudged Bridget, indicating Harmony.

"No worries!" Bridget was feeling fine. It was fun to be an older couple going to a wedding like this. *So many beautiful young women.* Having already had good conversations, and with a whole night and day ahead, she was relaxed and happy.

They docked and people filed off the ferry, bristling with packs and acquisitions. Old red brick buildings behind the small dock made a picturesque landing site. Off to the side of the small plaza there were three big carriages with two huge horses each. In spite of boisterous talking and laughing, they were soon seated in the carriages, eight or nine in each. She looked ahead to the first two carriages and observed Kathy sitting in the back of the first carriage with Luis and Roy. *I hope she doesn't try to get them to talk baseball with her!* she thought archly. No sooner had she had the thought, than just behind her two of Kathy's Tryouts started talking baseball. She turned to see Eric and Andy, the latter trying to explain the local scene.

"So everyone thought the Farmers were out of it back in June. But since then, they've played better than anyone. Now they're a game and a half ahead of Reno for the wildcard, with 15 to play. The Oaks have first place in the bag. Their magic number is four."

"I never figured out who's who here on the west coast," Eric admitted. "In Chicago I followed the Cubs, and even the White Sox a little, but the Midwest league never goes anywhere, so it was hard to get excited about the post-season."

"Whaddya mean? The Cardinals were the continental champs three years ago!"

"Oh yeah, okay, but still, the Midwest champ usually loses in the first round. Shit, we—I mean they—get swept as often as not!"

"The Mexicans are going to win forever. The Aguilas are SO good!" Andy was a huge fan, that was clear. Eric knew the basics, and enjoyed the game but he'd lost track of all the statistics and relative strength of the different leagues.

"You know, I think the Mexicans stack the Aguilas with all their best players. It seems like an all-star team! They've won seven years in a row, and only lost the World Series to the Cardinals in '54 and their first championship year when the Koreans beat 'em in the 2nd round."

Eric couldn't keep up with Andy's encyclopedic knowledge, and after a while the baseball talk petered out. "What's happening with the San Bruno case?" Andy asked, still miffed that he wasn't on it.

"Funny you'd ask. There's a young woman here," he stood up on his haunches. "There! That's her, the one with the red-brown hair in that turquoise tank top," pointing at Valentina in the back of the second carriage. "My girlfriend Emmy was talking to her on the boat and she knows some guy who said he was there when it started."

"Really?!"

"Yeah. I started to talk to her, but it was too hard while we were walking through Petaluma. We left it that we'd connect later."

"Hmmm. So any other breakthroughs?"

"Nope. Not yet. I'm going to visit fuel dispensaries next week. And I got the names of people who were treated for burns on the day of the fire."

Andy nodded seriously, remembering how all investigations seem so hopeless at the beginning.

* * *

"Look! Look!" squealed Harmony, pointing to the woods at the top of the hill. In the shadows of n'oak trees stood a black bear, apparently going after a beehive in the tree. The bear quickly dropped down when it heard the human commotion.

The carriages made good time, the steady clip-clopping of the horses laying down a soothing sound track for the wedding party. Water passed among the passengers under the relentless rural sun. A lucky few had parasols and umbrellas and they were putting them to good use. Dried grass and n'oak trees scented the atmosphere. Some dozed off, tiring as the journey stretched past the three-hour mark. Eventually almost everyone had fallen silent, either sleeping or lost in their own thoughts. The carriages followed a long dusty road over hills covered in grass, corn, marijuana, vineyards, wheat, and occasional apple orchards. Sprinklers sometimes doused them with light spray much to everyone's delight, rousing the drowsy passengers from their slumber.

Finally, when they topped a ridge, their destination appeared. Far below was a bucolic ranch with a small creek meandering through a golden valley. A sprawling farmhouse sat among vibrant green gardens, and a white tent in a pasture a short distance behind it. The carriages paused to give everyone a good look, leading to a pleasant buzz of anticipation for the final descent to Rolling Oaks Ranch. In ten minutes they were pulling in, everyone happily piling out of the dusty carriages.

Lily strode ahead, turning to address the whole party. "There are showers and changing rooms in the farmhouse," she gestured behind to the big house. "Your rooms are on the second floor. There are ten bunks per room, so feel free to claim your spaces. There are four small private bedrooms for couples."

Someone was calling from inside the house. A woman came out wiping her hands on an apron. "We have tents for anyone who needs privacy but doesn't get one of the bedrooms, okay?"

* * *

Eric sought out Emmy and stood quietly while the private room or tent options were presented. Emmy found him, putting her arm around him and giving him a warm squeeze. She was glad to have had a break. "Shall we just ask for a tent? I like sleeping outside anyway," she said.

"That works for me," he assented. So they went up to the farmhouse and found out that the tents were stacked in back. They had fun putting up the tent. Eric dragged in an air mattress and big cotton sleeping bags. When everything was set up they stretched out in the sultry air of the tent and started kissing, pushing the dripping sweat out of their faces.

"Maybe we should go take a shower?" Emmy suggested.

"I'd rather stay," Eric said, hoping she'd stay and have sex.

"I feel SO grimy. I'm gonna shower," and up she jumped, feeling not at all sexy in the dust and sweat. Seeing Eric's hangdog look, she bent down to give him a kiss and say softly, "later, honey, okay?" to which he nodded uncomfortably.

He lay back and closed his eyes. In the tent's dry heat, he soon fell asleep.

32.

Sheila! Are we out of soap?" yelled Jimmy from the shower. "Goddammit!"

Nwin burrowed under the pillow, trying to blot out the noise. He'd been at his cousin's house for almost a week, and it was getting kind of tense.

Sheila bustled past his place on the couch and into the hallway, rummaging in a closet. She opened the bathroom door, letting out the steaming roar of the shower, "Honey, here's a new soap."

"Maybe Nwin can go to the freestore?" Jimmy mumbled as Sheila was stepping out of the bathroom.

"I'm going to the restaurant. I'll see you tonight." Nwin heard Sheila walk past him again, stopping momentarily in the room. Was she looking at him buried in the couch?

Her boot heels pounded the wooden floor as she went into the kitchen, opened the fridge, and gathered up her things. On her way to the front door, she paused in the room again. "Nwin, you have to help out around here. You might start by getting up and talking to Jimmy about what he needs you to do."

She didn't wait for him to respond or even move. She left, shutting the door just short of a slam.

He flinched at the door, and then flipped onto his back, eyes wide open. His lower back throbbed as tension surged up his spine. Moving his feet slowly in circles he noticed that his left leg was kind of numb. Where would he go now? He obviously couldn't stay here any longer. He put his hands behind his head after scooting up on the pillow, closer to a sitting position, letting out a low groan as he maneuvered his lower back to avoid pain.

The shower stopped in the bathroom. He braced himself for Jimmy's emergence. After some minutes, the medicine cabinet opening and closing several times, the door opened.

Jimmy stood there literally steaming after his shower, glowering in Nwin's direction. Nwin's head was back in the corner, Jimmy standing behind his right shoulder.

"Well?"

Nwin turned stiffly to glance over his shoulder. "Mornin'. You need me to pick up some stuff?"

"That would be a start."

Nwin struggled to sit on the edge of the couch, pushing aside the sleeping bag. He looked blearily up at his cousin, who stood with his hands on his hips, sucking in air at a prodigious rate, a fierce expression sharpened by wet hair and face.

"Nwin, let's get right to it. This is a small apartment, and I thought a couple of weeks would be okay…"

Nwin looked down at his knees.

"Look, man, what's happening?" He came over and sat down opposite Nwin. "Is your back still bad? What are you going to do? What do you WANT to do?"

Nwin sat sullenly, shaking his head, unable to speak.

The shellfone on the kitchen table rattled and Jimmy went over, trying to mop up the water he was still dripping as he went. He picked up the palm-sized clamshell and flipped it open. "Hi Jen," and her tiny disembodied voice rose out of the shell.

"Jimmy, is Nwin there?"

"Yeah, Jen, he's right here. You wanna talk to him? Here—" and he brought it over and shoved it into Nwin's hands.

Nwin sat looking at the five-centimeter image of his mother, saying nothing.

"Nwin, what are you doing?"

"Nothing, just waking up."

"Why don't you come home?"

"Nah," and he looked out past the porch at the sunlight streaming down on the greenway, the willows swaying in the breeze. A few pedestrians and cyclists were moving up and down the path unhurriedly. A small fox darted out of some bushes and disappeared on the other side of the greenway, small dogs yelping in hot pursuit. Parrots noisily screeched in the palm tree next to the house.

"Mom," but words failed him. In a cold, hard spot in his chest his pulse quickened as he groped for what to say. He was sick of answering to his mother, to anyone.

"Nwin, are you alright?" she asked, and then swallowed a sob as tears began streaming down her face.

"Mom, I'll talk to you later, ok?" and he slapped the shellfone shut, his heart beating hard. He looked around and found that Jimmy had disappeared into his bedroom. He quickly got into the shower, immersing himself in the hot water. Slowly washing, he bent over so the hot water pounded his lower back muscles, loosening up his stiffness. He stayed in the shower until his hands were turning to raisins and his skin was practically aching from the needling hot water. Finishing with a vigorous toweling, he finally emerged from the bathroom almost a half hour after he'd gone in. Jimmy was sitting at the kitchen table, looking at some papers.

"So? You going back to your mom's?"

"No man. I'm done with living at home. Fact is, I think I'm ready to get out of this place altogether."

"Here?"

"Jimmy, you've always done me right. I 'preciate it, really I do. Thank you man," and he walked over and brought his arm around to give his cousin a warm embrace, which Jimmy returned. "I don't wanna cause you any trouble. I'll find another place to stay. But I'm thinking of getting the hell out of San Francisco."

Jimmy was surprised. He'd never heard Nwin talk like this. He'd never wanted to leave his hometown himself, except for the occasional vacation.

"Why?"

"I'm just sick of everything. I hate all this "do your share" shit!... "pull your own weight," all that... I can take care of myself. I'd be glad if I never heard "Nobody wants to, so we all have to" again!"

Jimmy laughed softly. "Yeah, that gets kinda old, doesn't it?" he sympathized. "But you know, no one lives in a vacuum. You can take care of yourself, but you can't do everything!"

"Jimmy, look—" and he fell silent again, not wanting to explode at his cousin. He did not want another condescending explanation about how he had to accept basic truths. "Let's just say I need a break, ok?"

"Sure, everyone needs a break... So you're thinking of taking a trip?"

"I don't know what I'm going to do. Today, I'll look for a different place to stay, so I can get out of your hair, okay?"

"Okay, but you can stay a couple more days if you need to. Sheila won't be so grouchy later, especially if she knows you're about to move."

Nwin poured himself a bowl of cereal. "You want me to get a few things today?"

"Yeah, that would be great. Here's a list," and he pushed a small shopping list across at Nwin.

Nwin read the list while he munched his cereal: "milk, soap, toilet paper, bread, cereal, mustard, juice, sponges."

"I'll go to the Central Freestore this afternoon, okay?"

"Thanks, Nwin." Jimmy rose and got ready to leave for the Community Workshop. "You know where I am if you need me, ok? I'll see you tonight." He grabbed his lunch, put his hat on, and departed, leaving Nwin at the kitchen table.

He finished breakfast and rinsed his dishes. Stuffing the list in his pocket, he grabbed a light jacket and threw it over his shoulder as he went out the front door. His back was feeling a lot better, no pain at the moment, just a little stiffness. He walked north along the greenway under hanging willow trees and the occasional palm. Thick impatiens bushes with pink and white flowers walled the west side of the path, giving way after a short distance to an old fence covered in morning glories, their vibrant blue blossoms basking in the bright sunshine. He barely noticed the people pedaling past him as he made his way down to the dock at The Willows. He glanced in to the commons and saw people scurrying back and forth in the kitchen area but he didn't see Sheila, to his relief.

A rickety pedal taxi bobbed on Mission Creek, its skipper sitting reading Dostoyevsky's *The Brothers Karamazov*, when Nwin approached.

"You taking people over to 7th?"

The skinny guy looked up, his wavy black hair partially obscuring his acne-scarred face. "No... You should grab a bike, or take a streetcar on Folsom."

Nwin shrugged and walked away, pondering his options. He didn't feel like bicycling, worried it would hurt his back. He decided to go to the café in Dolores Park, thinking he might run into Valentina. If he didn't find her there, he would try the ice cream parlor in The Wiggle. He could look for available rooms while he walked. So he started off along the creek, opposite the veloway. It was a beautiful day, although he hardly noticed, still feeling quite agitated.

"Hey Nwin!"

He looked across the creek at the veloway where Stefania was hailing him from her bike. She pointed to a small footbridge a short ways ahead where they were both heading. "I'll meet you up there, okay?" and he nodded.

They slapped hands when they met at the footbridge. Stefania had parked her bike on the other side and was leaning over the railing as he walked up.

"Look at all those fish! Can you believe it?" pointing into the shallow creek, which was in fact jammed with fish.

He shrugged and turned the other way, not wanting to bend over the railing.

"Hey, how's your back, anyway?" she asked him.

"So so. It's not a good idea to lean over like that, that's for sure."

"So what are you doing with yourself these days?"

"Not much. Been working on the Harrison Rose Gardens some. My "auntie" is the senior there..."

"Are you going to come back to the Rice Bowl? We could use you."

"My back is still pretty messed up. I might come back, but I don't know when," he said vaguely, skipping over the Angus problem. "Hey, you don't know about any empty rooms, do you?"

She put her thick thigh on the railing, showing off an elaborately designed pattern on the side of her boot. Her blonde hair had grown since he'd last seen her, curls hanging over her forehead and down to her shoulders now. Her elbow landed on her knee in time to catch her chin in her hand. She turned toward Nwin with a mischievous glint. "Matter of fact, I do. Who wants a room? You?"

He nodded. "I don't need much."

"My sister's house is looking for new householders. You're a gardener so that helps.

Play any music?"

He shook his head, already uncomfortable at submitting to this evaluation.

"I'm not sure… I think maybe I should just get a room in one of those old hotels on Mission Street or something."

"Eeewww!" she wrinkled her face up, "that seems so lonely and awful!"

"I don't know. I've heard different."

"Whatever suits ya."

"What's the news from Chile? I heard about the war starting. Must be the same thing you were talking about, eh?"

"Yeah, it's terrible." A cloud passed over her face. "Hundreds have been killed. My closest relatives are okay, but they had to run away from their farm because it's right in the war zone. They've gone to a nearby town to wait."

"They're not fighting?"

"Well, some of my cousins are. I talked to my uncle, and he's pissed, of course."

"Pissed at your cousins?"

"At the attackers firstly, but he's pissed that his sons would take up arms, too. Says it's just as bad."

"You agree?"

"I don't know, Nwin. It's so hard to figure how to deal. What do you think?"

He looked into the distance. He wondered what war felt like. It sounded exciting, a thrill of the forbidden. But he couldn't say anything like that.

"I don't think I could stand to be attacked and not fight back," he said truthfully.

"My uncle says he's organizing a big march—with my great-grandmother—to bring thousands of people to the conflict's front lines."

"Didn't they already shoot nonviolent resisters?"

Stefania looked frightened. "This time there will be too many. They *couldn't*— could they? I mean, how could they kill thousands of unarmed people who are trying to stop the fighting?"

Nwin stood up straighter, running his hands on his lower back, then stretched backwards, impatient with the conversation. "I don't know… seems like if they've started shooting people already, they would just keep on… Sounds like they want violence, doesn't it?"

"How could they? Who wants death and violence? Why, why?…" she trailed off, near tears.

Nwin remembered his chat with Joseph. "Terror breeds fear and creates power. It makes sense when you think about it."

Stefania looked at him with horror. "Wha? Are you out of your mind? What are you talking about?" His matter-of-fact tone deeply offended her. "What makes sense about mass murder?!?" her voice rose to a near shriek.

Nwin put his hands up. "Whoa, whoa—I'm not saying they're right. I'm just saying that there is a logic to their killing, at least it seems like there could be." He didn't feel a lot of sympathy for Stefania's anguish, nor did he see much reason to stay any longer. "Hey, I hope your folks are alright," he offered half-heartedly. He patted Stefania on the shoulder, and she looked at him coldly, stunned by his callousness.

"Bye…" she walked back across to her bike.

He left the footbridge and proceeded through a small grove of recently planted pine trees. Inhaling deeply, his nostrils filled with the perfume of fresh pine, while he kicked a tiny pine cone in his path. He walked quickly to escape the emotional cloud Stefania had wrapped around him.

War. What would war be like? He didn't feel afraid so much as excited and curious. The romance of war seized him. His imagination raced through images of leading soldiers through hostile territory, standing victorious on seized buildings, accepting the surrender of weak-willed diplomats like the idiots his mother had to deal with all the time in city politics. Maimed bodies, death, privation and misery, all failed to appear in his imaginary war scenario.

The pine grove gave way to an open path between buildings and the narrow channel of Mission Creek. Two folks in respirators and white suits came out of the building just ahead, carefully shutting the door behind themselves. They quickly pulled off the masks and took down their hoods, revealing two women, a pudgy blonde and a dark-skinned woman. Nwin kept an eye on them as he approached, but they were busy complaining to each other about their jobs.

"If Harriet keeps pushing us like this, I'm outta here!" said the Latina, while the blonde nodded vigorously. She pulled out a joint and lit it up, taking a deep drag.

"You can't quit! *Ching* Harriet!" the blonde was trying to keep her spirits up. Her companion looked at her, one hand on a hip while she puffed the joint, her skepticism etched in the wrinkles of her face. The Latina shook her head, unmoved by her coworker's exhortation.

"I'm gonna quit after this shift. She just pisses me off, her attitude, her bossiness, her condescension!"

Nwin drew alongside at this point. The Latina took a look at him with her blazing eyes, and responding to something, offered him the joint.

"Why not?" he said, smiling, and stopped for a hit. "What're you guys doing in there?"

"Plastic recycling," the blonde explained.

"This week, we're turning goop into kitchen utensils and storage boxes," said the Latina. "Aren't you impressed?" she took back the joint, sarcasm dripping from every syllable.

"The lifer has been torturing us for the past few days," explained the blonde, taking her turn with the joint. "We're not getting much support from the rest of the crew, who adore her," she said incredulously.

"So, why not quit?" asked Nwin, working a hit out of the much reduced marijuana cigarette.

The Latina had both hands on her hips now. "Damn right!" she directed to the blonde, "why shouldn't we?"

Nwin laughed, and wished them good luck, not wanting to get pulled further into their saga. "Thanks for the smoke," he waved, heading up the path while they continued talking animatedly behind him. He walked past some small boys who were throwing sticks into the rushing water. A very large matronly woman was hanging her laundry on a line that crossed the creek, her sheets dripping into the stream below. A solo trumpet blared from an open window in a building across the creek, competing with some electronic rhythms pounding out of another apartment nearby. He could see fog curling at the top of Twin Peaks to the west, and noticed the breeze hurtling down the creek. At

Mission Street he turned south for a block, darting between streetcars and avoiding dozens of bicycles to cross westward. The sidewalks were thick with people, fruit and vegetables poured out of storefronts, cafés and restaurants were jammed.

Jugglers were throwing bowling pins back and forth across the street, threading them through the passing cyclists, who found it irritating to try to ignore the flying objects in their path. One of the open-sided streetcars approached and the juggler nearest Nwin whistled loudly in some kind of signal. As the streetcar passed, he hurled his pins through the open car, just skimming above the heads of the passengers and below the roof of the streetcar. Everyone who saw it had a good laugh, especially his companions who caught the pins as they sailed out of the open streetcar, lunging to the side to keep up with the trajectory. But one pin hit an upright in the car and fell into the lap of an old man, who looked up alarmed. When he realized what was happening, he angrily flung the pin out of the car's side, a good half block up the street, where one of the jugglers retrieved it laughing.

Nwin continued to his favorite haunt in Dolores Park. He turned on 19th, swinging into the veloway to avoid the dense mob spilling out of a corner bar. Bits of conversation flew out at him, "shoulda won that by the 7th inning!"

"—in cold blood! They were unarmed—"

"...told 'im I wasn't gonna keep—"

"I could've caught that one!"

Inside was a big screen with a baseball game on it, but Nwin, not much of a fan, had no idea who was playing or where they might be at this morning hour, probably back east, or a taped game.

He ignored the boisterous scene and walked past Valencia, stopping to admire costumes being made by a group outside a workshop. Models were standing on pedestals while people bobbed and weaved around them, trying to attach last minute decorations or fix hems and seams. A short distance ahead on the right a furniture workshop opened to the street. This was not a Community Workshop, but an artisan's shop, Luigi Barraso's. He had a gondola workshop down on Shotwell somewhere near Mission Creek, but here they were making beautiful cabinets, tables and chairs. Nwin stopped briefly to smell the wood and to admire a nearly complete set of ornate chairs. He exchanged nods with one of the workers, and then walked another half block to the park, and up to the café.

Entering it, he couldn't see any familiar faces. In fact, it wasn't particularly crowded, still a while before the lunch rush. He ordered a cappuccino and sat down in his favorite corner against the bushes. He thought wistfully about Valentina, but he couldn't keep thoughts of her in his head, once again turning to his fantasies about war. He doodled with a scrap of pencil he found on his table, drawing a crude image of people shooting rifles over a hill.

"Nwin!" the harsh voice came from behind him. His shoulders rose reflexively while his head ducked. He quickly turned, straining to see who it was. The face was familiar... "Nance!" he sputtered. She had cut her hair very short, and dyed it light brown. Her cheeks and big lips hadn't changed, but she'd shaved her thick black eyebrows and drawn in some strange theatrical eyebrows instead. All in all the effect was very weird. Her appearance was radically different than the last time he'd seen her.

"Surprised? I guess you should be. We wrote you off after that little fiasco at the

Café Hurricane." She sat down across from him, not waiting for an invitation. She laughed unexpectedly. "I told you we were watching you."

"Who are you? What do you want?" Nwin was breathing heavily.

"We'll get to that in due time," she said, her face hardening as she stared at Nwin.

"You're part of that war in Chile, aren't you?!?"

She looked very surprised, but quickly regained her composure. "What makes you think that?"

Foolishly, he began talking quickly. "I know you were on the *Leopold Tanzania*, I saw you. And I know that captain is from Chile, and that you guys were up to something strange. You were doing something near the dock at Treasure Island." He told her everything he knew in a matter of minutes. She sat across from him impassively.

A minute of silence, then another. He wanted to grab her by the shoulders and shake her, demanding that she tell him everything, but he remembered her vise-like grip and decided to wait.

Finally, she cleared her throat. "Well, you are a resourceful young man. I thought as much." She looked at him intently. "Why do you set fires?"

He said nothing, his eyes flickered briefly at the question, but then he looked down.

"We observed you leaving San Bruno Mountain as the fire started."

He began to blush, wondering if that meant she'd seen him jacking off in his boat. There was no point in denying it to her. Maybe if he was straight with her about it, she'd tell him what he was now dying to know.

"You still anchored in the Bay?"

"No, the *Leopold Tanzania* left two weeks ago," she said circumspectly.

"But you didn't leave with it?"

"I did."

"Okay, look, I set that fire. I like fires… There. Are you happy?"

She leaned forward. "You like setting fires?" He nodded. "I can use someone like you."

"For what?"

"That will come… *if* you join us." She folded her arms, watching Nwin's face closely. "I'll tell you this. If you join us, you'll set more fires and have more power than you've ever imagined!"

"Are you part of that army in Chile?"

"I might be. If you want to find out more, you'll have to join us. In five weeks, there will be a ship leaving San Francisco." She pushed a slip of paper across the table to him and got up to leave. He took the paper, surprised.

He unfolded it and read, "*Republic of Texas*, Pier 1½, October 7, 0800 hours." When he looked up she was gone.

33.

The smell of ripe apples was strong in the waning heat of the late afternoon. Robin was beaming in front of the wedding party. Trish, clutching her father's arm, walked up the aisle wearing a peach-colored veil, a matching satin dress hugging her swaying hips. She was crying, and everyone was smiling and reaching out to touch her reassuringly as she passed.

Eric was near the back next to Emmy, just behind Kathy and Bridget. He was surprised to recognize Trish's father, one of the guys he'd met briefly at Worth While Books on one of his first days in San Francisco. He stood fidgeting with his hands in his pockets, wondering why he had come. Emmy elbowed him brusquely at the sound of his jangling pocket full of junk. He recoiled resentfully, wanting desperately to leave before the ceremony went any further.

A very tall woman appeared from behind the gazebo. She quickly shot a glance toward Emmy, surprised to see another woman matching her unusual height, but then returned her attention to the task at hand. Apparently she would preside over the marriage. A bright yellow gown flowed down from her shoulders, and a garland of flowers encircled her long white hair. When Robin and Trish were standing before her, she began a deep toning, and was soon joined by the rest of the wedding party.

Kathy sagged in front of Eric. She released Bridget's hand and grazed her with a gentle stroke as she began to move away from the wedding. She shot an arch glance at Eric, and with a quick jerk of her head, invited him to join her. He had warned Emmy that he would probably peel out if given the chance. When Emmy saw Kathy give him the signal, she understood. As the tone grew suddenly much louder, dominated by the higher register female voices, he gave Emmy a quick kiss on the neck. He tiptoed behind Kathy towards the house, far from the orchard where the ceremony was taking place.

The tone diminished as they put some distance behind them. They ran the last thirty meters to the porch, stifling giggles as they jumped up the steps two at a time, trying to muffle the noise of their boots hitting the wood. Eric took a last glance back and observed the party slowly assembling itself into a circle around the tall priestess, whose now shrill voice rose above the deep hum, although he couldn't make out what she was saying. Kathy grabbed his arm and roughly yanked him through the door.

"If you're so curious, you should've stayed there!" she scolded.

"It is kind of fascinating... in a sickening way," he chuckled, glad to be indoors and out of sight. "So what kind of priestess is she?"

"Some Church of Gaia type I suppose. I never pay much attention to the specifics of these things. We should have ducked out earlier, but I blew the timing."

"I don't think anyone paid attention. Emmy and Bridget knew..." he trailed off. Kathy walked over to the wine bar and poured glasses of red wine. They winked and clinked, sniffing and sipping the delicious late harvest merlot. Eric felt a surge of affection for Kathy, thankful that she shared his hostility to religious ritual. He sank into one of the big soft chairs in the sprawling farmhouse living room.

A local taxidermist's work was collected along the upper shelf that encircled the room: a raccoon, two ducks, a seagull, three parrots, a badger, an opossum, and a big elk's head with a full set of antlers. An old oil painting dominated the end of the room opposite the fireplace, depicting a party of early white settlers facing an attack by a huge grizzly bear. One man kneeled with his rifle pointing at the chest of the standing bear while the rest of his compatriots hurriedly ran from the campfire scene.

"Check that out," Eric gestured to the painting. "What a fantasy, eh?"

"Why fantasy? There were grizzlies all over California in those days."

"Yes, but—" and he stopped. He explained his take on the underlying pro-technology theme and she laughed.

"The grizzly is extinct, has been for practically 300 years. I don't think they were destroyed by ideology—more like hot lead!" She started sneezing violently.

"I suppose our friends out there would propose that we sing and hold hands to woo the bear with our naturalness," he dripped disdainfully.

"C'mon Eric! I don't like this stuff either," she sneezed twice more, and then wiped her nose, "but you don't have to make them into idiots!"

Embarrassed, he apologized.

Kathy drained her glass of wine and bounded up. "Let's take a walk. They're going to be at it for at least another 45 minutes or so. Whaddya say?"

"Sure—but are you okay? You having an allergy attack?" and he pushed himself up, finishing his wine and leaving the glass on the side table.

"Yeah, chingin' allergies! I got these pills," and she popped a couple as they left.

They went out through the kitchen and into the golden forest behind the house. The late afternoon sun streamed through the gnarly n'oaks, the smell of hot California countryside filling their senses. Flies buzzed and the occasional mosquito attacked, but it wasn't bad. Not like the forest hikes Eric had known back east, where the entire hike was spent fighting off the insect world, leaving little time to appreciate the great outdoors for itself. Deer bounded through the trees ahead but Eric was captivated by some wild fungi growing on a fallen tree, big flapping pink and orange pieces jutting out from a dark, wet log. He soon rejoined Kathy marching up a steep slope.

At the top, they came into an open meadow, golden grass swaying in a breeze that cooled them as they emerged. "Let's climb that," Kathy suggested, pointing to an outcropping of large granite boulders at the other side of the meadow. Eric grunted his assent, noticing that her allergies seemed to have stopped.

After a short while they were perched atop the highest boulder. Small ledges provided sitting spots facing the view eastward across the rolling hills, practically as far as the eye could see. Eric read the names carved into the rock, how long ago? "Susie + Johnny forever" How long was forever? Were they sitting here 10 years ago? 100? 200? Huge flocks of birds wheeled through the big sky before them. They sat silently admiring the view.

After a while, Eric asked Kathy, "Have you ever gotten into trouble?"

"What do you mean? Have I ever been investigated?"

"No! No, I meant trouble like people getting mad at you about religion, offending people by ducking out of a wedding... like we did here."

"Oohhh," she laughed. "I thought you meant trouble of a different sort—" she clapped her hands on her knees and began unconsciously stroking her soft green pants, unaccustomed to wearing long pants. "I've offended my friends and family MANY times... if that's what you mean by trouble!" she laughed again.

"Me too," Eric admitted. "Seems like such a contradiction."

Kathy raised her eyebrows, interested to see where Eric was going to go with this. He was grateful that she wanted to hear what he thought. He hadn't very often had the chance to explain his thoughts to someone that he respected.

"I mean, here we are living in a world that is built on respect for diversity, individual freedom, mutuality, the common good shared fairly... You know, the usual blather." Kathy nodded, smirking at the casual litany of qualities that had once engendered such fierce loyalty. Eric continued, "But people carry on with all these religions, cults, and clubs. It's like they have to join something to be part of a group…" he paused. He gazed into the distance, trying to find words, the passion that had so often inflamed him as he'd thought about this in the past. "What really gets me is how exclusionary it is. It's like they want to find some way to define themselves as 'in' and others as 'out', you know?"

Kathy nodded. "I'm not sure if I agree. I think you're partly right. People do need to belong, and it figures that they'd come together around shared beliefs or traditional practices. But I haven't found it so exclusionary, to tell the truth. Actually I've been invited countless times to join in!"

"Well sure, but then you have to become *one of them*!"

Kathy smiled. "You see, the exclusive nature comes as much from the perception of being outside as inside. It sounds like you notice being outside, and fear having to give it up."

"I'm not going to join anything! I'm a free person, and I don't need to be part of any group! And it's not fear" he said fiercely, "I'm definitely not afraid—shit! I've been told I was afraid before, and it just pisses me off!"

"I'm not saying you are. But you might stop and consider why it makes you so angry, what you're feeling that makes it such an important issue." She looked at him sympathetically.

He pulled his knees up to his chin, wrapping his arms around his legs, assuming a near fetal position. Resting his head on his knees, he took in her admonition and quietly stared at the distant golden hills, shadows growing longer and deeper. A cool breeze ran away from the setting sun, sending a bracing chill over them. They sat in silence for a while. He eventually released his knotted position, stretching his legs out before him. She sat unmoving, watching birds caterwaul overhead.

"Kathy?"

"Hmm?"

"How did you get into being a P-I?"

"Ooohhh. That's an interesting story." She looked back at the sun. "I'll give you the short version. Then we should probably head back." He nodded.

"I had been kicking around San Francisco for a few years, like everyone I guess. I was a little kid up in Ukiah, north of here, born 10 years after the revolution. The Die-off was devastating, but up in the Emerald Triangle so many people were stoners that there was a high rate of survival, including my parents. By the time I was in my mid-20s I had migrated to San Francisco. What a time it was! It was still chaotic in those days. I did reconstruction work, helping install the Shitsys, creek and wild corridor building. They used to call it 'restoration' but we were building that stuff from scratch, which they finally admitted in official parlance. Anyway, everyone was working a lot, doing amazing things. Daily debates raged about what to work on, where we'd go, how much to put into a given project. It was fascinating. And the city was changing before our eyes. We were changing it, making it so beautiful!

"Somewhere along the line I got tired of infrastructure work. I wanted something else, something more analytical, but I still wanted to be in the middle of things. I knew I wasn't an artist! I had been going out with Bridget for a year or so. She was—is—an amazing performance artist. She was still trying to find her style in those days, and I remember long nights at rehearsals. At an opening party, I forget which one... oh yeah, it was on a glass bottom boat floating off Rincon Hill," she was lost in her memories and far from the original point of the story.

"Uuhh, Kathy?"

Her reverie broken, she looked at Eric, remembering the original question, and burst out laughing. "Sorry! It's so easy to wander off track when thinking about the old days. Anyway, how did I become a P-I?"

"Right!"

"Actually I was on the right track there. See, it was at that party on the glass bottom boat that I met Virginia Moskowitz—'Moose' we called her. Anyhow, Moose had been a civil rights lawyer before the revolution. She was one of the chief architects of the new legal system. Thanks to her we kept some of the best of the old system—jury trials, assumption of innocence, evidentiary rules, a whole bunch of stuff like that."

"So she inspired you?"

"Sure did! But more than that, she recruited me! She saw something, I don't know what. She invited me to come to her office where she explained what they were trying to do, how the idea of the P-I had developed. I met the others who were working in the office, and it was just what I had been looking for.

"Moose was a civil libertarian of the first order. You couldn't find a less religious woman, I promise! I suppose she inspired me in more ways than one. She reinforced my aversion to religious groups and practices. Especially then, when so many people were starting new churches, new political campaigns that were driven by spiritual agendas, it was pretty lonely sometimes being one of the few who turned away from all that..." she trailed off, remembering some darker moments in her past.

Eric felt strangely elated. Kathy was just what he'd never known, an older, smarter person who he could actually look up to and learn from. He grinned boyishly, momentarily letting go of his thick character armor, and giggled.

"What's so funny?" Kathy frowned at him.

"Oh, sorry! I'm not laughing at you! I was just tickled because... well..." it was hard for him to say. He blushed deeply and looked away, his voice dropping to a nearly inaudible level, "I... like... you." He sighed.

She watched him tense up, feeling simultaneously sorry for him, and appreciative of his expression of affection, which she knew had been hard for him to do. "Hey," she touched him on the shoulder.

He turned back, and she was surprised to see that he was near tears.

"Hey, don't go getting all emotional on me now!" she scolded playfully. She gave him a strong squeeze, and he managed to smile again. "I think we'd better head back. I'm sure the ceremony is over by now, and we'll miss the champagne and cake—the best part of any wedding!"

He jumped up, relieved. His affection for her grew accordingly. He climbed down from the boulder, Kathy following. They went across the meadow back to the forested slope they'd come through an hour earlier. A small herd of deer at the far edge of the meadow froze as they passed.

"Hey, I just remembered! Emmy found a girl here who has some information about a witness to the fire," Eric blurted as they started into the n'oak grove.

"Really?" Kathy was immediately interested, and quickly discovered that he had already made a plan to talk with her. "Maybe we can get this girl to take a few minutes during the party, before everyone is too drunk to talk."

Eric readily agreed. They could hear laughter and clinking glasses as they bounded down the path towards the ranch. In the distance cows mooed. Cowpers Jays scolded them from the trees as they crashed downhill, precariously keeping their balance against the pull of gravity and the slippery acorns under their feet. Emerging from the trees, they could see the party going into the yard on the other side of the ranch house. A half dozen tents were pitched between the forest and the house, one of which Eric and Emmy would be sleeping in later. He told Kathy he'd meet her at the party, and darted over to his tent, where he quickly changed into shorts and a different shirt.

The tent flap opened just as he noticed rustling feet outside. Emmy ducked in, smiling wryly at him. "So—been hiding here all this time?"

"Kathy and I took a walk," he pointed back up the hill through the back of the tent. She changed her dress while he enthusiastically recounted his story. Before she donned her change of clothes she flopped over onto the makeshift bed, reaching her long hand over Eric's thigh and began rubbing.

"Honey, come here," she said coquettishly. "I've got an itch and I want you to scratch it."

He didn't need to be asked twice. No one noticed the vibrating tent during the next twenty minutes, nor did anyone come near enough to hear the gasps and moans that they couldn't help emitting in spite of repeatedly shushing each other.

"Oh shit, now everything is soaking!" Emmy groaned.

"Here," Eric flung her bag across the tent. "You've got some dry stuff in here." He also dug into his bag for another change of clothes, pushing their rumpled, sweat-stained clothes aside. After some minutes they were as normal as they were going to be, glowing with a post-coital buzz, and emerged from the tent. They went through the house to splash some water in their faces and wash up before joining the party. By the time they came out of the ranch's front door, arm in arm, they were a stunning couple, happy and at ease.

* * *

"C'moooon you guys!" Harmony was ahead, leaning from a small tree up the slope. Shelley and Valentina walked at a leisurely pace, having just left the circle a few moments earlier at the urging of Harmony, who was dying to explore the area.

"Trish was so beautiful!" exclaimed Shelley.

"It was so cute the way she was crying the whole time," agreed Valentina. "And Robin was stunning too. Did you see her eyes as Trish approached? Don't you think weddings do something amazing? I mean, I've only been to a few. People getting married practically vibrate!"

"I know what you mean…" Shelley shook her head, "Married! Don't think I'm gonna do that for a looong time."

"Me neither!" giggled Valentina.

A loud crash stopped them in their tracks. Harmony was ahead, but the noise came from the rise to their right. They grabbed each other reflexively and froze in their tracks. Bounding away over the hill and out of their sight was a black bear. They looked at each other with eyes as big as saucers, and then simultaneously whispered, "a bear!"

"Booo!" shouted Harmony, jumping out from behind a tree just ahead. They jumped automatically, and then laughingly began chasing her. Harmony was delighted to have their undivided attention now, and she scampered ahead, easily outdistancing her older sister and friend. She topped the small ridge they'd been climbing, and turned back to taunt them. But they weren't coming. She tried it again, but no noise. Cautiously she called their names, but no response. Frustrated, she started back down the hill, kicking a fallen branch aside. She was wondering where they went when all of a sudden Shelley jumped out in front of her yelling like a banshee, and hands covered her eyes from behind. She screamed and playfully fell to the ground, while Shelley and Valentina stood laughing over her.

"Okay, okay, you got me," Harmony admitted. She jumped up and joined the older two as they purposefully climbed the hill. The bear they'd caught a glimpse of a few minutes earlier was nowhere to be seen. The n'oak forest spread out below them, a trail skirting the slope heading down into the bottom of a box canyon. A small creek gurgled in the distance. Jays yelled incessantly as the girls stood under a stately tree, trying to decide whether or not to go down the trail.

"Let's go over there," Shelley suggested, pointing to a higher ridge a short distance to their left. Much higher hills loomed in the turquoise sky, still bright in the late afternoon sun.

Valentina announced, "I'd like to go back to the party pretty soon."

Harmony was noticeably disappointed. Shelley shrugged, unconcerned. "I hope they've got some good music at this party... There are no boys!" she complained. It was true, the party was about 80% female, and the males who were there were all in couples, gay or straight.

Valentina poked Shelley. "What do you care? These people are all too old for you anyway!"

Shelley gave her a dark look, resentful to be reminded of her age.

"I just hope they're done with all the ritual stuff before we get back," Valentina admitted. "I was starting to get sleepy back there," she laughed.

Harmony was offended. "That was SO beautiful. Besides, you have to do these things right, or who knows what kinds of problems you'll have later?"

Shelley grabbed her sister's ear and gave it a big-sisterly pinch.

"OW!" Harmony flailed at her. "Why'dja do that??"

"Since when are you superstitious?"

"Francesca was explaining it to me on the boat ride. She told me how the wedding had been planned for this time because it was awlspishis."

Shelley laughed at her sister. "Awlspishis, huh? You don't even know the word! It's 'auspicious'."

Harmony glared at her. "Yeah, well, I know what it means, it means it's a good time to get married, the signs are right, the planets are right, and the place is right... that's what she told me!"

"Okay, okay, I'm sure Francesca knows what she's talking about," said Shelley deferentially. Valentina, knowing her grandmother in a more intimate way, and having seen her spiritual assertions fail on plenty of past occasions, remained silent. They had gone down and now up again along the ridgetop trail.

"Let's go back," Shelley proposed, and they quickly agreed, all plunging down the trail until they ran into the pasture where the reception was spread out on tables under arching grape arbors.

* * *

Francesca was sitting near the end of one of several long tables. Bridget was next to her on one side, and Sue Billings and Paula Pandit on the other side of her. They were sharing a laugh about the blushing brides who had just sat themselves down across the table, plates piled high with the reception's culinary delights.

"You're not going to fit in that sweet dress for long if you eat like that!" teased Bridget.

Robin stuck out her tongue as she settled in to her seat, admiring the heaping plate of curried vegetables, clams, mussels, and Bay scallops. "This is nothing! Wait until dessert!"

Trish put her hand on Robin's neck, stroking her softly, then leaned over to nuzzle her. By contrast, her plate had only a modest serving on it. But then, she was rail thin next to the athletic Robin. She glowed happily on her wedding night, luminous in her lace dress, both shoulders bared to accentuate her delicately curving neck as it blended into her beautiful face, blonde curls bobbing in a short, stylish cut. Trish was not much interested in eating, all her attention was on her new spouse. Robin, for her part, was starving, and unable to ignore the steady ribbing coming from across the table. Luis and Roy were just sitting down with their dinner at the same time.

"Who is giving me the first dance?" demanded Luis of the newlyweds, who looked sheepishly at each other.

"That is a fine curry," complimented Paula, a native curry specialist. "Who is the chef?"

Before anyone could answer, Valentina and the girls ran up, breathless. Francesca trusted gesturing to Valentina to come over and talk to her.

As Valentina talked softly with her grandmother, Bridget and Kathy turned back to their scrumptious seafood. The memory of Eric's tip about the fire flooded into Kathy's mind. She guessed it must be Francesca's granddaughter who had the tip.

Eric and Emmy glided into the reception and sat at the other end of the table next to Luis and Roy, Sal and Janet, and some others. Kathy strained to catch Eric's eye, but he was completely absorbed by Emmy. When she looked later, he was involved in a heated conversation with Roy.

"But how can you say that?"

"Why? If they are attacking people, using arms, trying to take over, they lose their rights... it's that simple!" Roy put his fork down for emphasis.

"But you can't go killing people... that's what *they're* doing!"

"If these people have taken up weapons and turned them against peaceful people, knowingly and with intent to kill, why should we be concerned about their lives? They obviously have decided to sacrifice others' lives for their own interests!" Roy was a small man, with short black hair slicked-back. He had a tiny mustache, but was otherwise clean-shaven. His Adam's apple bobbed as his temperature rose with the discussion.

Emmy joined in. "But if we start killing people to defend a culture opposed to killing, don't we lose even if we 'win'?"

Luis hated these kinds of discussions. He was frustrated that the wedding party was being taken over by war talk. "People! Peeeeeople! Y'know this is Robin and Trish's wedding. I don't see how you can ruin it with all this arguing!" He folded his arms and glared at Roy first, then Eric and Emmy.

"Look Luis, we're not ruining anything, we're just discussing the situation."

"Can't you save it for later? Like after dinner?"

"Okay, okay," Roy patted Luis on his leg, and withdrew from the conversation.

Eric returned to his scallops, shaking his head. "I don't see why political conversations have to be off-limits...just because it's a wedding dinner." Emmy shared his frustration, but also chose to withdraw. She turned to Janet and made small talk about the sunset they'd just witnessed. Eric ate his dinner sullenly, wishing he could somehow get away from the table. He looked down at the other end where Kathy and Bridget and the famous Francesca Panduccino were eating, thinking they wouldn't be reluctant to talk politics.

A short while later he was at the dessert table getting a heaping serving of apple cobbler and vanilla ice cream when Kathy appeared at his elbow.

"Eric, who is the girl with the lead on the fire?"

"Her," gesturing at Valentina

They took their desserts to the table where the three girls were just getting up. Kathy and Eric asked Valentina if she would sit with them a few minutes.

"Sure."

"Valentina, tell us what you know, don't leave anything out, no matter how trivial." Kathy started, leaning forward with great curiosity.

Valentina told the story of Nwin Robertson taking her on a boat ride, going down to the site, walking around, his strange nervousness, his confession.

"So he said he was there when the explosion happened?" Kathy pressed her and she nodded. "But he didn't say anything about starting it?"

"No, no, definitely not. He wouldn't do anything like that."

"But didn't you say he thought old buildings standing in the water were an ecological problem?"

"Yes, but that would hardly prove anything would it?"

"Correct. But it does begin to provide a motive, admittedly a weak one," Kathy concluded. They continued a little longer, repeating the details for Valentina to confirm, making sure they had the story straight. She didn't know how to contact him now, except by way of the vyne. She thought he was living at home with his mother, but she wasn't sure. Eric watched her at work, impressed again at her sharpness and how her enthusiasm infected the interviewee and made them open up. She coaxed details from Valentina.

A rousing tune erupted in the barn. Everyone grabbed partners and hurried to the dance floor. Emmy came by and swept Eric up, grabbing him by the arm and refusing to let go even over his urgent protests that he wasn't finished with Kathy.

"This is no time to be working!" she admonished, enjoying the irony of being the one who was scolding.

Bridget and Francesca swooped down on Kathy and Valentina and dragged them off, too. Within a few minutes the entire wedding party was swirling around the big barn, dancing to the wild *vallenata* pulsing from the stage.

34.

Breathing hard, he finished climbing the fifth flight of stairs and stopped to sit on a bench. Chest heaving, he sat still, feeling his heart pounding. The sun was behind Twin Peaks now, the sultry mid-September air hung in eerie stillness, thick and hazy. Far below, Nwin could see streetcars parked in the ornate iron terminal at 17th and Castro. Hundreds of cyclists and pedestrians swarmed through the grand plaza where Abundance joined 17th and Castro, a huge replica of Michelangelo's David rose up out of a wide white marble fountain in its middle. Nwin hated the statue, like most San Franciscans.

Tourists with small backpacks and cameras hanging from their necks clattered down the steps, drawing his attention. They smiled and waved to him as they passed, which he returned with a nod of his head. *Why do tourists always wear baseball caps?* he thought, watching a squarish young woman at the back of the group who, like the other five members of her party, wore a green Oakland Oaks cap.

"Shit!" he reached around rubbing his lower back while trying to sit up straight on the wooden bench. "I've got to get over this back problem!" realizing that everything he could think of was dependent on not being hindered by his back pain. He decided to seek out an acupuncturist. *Mom knows a good one,* he thought, but dismissed it immediately, not wanting to turn to his mother for anything.

He got up and twisting from side to side, fought off a growing stiffness. He'd caught his breath again and up he went, two steps at a time with his long legs. There were occasional benches along the way, places to stop and rest. Sometimes there were people sitting on them, admiring the view, but mostly there weren't a lot of people up here on this hot late afternoon. His shirt, soaked with sweat now, clung to him, so he pulled it off, his lanky dark brown torso gleaming in the sun.

Next to the stairs trickled a small brook built at the same time as the stairs, modeled on a plan originally proposed by Daniel Burnham back in 1906. It had taken two big earthquakes, more than 200 years, and a social revolution, but San Franciscans had finally embraced parts of his plan during the city's 22nd century makeover. Nwin, of course, had never known the city before this 350-meter, 1000-step stairway had been built straight up the hillside from Abundance and Castro. Along the side cutouts horticultural designers had created different smelling spaces. He passed a small grove of California laurels with their elegant Bay leaves waiting for passersby to pick them for an upcoming meal. Atop the next flight of stairs was a jasmine-covered fence, with a small grove of n'oaks behind it. The perfume wafting across the stairway hit Nwin's nose like he'd stumbled into a beehive. He rubbed his nose and blinked away the powerful odor, reacting to its intense sweetness.

He resumed his climb into a cool breeze rolling down the hill, guessing that fog piled up just behind the city's highest ridge. After another 15 minutes of vigorous climbing he reached the top. The marble plaza here was as garish as the one below. Here the fountain was a mirror-like pool of water surrounding an oversized replica of the Italian sculptor Bernini's *Apollo and Daphne*, where Daphne is metamorphosing into a laurel tree to avoid abduction by the god Apollo. It had been installed to represent San Francisco's metamorphosis into an ecologically designed city.

Nwin barely glanced at the statue, bracing himself against the chilling wind rushing off the fog. Toweling off with his wet shirt, he sat down under the curving wall, built to shelter hill visitors from the persistent westerly winds while they enjoyed the view. He sat alone although a dozen others were sharing the sheltered benches that stretched 250 meters around the eastern edge of Twin Peaks' summit. Deep aquamarine Bay waters surrounded the cheerful city, aflutter with flags, colorful buildings climbing the hills, ant-like residents maneuvering through the streets far below. Windmills stood like sentinels on the southern reaches of Twin Peaks. More could be seen off on Bernal Heights, above his mother's house, and further away, on Bayview Hill. They were all turning steadily, exploiting the rush of cool fog into the hot inland air.

It was still afternoon, maybe four more hours of daylight. He had to find another place to stay. Three weeks until the boat. He wasn't sure he was going to go, but it sounded appealing. *Why stay in SF?* He was bored with everything—or worse, completely pissed off! *Abandoned buildings still sitting in the Bay. Idiotic committees that run the city, slogans everywhere.* And that ridiculous fight between gardeners and bicyclists. *They call that politics?* He wanted to be somewhere where real issues were being fought over, where people knew how to fight like it mattered!

He started daydreaming about Chile again. He tried to imagine life under the money system, but he couldn't. *You need money to pay for things? You get money for working and then use it to buy the things you need?* It seemed too crazy. *So complicated.* He hated a lot about life in San Francisco, but at least no one ever paid attention to how much you worked or where, and certainly no one paid attention to what things you took. *Why would they? There was plenty of everything…* He tried to imagine hoarding, but he was repelled at the thought of accumulating anything he didn't have need of. He knew there were some hoarders around. There'd been that guy in the Pyramid last year. *Shit, his whole place was full of junk! Books he'd never read, more music than anyone could possibly keep track of, clothes for ten people, three bicycles right there… what a nutcase!* Maybe the money system keeps people from collecting things they don't need. Finally it was incomprehensible.

He remembered Joseph, and his theory about fear, and that made some kind of sense. Money wasn't about stuff at all, but about fear and control. His heart quickened, Nance shot through his head as she sat across from him in Dolores Park, promising… something. *Individual freedom. Not having to answer to your neighbor. Control over your own life! Taking care of yourself instead of pulling your own weight, doing your Annuals, all that.*

Abruptly he got up and walked briskly back to the head of the stairs, starting down ahead of an older couple. He loped, using his knees to cushion the pounding effect of gravity on his spine. As tall as he was, he was able to scamper down rapidly, passing a lot of others going in both directions. In ten minutes he bounded off the stairway, skirting past the David fountain, bobbing and weaving through the throng. He was still shirtless, and just finishing his descent he was again warm and sweaty. Clutching his wet shirt, he realized he'd better get something else, so before taking the streetcar, he ducked into a nearby freestore.

A quick glance told him that there weren't any clothes in this food store, so he stopped a young blue-haired woman with fifteen rings tightly coiled around her elongated neck. "S'cuse me, d'ya know where there's a clothes place near here?"

She looked at his sweating torso, and then up into his face. Turning herself stiffly, neck and head and shoulders all moving together, she pointed across the plaza. "I'm sure you can find something over there at the bazaar."

He immediately felt stupid, having been by the bazaar on many occasions. "Of course, thanks!" He bolted across the plaza.

He rushed through the garish red door lined in shimmering aluminum and bright yellow lights. Neon bulbs crisscrossed the ceiling. Big tables covered in heaps of clothing were being picked through by dozens of people, mostly men, oohing and aahing over shirts, shorts, belts, scarves, you name it. Along the perimeter were racks of shirts, pants and jackets, organized by size, material and color.

Several loud wolf whistles rang out when Nwin walked in. He wasted no time. He went straight to the nearest shirt rack and put on a pale blue shirt with yellow pinstripes. His bare chest had already attracted too much attention. He glanced into the mirror, noting that a number of men were watching him. Luckily the shirt fit well so Nwin tucked it in, and practically ran out, a second barrage of catcalls and whistles chasing him through the door.

He jumped on a streetcar as it was starting to pull away, going north up Castro. Swinging through the open side door, he flopped down on an empty seat and took a deep breath, feeling as though he'd narrowly escaped.

"Hey, Nwin, what's twirlin'?"

He was startled to hear his name. It was Lupe, the hallmate at the Pyramid that he'd so often tried to avoid. "Oh, uh, hi Lupe. Howzit twirlin' with you?"

"Oh, where should I begin!" she said breathlessly. "We're having a big full moon party next week. Then it's Elijah's birthday the week after that… we're having a huge blast for that! And Halloween is coming. What are you going to be this year?"

Nwin shook his head. "You know, I haven't given it a thought. Sounds like you're in the middle of everything," his gaze shifted to the window, "as usual."

"So where are you living now? Did you move to another downtown tower?"

"No, I went home for a while after my father died," he stretched the truth, "but now I'm…" and he groped for something to close the conversation. After a moment of silence, she cut back in.

"Where?" She imagined he'd just forgotten to finish his sentence.

"Hm? Oh, uh… Listen, this is my stop… I'll see you around Lupe. Take care!" and he moved to the front near the conductor. They had already traversed the top of Duboce Triangle, curving to Divisadero Street. Streetcars piled up ahead of them, blocked by a demonstration passing on Haight Street. Placards waved in the dusk, white coats on most of the demonstrators. He disembarked and walked quickly toward the demonstrators.

They were yelling in a call-and-response cadence, "Search for the Truth… REEESearch! Search for the Truth… REEESearch!" Signs bobbed among the protesters, evidently medical and science workers coming down from the Parnassus Heights UC hospital complex. "Freedom to Research = Freedom of Speech" said one. Another said "Science and Nature, Together Again!" Yet others said "Support MacMillan, Open the Door and Open Your Mind!" "Talk to the Dolphins," "Interspecies Communication is the Next Frontier of Natural Evolution."

Nwin stood behind a boisterous mob of Integritistas, jeering at the passing demonstration. "Go back to your labs!" "Scientists Under Control!" "You have no right to redesign life!" "Don't Mess With Species Integrity!" and so on.

Others were standing quietly, watching the passing lab workers or the Integritistas on the corner. Nwin walked across the street to get a better view up and down Haight Street. A sea of white-coated marchers poured over the crest of Haight above. Down the street, an equivalent mass of white coats with waving signs was turning right on Rexroth, south of the Hayes River. Nwin waited until a gap appeared in the march and quickly darted across Haight Street. He squirmed through the mob on the north side. Streetcars waiting to proceed to the Castro were piled up like their northbound counterparts on the other side. A sparsely populated outdoor café sat at the corner of Page, but Nwin wasn't looking for a place to stop. He continued on Divisadero, looking into second floor windows, hoping to find a "Room Available" sign.

He walked several blocks before a few signs appeared. Two were in upper floors on Divisadero, but the one he liked advertised a room on Alamo Square, just a block east. He turned up Grove, hoping to get lucky. On Rexroth he soon located it, an elegant old Victorian, nearly 300 years old. Sure enough, a "Room Available" sign was in the window. Loud drumming echoed from Alamo Square across the street, and he wondered if that was why the room was vacant. He walked up to the porch, knocked, and let himself in.

"Hello? Helllloooo?"

No one answered. He slowly walked through the foyer and into the first room, a big living room with a piano in one corner, a working fireplace under an elaborate mantel, dusty old photographs of long-gone people filling the walls. He peered at one photo in particular, a portrait of a very old black woman. It must have dated from the late 19th or early 20th century.

"My great grandmother. Gorgeous, wasn't she?"

Nwin whirled around, alarmed that he hadn't noticed anyone enter the room. The woman who spoke was herself quite beautiful, but so white that it was difficult to imagine that the black woman in the picture could be her ancestor.

"Did you come about the room?" she asked, her warm brown eyes twinkling under curly jet black hair. "I'm Rochelle... Henderson."

He gave her the customary slap, introduced himself, and confirmed his interest in the room. "I'm not sure how long I'll be in the city, but I am looking for a room. It might be a month, or it may last indefinitely, depending..."

She was older than he was by decades. Her eyebrows rose with curiosity, little crowfeet lines appearing. "Depending?"

"Yeah, I may be going on a long journey. Been wondering if I should get out of town for a while."

"You're a native?"

He nodded.

"Are you working anywhere steady, or just covering your Annuals?" She backed across the room and sat in a plush chair covered with a fuzzy dark blue fabric.

He told her about the Rice Bowl and his back injury and the Harrison Rose Gardens. "But I'm getting ready to try some new things out," remembering his desire to learn how to fly, pick up some martial arts, learn Spanish, "I've been thinking about doing some Annuals in a Spanish-speaking workplace to develop my Spanish."

"Bien, bien! Cuántos años tienes d'Español?"

"Uhh, um—I haven't had any since I was a kid." He was glad he could at least understand her question.

"My father speaks Spanish at home. We are bilingual. So perhaps you've come to the right place?" She crossed her legs under a full-length, deep burgundy velvet dress, shiny dark brown boots adorning her feet. "Let me show you the room," and she got up and led him up to the second floor. Along the stairs another dozen photographs graced the walls.

"Where'd you get all these old pictures?"

"They're part of the house. This place goes back generations." They turned at the top of the stairs and entered the first room. It was a square room, maybe five meters on each side, very tall ceilings, and a large window facing the roof slanting down on the next building. "The light is good even if the view isn't so hot," she said sheepishly.

He opened a large closet. "Seems fine. So I could move in more or less right away?"

"Well, sure, but first you have to meet the rest of the family. Can you come back on Thursday night?"

"Yeah, sure, I guess so." He stood with his hands on his hips. "Hmmm, I wonder... would you mind if I used the vyne for a couple of minutes? I just want to check my messages."

"Sure, go right ahead." Rochelle left, calling over her shoulder, "My room is in the front of the building. Why don't you stick your head in and let me know when you're leaving, okay?" and he grunted his assent.

"Vyne!" and the large leaf began unrolling on the wall opposite the window. The little question mark blinked in the corner after the thin square drew itself on the unfurled surface. "Nwin Rob-ert-son, An-der-son Street, Ber-nal Heights, San Fran-cis-co" he uttered in staccato monotone. After a short pause, he called "Messages!" Seconds later a series of lines appeared on the leaf's surface, names, subjects, times and dates.

Jennifer Robertson, his mother, appeared six different times. A few old messages still sat among his incoming, dated more than a month ago. Had it been that long since he had checked it? Stefania, Rikky, Marco, Jerry, all pals from the Rice Bowl, all had messages during the time he was in the hospital back in July. Angus?!? Surprising that he would be getting in touch, especially a month after he'd left. Probably he just wanted to confirm that he wouldn't be coming back. Jimmy had left him a message.

"Jimmy Van" he called, and the leaf resolved into Jimmy's face:

"Nwin, don't feel like you've been kicked out. You can stay until you find something. Definitely come back tonight, so we can talk, okay? Vyne me if you're not coming, or call on the shellfone."

"Over." Back to the list. Stella Brooks. Who is Stella Brooks?

"Stella Brooks!" and a wide red-faced woman with long brown hair appeared on the leaf.

"Nwin Robertson. I'm Stella Brooks with the Public Investigators' Office on the Civic Green. I'd like to have you come in for an interview, or if that's not possible, please let me know where I can visit you. We'd like to talk to you about the San Bruno Mountain Fire. We've learned that you were a witness to it."

His heart leaped into his throat. *Chingale!—who told 'em that? Had to be Valentina,* he raged inside.

"Dammit!!" He tried to keep his composure. His heart raced, and he paced back and forth. He wouldn't respond to this Brooks woman. He wanted to talk to Valentina, but on second thought, what for? It was obvious that she'd told the P-I, but why? He paused, taking a deep breath, calling to the vyne "Nwin Robertson, over!" and watched while the vyne rolled itself up. He clenched his fists several times, his temples pounding with an erupting headache. Trying to calm himself with steady breathing, he slowly made his way down the hall to Rochelle's room where the door stood ajar.

"Rochelle, thanks! I'm outta here. I'll come back on Thursday, okay?"

"Yeah, great. Why don't you come about 8 and have dinner?"

"Sounds good. See ya!"

He ran down the stairs as though he was being chased, bursting through the door and into the emerging darkness. He had to figure things out.

35.

He jumped off the streetcar as it entered a sweeping left curve into the Fort Mason greenway leaving the Van Ness corridor behind. Eric tucked the newspaper into his shoulder bag, realizing he'd lost track of where to get off while reading about Sam MacMillan. Planning to engineer vocal chords, mouth and tongue into dolphins, MacMillan claimed, "I know this is a necessary and unavoidable step in evolution!" The thought reverberated through his head while he darted among bicycles to avoid an oncoming streetcar.

On the opposite side of the greenway he stopped to look at the Golden Gate. The two bridge towers stood at the Bay's opening. The south tower, closest to San Francisco, had been painted green by zealous eco-campaigners a century ago, years after the big quake of 2044 destroyed the bridge and left it leaning precariously over the edge of the Presidio. Two large windmills spun rapidly at its top, and a half dozen smaller ones extended from various spots along its tilting twisting uprights, catching the incessant wind to generate a steady supply of electricity. The north tower kept its historic red color and erect posture, but strange carbuncles sprouted from its sides where people had built apartments and studios. A suspension footbridge connected it to the Marin headlands, where the hillside was dry and brown in the mid-September sunlight. Eric breathed deeply, enjoying fresh sea smells, noting the large freight ship chugging into the Bay. Distant barking sounds reminded him of the dense population of sea lions that made a home of the city's northern coastline.

Eric took Franklin to the corner of Union and turned left to Van Ness. A dense vine-choked fence surrounded a large corner lot. Rising in the middle of thick trees was a gleaming silver silo. On the Union street side a driveway was open through the fence. Eric walked in along a small pedestrian path that wound through the thicket of trees inside the fence. The driveway was paved with large granite blocks covered in some kind of green moss.

A trike rolled through the driveway a few seconds after Eric, a one-seat cart with a small luggage carriage behind. He turned to see an elegant woman in black from head to toe with flame red hair steer her museum piece towards the silo, where a door silently slid open as she approached. Her cart had a hand-lettered name painted on the back: "Rambler."

A man with a clipboard in a white lab jacket met her, filling out some kind of form, which he had her sign. She re-emerged after a moment and went around the corner, Eric following, and entered a nearly invisible door. Eric caught up as the door was closing and squeezed in.

On the far wall a large map glowed with colored lines, which on closer inspection he recognized as a custom vyne display. Different people walked around casually; the redhead he'd followed in was heading for some chairs in a waiting area. He approached a counter where a young man in a white lab coat was hunched over a desk, filling out forms.

Eric explained that he was from the P-I's office. "I'm investigating where an arsonist got his gasoline. I wanted to check out your distribution procedures here, and see if anyone remembers anything unusual from about two months ago."

The young man remained very business-like. "We keep meticulous records here. No one gets a drop of gasoline without signing for it, and before that, they have to show their Dispensation Certification."

"Could I have a look at the allocations between July 15 and August 15 of this year?"

"Sure. Follow me."

They entered a side office, where a dozen people were busily working. Most of them were on vynes, apparently sending and receiving messages regarding supplies and shipments of the precious but toxic fuel, gasoline.

"Over there," the young man gestured, "is the record department. They have all the allocation forms for the past ten years, and they also have the supply records. You can be sure that it all balances—right down to the drop!" he said with equal parts pride and defiance.

Eric realized that any inquiry had the effect of making these people defensive, which was far from his purpose. He explained his mission at the record counter.

A middle-aged black man scrutinized Eric and briskly looked him up on the vyne before agreeing to help him find the records he sought. "You're not going to find anything. We're very careful about who gets gas here. Nobody comes in here and leaves with gasoline without a well-documented need."

Eric assured him that the Dispensary's reputation was exemplary. Nevertheless, he had to go through the records and see if anything turned up. The man led him to a desk with a vyne display already open on the wall, near a row of file cabinets. "You can find everything you need to know here," he said perfunctorily. Then he disappeared into another room. No one paid Eric any attention. He wasn't sure how the records worked, or what he was looking for. Glancing around, he wondered if anyone would be more helpful than the two he'd met already.

As though in answer to his confusion, a bookish young woman with big eyes came walking across the room. "Need some help? You look lost."

Eric smiled gratefully and explained what he was doing.

"Didn't they explain how the system works? Man, you'd think we were guarding state secrets here or something!" she complained. She shook her head in exasperation, but pulled up a chair and began running Eric through the categories and types of information he could examine. The system was quite straightforward.

"Thanks very much. I think I can do it now."

"Okay, good," she said, pushing back to leave.

"Can I call you if I have any other questions? What's your name?"

"Cecilia Forrester." she pointed. "You can just walk over if you need me."

He spent the next two hours poring over arcane forms, searching for anomalous purchases of small amounts of gasoline. Everything seemed quite regular and thoroughly documented. His mind blurred with the passing lists of small historical vehicles and heirloom devices that still used internal combustion for power. He wasn't going to find anything useful here. Robin was checking another dispensary in the south of the city. She wasn't going to find anything either. He remembered Stella saying that they had to do this first, but that later they'd follow up with remnant dealers. That sounded much more interesting, even a bit cloak-and-dagger. "Unregulated supplies…" he tried to imagine how he would find a lead, but was drawing blanks.

* * *

"Find anything?" Eric tossed his folder on the table as he slumped into a chair.

"Nope. You?" Robin was poring over her own files getting ready for the meeting.

Eric shook his head. "It's a wild goose chase. Stella coming?"

"She's s'posed to be here."

Kathy walked in briskly and sat down at the head of the table. Seconds later, Stella swirled in behind her, bedecked in cape and long dress that floated down as she sat. Anita, another Tryout, was the last to enter, furtively rushing to the far end of the room, trying to avoid notice.

Kathy took the lead. "I think we're closing in on this case. Robin, Eric, did you have any luck at the dispensaries?"

They both shook their heads, Robin muttering, "like looking for a shrimp in a whale!"

"Anita, you started compiling the medical reports?"

"Seven people were hospitalized with burns. Here's my list," and she passed it forward to Kathy, who gave it a quick, intense glance.

"Stella? Did you reach Mr. Robertson?"

"I've been trying to track him down. I leafed him and I talked to his mother, but she hasn't heard from him for two weeks."

"He's looks like our guy, but we need to connect a few more dots."

Anita piped up. "This came in from the Shotwell Community Workshop: instructions for making electrical timers on gasoline bombs. They found it behind the workbench in the electrical shop."

"Shotwell? According to his mother, that's the same place he went after he left home. His cousin works there," said Robin.

Kathy leaned forward. "We're close. Anita—go to the Shotwell Workshop. See if you can interview his cousin. I'm going to have another chat with Valentina Rogers over at the Panduccino's. Stella, give Robin and Eric an overview of remnant distributors. You guys divide 'em up and see if they recognize Robertson. If we can connect him to one of the remnant shops, I think we can make the case."

"Don't we have to find Robertson? What if he's about to start another fire?" Anita was trying to understand the procedure.

Kathy looked at her calmly. "Yes, we certainly do. But I want to remind you that our primary mission is to expose and explain. Finding Robertson and confronting him is going to be more feasible if we get our work on the vyne for all to see. Then it's everyone's job to find him."

Anita nodded. "So this isn't a hunt?"

"No. But we try to find him in the course of the investigation so we can ask him directly about our suspicions. It also discourages him from doing it again. He's much less likely to go forward if he thinks he's the primary suspect. Plus, if we can connect him to one of the remnant shops, they won't want to give him any more gasoline—assuming we're right about that."

* * *

It was strangely quiet considering how close it was to the city's bustling center. Eric was no more than 30 meters from the front of ABC Locks and Safes. It was a run-down storefront, dirty windows behind ancient rusting metal bars. He looked down at the note again, double checking his address, 136 Tailor near Eddy. Pius Lee Wong was the proprietor.

"Just approach them directly and quietly. They are the closest thing to a black market operation these days, so they're touchy about publicity," Kathy had explained to him. "They see themselves as an outpost of total freedom, no social control… and they do have their enemies."

He made his way through a small grove of trees, ducking under the one closest to the shop. The door gave way at his touch, propelling him into the dusty, cluttered store. Two old Chinese men were sitting at the counter playing Go. A young woman emerged through the bead curtain as soon as Eric appeared in the shop.

"Yes? Can I help you?" She brushed her black hair back from her face as she leaned into the counter, her tight bluejeans buckling over the edge.

"He walked closer and said in a low voice, "I'm with the Public Investigator's office. We're investigating an arson case. Do you recognize the name Nwin Robertson?"

"Why… yes."

"Has he gotten gasoline here?"

She looked over his shoulder at her father, who was staring at the back of Eric's head. He nodded.

"Yes, he has. He uses it for cleaning tools. At least that's what he told me."

"Have you seen him lately?"

"No, it's been more than a month, maybe two."

"When was the last time he got gas from you?"

"I'd say it was sometime around early July… I'm not exactly sure."

"You don't keep records?" he said incredulously, struck by the contrast to the hyper-regulated Dispensary.

The young woman's mouth twitched involuntarily, and she looked away. "No," she said curtly.

Realizing that he was intruding on a sensitive area, he withdrew. "I may need a statement from you."

She nodded almost imperceptibly.

He had what he needed for now. "Thank you." Eric left as quickly as he'd come. Stepping into the aromatic forest outside the shop, he breathed deeply, glad to be out of the dusty place. A sense of great accomplishment surged through him as he raced to Abundance to grab a streetcar back to the Civic Green and the office.

* * *

"**B**y the time I got back to the office, everyone was gone, so they don't know yet." Eric was sitting at the big dining room table with Gerald, William, Tanya and Angie.

"What is his name?" asked William.

"Nwin Robertson—"

"Wait a minute!" Angie Sung practically jumped out of her seat. "I know him! He was in the hospital… he collapsed with a bad back. He was unconscious when they brought him in." She was standing now, eyes blazing. "Of course! He was stinking of gasoline. I remember now, it seemed very strange, but it wasn't related to his injury, or so we assumed…" she trailed off, trying to remember.

"Angie, do you remember when this was?" Eric's excitement matched hers.

"Chingale… let's see… Late July? Early August? I'll have to check the hospital records."

"Can you look it up?"

"Sure, you want me to do it now?"

"Any information—his condition, what you remember, the dates of his hospitalization, etc."

Emmy came in just then, smiling and greeting everyone. She sat next to Eric, giving him a kiss on the cheek and a brief embrace. "What's up?"

They quickly filled her in. She put her long arm over Eric's shoulder and gave him a squeeze. "That's great. Congratulations! So I suppose that information from Valentina at the wedding was the break you needed, eh?"

"Yup. That unlocked the whole thing. Now we've got a ton of evidence. If we could confront him directly, that would ice it."

"Eric, I got that bookshelf for you," Tanya announced. "Do you want to come and get it right now? I have to leave and it's strapped to my bike."

Eric laughed, remembering their first meeting over a freight-laden bicycle. "Sure, sure." He got up.

"After dinner," Emmy said to him, "let's talk, okay?"

His heart sank. He knew what was coming. They hadn't slept together since the wedding. Gloomily he followed Tanya into the backyard, past the hot tubs and the jungle gym.

"Now what? You look like someone stole your toys!" Tanya said shrilly.

"I think Emmy's going to break up with me."

"Really? I thought you guys were solid, especially since you got your own room."

"Not really. I think she's fed up with me."

Tanya looked puzzled but held her tongue.

"And I think maybe she's met someone else…" he trailed off, defeated, his stomach churning anxiously.

"Here we are," Tanya announced, trying to be cheerful. "I told you I could get you a good bookshelf from the Community Workshop."

"Yeah, looks perfect," he replied without enthusiasm. He helped take it off the bike, after which she sped away on another acquisitive errand. He hauled it up to his room, and placed it on the bare wall opposite his bed. In the evening gloom, he found his room depressing. The bed was a mess, and all his books and clothes were scattered around the floor. He flopped onto the bed, curling up and pulling the blanket over his shoulder. In a few minutes he dozed off.

When he awoke two hours had passed. Laying there he remembered that the axe was about to fall with Emmy. Suddenly he was wide awake. Confused about the time, he looked at his clock and realized that he'd slept through dinner. "Shit!!" He took the back stairs, rushing through the yard to Trixie's kitchen.

Folks were already cleaning up, while a few still lingered over tea. At the stove he looked for leftovers, but everything was already clean. "I guess I missed dinner, huh?"

Vinnie was at the sink with an apron on. He heard Eric's whine and turned with his hands on his hips. Wagging his finger, he scolded Eric. "You know how it works around here. Be on time or no dinner. But you! You are lucky. Emmy put a plate aside for you."

"Is she still here?"

"No, she said she had an appointment or something. She left a half hour ago."

Eric took the plate to the kitchen table, where he dug in to tepid potatoes, salad and lentil stew. Feeling sorry for himself he slowly ate while housemates came and went from the kitchen.

"Oh there you are." Angie Sung came in. "Here's the info on Robertson you wanted." She gave him a sheet of paper showing that he had been admitted on the same day as the fire, August 12. The notes indicated the smell of gasoline, but there was no diagnosis of any burns, just damaged discs in his lower spine. He was sent to physical therapy after two days, and checked out that same day.

"Great, thanks Angie. Hey, what does this guy look like anyway?"

"Hmmm. He looks black, but he has thick straight hair. His mom looks Asian. He is quite tall, rather thin, and very dark-skinned. His hair was bleached blonde at some point, but it was growing out when I saw him. His eyebrows were kind of weird, too. I think he must've shaved them off earlier, because they weren't fully grown out when he came to the hospital. I remember trying to figure out why his face was so unusual. Hair, eyebrows, Asian features and black skin... he's actually very striking."

"It says here he hurt his back?"

"Yeah, he ruptured the disc in his lower spine."

"But he left the hospital after two days?"

"Well, he is young. The soft tissue drugs worked like a charm. If you can move and there's someone to help you, you're much better off at home than in the hospital. His mother was there with him."

"This is great." He was excited about going to work tomorrow with two huge breaks. Finished eating, he cleaned his plate and took Angie's report back to his room. He worried about Emmy for a while, then managed to get lost in his novel. Later, he dreamed about fighting, getting wounded, laying in mud with a broken back. When he woke up the next morning, his body was weirdly stiff and achy.

36.

Nwin rolled off the couch at the first sound of Jimmy and Sheila stirring. He'd come home after they'd gone to bed. Now he would have to talk to them.

Jimmy strode in and told him that he was being sought. "Nwin, you should call them. I'm sure you can clear this up." Kathy Fairly had called and so had Nwin's mom, after the P-I had contacted her.

"Why do they suspect me?" he said innocently, his heart pounding as he tried to imagine an escape. He stuffed his bag with his belongings.

"Who knows?" said Sheila. "You should call your mother, Nwin, just let her know you're okay." Sheila was irritated that Nwin wasn't more responsible.

Nwin scowled at her, sensing her underlying hostility. "My mother... I don't know what her problem is. She started hassling me... and now..." He trailed off, clenching and unclenching his fists as he stared at the floor. He wished she would just leave him alone.

"Okay, okay," he put up his hands. "I'll call my mom and check in with the P-I, too." He stared at his cousin defiantly.

"Look, don't get mad at me. I'm trying to help. I told 'em you had nothing to do with those instructions we found."

"You told them about that?" Nwin asked, anxiety betrayed in his voice.

"Well, sure... they said it matched some evidence they found at the place the fire started. Why shouldn't we turn it over?" Jimmy folded his arms.

"No reason. Nothing. I'm just surprised that... that... that you're helping the Investigators! That's all!" He slammed his last dirty clothes into his bag.

"You want some coffee, breakfast?" Jimmy asked, trying to calm things down.

"No. I'm heading out. I got a place."

"You did? That's great. Where is it?"

"Um," his mind raced as he decided to give a false address. "Out Mission on the other side of the Islais Bridge—on Silver."

"Yeah? What's the number, so we can reach you?"

"Umm, 243 Silver, just off Mission," he improvised. "A big white house with three floors. Palm trees in the yard, a small farm of fig and lemon trees, plus a vegetable patch, a few pigs." He went overboard describing his imaginary new home. "A woman named Rachel Emery."

"They already accepted you? Without meeting the rest of the household? And without a trial stayover?" Sheila saw right through his story, but she was more interested in Nwin getting out of her house.

Jimmy, for his part, had no reason to mistrust Nwin. He'd known him since birth, when he himself was just 13 years old. "I hope it works out for you, man. You need to get yourself back on track." He spoke with real affection, but Nwin could only hear condescension.

"Yeah, well, thanks." He gave his cousin a slap and a perfunctory hug, slung his dufflebag over his back, wincing at the jolt to his lower back, and headed out the door.

"Don't be a stranger!" Jimmy called after him. "And don't forget to talk to your mother. She's worried about you!"

Nwin maneuvered carefully down the stairs, wishing Mel and his cart were around. An old skateboard was sticking out of a pile in the corner. After strapping his bag to it, he towed it, noisily leaving the open space under his cousin's house. The bright morning light cast an early autumn orange hue. He squinted against the brightness.

Now what? He hadn't expected to be evicted so suddenly. He still needed a place to stay tonight before his household meeting at Rochelle's on Alamo Square the next day. *And what if they don't accept me?* He shook his head unconsciously, realizing that he was in a bind. Rage rose in him.

Valentina, that bitch!! Why did she report me? Chingale! He never imagined that he could be associated with the fires.

After finishing a roll and coffee at the Willows, he retrieved his luggage and went to the dock. He boarded a northbound ferry and peered over the shoulder of a man at his newspaper.

"THOUSANDS GATHER TO STOP WAR

VALPARAISO, CHILE—Tens of thousands of citizens gathered in the central plaza today, encouraged by speakers to enter the war zone and overwhelm the combatants nonviolently. People wept openly, hugging and singing, as they prepared to pursue the largest nonviolent military campaign in history.

Leaders of the Popular Assemblies in twenty-three Chilean districts, including the most populous urban areas, reaffirmed their plans to counteract the armed rebellion with mass resistance. Thousands of citizens converged on this coastal city to finalize the strategy and plan their tactical approach facing an armed and murderous foe."

Nwin sat back. His head spun again with thoughts of war. He couldn't imagine shooting a gun. Suddenly a dream he'd had the night before flooded his memory:

It was a dusty rock outcropping where he sat with three others, smoking. Sweat trickled down his back as the sun baked the exposed promontory. No one spoke and everyone moved in a strange, halting slow motion. Explosions echoed hollowly in his ears, and he looked around at his companions, who didn't seem to hear. He wanted to get up and look but he couldn't. His legs wouldn't move. Gleaming metal rifles lay across their laps, sweat running from his wrist onto the barrel where it quickly dripped off into the dust. Heads began popping up all around the rocks, peering into their hiding place. Familiar faces, Angus, his mother and father, Jimmy, Auntie, Rikky and Stefania, Valentina and Shelley, and then they all started laughing, pointing at him, ridiculing him. One of his companions in the outpost turned to look at him under the laughter. It was Nance. She grimaced at him, disdaining his inability to silence the laughing hyenas that surrounded them. His rage rose as he fought his paralysis, but he couldn't move.

That was all he could remember. He stood up on the ferry as it slowly churned in the channel. He moved to the back as the ferry steered around a rocky cliff, blasted away centuries ago by early settlers. He stared at the captain's thick arm on the tiller, her white bra visible under her sleeveless shirt stretching forward over her large bosom.

Catching himself before she looked at him, he turned around to see a school of silver fish flashing in the creek. Large feral pigs lumbered on the opposite bank, disappearing into a thicket of bushes covered in pale pink blossoms. A small skiff shot by in the opposite direction, much like his own, but occupied by children… He looked across the marshes to the city rising in the distance.

The Rice Bowl came up on either side of the creek's canal. Smoke wisps rose near the barn, the morning fire still burning down. He refocused his thoughts to his immediate predicament.

In two minutes they were at the 7th and Kyoto dock, where he disembarked. He made his way through the dense morning throngs. He pulled his bag across the wooden boardwalk, into the street and past the velome to the Rice Bowl's table. A small sign invited people to work in the paddies, and to sample their produce. Fresh flowers and a few bags of rice sat on the table for anyone to take. He looked down the road that led to the Rice Bowl's barn and warehouse. Someone he didn't recognize was working in the distance, far from the supply shack where he was going to stash his stuff.

The sun was hot already. In the shack he found a spot to put his bag, still attached to the skateboard. Closing the door behind him, he glanced toward his old workplace again. A cyclist came pedaling into view—it was Marco. He stood quietly, waiting.

"Hi Marco," he called as the bicycle came near.

"Nwin! What are you doing here?"

"I was just stashing my bag here for the day."

"Really? Why?"

"Oh, I'm moving to a new place, but it's not quite finalized yet."

"I thought you were staying with your mom?"

"I was, but I left last week."

Marco looked at him with unusual attention. Nwin quickly became self-conscious. "Why are you staring at me like that?"

"You look pretty much like you always did."

"What's that supposed to mean?"

"Nothing. This gal stopped by yesterday looking for you."

"Who?!?"

"Some woman from the P-I's office. Said they're investigating the San Bruno fire, and you might know something about it."

"Well? What did you tell her?"

"I wasn't here. I just heard about it. I don't know what they said. We haven't seen you for over a month. I'm sure that's all they said. Why? You don't want to talk to 'em?"

"No! Um, uh,… I'm *planning* to talk to them. I heard they were looking for me. I've been busy with other stuff," he said vaguely.

"How's your back? You coming back to work soon?"

"I don't know Marco. Since I stopped, I'm not sure I want to. What's happening with Angus now?"

Marco laughed. "Same as ever—still an asshole. What're you gonna do?" he spread his hands helplessly. But his smile showed he didn't have the same level of frustration with Angus that had plagued Nwin.

"Listen Marco. I'm going to leave my stuff here for a day, maybe two, OK?"

"Sure, man, no problem. That's a good place for it."

"I don't want to talk to everyone, or even have them know that I've been here. Do you mind keeping this to yourself?"

Marco looked at him, puzzled. He shrugged. "Sure, Nwin, whatever…"

Marco took off on his bike, while Nwin slowly walked back to the Crossroads. "Can't believe I left *Hot 1* over at Precita," he thought with irritation, wishing he had it here at the 7th Street dock. There was heavy traffic at the dock as he crossed the causeway and peered down, wondering what to do next. At this hour most of the traffic was commuting out to the University. Sun reflected in the Bay, obscuring the campus rising out of the water a half klick out. Squinting against the glare, he angled down the stairs towards the piers, moving without direction. Youthful technicians stood in a knot on Pier 16 awaiting the imminent arrival of their shuttle. Nwin moved towards them, curious about their animated conversation. He couldn't hear what they were talking about until he drew nearer.

"—was the stupidest thing we ever did! People said we looked like shock troops or something!"

"Frank, what the hell are you talking about? We looked great! We were huge, strong, silent, and self-assured!" A chubby black woman was poking her finger into the man's chest.

"Give me a break!" An older woman cut in, taking the man's side. "All those white lab coats! What an embarrassment!"

"Chingado!" the black woman whirled on her now. "You didn't even participate… In fact, I recall you don't even support MacMillan, am I right?"

"Darlene, I'm sick of your bullying. That demonstration was a larger version of the way you're acting right now!" Her body stiffened as she challenged the younger, heavier woman. "There are good reasons why many people are opposed to this. You're so arrogant! It's taken decades to earn the respect that science has now. *That's* what's at stake!"

"Calm down you guys," urged a professorial Arabic-looking fellow. "Here's the shuttle."

They stopped their conversation while they filed onto the shuttle, a furry gray device with thirty "seats" filling the floor. Nwin followed them on, curious to see if the debate would continue, figuring he could turn around and return on the next run. He sat on one of the fuzzy backless nodules that passed as seats.

The antagonists separated to opposite ends of the boat, so the debate died out. Nwin was sitting near the black woman Darlene who had been ardently defending the demonstration. He guessed it must be the same demo he'd seen the day before. The woman opened a thick textbook and buried herself in it. Quiet buzzing enveloped the shuttle as it started its run across Mission Bay. Nwin leaned forward, elbows on his knees, and stared at the passing water. A couple behind him discussed their dinner menu. He regretted coming.

At the Physics Building dock, a gleaming chrome sculpture swung out and down from the building's outer walkway, one story above the water. Contentious glares shot back and forth among disembarking passengers, but the debate remained closed for now. Nwin aimlessly followed up the cool smooth stairs. At the top, a glassed-in lounge beckoned so he went in. People sat around in small groups, studying, talking quietly. A busy coffee bar in the back stood next to a door, a "clinic" sign over it. He went over for a closer look, rejecting his instinct to turn back to the city. A few people glanced at him without recognition.

He entered the clinic. A young man asked, "What can we do for you?"

"Uhh, um, well, I uh,… I was wondering what you do here?"

"New, huh? We're an all-hours drop-in clinic. We do acupuncture, massage, and sleep therapy."

"Acupuncture?" He reached for his stiff lower back. "Y'know, I could use a treatment for my back."

"You've come to the right place! Follow me."

The young man took him to a dark room, turning on a soft light as they entered. "Sit there," pointing to a simple chair by a desk. "The doctor will be right in."

He sat for a moment in the dim light, feeling his sore back on the hard chair.

The doctor, a small Chinese man, came in, gruffly waving at Nwin without speaking. He pulled Nwin's arm onto a small pillow and took his pulse, delicately pushing his veins with three fingers, trying to ascertain where Nwin's *qi* was blocked. The doctor's bedside manner was entirely unfriendly. He still hadn't said anything. He looked at Nwin, and finally said, "put out your tongue." He pulled it like he was looking for hoof and mouth disease. "Okay," and he pointed to the gurney. "Lay there."

Nwin lay down, his face in a donut hole, and the doctor came over, pushing various points, imperceptibly slipping in the needles behind the prodding. Then he returned to each of the needles, twirling them in place. "Just rest." The doctor quietly left the room.

Nwin lay there, controlling his breathing, and soon was asleep. His forehead pressed against the padded circle, as he fell into a deep sleep. He dreamed that he had squeezed through the padded face rest, and was falling. Stars flew by as he zoomed through swirling darkness; then the swirl took a watery form and he was plunging into a whirlpool. His vertical speed lessened and he focused on objects in the surrounding wall of water. Toys from his childhood, his first bicycle, his mother's trike. Then people's faces peered through the water like visitors to an aquarium and he was a fish in the tank. He didn't recognize any of the faces, they all had big eyes and frozen expressions. The swirling was slowing, as was his descent. He could feel his feet below him now, and looking down, he stood on a grassy patch. The swirling water had subsided, and he was in a glass booth, a bright light shining down on him. The walls shifted from a cylindrical form to a four-sided box, with dozens of faces pushing at each of the windows. He turned around and around, confused, observed, self-conscious. He grabbed his elbows with his hands and looked down at his feet, trying to calm himself with the steady breathing he'd been taught as a small child.

Tap, tap, tap. He looked up to the sound, and found that the four-sided box was gone. He was in a huge open meadow surrounded in the distance by a forest. A mysterious wall with a thick closed wooden door stood before him. Tap, tap, tap. Someone was knocking at the door. He took three steps to the door and reaching the ornate doorknob, found he could not turn it. Tap, tap, tap, came the urgent knocking.

"Hey, I'm trying, but I can't open it." He heard some muffled yelling on the other side, but couldn't make it out. He fought with the door, pulling and pushing, putting his shoulder into it. Deeply frustrated, he stood back, hands on hips, staring at the door. He looked from side to side, the only boundary a forest a kilometer away. He stepped to the left side of the door while the knocking grew louder. He looked around the side of the wall with the door, and immediately a cool air rushed at him and he fell into blackness. A tiny voice called him. "Nwin, Nwin… Use your head!… Open your mind… open your heart…" But he was spinning wildly again, and everything was black. Then he woke up as the doctor twirled the needles in his back again. As he regained consciousness, he heard the tinkle of needles landing in a small metal container, and realized that the doctor was taking the needles out, finishing his treatment.

"Sit up now," the doctor ordered. "Feel better? Looser?" he pointed to Nwin's lower back. "Looser?" Nwin looked at the crags and wrinkles in the old doctor's face, trying to figure out what he was asking him. The doc must be over 100, he thought. "Your back, is looser?"

He rotated his back gently. "Yes, it's much looser, thanks!" Why hadn't he gone for acupuncture before? He put his clothes back on, and the doctor gave him a pile of small black pills.

"Take six with meals," he ordered. "Three days, you come back if you need, okay?"

Nwin nodded, and watched the old doctor leave the room. He finished putting his clothes on, still affected by his weird dream. That voice, it sounded so familiar… He went back into the lounge, and something about the upholstery triggered the memory he was groping for. "Joseph!" Last time he'd seen him was at the BioManufacturing Building. He looked at a clock—it was almost 11 o'clock, too early for Joseph. At the exit he stopped to read a big poster on the wall.

"Showdown! MacMillan vs. Floyd, the Debate of the Decade!" In smaller print, the poster described a public debate over the infamous MacMillan proposal to give speech to dolphins. He didn't like it. Aggravated by the thought of human domination of nature, he walked away hurriedly. His stomach rumbled, his head swamped by anxieties. His mother, the investigation, his hope for new housing, the ship leaving in October, Valentina's betrayal. His head spun from item to item, finding no peace or comfort anywhere. Everyone was against him and he had to avoid traps. He looked around, panicky, expecting strangers to accost him.

He ran down the stairs to the dock and jumped on a regular ferry, line 6 heading northward to the Central Train Station where he got off.

He darted under a scaffold where workers were restoring an old mosaic mural. It depicted a huge tidal wave washing up on the western side of the city, sunset bungalows swept up and pushed along in the gargantuan surf. It never happened that way, Nwin knew, but the waters *had* risen, albeit less dramatically. Again he smelled the strong presence of pot smoke sickly sweet and repulsive. Heading north towards the 3rd Street streetcars, he hopped on one as it pulled away, climbing to the sunny second deck, unconsciously stroking the smoothly polished bamboo railing that twisted up the spiral staircase. He flopped into a seat, looking around at a group of young people with backpacks.

He made eye contact with one of the women, about his age. She stared back, and began smiling. "Nwin, don't you recognize me?" she laughed.

"Huh?" he shook his head, as though trying to clear cobwebs from his eyes. The face was familiar and he struggled to put a name to it. "Maria?" he finally croaked.

She extended her hand for a slap. "How long has it been? You still living on Bernal?"

Memories flooded into his mind. Maria lived a few blocks away, one of the kids he had been schooled with. They had gotten into various mischievous adventures, like the time they had built a dam across Precita Creek. It had worked a little too well, backing the creek up until it pooled over its banks, flooding some nearby houses. He suddenly remembered her tear-stained face after he was caught for starting the big fire on the hill, a fire that had killed two of her pets.

"It's been five years—at least!" he returned her slap and looked at her again. She was a striking, dark-haired beauty, a small mole on her left cheekbone just where it had caused her so much torment as a small child. Now it almost looked like a cosmetic addition, fashionably harmonious with her classically beautiful face. Her thick black eyebrows arched as she returned his scrutiny, her own memories dancing behind her eyes.

He filled her in on his father's death, which reminded her about the accident Jeffrey Robertson had suffered, a mini-trauma for all the neighborhood kids when Nwin's dad was suddenly laid up, giving them all a dose of vulnerability. He spoke briefly about the Rice Bowl, hurting his back and moving back home.

"And now? What's next for you?"

"Well, I just got an acupuncture treatment," and he twisted and turned in place, still astonished at how much better he was. "So I can stop worrying about my back so much," he confided, surprised that he was telling her so much. He felt ambushed by the combination of his inbetweenness and stumbling into an old childhood friend.

Maria told him about the Giant Sequoias in King's Canyon where they had been. "There's this huge tree, they say it's practically 3,000 years old. The first settlers who named it called it the Karl Marx Tree. They were the ones who built the first road into the giant trees, radicals called the Kaweah Cooperative. Then their land was seized by the U.S. government and turned into a park at the end of the 19th century. The government renamed the tree after the general who destroyed the south at the end of the first Civil War, General Sherman."

One of her companions leaned over and said "Now it's called the Califas Tree." He looked intently at Nwin, but Nwin kept his attention on Maria. Indifferent to the details, he was attracted to Maria's enthusiasm. He was dumbfounded that the mousy little girl he'd known had turned into this beautiful woman. Maria elbowed the fellow out of the way, sensing his jealousy, and shot him an angry look. Then she refocused on Nwin.

"I'm beginning an Apprenticeship."

"Really? Already? At what?"

"Landscape design, horticulture."

He smiled, remembering one of his coworkers at the Rice Bowl who had been trained in horticulture. There had been endless fights between his sense of how things should be done, and the practical arrangements the rest of the people made every day. "Don't you have to study biomanufacturing as part of that?"

"Yeah, but that's not until the third year. I spend the first two years in field work. One year on an urban conversion project, and one year on a truck farm within an hour of the city."

The double-deck streetcar slid to a halt next to Yerba Buena Gardens, protected by the seawall that ran along the east side of 3rd from Howard to Abundance. An elevated diagonal skybridge departed from the terminus, soaring over the gardens towards the south Union Square docks at Abundance and Stockton.

"Where're you headed?" Maria asked him, as she and her friends began leaving.

"Not sure. I'm taking the day off," he declared.

"We're going to an all-night dance party later at Immersion. You want to join us?"

They slapped goodbye and promised to meet up again, if not at the dance, then they'd vyne each other. He stood on the platform watching Maria and her friends waddle off under their backpacks across the skybridge. He went in to the gardens, running down the stairs into a subterranean labyrinth.

Sometimes concerts and conferences were held in the sprawling basement, but mostly it stood silent, an empty relic of a long-gone era of commercialism and an obsolete "convention business." Nwin plunged into Yerba Buena Caverns, a famous diversion for city dwellers, an ever-changing labyrinth full of booths offering special foods, gadgets, short-run clothes, shoes, and one-of-a-kind art productions, all locally produced. Jokesters and clowns roamed around, regularly tricking unsuspecting visitors. It was a menagerie, a playground for home-made madness and whimsy, made by and for San Franciscans.

"Here's a tall one!" screeched a face peering from a small window at an improbable angle at the bottom of the stairs. Nwin cringed when the voice blasted him. That sent him right into the arms of a waiting host, a man in giant oversized golden slippers with long ball-tipped points sticking out in front of him.

"Ah ha! Welcome my friend," and he bowed low, "I am Abner...at your service!" He was a pale fat man of indeterminate age with a wispy goatee and mismatching bushy eyebrows, one blond and the other black.

"Uh, hi Abner. I was just going to take a shortcut through here."

"A SHORTCUT?!?" Abner bellowed. He turned from side to side, repeating it, louder and louder. Laughter started rolling through the entire hall as the word bounced through the labyrinth. Finally, amidst a jocular buzz, Abner clapped Nwin on the shoulder and asked him, "Have you worked here yourself?" an obvious requirement for anyone to know how to use the place as a shortcut.

Nwin grinned from ear to ear, stepped two strides back to his right, gave a small wave of his right hand, flattening his palm and bringing it down into a garish welcome sign, where a clown's face leered, forming an O with its mouth. Nwin's palm carefully struck the 'O' and the wall spun around, taking him to the other side, laughter peeling through the air behind him.

He was at one end of a long corridor. Magnetic cars hovered on the far wall. He climbed into the first one and it immediately sped down the hallway, almost before he could get his hands and feet inside. His back twinged unhappily under the torque of acceleration. "Shit," Nwin muttered to himself, trying to sit comfortably as he hurtled along. In 200 seconds he reached the other end. After he climbed out he carefully twisted and turned his torso, testing his back, but luckily it didn't complain any further. Relieved, he ran up to the gardens behind the Old Mint Museum. A class of kids was noisily exiting the Museum, excitedly describing artifacts of old San Francisco.

"That fire truck was the dew!" a frizzy redheaded girl cried.

"The stagecoach was better!" said a boy who Nwin thought could be a younger version of himself.

"Can you believe that they had people walking around with all those guns? And wearing that stupid blue uniform? How could anyone respect someone wearing something that looks so silly?" laughed another girl.

Nwin realized that it hadn't been *that* long since he himself had been one of those kids. He walked through the green courtyard absent-mindedly, stepping aside to watch an old woman on a wooden bicycle slowly threading the narrow bike path in the broad pavilion. He angled to a deserted café and sat under a beautiful Japanese maple tree. The tree was flourishing in a dark corner of the pavilion, shaded by old hotel walls. Sun bleached the rest of the block-long open space filled with cafés, benches, and low trees and bushes.

From the next table he grabbed a newspaper and a magazine, copies of *The Free Radical* and *The Dock of the Bay*. *The Dock of the Bay* had a cover story on rogue species invasions featuring a sensationalist image of a flying reptile with a bleeding baby in its mouth. Inside it promised more prosaic pieces on sand farming on the coastal plain, combating fruit flies, composting chemistry, favorite local recipes, and a feature on Seals shortstop Billy Bonds and his storied baseball family. Nwin tossed it aside. *The Free Radical* had a huge rat on its cover with human facial features, and a name tag saying "Hi My Name is Greg Duvall!" The monster rat filled most of a San Francisco intersection as tiny protesters waved Recall picket signs in the background. Flipping it open, he passed the piece on the Duvall recall campaign, barely noticing the columns dedicated to regional reports from around the Bay. An exposé by a lab worker at UC Mission Bay caught his attention briefly, until he realized that the author was a member of the Garden Party Steering Committee, after which he lost interest. "Chingin' Garden Party!" he muttered, flipping pages.

He stopped on a full page photo spread of marching troops in green khaki uniforms. "Inside the Reagan-Pinochet Freedom Brigade!" was the headline. He hunched over the magazine hungrily. The article was a translation of a piece that had appeared in a Chilean magazine six months earlier, before the recent outbreak of war. Photos showed a town that looked like a strange 20th century Disney suburb: Tidy rows of cookie cutter houses, green lawns, ethanol-powered cars from the mid-21st century, old flags flying from houses. Nwin couldn't recognize most of the flags, except the old U.S. and Confederate flags.

> "San Fernando, O'Higgins, Chile—Everyone here is in the militia. It's considered mandatory. Local authorities are not challenged. Those who object to the militarization of daily life are "invited" to leave.
>
> Accusations of brutality, violence, and even murder have not been proven. To a person, men, women and children all deny that there is any coercion involved in this community's ardent embrace of the iconography of pre-revolutionary states.
>
> On a sunny Saturday morning this past December, the citizens' militia gathered on a local football field to prepare for a Christmas pageant. Citizens in a neighboring region have accused the O'Higgins communities of organizing a military force, and worry that they will be the victims of it. But locals interviewed scoffed at such charges, gladly taking this reporter on a tour, allowing me to choose any place I wanted to go.
>
> "We are not violent or warlike. We just think some things were better in the pre-revolutionary societies. They were much more efficient for one thing!" bragged Daniel Ortega Johnson, my guide during a

two-day visit to the area. "People were proud of their country, and families stayed together, people had respect, it was a time of well-organized growth and learning."

But as I watched the militia drill that balmy Saturday morning, it was hard to imagine that the strictly disciplined ranks were being trained for a Christmas pageant. Target practice echoed in nearby hills that afternoon. When I asked why they used guns and bullets, I was assured it was all in good fun, part of the strict athleticism of the community. They planned to win the gold medal in the next Olympics, they said."

Nwin gave up on the article, which had no news on the war itself, being too old. He stared at the photographs, trying to find Nance, but to no avail.

A small parade appeared in the distance, a large bass drum thumping beneath the strains of several mournful trumpets and trombones. It looked like a wake of some sort, and it grew larger as Nwin watched. Several hundred people followed the band, some wearing black, but many more carrying on in typical festive San Francisco style, dressed in all sorts of garish outfits, some on stilts, a few blowing clouds of fire. When Nwin observed the fire breathers, he immediately rose and began walking towards the spectacle.

He fell in to the stream of revelers. He was surrounded by a group wearing masks and waving golden wands that emitted some kind of lighter-than-air sparkling golden material, which filled the air. It stuck to his skin and clothes, and as he brushed at it, it seemed to adhere more thoroughly. Sighing, he knew he wouldn't be able to get rid of it without laundry and a good shower, so he stopped and let them pass.

The next contingent was all in black, toning a deep hum together. He let them pass too. Fifteen or so unicyclists were next, all but two keeping themselves going effortlessly. One, a stocky, muscular girl, fell three times in a row, and finally, laughing, just started pushing her unicycle in front of her. She looked at Nwin who towered over her bobbing associates. "You wanna give it a try?" offering him her unicycle.

"No thanks," he smiled. "I can't do it!"

"It's not as hard as it looks," she said encouragingly, but her own experience belied that.

"What is this parade for anyway?" Nwin asked.

"I think it's a wake. Elmer Eddings—you know him?"

"Eddings? He was an old revolutionary wasn't he?"

"I think so. And he was a writer, too."

"Yeah, I've heard of him. But I didn't know him."

"Me neither. We were practicing when they came by, so we figured we'd join in," she giggled as one of her companions took a spill just ahead. "Francine! You look like me!" she shouted.

Francine looked back, chagrined, and waved dismissively as she got back up and roared ahead.

"Aaah, she's actually a good unicyclist."

"Do you know where this is headed?" Nwin continued.

"I assume we're going to the Civic Green… I think there's a ceremony or party or something."

He stepped back from the unicyclists. At the back a tall couple in flowing black robes nodded their heads as he fell in beside them.

Silence suited him now. It had already been a long day. Where was he going to stay tonight? Of course he could crash at any of the numerous hostels or dormitories. He could even go and stay at one of the hotels. But something held him back.

The march turned up 7th from the Mission greenway, veering to the east of the streetcar corridor. Bicycles waited at 7th to bring up the rear, filling the veloway into the Civic Green. At Abundance several other parades converged from other directions.

Soon they entered the sloping Green, most paraders finding places to sit on the lawn around the stage at the bottom of the bowl. Nwin waited to see what would happen, which didn't take long.

"My friends," said the choking voice of an old black woman dressed in black, veiled with an elaborate hat on. "Thank you for coming. Elmer would be proud." A chant went up, "Edifier, Edifier, Edifier," and Nwin remembered now that Eddings was revered as The Edifier for his clear writing and frequent political interventions in the early days of the revolution.

Leaning over to the elderly couple next to him, he asked, "Do you know how old he was when he passed on?" They looked like Eddings' contemporaries.

The old man, white hair, deep craggy wrinkles in his café au lait face, smiled at Nwin. "Elmer? Shit, he was 136! He didn't want to go, either, let me tell you!"

"You were friends?"

"Hell yes, me and Elmer go WAY back, I mean WAY WAY back, before the Die-off and the Revolution."

"No shit?"

His wife was shushing and elbowing him, but the old man was happy to talk about Elmer and his shared past. He grew animated, overcoming the somber sense of loss that had dominated his day so far. Struggling to rise, he spoke quietly to his wife, and then offered Nwin his arm.

Nwin bounded up, automatically respectful of the elderly man. As soon as he made contact, the old man's weight sagged on to his arm.

"Let's go over there," the old man pointed, "I need a drink."

They sat at one of the cafés surrounding the plaza. The man, whose name Nwin learned was Abraham Miller, or Abe, ordered a whiskey. Nwin went for a beer. While they waited for their drinks, Abe pulled out a very large joint and fired it up. Then, as he exhaled, he began reminiscing, passing the joint to Nwin, who demurred.

"This is the shit that saved our lives, man!" he insisted. "If we hadn't been stoned, we'd have died, it's that simple!" Nwin grudgingly accepted the joint and took a shallow puff. "No man, take a REAL hit!" Abe demanded. Nwin complied, realizing that it would be impolitic to refuse at a time like this.

Abe, well over 100 himself and like all old folks, fond of storytelling, started in on the story that Nwin already knew well, like everyone everywhere did, about how pot had saved the world. Nwin sat quietly, feeling the strong drug begin to show up in his limbs, behind his eyes, and in the warm buzz that overtook the back of his brain. A waiter invisibly deposited their drinks as the story continued. Nwin's mouth had completely dried out and he glugged the beer like a man dying of thirst.

"So we'd been stoned, wondering how we were going to fight the government's plans to build more jails. We decided to take a walk, and when we came out—we were over in Oakland on that fateful day—there were bodies lying everywhere! We couldn't believe our eyes!"

Nwin faded out the story. He'd heard it so many times, how people who survived ran around in confusion, how it slowly dawned on them that being stoned was the antidote, getting everyone to smoke who hadn't already, wondering if they would survive if they stopped being stoned after a night's sleep, and so on.

Nwin got so stoned so quickly that he couldn't focus on Abe and his story anyway. He gulped his beer, which only made him thirstier, and then his head started to spin. Abe was droning on, smoking like a chimney, not noticing whether or not Nwin was with him. Just having him sitting at the same table was enough.

"So the Swiss started shipping pills all over the world, trying to nip the epidemic in the bud—ha ha ha!" It was one of Abe's favorite jokes. "And it worked. After that horrible month, it stopped." He stopped and downed his remaining drink, immediately calling for a refill. Meanwhile, in the distance, the ceremony was continuing but Abe had forgotten about it completely.

Nwin tried to gather himself, clearing his throat and finally cut in on Abe. "Hey Abe, man, that's a great story, but don't you think The Edifier would expect you to be at his wake?"

Abe's bleary eyes suddenly focused on Nwin, who was having plenty of trouble focusing his own vision. "Damn!" His memory was definitely slipping. He pushed back from the table, and walked purposefully, like a much younger man, back to his seat. Nwin stood up with him, but quickly moved in an opposite direction, far too stoned to listen more to the ceremony or Abe.

Leaving the throngs behind, he walked unsteadily toward the streetcar stop in front of City Hall. He boarded a waiting streetcar unconscious of its destination or direction, but clear that it had an open top deck. He pulled himself up the spiral staircase and flopped on the first seat on the top, slumping against the side. When the streetcar started a cool breeze whistled over him, jarring him out of his deeply stoned state. He sat watching the streets go by, looking up to see flapping flags and banners, flocks of birds, filaments of soaring lights just starting to illuminate the falling dusk. He closed his eyes briefly, but the spinning worsened dramatically, so he quickly opened them again. He wasn't tired, just terribly stoned.

I should walk, he thought, *a strenuous march uphill should help sober me up*. The streetcar approached the western slope of Russian Hill, still on Polk Street. At Greenwich he hopped off and entered the familiar terraced gardens, up past the orchard and the vegetable gardens, through the taro patch irrigated by a small stream running through a stone-lined channel. When he skirted a billowing patch of gorgeous pot plants, they seemed to reach out for him, making him uneasy. Then he took the old stairway for the rest of the climb, finally emerging at the top of the hill, a short walk from his favorite tree. After two minutes of vigorous climbing, he was perched on his favorite branch just in time to catch the last bit of pink and orange through the aptly named Golden Gate. He sighed deeply, relieved to be once again comfortably ensconced in his childhood retreat.

He stroked his name where he'd carved it years ago, and looked up to see the hawk nest where it had been for at least two years. A squirrel chirped at the end of a nearby branch, and he chirped back, feeling that he was being welcomed home. Just as he felt fully enveloped by a sense of familiarity and security, he remembered his conversation with Valentina about tree climbing and his unfulfilled promise to show her this place.

Glad I never did that! he thought bitterly. Anxiety surged through him, obliterating his fuzzy stoned-ness, and ruining the comfortable homey feeling he'd been appreciating. Small ships dotted the darkening Bay as he realized he didn't know what was next for him. *Those photos of Chile were NOT inspiring!* But he probably couldn't stay here much longer. He was sure to get caught eventually by the P-I and what if they had put a case together? What would people do to him? *I didn't mean to burn anyone's house down! That should help, shouldn't it?* He fidgeted in the tree, wanting to escape this train of thought, but couldn't.

The wind was blowing now, so he pulled his shirt close and drew his arms inside, huddling for warmth but starting to shiver. He wanted to stay, but angrily realized he'd already lost what he came for. He shook his head vigorously, trying to clear his intoxication. A couple strolled beneath the tree, lost in romantic mutual absorption. Nwin silently gazed down, watched them stop, embrace and carry on a prolonged kiss. It was a strange view, looking straight down on the noses and tongues meeting and parting, whispers and giggles. Nwin fought his shivers ten meters above the lovers. Finally they moved on, walking arm in arm towards the descending path over Lombard.

Fluttering bright blue and purple lights suddenly illuminated Aquatic Cove. A red sign flickered on, too, *IMMERSION*. Nwin remembered that Maria—the suddenly beautiful Maria with her winsome smile and sculpted face—invited him to meet her there for a dance. Freezing by now, the thought of immersing himself in warm water was very appealing. He clambered down from the tree and began the short walk downhill to Aquatic Cove and the entry to Immersion.

He approached a tall arching pier bulkhead that had been relocated to the corner of Hyde and North Point. Though it wasn't even 9 p.m. yet, cable cars were already disgorging throngs of revelers, while cyclists were beginning to fill up the velome lot just across the street. Nwin noticed many people adorned in flashing neon tubing, and looked down at his own rumpled, dark clothing, feeling out of sorts. An old man hailed him from a small booth just off the side of the entryway.

"Young man, you need color, some light..." the arthritic hands clutched a bright pink vest, which he waved briefly, and then exchanged for a small tangle of pulsing tubes.

Nwin accepted some lengths of electric purple tubing and wrapped them around his black clothing, the sharp contrast meeting with his satisfaction. "Thanks, man." The old man nodded, and turned his attention to the next passerby.

He walked through the tall gateway with a cluster of others, and entered a downhill slope. People ahead were following stairs through two giant, neon doors, adorned by a man on the left and a woman on the right. Dressed like old-fashioned dance hall hosts, the man wore a big top hat, long tails and striped pants, the woman dressed in a tight, low-cut red dress covered in frilly sequins. A big neon sign hung across the ramp, spelling out, *"Desmond and Molly Jones Welcome you to Immersion."* The Jones's had invented the underwater dance club and its enabling technologies decades earlier and most of the signage dated to pre-revolutionary times. Desmond and Molly were long gone, of course, but their place lived on, thriving on the north edge of San Francisco.

Nwin followed the throng to the left. As they passed through the door a shower of clear liquid inundated them. Initial contact with the warm, translucent goo stung a bit, but it quickly formed a surface over one's entire body without blocking air, visibility, or tactility. The goo adhered to everything, and continued onto the floor and up and over the next person, steadily covering every person who passed through. Nwin followed the people ahead of him as they excitedly walked into the water. Like the first time he' come, it was strangely disorienting to be covered in goo, and then walk into the dark waters of the Bay until you were five meters under water.

An underwater doorway glowed green and opened and closed ahead as people entered. Inside, Nwin found himself in a swirling light-filled place, not a room exactly, but cozy and close nevertheless. A deep throbbing bass grabbed everyone by the backbone and hurled them onto the dance "floor"—a flashing, multi-colored, semi-translucent platform that was a step up from the cement stairs they'd entered. Couples and small groups were already merged together, dancing wildly around the floor.

Before he was ready to abandon himself, an apparition approached, a tall, thin albino, eyes blazing gold with a strangely inhuman luminescence. Both hands, draped in white robes under the goo, reached out to take Nwin's. In seconds their coatings had reoriented themselves to form a bubble in which he stood with the albino, whose eerie smile revealed teeth filed to points inside of blood red lips.

"Helloooo," the albino said breathily. "I haaafve sommm'ting for yoooou," and she breathed a cloud of white gas into Nwin's face. He made no effort to escape it. He hadn't planned on tripping, but once he entered the tank, memories of the last time set off his nervous system and he was practically hallucinating already. He smiled, breathed in the gas, and bowed deeply, as was customary, to the bringer of visions. The albino released his hands and once again the goo closed in tightly around him as he immediately felt the rush beginning.

Now the music was overwhelming. In the warm, close surroundings he merged with the movement and sound. As he swirled around the dance floor, his vision repeatedly locked onto tracers of neon color flying across his vision, interrupted from time to time by parrot fish, simulacra projected by the club's cameras, swimming in front of his eyes.

A warm hand grabbed his and spun him around. The goo lifted and in the bubble he was face to face with Maria. "Hi Nwin!" she smiled lasciviously. He pulled her towards him, guessing that she was as high as he was, and together they gyrated to the music, bodies pressed close. The albino's drug, probably Q but he wasn't sure, made every part of his body feel like an erogenous zone. Maria wrapped some tubing around their waists, firmly joining them, before she reached out to a cluster of friends nearby. In seconds she and Nwin were in a much larger bubble, dancing and groping with at least a dozen others in various stages of undress. Nwin felt his shirt coming off, but had no sense of doing it himself. He was staring at beautiful bared breasts—then he suddenly realized it was Maria. Behind her two other women were pressing together their naked bodies, while two couples were on the floor in a jumble.

It was a quick and furious introduction to Maria and her randy friends, but it was only just beginning. Hours and hours went by, dancing, having sex with strangers, dancing more, and somehow never tiring. When the darkness began to break, a cold emptiness gripped Nwin. The buzz rapidly wore off with the arrival of dawn, and his exhaustion was palpable. Looking around he didn't recognize anyone. Maria was nowhere to be seen. In fact, he couldn't remember when he'd seen her last. It seemed like days had passed. *Immersion* was a place that depended on darkness, and the all-nighters began slowly filing towards the exit, exchanging last kisses and embraces.

He emerged from the water and walked back through the entryway, the machines now vacuuming the goo from him as he passed through, then blasting him with warm air. Sinks stood to the side, where most patrons were washing off makeup and trying to prolong their consciousness with splashes of cold water. Nwin rearranged his clothing after a brief washup, and on the way out, deposited his tubing at the now unattended booth.

The sun was low in the southeastern sky, silhouetting Coit Tower briefly. He walked absent-mindedly towards North Beach as early morning commuters began to fill the adjacent veloway, remembering the last time he'd been awake at dawn. The memory of starting the fire made him anxious about the investigators who were still trying to find him.

He needed to sleep. Tonight he could return to Rochelle's place on Alamo Square. If that worked out, he could probably lay low there until October, until the ship. Nance's offer seemed like his only alternative to getting embroiled in a public trial here, assuming they'd catch up with him eventually. His mother—he flashed on how upset she was going to be, or must be already, since they'd contacted her. His stomach churned. Then Maria was in his thoughts, the unbelievable night he'd just had. He wanted to find her again! He kept walking, thoughts jumping chaotically from anxiety to desire to fear to hope. He needed to sleep.

37.

Eric clutched his knees to his chest, an involuntary shiver running through his body. She told him to wait here, in his room, and she'd be up in a few minutes. At breakfast Emmy had been her usual cheerful self, but Eric thought he could see a certain coldness.

This is it, he thought, fighting against the tears that were already trickling from his eyes. "SHIT!" he slammed his forehead into his knee. He heard footsteps on the back stairs. He cringed, bracing himself. The door opened and in walked Emmy. She had a black turban wrapped around her head, her eyes brightly glowing in her dark face. She forced a smile on entry, dazzling even when insincere. She was wearing a form-fitting jumpsuit with zebra stripes that emphasized her elongated form and remarkable height. Eric, as usual, was bowled over by her appearance.

"Eric," she sat down next to him, turning halfway to face him. She gently unwrapped his arms from his legs, pulling one leg and then the other down, and took both hands in hers, staring into his face. She leaned over and kissed him on the forehead.

"Why don't you just get it over with," he said morosely.

She recoiled, disappointed at his rising bitterness. There was nothing she could do to make this any easier. Her gaze hardened, but she wouldn't let go of his hands.

"I'm sorry—"

"No you're NOT!"

She scowled at his childishness. "You've been a sweet lover. But obviously—"

He jerked his hands back to his face as tears began, unable to stifle his sobs.

She tried to hug him, but he was so stiff and cold that she gave up. She rose from the bed to tower over him, reflecting unconsciously the power dynamics that had finally taken over the relationship. "I'm sorry, Eric. . ." She trailed off into silence, the room filled with his snuffling. "I hope we can still be friends. We've had some good times together, and I'll cherish those memories."

"How can you do this to me?!?" he suddenly screamed, and then broke down crying harder than ever.

Quietly she stood there, hands on hips now. Softly she said, "I'm not doing this TO you. It's not working out for us, Eric. You must see that?"

"NOOO!" but he really did, and was just carrying on the role in which he'd already trapped himself.

"Look, I'm willing to talk more, but later, when you're not so upset, okay? They're expecting me at the Theatre. Hey, I was going to tell you last night, I got the part!" she said and immediately felt guilty for having good news about herself at a moment like this.

Pathetically he watched her near the door through his tear-stained face. "Well, GOOD for you!" and like a spurned teenager, hurled himself into his pillow. Emmy slumped, saddened to have hurt him. She barely whispered "goodbye" and walked out.

Face down, he stopped crying right away, feeling more embarrassed than anything. He lay there, a final great sob shuddering from him. He lost his girlfriend.

Full of self-loathing, he daubed his swollen eyes with his soiled pillowcase. He lay there, paralyzed with grief and humiliation. He started crying again, feeling sorry for himself. *I bet she's already getting it on with some actor she met,* he thought angrily. But even jealousy wasn't enough to move him out of his self-pitying bed. He reached down and tried to arouse himself, thinking of some of the unforgettable sex he'd had with Emmy, but his grief was stronger. Disgusted, he forced himself out of bed.

He took a long hot shower. In the mirror a sickly white boy, swollen red eyes, scrawny and hairless looked out at him. "Ecch!" He threw his towel into the hamper. He got dressed and hurried out of the building. His room was not the place to be.

In the Panhandle, he was surprised at how pleasant the warm late September air felt on his face. The gardens smelled as sweet as ever, and people were friendly, smiling and waving as he passed them on his bike. His personal catastrophe was invisible to them.

He felt incredibly relieved that he had his job to go to, and was anxious to get there. He had breakthroughs, solid information that was going to ice the arson case on Robertson. He wondered if his colleagues had come up with anything since yesterday. Had anyone found the guy? He rolled with traffic to Rexroth, past the ice cream parlor and then wiggling over the Sans Souci Bridge, along the crumbling mural. He pulled over at Angelo's Juice Bar on the slope above Market Pond. It was almost 10 a.m., and there were dozens of commuters stopping for juice or coffee. He ordered his favorite combination of orange juice and passion fruit and waited while Angelo, a friendly man with a handlebar mustache, prepared it. Elbows on the counter, he closed his eyes to face the warm sun, comforted by the buzz of familiar sounds: bicycles clacking along, the juicer grinding fruit, conversational buzz rising and falling from table to table, in the distance a streetcar gliding over the Market Pond, clanging its bell.

"Hey, aren't you..." the woman's voice broke the spell. Sitting alone at a nearby table was a short, squarish woman. It was Victoria, the girl he'd met when he'd first arrived at the Tweezer Hostel. Her brown hair was altered—curled or cut, he wasn't sure.

"Yup, Eric, hi," he walked over and slapped hands with her.

"*Jugo!*" called Angelo in Spanish.

Eric retrieved his drink, and returned to Victoria.

"What are you doing now?" she asked eagerly. "I just got back after two months in Mexico. I think I'm going to stay for a while."

He didn't bother mentioning his miserable personal situation, instead telling her about his success at work. "So we're close. With the evidence I'm bringing in today we should be able to publish the facts… at least if I understand the process correctly."

"That's so great! Congratulations! It sounds like an interesting gig."

He agreed. Victoria was ebullient—her cheerfulness was a pleasant antidote to the crisis he'd left at home. Maybe he should move out of Page Mews? Now that he had his own room, it wasn't urgent. Having to eat dinner with Emmy, meet her new beau—a supposition that hadn't actually been confirmed yet, but he knew it—was going to be horrible. Victoria's interest was good for his bruised ego.

"So where are you staying?" he asked her.

"I'm crashing with some friends near Mission Creek, but I'm going to find a room of my own. Any suggestions?"

"Well…" he thought about his room, but then thought better of it. "I'll keep my ears open. I'll vyne you if I hear anything. What's your last name?"

"Matthews. I redirected my address to San Francisco yesterday, c/o Mission District General Delivery, okay?"

He drained his juice. "Gotta get to work. It was great to run into you again. I'll be in touch."

She got up to give him a warm squeeze, which pleased him.

Biking down Abundance he felt strangely buoyant. *Hmm, maybe breaking up with Emmy isn't going to be the end of the world after all*, he thought, but his heart ached at the thought. His brief sense of well-being passed as quickly as it had appeared. A lump appeared in his throat as he pedaled deliberately, his unfocused vision tracking potential obstacles. He made his way through the multitudes at Abundance and Van Ness and in another couple of minutes he was dropping his bike at the Civic Green velome.

"Hi Eric," greeted Tina cheerfully. Her hands were blackened with grease, even her face had a smudge, but it only emphasized her pixie-like demeanor. Her short blonde hair was tied up in two pigtails, and her tiny frame was hidden behind a floppy work apron.

"How's that *Bambu* doing? Still riding smooth?"

He looked at her, surprised at her solicitousness. *Is she trying to cheer me up?*

"It's riding great. But the brakes are squishy."

"I can fix that in a jiffy." She grabbed the bike from him.

"No hurry!" he protested. "I'm at work until mid-afternoon at least."

She looked back at him over her shoulder.

Is she flirting with me? Am I going crazy? His thoughts raced as he stood there, dazed and immobile.

"Okay, see you later then," Tina said, her tone offering no clue about her attitude. He thanked her and departed.

The Green was already filling up in the late morning sun. A bluegrass band was tuning up for the lunchtime concert down on the stage. *Shit, what time is it?* He hurried across the Polk veloway towards his building at the corner of Grove. He ran up to his office, noticing that it was past 11 already.

"Hey Eric," Stella called from her office as he hurtled past.

"Huh? Oh Stella!" he skidded to a halt, "I got it!"

Stella rocked back in her big chair. She folded her arms, looking expectantly at Eric as he came in, fumbling with papers.

"Here!" and he produced the medical report that Angie had given him the night before. Before she could begin reading it he began stuttering with excitement. "Y-y-yesterday... I found it! The rem–remnant dealer!"

Stella looked at him, surprised by his uncharacteristic stuttering. "Calm down, Eric. Take a deep breath and tell me what you found."

He took a deep breath, and went for a drink of water, breathing deeply several times before continuing. He stood at her desk and looked at Stella with unconcealed pride.

"I got a confirmation that Robertson picked up gasoline at the Wong's place on Tailor. And even better, one of my householders is a doctor at General. She treated him the day of the fire and says he stunk of gasoline."

"He was burned? I didn't see his name on Anita's list."

"Nope, that was the lucky break. He was hospitalized for a back problem. But Angie, my householder, remembered that he came in reeking of gasoline."

"Let's call a meeting with the others, and put it all together. I think we have enough evidence to publish."

She and Eric gathered Kathy, Robin and Anita to meet in the conference room. Eric was trembling with excitement. He made a quick detour to deposit his things at his desk. He was hurrying back to the conference room when he almost ran into Pops O'Hair.

"Whoa there young man! Where are you rushing off to?" Pops inquired jovially, having just barely avoided the collision.

Eric beamed at him, breathless, "Solved the San Bruno Mountain fire case!"

"Really?"

"Yeah, we're going to plan the final steps now," gesturing towards the conference room.

"Mind if I tag along?"

"Of course not!" Eric clapped him on the back like they were old friends.

Pops was surprised that the reticent Tryout had become this confident, enthusiastic investigator already. He thought he'd seen something in him, but this considerably exceeded his expectations.

"Hey Pops," Bill Mooney called from his office. "C'mere a sec, wouldja? I've got a lead on the Duvall case."

Pops squeezed Eric's arm and waved at him, indicating he'd be along in a minute. "You've heard about the Duvall recall, I'm sure?" he assumed as he disappeared into Mooney's office.

Eric was curious to know more, but his momentary distraction was soon forgotten as he entered the conference room, where Stella had already informally told everyone what he'd found.

"Great job Eric!" Robin said.

"I can't believe he was in the hospital and not on my list!" Anita complained, frustrated that he'd been right under her nose.

Eric looked at her, gloating inside, loving the attention. "Hey, I got lucky... you know he wasn't in for burns, right?"

Kathy watched Eric intently. She was pleased that he answered Anita with some humility. "Eric, what did you get at Wong's place? I hear it checked out?"

"The woman there confirmed that he'd been there. Picked up five gallons of gasoline in late July or early August, she wasn't sure exactly."

"No records, huh?"

"Nope." Eric looked around at the faces of his colleagues. Pops walked in just then, and quietly sat at the edge of the room. "We did this together, you know. I mean, I wouldn't have known what to look for or how to go about it. Moreover, it's pure luck that I was sent to the Wong place, and then my householder happened to be his doctor, and happened to remember enough to help us."

"Some things are meant to happen," said Stella. "The goddess works in mysterious ways."

Pops snorted derisively. Kathy looked back and forth between Stella and Pops, ready to intervene if they launched into their typical spat. She had no sympathy for Stella's superstitions, but she had to keep meetings from deteriorating. Stella just glared at Pops. Meanwhile, Eric was shuffling his papers. She jumped in.

"Eric, you've done a bang-up job here. Frankly, none of us would ever solve anything if we were working strictly alone." She shot a look at Stella, who was withdrawn now, her arms folded over her sprawling torso, but still listening closely.

"Stella, I think we have enough to publish, don't you?"

"Definitely! But it would be great if we could find Mr. Robertson and get his statement. What we have is a very strong circumstantial case. It's possible that Robertson can prove his innocence. I propose we wait a few more days and see if we can find him." Sighs audibly escaped Eric and Robin, both impatient to chalk up this case as solved after working on it all month.

Pops piped up, "I'm willing to try to find him. Do we have leads on where he might be?" Pops was the P-I's top sleuth, with years of experience at finding people they needed to interview, both suspects and recalcitrant witnesses.

"I called his mother and his cousin," Stella offered. "But neither knows where he is. The cousin thought he'd moved to a new place down near Islais Creek. He couldn't remember the address, but he said it was somewhere on Silver Street."

"No, Bill needs you on the Duvall case, and you've already got three others," Kathy said. She was the leader of the office, and it was her role to allocate the staff. "I was planning to revisit the girl, see if she's had any new contact. She might remember something else that would help find him. Eric, you go to the Rice Bowl where he used to work. Ask around, see if his friends know where he liked to go. Also, he has a skiff somewhere. See if you can track it down. Robin, you work with Stella on the report, okay? Vyne the Wong place and tell 'em we need a statement by vyne or on paper."

The meeting was over. They made a plan to check back with each other at the end of the day, around 5 p.m.

* * *

Kathy was checking her numerous pockets. "Got pens, the map," and she groped through some folders on her desk. She grabbed Valentina's statement about her trip with Robertson to the crime scene and folded it into one of her pockets. Her shell-fone began clattering in her back pocket. Like most people she didn't use it much but sometimes Bridget would call her for a quick consultation. She pulled it out and flipped it open, revealing a blurry image of Bridget.

"Hi sweetie. Tonight's rehearsal has been cancelled because we're having it this afternoon. So I will be home after all."

"Great! Clams and asparagus?"

"Mmmmm, sure! You cooking?"

"Well, that's not what I meant!" but Kathy laughed and agreed. "Hey, is Francesca there? I need to find her granddaughter."

"Hold on," and Bridget called to her collaborator. Francesca appeared in the shellfone. "Looking for Valentina?"

"Yeah, I need to talk to her again about the fire case."

"She was out on a ferry run to Benicia this morning, but she's supposed to be back by 2. I left her a message that we moved up the rehearsal, so I hope she comes. She's doing the lights."

It was 12:30. "Where does the Benicia ferry come in?"

"I don't know and I'm not sure what time either. You'll have to look it up. See you later." Francesca was being called away from the fone. Bridget reappeared.

"Are you coming here?"

"I don't think so. Valentina is coming in on the Benicia ferry. S'posed to be back by 2, probably sooner at the docks. So I'll find her there. Say, you don't know where the Benicia ferry dock is do you?"

"Me? No way!.. See you at dinner."

"Yeah, 7:30 or so. Bye!"

She clapped the shellfone shut and shoved it into her back pocket. Hunger rumbled in her gut. She called "Vyne!" It unrolled on the wall, awaiting her request with a blinking question mark. "Ferry service from Benicia to San Francisco." It displayed a schedule, 16 ferries a day going back and forth. Most of the runs were locals, stopping at many points en route, but there were two nonstop express runs in the morning and the evening. She looked for a 2 p.m. arrival and found the closest was 1:42, at the Central Train Station. "Kathy Fairly, over!" and the vyne rolled back up as she hurried on her way.

* * *

On her Red Fury bike, Kathy whisked across the back of the Green, between the Asian Art Museum and the Library, joining the stream of traffic passing to the right of the ancient Pioneers Monument. She hated the statue's blatant racism but grudgingly supported its preservation when it had come up for public debate more than thirty years earlier. "It's an insult, but it's a bracing reminder of the world before, too," argued "Moose" and she had to agree. Now she pedaled calmly along the greenway down to Abundance, past a variety of fruit and vegetable booths in Farmers Plaza, all of it grown in the city's farms. Several stands bulged with ripe apples, her favorite, so she stopped for a gleaming Golden Delicious.

"Hi Kathy!" came the cheerful salutation from her old neighbor, Doug Wilkins. Gray and grizzled, he'd known Fairly since the old days. They had so many shared memories that neither could imagine San Francisco without the other, even though they rarely spent time together on purpose.

"Doug! What's twirlin'?" She selected some apples and put them in her commodious pockets.

"Have a nip?" he asked her, eyes twinkling, obviously having been nipping all morning. He held forth a bottle of Wilkins AppleJack, his own apple cider, distilled in his Mission District backyard.

"Doug, I'm working!" she protested half-heartedly. He held it to her steadily, and she relented, taking a burning quaff before handing it back. She wiped her mouth on her sleeve, as the warm buzz descended into her chest. "Man, that's even better than last year's!"

"I thought you'd like it. Want to take a bottle home? I save 'em for my favorites."

"Sure, thank you. That's mighty kind." She held the bottle before her, admiring the label's portrayal of the bucolic farming community between Noe Valley and the Mission where Doug and his friends grew apples, oranges, walnuts and avocados. She held the liter of Doug's special cider proudly, as if she had won a trophy, thanked him again, and slipped it into her left leg pocket. "You and Bill should come over for a barbeque," she suggested as she pulled away.

"Just say when!" and they waved farewell, happily connected through the years and in the moment. Kathy fumbled with her pedals, one foot determined to slip off, but finally found her rhythm as she turned onto 7th, heading southward towards the Crossroads. She could smell the telltale shift in the air that confirmed it was no longer summer. The midday sun was already shifting southward after the equinox, casting shadows backwards from everything in her view.

At the Crossroads she checked the big solar clock. It was a few minutes after 1, so she had more than a half hour to finish the rest of her short journey and time to grab a bite to eat. Just a short way down the Kyoto Causeway was Gwen's elegant curving façade. "I never get down here," Kathy muttered to herself, delighted to stop at the popular seafood place and indulge her hunger. After parking at the velome she meandered over to Gwen's, found a spot overlooking Mission Bay, and ordered the striped bass. It wasn't too crowded, surprisingly, so she spent the time staring at the glimmering Bay waters, admiring the UC campus and its whimsical embellishments rising in the distance. The scooping chrome dock on the Physics Building reflected in the water. The roof area seemed more like an amusement park than anything else: soaring skybridges twisting among translucent sculptures, spires, and archways. Compared to the seriousness of the business conducted inside, the rooftop decorations seemed all the more incongruous.

Her fish arrived and she attacked it with ravenous hunger. The morning's accumulated tension and frustration sent her fingers flying across the plate. She hurtled mouthful after mouthful towards her waiting palate, as inelegantly as she had ever eaten. Her carefully constructed table manners were sacrificed to her frenzied pace, ending only when the plate was empty but for the fish bones. She sat back, struggling to stifle an enormous burp before it enveloped the entire deck.

On the way out she dropped her plate in the dirty bin, and went back to the kitchen to thank the chef. "That was perfect! Thanks so much!"

The chef, a gaunt Italian-looking guy, broke into a satisfied grin, putting his hands on his hips. "So you like that lemon pomegranate sauce?"

"Is that what that was? Yeah, great, really tangy!" With a wave of thanks she departed.

She got to the Central Train Station at 1:45, kicking herself that she hadn't made it earlier. Checking the arrivals, the Benicia Ferry had been on time at 1:42 at Pier B9. She quickly left her bike at the shack and hurried out to the piers, fighting through travelers coming and going. People were still disembarking at B9, so she relaxed. By the time she reached the ferry, an elegant modern waterwalker called *Twinkle Toes*, the passengers were all off. Valentina Rogers came down the ramp ahead of two young men, all three in ferry crew coveralls. She was laughing and waving them off as they enthusiastically pursued her.

"You mean you *don't* like dancing?" the taller of the two sarcastically said to her.

"After last night, I think we know better than that," said his companion with a nudge and a wink, annoying Kathy. But Valentina was laughing and obviously enjoying the attention. As she came off the ramp she noticed Kathy.

Her face fell as she guessed why she was here. "Is it about Nwin?" to which Kathy nodded.

"I'd like to ask you a few more questions. Wanna grab a coffee?"

"Sure. Give me a minute to change, okay?"

"No problem. I'll wait for you at the main door."

* * *

A few minutes later they were sitting down at the station's small café immersed in dense clouds of marijuana smoke.

"Whew!" Valentina waved at her nose. "Why do so many people want to get stoned at the train station?"

"Valentina, I was looking over your statement. I just want to ask a few followup questions."

"Sure, ask away!"

"How long have you known Roberts—uh, Nwin?"

"Well, I met him at the Rice Bowl when I did Annuals out there last May I think. Not long."

"Do you remember any of his friends? People he was particularly close to at the Rice Bowl?"

"He was pretty good friends with a guy named Marco, and a girl named Stefania. They're a couple I'm pretty sure."

Kathy jotted down the names. "And do you recall if he had any enemies?"

"No, not really. Everyone was on the outs with the oldest lifer there, a guy named Angus. He was impossible!.. part of the reason I didn't go back after a few days."

"Can you describe Nwin's skiff? Does it have a name? Any particular colors or distinguishing characteristics?"

"It's called *Hot 1*. I suppose it's like any other. There's no place to sit. It's just a one-person boat."

"You said he spoke angrily about flooded buildings. Did he say anything specifically about removing them?"

Valentina leaned forward, eyes widening. "Now that you mention it, I think he did. We were arguing about science and he said the UC scientists ought to be directing their efforts to undo the 'mess' as he put it. I thought he had crazy ideas."

"Like?"

"He thinks submerged buildings cause ecological damage, but that's just wrong. He wasn't easy to argue with, though. He got kind of mad."

"I remember you mentioned that last time. Do you remember anything else?"

"No, I've told you everything. I didn't know him that well. We hung out a couple of times, and then the boat ride. He got nervous at the fire site, and admitted that he'd seen it start."

Kathy put her pad back in one of her numerous pockets, and drained her coffee. "OK, thanks Val."

"I wasn't much help was I?" she said, a little embarrassed.

"You never know. You better hurry to the rehearsal. I've got to get back to work. Are you cycling or taking the streetcar?"

"I'm on the trolley. I knew I'd be too tired to pedal all the way back across town after being up since 4 a.m., y'know?"

* * *

Eric found the Rice Bowl easily enough. Showing up at the end of lunch had worked pretty well. There weren't many in the big barn when he walked in, but a few key people were still there. He introduced himself and was directed to Marco, a fellow cleaning a wheelbarrow in the back.

"Hi, I'm Eric Johanson, from the P-I's office in the Civic Green."

"Hey. Marco Stillweger. You looking for Nwin Robertson, too?"

"Yes I am. I guess Anita was here a few days ago, but that was before we found a few more bits of crucial evidence."

"Really? Like what?"

"Well, I'm not supposed to talk about it until we publish our report. But let me just say that everything points to Robertson as the guy who started the fire. But ALL the evidence is circumstantial, so we could be completely wrong. We need to hear his story."

"I told him!" said Marco with some exasperation. "He said he was going to contact you. He still hasn't?"

Eric shook his head. "When did you speak with him?"

"Yesterday. He came and stashed his stuff."

"Really? Where?"

"I'll show you, give me a sec."

Eric strolled around the barn, smiling at some of the funny drawings adorning the walls, obviously caricatures of people working there. Two women were quietly chatting in the kitchen area. As he approached they stopped talking.

Stefania had been waiting for Marco to finish so she could have lunch with him. She knew Eric was here looking for Nwin, and felt defensive on Nwin's behalf, even though the last time she'd seen him at Mission Creek he had been mean to her. "So you're looking for Nwin, huh?"

"Yes, that's right. Did you know him?"

"Of course, he worked here for months," she said condescendingly.

"Have you seen him lately?"

She looked intently at Eric, and could see no malice in his question or his bearing. "Yes, as a matter of fact, I ran into him just a few days ago over by The Willows."

"Go on," as he began jotting notes.

"We chatted about the war in Chile. He had a whole explanation about the fighting." She looked away, saddened at the thought of her family's plight. "And he seemed not to care, to tell the truth."

"You mean he supported the war?"

"No, no, of course not! But he had a strange take on it, emotionally. He was very matter of fact."

"Well, it is pretty far away."

"Not for me. I have family in the war zone."

"I'm sorry."

Marco interrupted. "Follow me." He gave Stefania a squeeze, saying, "I'll be right back. Just going to show the investigator Nwin's stuff."

Stefania and Liza exchanged a meaningful glance, but said nothing.

"I thought it was pretty strange when I found him stashing his stuff in the shack. It was yesterday morning. He hasn't been here for over a month, closer to two," Marco explained as they walked down the dusty road.

"So you know him pretty well?"

"Not really. I suppose I know him better than most people here, but Nwin's a loner. Working here seemed good for him, except for his endless fights with Angus."

"Oh?"

"It's a long story. Angus is a lifer and has a problem with young people. We tolerate him because he has a lot of great qualities too, and he's got rights here for sure. But he can be a huge asshole. Unfortunately he and Nwin used to tangle a lot, especially in the last few weeks before Nwin left."

"You said working here was good for Nwin. Why?"

"I think he liked farming—here we are." He opened the dusty old shack and in the back corner stood the dufflebag that Nwin had left the previous day.

"I don't want to go through his stuff. I'm sure I don't have the right to," Eric declared. He looked back and forth up and down the road, trying to decide what to do. He certainly wasn't going to wait here until Nwin came back. Who knows how many days that might be? Marco looked at him expectantly.

"I'm just going to leave a note on his bag. That way we can be absolutely sure he knows we need to speak with him."

"Whatever you want, man." Marco moved a short way down the road and began pulling weeds from a patch of marijuana.

Eric pulled out a pad and wrote,

"Dear Nwin Robertson,
Please contact the Public Investigator's office in the Civic Green.
We have been investigating the arson fire on San Bruno Mountain and

all the evidence so far is pointing at you. We would like to hear your
side of the story before we publish our findings.
  Sincerely,
  Eric Johanson, P.I.

He folded the note and carefully tucked it into the straps of the dufflebag. He
thanked Marco for his help. "Those are some beautiful plants!" he said appreciatively
about the pot.

"Thanks. You want buds? Here," and Marco grabbed a few rich buds, hanging
limply in the mid-afternoon sun, resin glistening on their tips. He put the sticky, pungent marijuana into Eric's hands.

"I don't smoke much, but I'll make sure these are put to good use!"

"Good luck. I guess we'll see what happens in the news, eh?" Marco said sadly.

"I suppose so," Eric agreed. They slapped goodbyes and Marco headed back to the
barn, while Eric started back to the Crossroads. Once again, his mind flooded with the
pain of his lost romance. He jammed his hands into his pockets and stared at the ground
in front of his feet. He walked automatically back to the velome where he'd left his bag.
At the Crossroads he avoided the bustling traffic that filled the busy intersection.

In his preoccupation, he didn't notice the tall young black man behind a light pole
at the corner, watching him over his shoulder.

38.

Voices buzzed in the distance, slowly approaching. Something very cold and hard
was pressing into his cheek. Cold air rushed over the right side of his waist. He
became aware of his weight pressing into the ground as he regained consciousness. Groggily he opened his eyes, and found himself peering through a jungle of grass
blades, bright colors and movement filling the long view. He pulled his shirt over the
bare spot where cool air had been running over him.

A brass band began a mournful dirge, leading a funeral from a nearby church.
Nwin slowly rose to his elbows, his head throbbing, his back as stiff as a board. A few
yards from his spot he observed a couple lying on each other, reading newspapers.
"Hey," his voice sounded as though it was coming from somewhere far off. "D'ya have
the time?" His vision was back in focus now, and the tall spires of the church across
Washington Square removed any doubt about where he was.

"It's about 12:30," the woman announced, hardly taking her eyes off her paper.

He'd been asleep in Washington Square for at least five hours. No one was paying
any attention to him. He sat up, rubbing his temples, trying to reduce the pounding
between his ears. No sooner had he smacked his bone-dry lips together at the thought
of a drink than his stomach loudly rumbled, demanding that it, too, be satisfied.
Struggling against his recalcitrant limbs, he slowly rose to his feet, unable to hold his
head and work on his lower back at the same time.

After a quick snack and coffee, he made his way to a velome, shaded beneath several large cypress trees in the corner of Washington Square, where he found a suitably

tall bicycle and began pulling it from the rack. The attendant watched him, his piercing black eyes emerging from tangled long hair followed Nwin.

"What're you looking at?"

"Nothin'. Jus' noticin' that'cher takin' the tallest bike in the place. But looks like you need it, so g'wan an' take it."

Nwin glared at the mechanic, his rising anger and paranoia bubbling dangerously close to the surface. But he prudently rode away, taking his rage out on the climb up Stockton Street. He soon entered the bulging produce market area of Chinatown. It was slow going because bike traffic was thick. Jammed streetcars glided along the middle of the street, and freight bikes were everywhere unloading cartons of produce into the busy shops. He passed a row of stately palms to reach the old tunnel ruins. From here he followed the twisting roadway up into a grove of orange and lemon trees, too self-absorbed to notice the sweet singing of the fruit farmers working their trees.

But they noticed him. Three young women were perched in an orange tree, in midverse when they observed Nwin pedaling furiously over the near crest of the hill. One, a gangly blonde, elbowed her companion, who shushed the third. Beth, the blonde, pulled a ripening orange from the limb and hurled it at him as he passed, but it soared over his head, unnoticed. Giggling, this time all three repeated the gesture. Oranges whacked into Nwin, two direct hits and the third bouncing into his wheel, knocking him sideways, not off his bike but enough to send him wobbling in to a nearby ditch.

"What the hell!" he yelled, but before he could focus his anger he was falling into the ditch. "Shiiiittt!" He couldn't regain control over the bike and down he went. He breathed anger but was tangled with his bike, lying on his back staring up into the branches of a dense green orange tree, unripened fruit hanging from the branches. Where the air had been filled with melodic singing, and then giggling moments earlier there was now silence, broken only by a distant screech of a seagull. Anxious whispers and scurrying footsteps preceded the appearance of three worried faces over Nwin.

"Are you OK?"

"I'm so sorry! That was terrible!"

"Help him up, here—grab that handlebar, wouldja?"

The women worked frantically.

Speechlessly he lie paralyzed with his mouth wide open. His boiling rage was like a furiously spinning ball, but strangely it was shrinking, rushing toward a vanishing point somewhere deep in his chest. He floated, as if apart from his body, watching the rage shrink while his female attackers fretted over him. His leg was tangled in an improbable pretzel with the bike. When they began jostling him, a searing pain shot through his entire body. He gasped, still speechless, and then the vanishing point rapidly spread out to engulf him in darkness.

* * *

"At least it's not broken!"

"He's gonna be okay?"

"Yes, he'll be pretty sore, but it's all muscular. He's a lucky young man."

Nwin emerged from a dark fog. Before opening his eyes he felt the wool blanket under his elbows and hands. He slowly checked for sensation throughout his body and found that he was lying on his back, stretched out on a hard surface, covered with a blanket. He opened his eyes, squinting against the bright sunlight shimmering through the trees overhead. His nostrils filled with the sticky sweet smell of the orange grove.

Surrounding him were the three women who had brought him down with their barrage of fruit, plus a very thin fellow in an ink-stained smock. The guy seemed to be the medic. "How're you feeling? Where does it hurt?"

Nwin tried to say something, but only managed to utter an unfocused groan. He cleared his throat. "Where am I?"

"You're in Citrus Heights, east slope of Nob Hill," one of the women said. She pushed her black hair out of her worried eyes. "You were bicycling along and we—um, well… we knocked you over," she said ruefully, looking quickly at her companions, who both hung their heads and nodded their heads guiltily. The tall blonde took Nwin's hand, tears welling in her eyes. "It's my fault. I saw you first and I started it. I'm truly sorry."

Nwin pulled his hand away, confused to find himself flat on his back, the object of so much emotional attention. *Who are these people?*

The medic was talking, but Nwin saw his lips moving without hearing anything. Focusing more intently on him, he started hearing what he was saying.

"—easy for a few days. You took a pretty hard fall I'd guess, but you're young. You got banged up, that's all."

"Aaaagh!" Nwin tried to sit up Pain shot up his leg through his lower back, and he fell back with a thump.

"What is it?!?" the medic asked, deeply sunken eyes peering at him through his knitted brow.

"My…" he gasped as a spasm shot through again, "my back." Nwin briefly explained that he'd had back problems that had only just been cured, thanks to the acupuncture treatment… yesterday? Could it have been only yesterday?

The ink-stained pressman drew back, having reached the limits of his medical skills. "Hey Rita, isn't your aunt a doc? She does acupuncture, doesn't she?"

The black-haired woman nodded. She had a hint of Asian heritage around her eyes, although he almost didn't see it. "She's close. I'll get her," and off she ran, hurling her apron aside. The third girl, who couldn't have been much older than Nwin, tried to improvise a pillow for him, but moving his head only aggravated the pain in his lower back.

"Can I get you anything? Water? Something to eat?" she asked.

"Uh-unh," he grimaced.

"We'll be right over there, if you need anything, okay? She's Beth and I'm Dru." They went back to the other side of the road and began organizing their tools, clattering rakes, shovels, and shears.

"Hang in their buddy. The doc is comin'," said the pressman reassuringly. And in fact, she came running up a few minutes later with Rita, stethoscope hanging out of one pocket, a small doctor's bag in her hand. She kneeled by Nwin's side, touching his forehead, pressing his limbs gently but firmly. He watched her numbly, feeling an eerie sense of déjà vu. The doctor looked very familiar.

"Rita told me you had a bad fall?" Nwin nodded. "And that you've had back problems?" He nodded again. "Have you been treated for the back?"

"Well, I was in General Hospital about six weeks ago, and then yesterday I got an acupuncture treatment at the Mission Bay clinic."

"General? Who was your doctor?"

Then he recognized the resemblance. "Son or Song?" he said, unsure if he remembered the name right.

"Angie Sung?"

"I think so."

The doctor looked up at Rita, smiling, shaking her head. "Small world, eh?" then turned back to Nwin. "She's my sister, Rita's other aunt."

While she checked Nwin's pulses, she got him to explain as best he could what treatments he'd received in the hospital and from the acupuncturist.

"We're going to turn you over. It's probably going to hurt. Keep breathing. I'm going to try to stop the back spasms." The doctor, along with her niece and Wadsworth the pressman, carefully rolled Nwin over, to which he nervously and painfully submitted. She worked needles into various spots. Then she began working on the soles of his feet, and after that she put needles into various spots on his scalp. "Don't move. I'll be back in fifteen minutes. You'll feel a lot better."

Nwin lay dazed amidst warm breezes and earthy smells, sounds of passing cyclists, screeching seagulls, and a nearly inaudible musical humming that seemed to be coming from the women across the road. He couldn't imagine what he was going to do if this treatment didn't get him back on his feet.

Gotta get my stuff, my boat… gotta go to the Alamo Square place tonight… his head swirled with anxious thoughts. It seemed like she'd just left when the doctor reappeared.

She pulled out the needles. "Hey, I'm going to do one more thing before you try to get up. I spoke with my sister and she looked up your skan. Here—" and she manipulated his lower spine, pushing a particularly sore spot. Suddenly something seemed to pop into place, and she pulled back, beaming. "There!"

Nwin groaned as he tried to get up. It hurt but it wasn't agonizing. He pushed a little further and felt no worse, so he cautiously got up on his knees, hands on his thighs. It seemed miraculous but he didn't feel too bad. His back was sore to be sure, but nothing like the sharp pain he'd been in a little while ago.

"Wow!" he twisted very gently, rubbing his lower back, and beginning to grin. Beth and Dru came running over to join Rita and the doctor, Laurie. "How is it? Are you okay?"

"Well, I think I'm going to be able to dance again!"

The women laughed. "I get the first dance!" declared Rita, "My aunt cured him so he's mine!" The other two poked her and laughed along. "I oughta get something for being the one who started all this!" joked Beth. Nwin didn't mind the playful bantering, now that he could move under his own power again. He stood up and kept moving his torso.

"Maybe I'll come to you again if I need another treatment."

"Sure, you do that. Here's my address," and Laurie handed him a card before heading back to her office, gratified by the good results.

After the doctor left he turned back to the three women. Rita's smile was electrifying, he finally noticed. Dru and Beth were pretty cute, too. Maybe he should just hang around here and see what developed. He walked around a bit, relaxing as he realized he was going to be okay after all.

"Shit," he saw his twisted bike. "I gotta get another bike. 'S there a velome nearby?"

Beth, who was pretty tall herself, said, "Hey, take mine. It's the least I can do." She waved toward a high riding silver bike leaning against the wall. "I'll take the one we broke and get it fixed."

"You hungry? Wanna have lunch?" Rita asked, reaching out to delicately stroke his arm. The erotic tension was unmistakable. Last night's bacchanalian revelry came rushing back to him.

" I just had breakfast a little while ago. I'm not hungry at all." He returned her gaze, smiling and took her hand in his. "I'd love to see you later. I have to take care of some things first. Where can I reach you?"

She gave him her address, which turned out to be in the Pyramid on the 17th floor. "You been there long? I used to live on the 33rd floor."

"Really? I've been there for almost two years. When did you live there?" They chatted about how odd it was that they'd never met. "There are a lot of people living there, I guess," she conceded. He promised to vyne her. He mounted the bike Beth had given him and took off down the southern slope to the Union Square docks. Leaving the bike in the velome he caught a southbound express ferry heading to Redwood City. He rode in the warm sunshine, past the first stop at the Central Train Station, and then got off at the Precita Levee.

There, he disembarked into a throng of folks getting ready for their trip to Treasure Island.

"I never found that vintage available anywhere!" exclaimed one man, who had somehow acquired the day's order form before boarding the ferry. Nwin walked past them, all chattering about their biannual trip to the island. He proceeded to the small boat dock further south, passing a swimming pool built into the lower floors of the Arcobolo that sat above the Levee. Typically the pool was surrounded by naked bodies, in various states of browning and pinking. He spent no time ogling this time, though. Finding his stairway down to the floating dock, he found *Hot 1* where he'd left it several days earlier.

He was soon maneuvering through the taxis, ferries and barges to the Bay. Potrero Hill rose to his left as he skirted the shoreline, avoiding the fences of the aquaculture farms where oysters and clams were produced by the ton. A flock of parakeets native to the hill swooped out over his path before heading back to the stately palms silhouetted along the top. The big pot farm below the P O T H I L L P L A T Z sign was shimmering emerald green in the bright sunlight. Sitting in the bottom of *Hot 1* out on the Bay on a warm afternoon felt happily familiar, although his body was beginning to complain. He wasted no time and headed straight for the docks at The Crossroads.

Moving gingerly, he tied up and crossed the Kyoto Causeway that separated Mission Bay from the busy intersection. It was mid-afternoon now, almost 3 o'clock on the big Crossroads clock. On the dusty road to the Rice Bowl, he stopped abruptly when he noticed the shack door open. He moved to the building wall and watched. It was Marco who backed out first followed by a stranger. He slowly walked back to the bustling intersection. He found a lamp-post from where he could see down the road. Marco and the stranger were talking at the shack. *Who the ching is that?* he wondered, worried. *And what is Marco doing, showing him my stuff?* He turned to see Rikky heading towards the Rice Bowl across the sprawling intersection, and he quickly ducked behind his pole. He didn't need to explain anything to anyone right now.

He watched Rikky pedal down the road and wave to Marco and the stranger, who were grabbing some buds from the billowing pot plants next to the shack. Then Marco and the stranger parted, Marco heading back to the farm, while the stranger walked towards Nwin with his hands in his pockets, looking at the ground. Nwin sized him up. A young guy, tall with greasy brown hair hanging over his face. Nwin made sure the pole stayed between him and the stranger. The man passed behind him, completely lost in thought.

He waited a few minutes while the guy disappeared into the velome and then re-emerged on a Bambu bike, which Nwin immediately recognized. *At least he has a dew bike!* After the stranger rode away, Nwin, very alert to anyone coming or going, proceeded up the road towards the shack and his bag. No one appeared before he ducked inside the dark shack.

He flipped on the light and found the note that Eric had left on his bag. He read the terse message and muttered "my side of the story—Chingado!" He crumpled the paper and threw it into the corner. His jerry-rigged skateboard cart was still under his bag, so he pulled the contraption out onto the road, but not until he had carefully checked to see if anyone was coming. The coast was clear, so he headed to the Crossroads, noisily towing his bag, kicking up a small dust cloud. He also grabbed a few ripe buds of marijuana from the big beauties lining the road. *Might need these later,* he thought absent-mindedly.

He reached *Hot 1* without a hitch. He was relieved when he was underway with his belongings. It was still hours before he was supposed to show up at Rochelle's on Alamo Square. He decided to use the vyne, so he flipped over to the campus again, figuring it was a good place to branch in from since no one would be looking for him there. He pulled up at the Biomanufacturing Building, and made his way up to the lounge, past the marquee sign at the entrance promoting "The Big Showdown" between MacMillan and Floyd, September 30.

Various private vyne booths were open, so he grabbed one and shut the door behind him. "Vyne," he said calmly, and the leaf unrolled, casting a green glow in the small booth. "Nwin Robertson, Bernal Heights, messages." A half dozen messages from his mother, a couple from his cousin Jimmy, even one from his Auntie—that was unusual, she never used the vyne as far as he could remember. Someone named Kathy Fairly had a message, as did a woman named Robin Davis. He decided to go through them, starting with the first one from his mother. "Jennifer Robertson" he called and the vyne immediately produced a milky green image of his mother. After a brief hestitation she started talking and moving.

"Nwin, will you please come home? I'm sorry I got frustrated with you." And that was all the first message held. The next one was quite different, his mother crying heavily before she had even leafed him. It made him angry to see her crying and begging him to come home. "That's such bullshit!" he exclaimed. Maybe she was humiliated by it too, because the next message was a complete turnabout. She was calm, reserved. "The P-I wants to interview you about the San Bruno Mountain Fire." Now she was worried, imploring him to contact her, at least to leaf her so she could know he was okay. Then there was the invocation of family. The P-I was contacting everyone. She was embarrassed that he seemed to be hiding. He went on to the messages from Jimmy. The first one invited him back again, but he could hear Sheila in the background complaining! Then Jimmy quite seriously warned him that he had better have a good alibi, because it seemed that there was a big case against him for starting the fire. When he checked the message from Auntie it turned out to be a nonmessage. She briefly flickered across the screen, but had failed to say anything before transmitting the message. He called for the message from Kathy Fairly, not knowing what to expect. It was a text message, something he hadn't received very often.

> "Nwin Robertson. This is Kathy Fairly, chief of the Public Investigators' Office in Civic Green. We want you to come in and talk to us about the San Bruno Mountain Fire. There is a great deal of circumstantial evidence accumulating that all points to you as the person responsible for that fire. We will be publishing the results of our investigation by October 4. You should make a statement, present any alibi or evidence you have that would counter the case we've got. Please contact me as soon as you get this message."

"Shit!" He called for the last message from this Robin Davis. An athletic young woman with short black hair and glasses appeared. "Nwin Robertson. This is Robin Davis from the Public Investigators' Office. Time is running out to include your side of the story. We think we have a very strong case proving you are the arsonist who started the fire in Guadalupe Canyon. If you want to contest this conclusion, you must—I repeat, you MUST—come in and make a statement. After we publish our report, you will be subject to citizens' arrest and a jury trial which could lead to expulsion and forced exile. Contact us immediately."

He watched her image flicker out. There weren't any other messages. He had been planning to leaf Maria and that girl he met today, Rita Jefferson. But now he felt anxious and trapped. "SHIT!!" he slammed his fist into the booth's wall. He left the booth and began pacing back and forth. Voices rose near the windows as people gathered, pointing to the water. His curiosity aroused, he walked over to see a small whale rolling on its back, waving its fins in the air. He didn't care, so he kept walking along the windows, staring at dozens of small boats crisscrossing the channel between the Kyoto Causeway and the campus, avoiding the whale's patch of Bay.

"Hey... Hey Nwin!"

He whirled around, eyes bulging, his heart in his throat, fully expecting a hostile stranger to be accosting him. But there was Joseph, calmly sitting back in his favorite chair, smiling enigmatically, thumping his walking stick a few times in front of the chair next to him, inviting Nwin over.

"I'm surprised to see you here, Nwin." Joseph didn't move, staring straight ahead. "I heard you were on the run. Are you on the run?"

"Me?" Nwin almost choked on the question. "No! I'm not running, why should I?"

"The whole family knows the Public Investigator is looking for you, thinks you started the San Bruno Mountain fire."

"That's bullshit!"

Joseph slowly turned to Nwin, who looked away. Joseph stared at him until Nwin turned back and their eyes met. Then, as though mesmerized, Nwin couldn't turn away while Joseph kept his eyes locked on Nwin's.

"You're not a very good liar," Joseph concluded, sitting back into his chair. "I guess running makes sense when you can't tell a convincing lie."

Nwin was enraged. How dare he call him a liar? But he *was* lying, and the old man could see it. *Shit!* He tried to compose a response that fit the circumstances, but he couldn't come up with anything and remained mute. Finally, after what seemed like a mini-eternity, he spoke. "I'm getting out of San Francisco."

Again, Joseph turned, leaning forward on his walking stick, and looked carefully into Nwin's face, while Nwin stared straight ahead, trying to be inscrutable. "Sounds like you can go on your own, or they'll send you away when they catch you... And where do you think you're going to go?"

"I dunno," he lied.

"You could ask for understanding," Joseph suggested softly, already tacitly offering it.

"What?!? From who? For what? I didn't do nothin'!" he raged. Joseph shrugged and said nothing further. Nwin twitched with anger, utterly trapped in his lie and too proud or frightened to confide even in Joseph, who was offering him only support. "This is BULLSHIT! Why is everyone against me?! I hate this place... I hate everyone in this stupid city. I don't know why I stayed here this long!" and with that, he got up and stomped off, not looking back at Joseph, who placidly watched the boats go by, sorry that Nwin was so lost. He was also sorry that he hadn't asked him for a little bud, which he was sorely wanting.

Twenty minutes later, Nwin was cruising on the Bay again. Joseph frightened him. He called him a liar! Was it that obvious? No way he was going to the P-I if he couldn't maintain his innocence. He fumed in his skiff, composing his denials, trying to control his breathing, maneuvering through traffic. Unconsciously he steered on the familiar path towards the Pyramid. He skirted around the Rincon Station and headed up the California canal, Nob Hill looming straight ahead. He peered halfway up the hill to the edge of Citrus Heights, imagining the women he'd met earlier, wondering if he would get a chance with Rita before he got out of town. He became aroused at the thought of her, and almost crashed into a taxi that barreled across his path. Refocusing on navigating he veered right and left into Halleck alley, avoiding big elephant seals when they dived from the ruins right in front of him. He slipped into Leidesdorff and pointed at the Pyramid's orange façade, but as he neared it, he realized he was either going to stop and search for Rita or he'd have to keep going. A minute later he was tying up at the guest pier.

She's probably not even home, he thought as he started up the ramp towards the 2nd floor lobby. He dismissed his thoughts, keeping an eye out for former neighbors that he didn't want to see. At the big desk sat two attendants, helping the half dozen people distributed around the counter. He ignored them and went to the small vyne near the elevators, glowing with a dedicated display of the building's residents. He uttered "Rita Jefferson," and it displayed her name and the number 1443. He entered the elevator and punched 14, waiting while several others entered their destinations. Moments later he was knocking at 1443. He waited and then knocked a second time.

"Shit!" he slung his arms down, defeated by Rita's absence. He walked slowly back to the elevator where he unconsciously hit his old floor 33. Lost in thought he suddenly realized what he'd done and stopped at 31 to enter the dining hall. Nobody like Lupe was around so he served himself lasagna, along with some roof garden salad. He sat by a window, suddenly quite hungry, and while he ate, stared out at the golden light illuminating the surrounding buildings and the aquamarine Bay.

"Nwin!" he froze as he heard his name and a hand on his shoulder simultaneously. His mouth full, he turned slowly to find Johnny Templer standing over him, a stern look on his face.

"Mmphf," he chewed and swallowed hurriedly. "Hi Johnny, what's up?"

"What are you doing here? Didn't you move?"

"I stopped by to visit a friend, but she wasn't home."

"What's this I hear about you being in trouble?"

"Me? Trouble? What're you talking about?" he played innocent, employing the expressions he'd been practicing on *Hot 1*.

"Nwin," he leaned over the table, looking hard at Nwin, who was doing his best to focus on his meal. "Don't bullshit me. Call your mother! She's frantic, she's been calling everyone… even me! And I haven't seen her for years, nor you for months. Your father would be angry, I can tell you that!"

Nwin scowled. "Johnny, I don't want to hear it." He kept his head down, shoveling in another mouthful of lasagna.

"I'm going to leaf your mother and tell her you were here. You better talk to her!" he repeated, and then he left.

Nwin lost his appetite. He swallowed what was still in his mouth, but he left the rest of it, carrying his tray automatically to the disposal station, where he put everything into its proper bin. Looking around furtively, he went to the poles where he rapidly descended. At the 14th floor, he decided to give Rita another try.

Much to his surprise, the door opened within a few seconds of his first knock. Rita stood there, wrapped in a towel, just out of the shower. Steam roiled through the apartment behind her. "Hi," she smiled demurely, almost as though she'd been expecting him. "Come on in. Give me a sec while I get dressed OK?"

He walked to the windows, his heart beating furiously, trying to decide what to say. After some minutes, she came out, wearing a snug brown suede top, cut low to reveal a beautiful bosom. She wore a matching pair of skintight pants and some high-heel boots. Her hair was pinned back, giving him his best look at her beautiful brown face, her white teeth flashing in a winsome smile. She embraced him.

"How're you feeling?"

"I'm okay, actually."

"Great! You must heal fast… I'm surprised to see you already."

"Yeah, I wasn't planning to be here but I was passing by and thought I'd pop in and say 'hello'."

"I'm glad you did," she purred, taking him by the arm to the couch. She wasted no time, and immediately began stroking his thigh. It didn't take long to get through the preliminaries, what with his predisposition and she having spent 25 minutes in a hot shower fantasizing about him.

* * *

Afterwards, she was hungry, but since he'd just eaten, he begged off.

"Well, I've got to eat, I'm starving, especially after *that*! Do you want to stay overnight?"

He laughed softly, seeing a strange justice in this turn of events. "Rita, I, er, ah… well, it just so happens that I'm between places."

"Really?" she said with undisguised surprise. "You can stay here. It's a big place, and I'd love to have you."

"I accept," he said without hesitation. They left together, he to get his stuff out of his skiff and re-dock it in her residential slot, she to eat. As he was returning to the apartment, he felt suddenly lighter, like his luck was turning. Finally someone was on his side! He took a happy swing at the dangling sign hanging over the hallway, "No One Wants to, so We All Have To! Do Your Annuals!"

"*Ching* your goddamned Annuals!"

39.

Kathy was waiting in her office when a disconsolate Eric walked by. He hadn't found anything at the Rice Bowl besides a rumpled dufflebag and some curious but not very helpful former workmates. But he was hardly thinking about the case as he entered the building. Instead he was going over the conversation he'd had with Emmy that morning moment by moment. *If I'd reacted differently I might still have a girlfriend!* He felt more and more sorry for himself.

"Hey! Where you've been? I thought you were going to get back an hour ago." Kathy came striding into the hallway.

"Huh? Oh yeah, sorry! I got distracted on the way back, ended up riding up to Market Pond…" he trailed off, realizing that he had forgotten he was supposed to meet Kathy. He couldn't snap out of the fog his depression had brought down over him.

"Did you have any luck?"

"I met some former coworkers. He was there yesterday morning, and left his dufflebag in a shack."

"You're kidding! Is it still there?"

"Yeah, why?"

"Did you wait for him to return?"

"Well, no one knew when he was coming back. I left a note."

"Saying what?"

"That we need to talk to him, that we have a strong case and he needs to make a statement."

"Hmm. Well, we just keep missing him. A message came in a few hours ago from your householder, the doctor." They walked in to Kathy's office.

"Angie?"

"Yeah. Her sister, who is also a doctor, treated Robertson for back spasms after he had a bike accident in Citrus Heights earlier this afternoon."

"Did anyone get there in time to interview him?"

"Nope. By the time we got the message he was long gone. The doctor knew we were looking for him, but after treating him, she went back to work. I called to ask if she'd told him that we were trying to reach him, but she hadn't. Frustrating, but it's not her job and at this stage it's not a public matter. After we publish, then she has some responsibility."

Eric was still distracted.

"She wasn't too friendly when I spoke with her. I think she thought I was pressuring her to do our investigative work." Kathy shook her head. He stared at the wall, not focusing on their work.

"What's going on Eric?"

His head whipped around at the question, and he looked at her with fear in his eyes.

"Whoa, whoa!" she put up her hands. "You're upset. Is it about missing our guy at the Rice Bowl?"

"No!" He was breathing too hard and, panicky, his eyes darted around, trying to find something that would take him off the spot.

"Jeez! What's is going on?" Kathy came around her desk and put her hand on his shoulder. "You need to say it, c'mon man, spit it out!"

He began sobbing convulsively, unable to speak or stop. Finally he regained his composure. He looked at Kathy, no longer fearful, but deeply embarrassed.

"Hey, we've all been there. You'll be okay. Tell me what's up."

He spilled his story about Emmy. He'd been more and more insecure and whiny in the relationship. It had gotten worse as he'd realized he was doing it, and finally, she'd broken up with him that very morning.

Kathy sat on the edge of her desk, gently patting his shoulder. She felt sorry for him. She hadn't seen much of the whiny insecure Eric that he described. His competence and occasional bursts of enthusiasm were deceiving, because he now was a helpless boy. But she'd been around long enough to know that it was in the intimacy of the bedroom and people's hearts where real madness lies. And this wasn't madness, he was just young and very inexperienced.

He sat back, his face puffy and red. She went to the window, not wanting to focus on his misery. "So, Eric," she turned back to him. "We've got work to do!" Nothing soothed romantic heartache as well as a new romance. But absent that, the distraction of hard work was pretty good.

The shellcom on the desk crackled to life as Leigh's voice broke in. "Kathy, there's an urgent message that just came in, addressed to Eric. Is he in there with you?"

"Yes, Leigh. We'll take it here." She turned to the vyne, hanging open on her wall. "Eric Johanson, messages!"

On the leaf a milky green image formed of Marco, the guy at the Rice Bowl he'd been with a few hours earlier. "Eric Johanson, this is Marco Stillweger at the Rice Bowl." The time flashing in the corner was 17:52, just two minutes ago. "I thought you'd want to know. I was leaving for the day, and I took a look in the shack on my way out. Nwin's bag is gone. And I found this," he held up a crumpled piece of paper. "It's your note. I guess he came after we met, but no one saw him as far as I know. That's all." The image faded away.

Kathy was jotting down notes furiously. Eric looked at her. "What now?"

"He was in Citrus Heights at around 14:30, and according to the doc, pretty badly injured. What time did you meet Marco?"

"Must've been 15:30 or so, I'm not sure."

"If it was 15:30, or even 16:00, then that means our guy made his way from Citrus Heights to the Rice Bowl after you left, say by 16:00, and got his stuff before Marco discovered this, say at 17:40 or so. Then where would he go?" She sat tapping the pencil into the pad.

"He's moving around. Do you think he's trying to hide?"

"I think so. He knows we're trying to reach him. His cousin and his mother haven't heard from him for over a week, but we know he's still in town. Valentina mentioned that he was friends with Marco and also a woman named Stefania. Did you see her?"

"Yes, as a matter of fact I did. She told me about a 'strange encounter' with him on Mission Creek. They talked about the war. She remembered that he was calm, interested and not at all upset."

Kathy chewed her pencil, trying to pull something out of these disparate bits of information. "I think this young man is fascinated with violence, certainly with fire. I'd guess he's trying out various ideologies to justify his obsessions, but without talking to him, it's impossible to tell."

Anita came bounding in. "Hey you guys, guess what?"

They looked at her, eyebrows raised expectantly.

"I found the place in the library where the arson instructions came from. And the clerk ID'd Robertson. He got the documents back in July."

"Great job, Anita! We'll publish in the next day or two. We're trying to figure out where he is going next. He's been seen twice today, but we haven't managed to contact him. Anita, have you given that to Stella or Robin yet?"

"Nope. But I will. Hey, are you guys going to The Showdown tonight?"

"I was thinking about it. But I have dinner plans with Bridget so I guess not."

"What's The Showdown?" Eric asked.

"Sam MacMillan and Cameron Floyd are squaring off in a public debate—"

"Oh yeah! I heard about it. The whole speech-for-dolphins thing, right?"

"Yes, but it goes a lot deeper," Anita was excited. She was at least ten years older than Eric, but as a Tryout, was in a similar relationship to the work. Now that she was talking about the Showdown, her deeper involvement in the issues of the day became apparent. Eric looked at her brown hair tied back in a ponytail, her pale blue eyes like saucers in her freckled face. She was tall and athletic. She wore unflattering work clothes, a loose-fitting plaid shirt hanging over her denim pants. A hint of cleavage flashed at the top of her unbuttoned shirt when she leaned forward to describe the upcoming debate.

"MacMillan's campaign for the right to go beyond current species boundaries is a Trojan horse for a whole range of biotechnological innovation. Some think it's great, but most people are still categorically against it."

"For historical reasons," Kathy piped up.

"Of course." Anita acknowledged. "He's pushing to give voice to the dolphins, but right behind it are dozens of proposals: giving wings, fins, horns and claws to humans; creating a whole range of new virus-borne agents to extend age-blockers past the 200 year range; putting vyne-linked 'eyes' into birds and fish. Every crackpot idea you can think of is waiting in the wings."

"Where do you stand on all this?" Kathy asked pointedly.

Anita sat back, folding her arms, and grinned. "I love it! I actually don't care too much one way or the other. I'm more interested in the politics. I'm fascinated by the arguments, the factions, the characters!"

Eric saw Anita in a whole new light. "I had no idea," he mumbled, capturing his reaction to what she'd been saying as much as his own reaction to her. "What time is it?"

"It starts at 21:00. The format is formal. Each will make a speech and then opinions will be gathered afterwards over the vyne, where the entire discussion will be available for later viewing. The program will last less than an hour. It's hard to imagine that anything new will come out. Everything has been hashed out in the press and in discussions for months. But this will be a chance to hear two of the better speakers make clear opposing statements."

"What's going to happen then? Is there going to be a referendum or something?"

"Not yet. This debate is hot here in the Bay Area, but it's just beginning in other areas. What gets said here will go into the world for months to come. It will be at least a year before anyone formulates anything to vote on. MacMillan and his camp know they have a lot of convincing and inspiring to do to gain popular support. They could seek Resource Review Board approval soon to start setting up some laboratory simulations. This debate will give us a good idea about whether or not they'll get that opportunity."

"Can I go with you?" Eric asked Anita directly. Kathy got a sudden whiff of his interest.

"I'm going with some other friends, too, okay?"

"Sure. Is there an eating plan beforehand? I'm pretty hungry all of a sudden."

"We're meeting at Gwen's where I have a table reserved. I'll just leaf 'em that we have another at our table. We leave in a half hour. We'll have plenty of time to pedal at a leisurely pace."

"If you guys are finished making social plans, I'd like to finish this Robertson case up."

They focused for a few more minutes as Kathy summarized the day's developments, Eric and Anita chiming in their details. Then she tore off the sheet and handed it to Anita. "Deliver this to Stella or Robin with your library report, okay?"

Eric joined Anita as they left Kathy's office.

"Do you think we're going to find Robertson? What kind of alibi could he have?" Eric bubbled enthusiastically.

"Yeah, this case seems airtight. But what do we know? This is our first arson case!"

Eric was silenced by that obvious fact. He had had a sense of achievement, partly because Kathy relied on him in the investigation. But Anita's sensible admonition stung, and he realized that he'd grown cocky again. His morale, soaring a moment earlier, began its inevitable descent. He slowed down, fighting a welling despair. Emmy reappeared in his thoughts and he ached, suddenly exhausted emotionally.

"Hey, you ok?" Anita stopped, noticing that Eric was visibly slumping. Embarrassed, he drew himself up. He took a deep breath, trying to jump off the spiral sucking him down. "I'm fine," he reassured her. He didn't want to share his grief with Anita. Hoping to get off on a different foot, he forced a smile. "I'm really tired... haven't been sleeping well lately."

"You want to grab a few winks before we head off?"

"That's a good idea. I'll go rest in the lounge. Will you wake me when it's time to go?"

"Sure!" Anita patted him on the shoulder. "Have a good nap!"

In the lounge, he curled up on the big soft couch, falling asleep almost as soon as he hit the upholstery.

* * *

Her pleasant sing-song call, reminiscent of his mother, roused him from a deep sleep. A short while later, he was riding on the back of a recumbent tandem bicycle, leaving Anita to steer through the dinnertime masses. air streaming through his hair. Flocks of birds swarmed through the sky. Centuries-old buildings at the intersection of 7th and Abundance stood nobly where they'd been since the beginning of the 20th century. A floating eyeball over a crescent moon surrounded by seven stars decorated the Odd Fellows Hall, long abandoned by the provocatively named group, which itself had vanished in the forgotten past.

"Hey," his voice had a gravelly quality, still not fully awake, "this is the *dew*! You wanna drive me everywhere from now on?"

Anita giggled as she braked suddenly to wait for cross traffic at The Ruins, a huge 21st century government building at 7th and Stevenson that was now home to several thousand people. "I don't think you'll want me as your driver after this ride," she laughed.

"Wha- wha- what're you trying to say?" Eric stammered, feigning fear.

"Oh, nothing—just don't ask my friends how I drive!" Anita guffawed, cheerfully steering them past the old Federal courthouse, across the wood-covered Mission Plank Road, and into Natoma Alley. He peered into openings between old wooden Victorians sitting cheek-by-jowl with boxy 21st century lofts, warehouses, churches, offices and exotic recent structures that looked more like piles of collapsing dishes or slumping cones with skybridges bursting out of side walls. Whatever the architectural mix, they were usually joined together into block-sized complexes with open interior courtyards full of playgrounds, gardens, swimming pools, small forests, decks and greenhouses.

"So Anita..."

"Yes?"

"What did you do before you decided to Tryout at the P-I's?"

"I was a reporter at the *Call* for four years. Before that I was playing basketball and soccer. I blew out my knee during the 2151 West Cup. I was a midfielder for the San Francisco Parrots... Collided with Ruth Emory from the Riverside Ravens during the first half."

"*Chingo*—how awful!"

"Yeah. Well, we won 2-1, but by then I was in the hospital. I did rehab after surgery, but I never regained my strength or speed. Plus I just lost my passion."

"You must have been good?"

They were stopped at Bryant waiting for cross traffic to clear. She looked back at Eric. "I won the MVP in '50, and almost got it that year too," her face tightened with grim pride.

"I'd love to see you play... got any old recordings?"

"Nah!" she shook her head vigorously. "I never went in for that. But you can see any game in the past 50 years at the Women's Soccer Hall of Fame down in San Jose. They keep 'em all on file."

"Maybe I will." They wheeled on to the Kyoto Causeway, turning right past Gwen's before stopping at the Crossroads velome. "Then you were a reporter? What was your beat?"

"When I quit I was the political reporter. You know the *Call*—"

Eric put up his hands. "Actually I don't. I haven't taken the time to analyze the local press."

They strolled along the causeway towards Gwen's.

"*The Call*, officially the *San Francisco Call of the Wild City*, probably the most pro-Garden Party and pro-nature of the dailies." She made quote marks with her fingers as she said "pro-nature."

"They started the campaign to introduce wolves to the wild corridors, and decades ago, they were the impetus behind building and restoring the creeks and waterways, tearing up streets. *The Dock of the Bay* is the biggest regional newspaper. It covers the greater Bay Area three times a week. They tend to be middle of the road, lots of basic news on what's happening in various neighborhoods, the best reporting on community council meetings, a big opinion section with lots of ongoing debates. *Why Red?* is still mostly called '*Wired*,' since it has always been unabashedly in favor of using technology instead of human work. It has its roots in the pre-revolutionary period when it was the voice of abolishing the Economy, seeing it as the greatest impediment to the full development of humanity's technological potential. They were early enthusiasts for the vyne, before it was universally adopted."

"*Why Red?* Is it also meant to be taken as a post-Economic name?"

"Yeah, yeah, that's the joke I guess. Anyway, here we are. But just to finish," and she stopped before they entered Gwen's elegant curving wooden façade. "There are over a hundred neighborhood papers all over the Bay Area, at least 20 in San Francisco. Then there are a dozen magazines. My favorite is *The Free Radical*, a monthly that does general analysis, news from around the world, opinion and debate, long feature articles, that sort of thing. Great photography! The editor is one of tonight's speakers, Cameron Floyd.

"Before the political beat, I was a sports writer. Covered the women's soccer and basketball leagues at first, but eventually I was following the Seals, and for a little while I had a column. I still follow sports pretty closely but not in the *Call*. I read *Sporting Games* for local sports. Sometimes I take a look at *Green Gardener*, a journal that is half gardening in Bay Area microclimates and half about Garden Party politics, with reports from chapters all around the area, plus highlights from around North America, and usually a short feature on developments somewhere else in the world."

"Wow! You know your stuff. Thanks!"

"My pleasure. As a P-I. you can track a lot of things and find what you're looking for if you know what to read."

Eric nodded. They pushed through a huge wooden door with ornately carved panels. Each panel had a different colored pane of vibrating and flashing glass, as if it were an insane blinking face. Anita knew the table she'd reserved, and greeted the host familiarly, who waved them past.

Eric followed her to a window overlooking the sunset's golden light on Mission Bay. Three others were already seated. Nearest the window sat a heavy-set man, his jowls jiggling with jovial laughter as they arrived. "This is Jeremy Epstein," said Anita. The two women got up to greet them, kissing Anita simultaneously on either cheek, provoking a gleeful chortle from her. "And this is Grace Ullmer and Esther Smith, my oldest friends, former teammates!" Eric greeted them in turn, first Grace, a very tall, thin woman with bird-like features, her black hair tightly wound into a small bun, an elegant black sweater hanging loosely over her bony torso. Then Esther, Grace's polar opposite, short, thick, muscular, cherubic good looks beneath wavy blonde hair.

"Great to meet you! So you played soccer, too?"

"No! No, we were basketball teammates. Didn't she tell you about our championship season?" Grace leaned forward, hawkish, eyes glinting, mouth twitching in a tight smile, an old irritation rekindled. She glared at Anita. "You told him about your soccer career I suppose?"

Anita cast her eyes downward, nodding. "But I was getting to basketball, too, we just didn't have a chance yet!" she protested.

"Oh come on you two. Don't start that again!" laughed Esther. "What'll you have to drink?"

They all opted for very dry white wine, except Jeremy who was already halfway through his first pint of Angkor Steam beer.

Eric opted for fresh coho salmon, as did Grace, while Esther went for fried calamari, Jeremy decided on a Mexican Snapper dish, and Anita picked the day's special *marisco*.

The women soon disappeared into a ferocious argument on the upcoming basketball season, but Jeremy and Eric fell into conversation about the debate.

"Do you know the speakers we're going to hear?" Eric asked.

"Sure, I've been following this since it erupted last year. It was on low simmer until late summer, but everyone is getting ready for a major fight now. The Garden Party is mobilizing its members, and will probably have a lot of people in the audience tonight. Floyd—you know him?"

Eric shook his head.

"Cameron Floyd edits *The Free Radical*. He's a flamboyant writer and publisher, comes from a long line of revolutionary agitators. He was married to Rosalind Rogers, the current chairwoman of the Garden Party." Jeremy drained his beer. "They divorced years ago, but politically they remain close. I expect he'll argue from a point of view not too different than the Garden Party."

"Which is what?"

The wine arrived, along with salads. Jeremy quickly took another long draught of beer, and then a big bite of salad before he answered. "Mmphf," he started gesturing with his fork while mumbling through his full mouth. "You can get a copy of the Party manifesto almost anywhere… seems like everywhere I go someone is handing them out."

Eric was surprised, because in his nearly three months in the city, he hadn't seen anyone doing that.

"Anyway," Jeremy assembled another bite of the baby greens soaked in garlic-balsamic vinaigrette, "Floyd will be against increased technological intervention, against allocating more resources for MacMillan's proposal, against the expansion of work and projects. He argues that we should all slow down and take it easier..." After quickly gulping part of his next mouthful, he blurted, "or something like that."

"And what about MacMillan?"

"Samuel MacMillan is a master inventor. I watched him in the soapbox corner at the Civic Green recently. He was airing out some of his ideas and was quite persuasive. He's bucking a lot of history, though."

"I'm just learning about this whole thing, to tell the truth."

"This debate is over MacMillan's proposal to give voice to dolphins. But the conflict dates back to the 21st century, the Die-off and the Revolution. You know the basic story—countless renegade laboratories conducted experiments back then, and all kinds of strange hybrids and genetic monsters had been grown. Back in the Money Era, anyone with a modest amount of money could buy a working lab and start mixing and matching. Thousands did, thinking it was a new Gold Rush. That set off a horrifying era of Frankensteinian competition to see who could make the weirdest or most marketable creatures. Talking pets, self-herding livestock (who soon broke out of their ranges), sentient botanicals who claimed universal consciousness and "human" rights for the plant world, photo-synthesizing human cell lines. There was an insane proliferation of ethical dilemmas." The women stopped to listen to Jeremy's briefing. Their dinners arrived, and after a few minutes of clinking silverware and intent dining, Jeremy continued.

"The pandemic of 2074 killed three and a half billion people across the planet in just two months, sparing the pot heads and those who were never reached by the virus. When people learned that the cause was an engineered virus made at a rural Texas lab, the survivors violently shut down research labs wherever they could find them. Farmers with pitchforks attacking remote scientific outposts—it was right out of Mary Shelley!" he chortled. "Biological and nanotechnological experimentation was stopped for a half century before it resumed after the Revolution ended the Money Era.

"Now scientists claim to be artists, arguing that scientific research and experimentation is as artistic as any other human activity. And everyone, whatever type of art or work they do or propose to do, has to marshall the resources—resources subject to popular control."

Anita, who had been fidgeting through Jeremy's long explanation, finally took over the narrative. "The best example of how technology evolved in the post-Economic world is the Vyne. At first it seemed like a crackpot idea, but eventually it was recognized and embraced. After all it is both a source of nearly unlimited clean energy and a global communications system. But the vyne has no self-consciousness, no mouth or vocal chords. Mixing human physical attributes into other species is considered off-limits by nearly everyone, and giving humans characteristics from other species is also forbidden."

Esther had finished her calamaris and took her turn. "Now Sam MacMillan is trying to get formal approval to do just that. And he's using the arguments of the best artists and inventors. Cameron Floyd has his work cut out."

Anita again, "Floyd has always defended artists, their need for uninhibited freedom to create, against enforcement of their Annual labor commitment, and that they should be given whatever resources they requested. He argues that society can only gain by sustaining a diverse body of creative talents in whatever they choose to pursue."

Jeremy jumped back in, "But this is different!"

"That's the debate, isn't it?" grinned Anita.

* * *

They rode a shuttle across Mission Bay to the campus. They joined the crowd flowing towards the Morales Auditorium and took a seat. On stage were three chairs, Sam MacMillan on the right and Cameron Floyd on the left. In the middle chair sat a woman, with dark short hair in a nondescript navy blue suit.

Anita pointed out a few familiar faces in the audience: "That's Giselle Carrera the painter, he's Phillip Benjamin, Cameron's co-editor at *The Free Radical*, that old blonde guy is Herman Aaronsen the poet. Over there is Francesca Panduccino—"

"I met her at Robin's wedding. She's pals with Kathy, collaborates with Bridget, Kathy's mate."

"Oh yeah? Interesting. Lucky you... you know she's a famous revolutionary?"

"Yeah, but I don't know the details."

"Remind me to tell you some time. Anyway, her eldest daughter is Rosalind Rogers, the Garden Party chair, and she used to be Floyd's wife years ago." Anita observed a group of women whom she knew from Women's Night at the Toro Negro bar on Valencia, but she didn't see any reason to point them out to Eric. "Oh, there's Rosalind Rogers herself!" down in the front row surrounded by Garden Party militants all wearing garlands and carrying bouquets of intensely fragrant flowers, the smell filling the auditorium as subtle political pressure.

* * *

"Your attention please." The woman in the middle spoke through some kind of invisible amplification system, and the audience quickly quieted down.

"I am Phyllis Fortney, tonight's moderator. I teach experimental horticulture here at UCSF. This evening we have a debate between Cameron Floyd and Sam MacMillan on the subject of adding human characteristics to other species. Specifically, MacMillan proposes to grow a small batch of experimental dolphins with human vocal chords and tongues."

Many in the auditorium shook their heads disapprovingly.

Sam MacMillan was a powerful character. Tall, blond, beaming and confident, his long shiny hair was flowing freely. "Sam MacMillan will go first, with a prepared statement not to exceed 15 minutes."

The audience applauded politely.

"Thank you Phyllis," boomed MacMillan. His deep mellifluous voice was riveting. "I propose to create the ability to talk to our friends in the Bay, the dolphins—or more accurately, to give the dolphins the ability to talk to us. Decades of working with sign language and trying to decipher their language has not achieved the breakthrough that I am convinced can be reached with this experiment."

The crowd muttered restlessly, disapproval skittering around the floor.

"I know many of you are opposed to such work on principle. I share your concerns. I, too, worry about this line of work."

Grace Ullmer fidgeted, already opposed to the proposal, and struggling with her urge to break in to MacMillan's smooth speech. She already had two points to raise, and was hoping Cameron Floyd would be quick on his feet. "God, the hubris," she muttered angrily. People behind unanimously "shushed" her.

MacMillan was continuing, "... The scientist's passion is a social force, as we all know. But to see it only as malevolent, as something society must block, check, and restrain, is a terrible mistake. The true essence of the scientist's passion is no different than that of an artist!"

Murmurs cascaded around the room, a number of people declaiming, "Come on!" "That's ridiculous!" "Artists don't kill 3 billion people!"

MacMillan put up his hands, "Please, let me finish. We are in a new era. Scientists are no longer doing secretive, profit-driven research. This is not about personal gain or fame. We are committed, like everyone, to the improvement of life for all."

Whistles and catcalls rang out. MacMillan continued doggedly, "Moreover, my very presence here is evidence of a radically different social system in which this work, with your approval, will take place.

"The dolphins are our natural allies. They are our best hope to understand and repair the damage we've done to the oceans. They may even be able to help us anticipate further changes in sea levels, which have only stabilized for the past 50 years. Don't forget the catastrophes of the 21st century!" he wagged his finger pedantically.

Eric leaned over to Anita. "What's twirlin' with these people?! They aren't giving him much of a chance, are they?"

Anita whispered back, "Yeah, I'm surprised. Looks like he's walked into a trap."

Sam MacMillan was getting angry. He rarely had met with such abuse and hostility. In the front row Rosalind Rogers sat with a self-satisfied smirk on her face. MacMillan, not as savvy politically as he had imagined himself, suddenly realized that the audience was packed with Garden Party stalwarts. He knew there was no way he'd gain their support, so he stopped trying to be diplomatic and just went to the heart of his feelings.

"Our work, no, *our art*, is a *solvent*, dissolving the staid boundaries of our lives, tearing open new possibilities in the very fabric of our material world. We can bring the accumulated human wisdom and creativity of centuries to the process of evolution itself! We don't act blindly, or with arrogance, no! Our mission is to discover in creation the new, the unknown, the *unimaginable*! Give us the resources, give us your support, and we will expand the family of life on earth, we will open the conversation with our ocean-going brethren, we will open a new dimension in the art of life!

"Thank you!" and MacMillan sat down.

A small part of the audience erupted in cheers and foot-stamping applause. Many sat silent, and some few booed under their breath.

Eric felt chills coursing down his spine. MacMillan's words had been powerful enough, but the audience's energy was whipsawing through his body. He shuddered. Emotions swirled through the hall, anger and defiant jubilation crashing into each other.

Phyllis Fortney was speaking again. "Thank you Sam MacMillan. Speaking for the opposition is Cameron Floyd, who I think needs no introduction!"

People applauded as Floyd stood up to speak. He wiped his unkempt brown hair from his eyes. He wore a green cardigan over brown corduroys, looking the part of a comfortable middle-aged academic even though he wasn't. White hair speckled his sideburns and turned his beard into a salt and pepper mask. He looked at Rosalind and gave her a wink and a smile. She returned the gesture with her own, two thumbs up.

"My friends," Floyd began, feeling the support ripening, just waiting for him to pick its fruit. "Mr. MacMillan has made a strong statement. I found myself swayed by his conviction and eloquence." He turned and nodded to MacMillan, who crossed his leg and waited for the niceties to conclude.

"To tell the truth, I wouldn't mind talking to dolphins myself!" Everyone laughed along with him.

"But my esteemed colleague has invoked a new frontier. It's not a new frontier. It's the same old frontier that has led us astray so many times in human history. His scientific passion does not lead to a nuanced embellishment of the world we already inhabit, far from it! His passion reaches for something unknown, out beyond us. This place of unmeasurable achievement serves as a mythical carrot, pushing us to experiment, to violate vital barriers between species, to impose our human traits on a species that hasn't asked for it!"

Chuckles rippled at the irony of Floyd's turn of phrase. He had to stop and smile.

"Hmm, yes, how *would* they ask for it, anyway? Well, that's one of the main problems with this whole proposal. In its essence it smacks of the arrogance that nearly destroyed humanity a century ago. Oh sure, you can say this experiment is controlled and measurable. It doesn't involve viral or bacteriological agents. All true enough. But the assumption that it is our place to abrogate the integrity of existing species is precisely the problem. It goes much deeper than the specifics of this particular experiment."

Anita was enjoying this. MacMillan was good, but Floyd was too. Garden Party cadre were arrayed throughout the auditorium. Anita was annoyed by their uniform reactions, almost like they had been coached on how to react. (In fact, the Garden Party had prepared its members for this during the past couple of weeks, circulating position papers and benefiting from the close collaboration of Rosalind Rogers and Cameron Floyd. Rogers had helped Floyd frame his arguments, and of course she was one of the Party's chief ideologues.) The Garden Party was usually right about most things, but lately Anita had seen it in a different light. She was disturbed by the Garden Party's growing intolerance for other people's views and what she suspected was an increasing corruption. The more she thought about it, the more she could see cult-like behavior where she had never seen it before.

Floyd was still speaking. "As you know, I support the development of new technologies, but only those that strictly preclude consciousness or communication. So bio-boats, the vyne, biovators, shellfones, velocipedes, bio-roofs and so on, are all magnificent examples of scientific creativity in the service of humanity and art. Household items like vacuums, rugs, windows, bio-bulbs, along with hybrid foods, have made our lives immeasurably better. Breakthroughs in photosynthesis and low-wattage electrical transmission that came with the vyne have radically reduced our impact on planetary ecology."

Rosalind Rogers was exhilarated. She'd worked hard with Floyd to get the argument right. She was frightened that MacMillan might get approval for his experiment. Her friends and colleagues had turned out in good numbers and were helping shape the audience response. The debate was to be transmitted by vyne, so getting audience response across was something to which she'd also given a lot of thought and planning.

Floyd was wrapping up, "MacMillan's plans threaten to dissolve the necessary boundaries between improving human life and dangerously changing the web of life. Let us stay off the wheel of upheaval and uncertainty promised by these plans. The unexplored frontiers of human sociability are as numerous and untapped as any scientific or biological frontier. Let us take risks with the limits we impose on ourselves, let us take risks with our hearts! Thank you!"

As Floyd sat down, the audience cheered wildly, although whistles of disapproval were also audible. A fair number of people, many wearing white lab coats, rose and left abruptly, upset by the Garden Party stalwarts. A small scuffle erupted across the hall when a lab coat grabbed a bouquet from one of the Gardeners and threw it down and stamped on it. But they were quickly separated, and nothing more happened beyond a few heated gestures and dark looks.

Eric, Anita and the others got up as the moderator thanked the assembly and encouraged everyone present and watching over the Vyne to contribute their opinions, which would be gathered to further the debate.

"So what did you think?" Anita put it to Eric first.

"Uuhhh, well... It was interesting."

Jeremy piped up, "I thought I was going to die in there! The flowers were so intense... I bet MacMillan wondered what was going on!"

They boarded a shuttle, fighting their way through a dense swarm, buzzing about the debate. Grace nabbed a corner for them, and once the shuttle was underway, she declared, "Obviously Floyd won. I mean, MacMillan made his argument and Floyd took it apart. I can't see how anyone would still support the proposal!"

Esther folded her arms and shook her head. "You weren't listening, were you? MacMillan used Floyd's own arguments about freedom and individual creativity. How can you say that Floyd won? I thought it was a draw, or maybe MacMillan came out slightly ahead."

Grace looked at Anita and the men with a confident gleam. "So? I know Esther is going to disagree with me, but what about you guys?"

Eric felt completely swayed by both speeches. "I'm going to agree with Esther. It was a draw." He felt like a wimp.

Anita leaned forward smiling. She looked sidelong at Eric and then Jeremy. "But what do you think? If you had to choose right now, would you support the proposal?"

Eric looked at Jeremy. He shook mirthfully, laughing as he answered. "Anita, my love, you are so demanding! I would vote yes... because I agree that we need to loosen up and go forward with new experiments. And if we take it slowly, we can still pull back if it seems to be going wrong. A few dolphins with big mouths? I say yes!"

"Imagine how talking dolphins will change the underwater club scene," Esther said sardonically.

Anita sat back, folding her arms. "I'm glad we don't have to make a decision yet. I'm with Eric, it was a draw. There are strong arguments on both sides."

Eric smiled with relief. They docked at the Crossroads, and made their way back to Gwen's for a nightcap. After an inconclusive hour of drinking and arguing, they broke up to head home.

It was a very dark night, illuminated by the orange-green glow of the fog-piercing streetlamps. It was also a lot colder, the end of September bringing a change in the weather. They chugged up 7th street on the tandem, avoiding the smattering of pedestrians and cross traffic along the way.

"What do you think of Kathy?" Eric asked.

"I like her pretty well, so far. I appreciate her toughness."

"Yeah, me too. Plus, at Robin's wedding, I got to hang out with her. She's as religiophobic as I am."

"Really? I was wondering about that."

"You?"

"My mother was a Buddhist and my dad was some vague Green Christian, but nothing very strong. So I ended up without much... but it doesn't bother me either."

"I HATE religion and ritual!"

She braked to a halt at Abundance and 7th. She smiled up at him as he got off the bike. "I'll be sure not to invite you to church!" she laughed.

He smiled weakly, wishing he could think of a graceful way to prolong the evening. "I had a great time. Thanks for taking me along."

She put her arms around him in a warm embrace. As they separated, she leaned in and gave him a big kiss. She smiled, jumped back onto the front of the tandem, and sped off northward, waving over her shoulder.

He stood at the corner, grinning like an idiot. An O-line Oak streetcar appeared and he scurried across to catch it. Slumping tiredly into a seat, he thought happily about his new friendship with Anita, and the interesting evening. After a speedy, uneventful ride home, he walked a block to the Mews and it wasn't until he got to the backyard that he remembered about Emmy and all the grief he'd been through earlier that day.

"Chingale! What a day!"

40.

Nwin woke up to loud knocking. He groaned and turned over, confused about where he was. After a moment he remembered the warm body next to him was Rita and that he was in the Pyramid.

The knocking at the door was insistent. Rita donned a swirling bathrobe and walked across the room as the knocking continued steadily. "Shit, it's only 8:15! Who would be knocking this early?" She opened the door.

An attractive middle-aged Asian woman stood there, dressed in black, looking frantic. "Hello." She was confused. "I'm looking for Nwin Robertson. Is he here?"

"Who are you?"

"I'm his mother, Jennifer Robertson," and she perfunctorily slapped hands with Rita, groggily going through the motions.

Rita called from the door "Nwin, it's your mother!"

Hearing her voice, he was already putting his clothes on. "Shit!" *How'd she find me here?!* he thought frantically.

Jennifer walked into the plain comfortable apartment. Rita went to the bathroom.

Jennifer watched Rita cross the room, a very pretty girl who she immediately guessed had one black and one Asian parent, like Nwin.

When Nwin emerged, Jennifer rushed over to him, throwing her arms around him. "Nwin, why haven't you come home or at least called?"

He stood there sullenly, unable to speak after a desultory 'hello.' His mother clung to him, and then started shaking and sobbing.

"Nwin, Nwin…" through her tears, "did you start that fire? They say it's you."

He sighed deeply and shrugged, withdrawing from his mother, who was still sobbing and trying to hold him close. "I didn't do nothin'!" he declared.

"Why do they think it's you?"

"I don't know."

"They told me you admitted to being there when the fire started."

"That's bullshit! I said I saw it start—I was on the Bay that morning. I told a friend, and I guess she told them. I didn't."

Jennifer looked at him through her tear-stained face, her eyes wide and full of fear. "You have to tell them you didn't do it!"

"What's the point? They've already decided it's me. I don't see what good it'll do."

"Nwin!" Jennifer gathered herself up with all the maternal power she could muster. Just then, the bathroom door opened, and Rita came out. "I'll leave you guys alone, just give me a sec while I get dressed." Nwin wanted Rita to save him from his mother, but she heard their exchange from the bathroom and was in a hurry to get out of the apartment. She disappeared into the bedroom and closed the door.

"Nwin, you have to make a statement. If you don't, it's like conceding your guilt!" Jennifer had been around city politics for many years. She knew a person could contest even the worst accusations, but you had to make a defense. Ignoring the process was the worst approach. Besides, how would she explain it to the rest of her family? Not to mention her neighbors, and her fellow councilmembers on the Bernal Heights Council? The shame rose in her, inflaming her anger towards her son. "I can't believe you! You didn't do this, did you?"

"I TOLD YOU I DIDN'T!!" he yelled. He walked over to a chair and sat down, putting his head in his hands. "Is everyone against me?" he asked no one in particular.

Rita reappeared and walked across the room hurriedly. "I'll be in the dining room on 12, OK?" she said to Nwin, who nodded absent-mindedly, watching her curving figure sway through the door. "It was nice to meet you Jennifer," she said neutrally before the door closed.

Jennifer had reached the end of her patience. Her grief and shame were overtaken by rage. "I don't know what's wrong with you! I've had enough of this. You will come with me, RIGHT NOW. We are going to go to the P-I's and you WILL MAKE A STATEMENT! Do you UNDERSTAND?" She used a voice that left no doubt about her authority.

Nwin was frightened. He had managed to avoid his mother for a long time, but here she was, nostrils flaring, hands on her hips, demanding his obedience.

"OK," he mumbled. "Let's get it over with." He rose, humiliated and defeated, hanging his head. He would just have to go through this. He wasn't going to admit anything, that's for sure.

"Good. I'm glad you're finally going to deal with this. I can't believe you haven't done this already. I've been contacted at least five times by the investigators. Not to mention your cousin Jimmy, Auntie, and who knows who else? The whole family is in an uproar."

"Alright, alright," he put his hands up in resignation. "Let's go."

"What about Rita? Don't you want to tell her where we're going?"

"I'll leave a note." He fumbled in a drawer for a pen and pad. "How did you find me here anyway?"

"Johnny Templer vyned me. Said he saw you here yesterday. I was so worried. I did-n't know I'd find you here. But I looked around the docks, and found *Hot 1* parked in the slot for this apartment, so I thought I'd knock. And you were here, thank goodness!"

Nwin scribbled a short note: "Going with my mother for a few hours. Back later, Nwin." No point in telling her anything more at this stage. Who knows what she was thinking after this scene with his mother, anyway.

* * *

Stella Brooks arrived early that morning. She hadn't slept well. One of her five cats was sick and she had to get up every four hours to medicate it. She'd been up since 6:30. It was now after nine and she'd spent an hour with reports and memos from various staffers. Anita's account from the Library, Eric's report on his visit to the Rice Bowl, Kathy's notes about Robertson's movements the day before, including an appended note that he'd retrieved his bag from the Rice Bowl after Eric was there at 4 p.m. Kathy's memo also described a bike accident Robertson had been in, and the doctor who had treated him, Laurie Sung. She read that Dr. Sung was sister to the doctor who lived at Eric's place, the same one who had told them that Robertson had been in the hospital smelling of gasoline the morning of the fire.

"Small goddamned world!" Stella shook her head at the curious coincidence. She sipped a big mug of tea and mulled over the story's details, outlining in her mind how she should write it up. Clanging streetcar bells and loud voices erupted outside, so she went to see what the ruckus was. People were standing around gesturing a half block away next to a stopped streetcar, but Stella couldn't see much. She started to turn back from the window when out of the corner of her vision she observed a couple walking toward their building, a short woman in black followed by a tall young black man.

She leaned into the window, peering down. It sure looked like Robertson, but she had never seen him in person. It seemed terribly unlikely that he would just suddenly show up at their offices. The couple disappeared through the front door below, and she returned to her desk.

Two minutes later, she looked up to see the woman and boy, as she could see he was now, walking slowly past her doorway.

"Hello? Can I help you?" Stella called out.

The woman turned, taking off her dark glasses and brushing her hair back with one hand. "Yes? Yes, please. I'm looking for…" and she fumbled for something in her purse. She pulled out a scrap of paper, "Kathy Fairly? Or Robin Davis?"

"They're not in yet. Maybe I can help you?" Stella was walking around her desk towards the doorway. "I'm Stella Brooks," and she extended her hand to slap.

"I'm Jennifer Robertson and this is my son Nwin. We've been asked to come and make a statement."

"Yes, yes of course! Please come in. I can help you, I'm just working on that report now." She looked at Nwin with avid interest. So here was their guy, obviously dragged in by his mother. What a surprise! He was a big fellow, over six feet tall, much taller than his mother, but there was no doubt that she was powerful too. The boy looked sullen and intimidated.

"Thank you for coming in. We are anxious to hear your side of the story Mr. Robertson."

"Call him Nwin," said his mother, who looked like she was ready to conduct the interview herself. "Do you have any evidence we can look at before we make a statement?"

Stella raised her eyebrows as she flipped through the papers before her. "Well, there is some physical evidence that pertains to this case. And there are a number of reports that taken together paint a strong circumstantial case against your son, Mrs. Robertson. Here are some relevant affidavits you can look through. I'll get the physical evidence while you have a look." She extended a folder to the Robertsons. She took a deep breath, wheezing slightly, and realized her lungs were tightening up in the face of the important interview she was about to administer. She left the room, heading to the evidence room upstairs.

Jennifer opened the folder. Flipping through the pages she quickly determined that most of the affidavits were descriptions of the fire, and then descriptions of finding evidence of arson at the point of origin.

"Look here, Nwin. They found some kind of gasoline bomb in a submerged warehouse near the place the fire started."

He took the paper from her, and examined it cursorily, not recognizing anything of his own experience in the dry account of the blackened ruin from which the investigator had fished a white plastic bucket.

Jennifer kept perusing the file. News articles on the fire's progress were also included, as were accounts from the volunteer fire brigade, with a list of injuries incurred during the long morning fighting the fire.

"Hey look. Here's your medical report from General Hospital. Says you smelled strongly of gasoline when they brought you in. Is this true? When I arrived you'd already been washed." She turned to look closely at her son. "Why would the doctor make something like this up?"

He wouldn't look at her as he shook his head, staring at the floor. He muttered a denial, "I don't know what they're talking about!"

Jennifer got worried and returned to the papers before her. She kept flipping through various investigators reports, checking gasoline distributors, remnant dealers, "Oh, here's another one… Nwin!?! What is this? A place on Tailor, one of those remnant dealers, says you got gasoline from them."

He walked to the window. He imagined crawling on the sill and getting away. But there was no clear way to hold on. He turned, ignoring his mother's imploring questioning, and looked at the door, thinking he could bolt.

"Nwin!!" his mother's voice was growing increasingly panicky. "The librarian said you were the one who made copies of instructions on setting fires with gasoline bombs. NWIN! Is this true?!?"

He had to get away. He moved towards the door, like an irresistible force was pulling him. He watched himself walk towards the door, hearing his mother in the distance, calling him urgently, yelling. She got up as he was getting closer to the door, he was almost there, just a little further, and—

A large cart filled the doorway, pushed by the fat investigator woman. He stopped abruptly. Brooks stopped pushing the cart just before running right into him. But she was blocking the door! *SHIT! SHIT! SHIT!* He looked left and right, and found no other doors. The open windows were too far off the ground. *TRAPPED!* His mother grabbed his wrist and dragged him to his seat.

* * *

"Mr. Roberts—uh Nwin. Where are you going?" asked Stella from behind the cart. His eyes darted from side to side, panicky, nowhere to go, his mother surging towards him. Suddenly he sagged, his shoulders slumping, and his mother took him by the wrist and led him, stumbling back to his seat. Stella watched the fuming mother and the sullen son.

"Can I get you something to drink? A bite to eat?" she asked solicitously.

"No thank you." Jennifer Robertson's face twisted in rage and fear.

"Here is the physical evidence we've collected," Stella wheeled the gurney next to the table. She held up the first item, the Earth Liberation Front instructions discovered at the Shotwell Community Workshop. She handed it across to the Robertsons. "This is the paper we found that corresponds to that librarian's affidavit," she pointed at the folder. "And we know that Jimmy Van is Nwin's cousin, and he's the Shotwell Workshop coordinator, so there's a plausible explanation for Nwin having been there even though no one claims to have seen him using the electric workshop."

"Then there's this," and she groaned as she lifted the plastic bucket from the lower shelf. "As you can see, it still has the ignition system attached," pointing to the soggy flare taped onto the lid of the bucket. Gasoline stunk up the room. "We assume this was one of several bombs, but it fell off the wall and into the water before it could ignite. The lid stayed on too, so the gasoline is still in there."

Jennifer felt helpless in the face of the mounting evidence. She knew Nwin had always played with fire. Combined with the circumstantial evidence, she was losing confidence in his innocence. But she stifled those thoughts and remained silent during the presentation.

"The rest of the evidence all depends on putting things together. Like the doctor's report when he was hospitalized with his back injury; or the account provided by ah… uh…" Stella reached for the affidavits and flipped through until she found what she was looking for, "Here! This story by Valentina Rogers." She looked up at Nwin for a reaction, but he remained impassive, staring at the table. She glanced at the mother, who was clearly on the verge of tears.

She started at the name. "Valentina? Nwin, isn't that the—"

He waved her off. "I took her on a Bay cruise, we went by the fire site, that's all."

"Ahem," Stella cleared her throat demonstratively. "Nwin, are you ready to give your side of the story?"

He scowled at her, but his eyes belied a real fear. He squirmed in his seat.

"Nwin, come on now. You didn't do it, you told me, so you need to make a statement."

"Mrs. Roberston, if Nwin is uncomfortable making a statement on his own, you do have the option of waiting for an Advocate to help him prepare his case. There's no obligation to speak now… although I must admit," she smiled, "I'm extremely curious to hear your side of the story." She returned her gaze to Nwin.

"Stella! What have we here?" Kathy Fairly burst in. She wore her baggy shorts as always, her thick calves stolidly carrying her into the room. Her loose-fitting blue work shirt billowed as air flowed into it with the force of her entry. Stella quickly apprised Kathy of the situation and introduced her to the Robertsons.

"Mr. Robertson—Nwin—is about to make a statement, I believe. Or perhaps he's going to wait for an Advocate."

Kathy perched on the edge of the table, taking in the plastic bucket, the folder bulging with affidavits and slips of paper. The case whizzed through her mind, rushing to the forefront with the long-awaited appearance of their prime suspect. She leaned towards the Robertsons.

"I've been a P-I for almost three decades. I have rarely seen as much circumstantial evidence in a case as this one. I would recommend that you meet with a Public Advocate before making a statement. But of course, if you prefer, we can take your statement now." She sat back, watching Nwin closely, occasionally glancing at his mother.

Jennifer spoke quietly to her son. "Nwin, I think we should meet with the Advocate."

"What for?!?" he flailed his arm, almost whacking her in the face. She recoiled and suddenly all her fragility vanished. She stood up abruptly. To Kathy and Stella she spoke in a steely tone: "Please excuse us for a moment." The two women departed the room without delay.

* * *

In the hall, Stella and Kathy walked a short distance away from the door to the conference room.

"Whaddya think?" Kathy asked.

"This might get ugly. The mom came in pissed off, then after seeing some of the affidavits, I heard her yelling at him just as I came back with the evidence cart. In fact, I'm pretty sure the kid was trying to run, but I entered the door before he could."

"Really? Do you think it's safe to leave them in there?"

"He's not going to attack his mother, Kathy, be realistic!"

"There's something not right about this guy. He doesn't seem to have the usual emotional buttons, know what I mean?"

"No."

"You've seen more of him than I have. He seemed frozen."

"He's a normal teenager. I've seen it plenty of times—you catch a kid misbehaving, he denies it completely."

"Can we wait for the mother to solve this? This young man is a menace."

"Yeah, that was a helluva serious fire he set, and he clearly went to an awful lot of trouble to do it."

"NOO! Chingale!" roared Nwin in the closed room.

"Shit! Let's go," Kathy made a beeline for the door, opening it at the same time Nwin reached for it from the other side. His mother was rushing up behind him, anger twisting her tear-stained face. "Excuse me, is everything alright here?" Kathy asked with a false innocence. Nwin stopped abruptly, intimidated by Kathy's bulky presence, even if he towered over her. She blocked the door, and attacking the P-I was still beyond anything he was prepared to do. He stared at her with undisguised hatred. She returned his glare with an unnerving calmness, crossing her arms as she stood in the doorway. "So how are we going to proceed? Have you arrived at a decision?"

Mrs. Robertson was standing just behind her son and once again took his wrist to pull him back to the chairs. He ripped his arm from her grasp, whirling on her. "Look, there's nothing I can do, okay? They're going to accuse me of this. I can't prove I didn't do it any more than they can prove that I did."

"Nwin," sobbed his mother, "can we meet with an Advocate—pleeease?—and at least see what our options are?"

"That's good advice son." Kathy was leaning on the door jamb now. Nwin whirled back to face her.

"Who are you calling 'son'?" He stood there, flexing his muscles, clenching and unclenching his fists. Kathy pulled out a toothpick, casually leaning in the door, and watched him, waiting to see what he would do next. His mother pleaded with him to sit down. Suddenly, the young man sighed deeply, and sat by his mother. She put her hand on his arm, but he shook it off.

"We'd like to make an appointment with the Public Advocate, please," Jennifer said.

"No problem," Kathy said, having moved into the room, followed by Stella. Behind Stella, Eric appeared in the doorway. "Am I interrupting?"

"Eric, hello, not at all. Come on in," Kathy encouraged him. "Eric Johanson, meet Nwin Robertson and his mother Jennifer Robertson."

Eric slapped hands with Mrs. Robertson, but Nwin wouldn't make eye contact or say hello, let alone slap hands. Eric looked down at the top of his head, strangely unmoved by the presence of the man he'd been seeking for weeks. There was no sense of victory looking at the teary mother next to her sullen teenage son. He felt uncomfortable and wondered what to do, automatically moving towards the door. He wished he hadn't entered this awkward situation.

"We're going to arrange a meeting with a Public Advocate," Kathy explained to everyone in the room.

At the door, Eric said "I'll be in my office if you need me," and he left hurriedly.

* * *

Nwin planned the next few days. He had to escape his mother, that was the first task. *So much for staying with Rita!* He had to get his stuff, and get out of there quickly.

His mother clutched his arm as they approached the Public Advocate's office. "We'll meet the Advocate and make an appointment to come back later, okay?" she said. He said nothing. He focussed on his overwhelming desire to get away. At the Advocate's office they entered and sat down. In a minute a short-haired, clean-shaven young man emerged from the inner office. "Are you the Robertsons?" Jennifer took over, explaining the situation, but the young man, who called himself Felton Dangerfield, already knew all about it. He smiled reassuringly, which made Jennifer feel better.

"You're innocent until they prove otherwise. It's great that you came here before making a statement. It's incredibly easy to say the wrong thing, even in good faith and in total innocence. I wish more people understood that!" He was strangely upbeat and exuded confidence. "You'd be surprised at how difficult it is to prove guilt with circumstantial evidence. I just took a glance at their case while you were walking down here, and I think you can beat this!" he gleamed.

"You already?—"

The fellow put up his hands as he rose from his desk. "We're all in the same building, Mrs. Roberston. This is one of the bigger cases to come along in a while, and when you showed up here this morning, it didn't take long for word to spread. I figured you'd end up here before the morning was over, and voila! Here you are!" He spread his arms wide, as though welcoming them to his ranch or something.

"Mr. Dangerf—"

"Felton, please, call me Felton. And may I call you Jennifer? And Nwin?" he asked each in turn, Jennifer nodding with relief while Nwin barely acknowledged him. "We've got a lot of work to do. Do you want to get started?"

"I was just going to say, I think we need to come back later. It's been a tough morning already."

"No problem, Jennifer. I understand. When would you like to get started? And by the way, you don't have to be here if you don't want to—or, if you Nwin, would prefer to work on this without your mother. It is YOUR case, after all."

That got his attention. Nwin looked at this strange, squeaky clean man and wondered why he was so enthused. What did he get out of this? On the wall behind Dangerfield was the usual sign: "No One Wants To, So We All Have to. Do Your Annuals" but 'Annuals' was crossed out and replaced with a hand-scribbled 'Advocacy.'

"What's that?" he asked.

Dangerfield turned to see what he was pointing at. "Oh that! My girlfriend gave me that when I finished my Apprenticeship two years ago."

Jennifer was surprised that this young man could have already been through an entire five-year Apprenticeship. "Excuse me, but if you don't mind my asking, how old are you?"

Dangerfield laughed. "You aren't the first to ask, believe me! I'm 37."

"And you're just using the regular age-blockers? That's incredible!"

He ran his hand over his full head of dark brown hair. "Lucky genes I guess…" He didn't bother to say that he didn't use age-blockers, although there were mornings when he peered into his face in the mirror and wondered if he should.

They made a plan to start the next afternoon. Jennifer and Nwin thanked Felton and made their way out to the Civic Green. It was after 11, and the noontime concert band was setting up in the bandshell.

"Hungry?" his mother asked him.

"Nah. Look, I gotta go."

"Where?" Jennifer was suddenly worried. "Why don't you come home with me?"

"I'll meet you here tomorrow. I've got stuff to do."

"So you're okay with me being there?" she asked anxiously.

"Sure, mom, no problem," he grimaced unconsciously. "I've got nothing to hide."

She smiled wanly, trying to find some reassurance. He put his arm around her, which was surprising, and gave her a perfunctory squeeze. "See you here at 1 o'clock tomorrow, okay?" trying to sound positive.

"Okay, Nwin. okay." She trailed off. "Where can I reach you? At Rita's?"

"Yeah, I'll be there later," he said over his shoulder as he walked into the Green. His mother stood hugging herself and watched him disappear, chilled even though the midday sun was quite warm.

41.

E ric!" Anita's voice rang out from the hallway before she entered. "Eric, will you do this interview with *Dock of the Bay*? They're doing a feature on the arson case."

"Why me? I think Kathy should do it, or Stella."

"They're both out on other cases."

"I'm on another case too!" He pushed aside the documents. He was trying to learn enough about biomanufacturing to be able to investigate misuse of laboratory resources. "Alright, I'll do it."

Their arsonist, Nwin Robertson, had disappeared again. He skipped his Tuesday appointment with Dangerfield, the energetic Public Advocate. Yesterday Stella had published the Public Investigators Official Report on the San Bruno Mountain fire investigation on the vyne, and it was all over the morning papers. Journalists wanted to examine the personal side of the story—both the accused and the investigators.

"Man, I so wish I was anywhere else," Eric grumbled to himself as he prepared for the reporter's arrival. Anita stood at the door gesturing down the hallway.

"She's a decent reporter—won't butcher your quotes," she reassured Eric. Anita gave him an easygoing friendship and workplace camaraderie. He watched her at the door. Today she was wearing a whimsical fringed leather skirt that extended below her knees. Her dirty old sandals that she wore almost everyday were flaking dried mud on the floor. She leaned coyly against his door, folding her arms and giving him a mischievous smile.

"She's a cutie too, so watch out!"

The woman entered, shooting a stabbing look at her old colleague. She wore her black hair like a hat, but on closer inspection, he could see it was densely curled.

"I'm Judith McLaughlin, how do you do," she extended a long, tapered hand from a dark green cashmere sweater, fitted tightly over her shapely figure. Her green eyes flashed behind thick brown-rimmed glasses, set off by ample red lipstick-laden lips. She smelled too, some kind of floral bouquet that for once, Eric actually found pleasant.

"Please sit down," he urged her after introducing himself and exchanging a light slap. She wore sensible flat leather shoes and her plaid skirt parted at a slit as she sat down, revealing a very white, milky thigh. Eric struggled to divert his gaze.

"Sorry about Anita, she's always trying to get my goat," Judith confided. "We worked together for some years, before she went to *The Call*."

Eric waved his hand like he didn't know what Judith could be referring to, but his heart was pounding, finding her enormously attractive.

"So, uh, aahh...

"Eric," he reminded her, crestfallen that she hadn't taken his name in.

"Yes, Eric...." she fumbled through her notes. "Can you tell me about the investigation?"

He gave her a quick account while she jotted.

"And you met the apparent arsonist? Nwin Robertson?"

"Yes, very briefly this week. I was following him around for a month, so when I finally met him—"

"Yes?" she leaned forward.

"It was disappointing. He is a confused young man." Eric felt uncomfortable characterizing anyone as a boy or a young man, so close to both categories himself.

"Was he defiant? Angry? Do you think he's psychotic?"

He sat back, surprised by the harshness of her question. "Definitely not. I mean, he was sitting here with his mother and my colleagues when I walked in. His mother had been crying—"

"Really?" McLaughlin scribbled furiously. "And how did she seem? Was she a controlling type?"

Eric was intimdated by McLauglin's aggressive questioning.

"I'm sorry. I don't know enough to help you. I only met the mother and the suspect for a couple of minutes. Anything I say is based on the shortest of acquaintances under most unflattering and difficult circumstances." He surprised himself with his well-formulated deflection. She stopped scribbling and looked at him with a penetrating gaze. He squirmed.

"Maybe I could ask you some personal questions?" she suggested softly, irresistibly. Eric nodded. He felt stupid before she even got to the next question.

"How long have you been a P-I?" He explained that he was nearing the end of his three-month Tryout. "And do you think this office provides adequate training? Do you think you were given the tools—I mean conceptual tools—to carry out this important investigation, with so little experience? You were the chief investigator, weren't you?"

"Absolutely not. Where did you get that idea? I was working under close supervision. The chief of the department, Kathy Fairly, directed me—an experienced Lifer, Stella Brooks, helped too. You should be interviewing them instead of me!"

McLaughlin scribbled intently. "Can Fairly or Brooks speak with me today?"

"I think they're out on assignment."

Anita came back in, and seemed to have been listening at the door. "Judy, give him a break! I told you Fairly and Brooks were out today. You can get 'em on Monday. Fairly might be in tomorrow, but Brooks never works weekends. Have you gotten a story from Eric?"

McLaughlin stood up, straightening her plaid skirt and brushing out the wrinkles in her cashmere sweater. Irritated that Anita had interrupted her, she gave Eric a winning smile, extending her hand for a farewell slap. "Thanks very much, Aaron—I mean, Eric! You've been a great help." She walked briskly through the door, while Anita hung back, watching her leave.

"You alright?" she looked at Eric. "She's a force, eh? You wouldn't believe how many times she's reduced interviewees to blubbering hysterics!"

"Anita? You coming?" Judith McLaughlin had poked her head back in the room.

"Yeah, sure, Judy. Give me a sec. I'll meet you at the front desk." Judith McLaughlin waved again and disappeared. "She can be such a pain! A great reporter, but an incredible prima donna!"

"I guess she went easy on me," he said in a low tone, still unnerved, the sweet smell of her scent lingering in the air.

"Next week, we're supposed to get cracking on the UC case, right?"

Eric nodded, reaching for his pile of papers. "I'm trying to get ready. I don't see how are we going to just walk in there and start looking around... It'll be so obvious!"

"That doesn't matter. In fact, it's supposed to help. The Public Investigator is brought in to uncover misappropriations, unauthorized resource diversions, unjustifiable wastage. Everyone knows what we're doing when we're there. An investigation can often stop the problem without taking any further action. We're trying to expose first, explain second." Anita had reported on Public Investigations many times as a journalist.

"It's impenetrable. I don't know how we'd even be able to recognize a problem if we were looking right at it!" He was exasperated and overwhelmed.

"We'll figure it out, don't worry!" Leaning on his desk, she peered into his face. "Relax Eric! We just do the best we can. Someone there complained, so I assume we'll be pointed in the right direction."

"And how do we avoid being used in an internal rivalry?"

Anita shrugged. "We don't! At least not until we get in there and do some interviews. You know the drill."

"Not as well as you."

"You'll be fine—and so will I!"

Eric smiled cautiously. "So what'cha doin' this weekend?" he asked hopefully.

"Sunday I'm going to the playoffs in Oakland with Grace and Esther."

"Oh yeah? Who's playin'?"

She shook her head, amazed that anyone could be so oblivious to the epic pennant race that had just concluded and the gripping playoffs that were already unfolding. "Oaks and Slugs—c'mon, you MUST've heard about it!"

"Nope."

"What planet are you living on?" she scolded. "Tomorrow I'm going with Jeremy and his queer pals to the Folsom Street Fair. Wanna come?"

"Street Fair?"

"Oh HO! You don't know about the Folsom Street Fair?!? You HAVE to come!" Anita was chortling in a way that made Eric feel stupid. "Come on Eric, stop moping like that... look, meet me tomorrow at Angelo's Juice Bar at noon. You know the place?"

Realizing with some surprise that he did, Eric nodded automatically. "Yeah, sure, above the Market Pond right?"

"Exactly. It'll be hot, so be ready for a day in the sun, ok?"

"Bands? Food? That sort of thing?"

"Yes, all that and *much more*. Trust me," she said mysteriously. And then she left.

He looked at his research with dismay. It was already lunchtime on Friday. They'd completed the job on the San Bruno Fire. He got up from his desk, beckoned by the warm sunny day. "I'm calling it a week! See ya Monday!" he called to Leigh and Andy as he walked down the hall to leave.

* * *

The warm afternoon sun caressed him as he started out. By the time he reached the top of Alamo Square he was soaked with sweat. He flopped into the grass to the sound of bicycle bells tinkling in the distance. He folded his hands under his head, staring at puffy white clouds in the blue sky.

This is the life! he thought to himself. *Why can't I feel like this all the time?* An unfamiliar contentedness swaddled him in a warm cocoon. He was almost dozing off when he heard giggles not far away. It sounded terribly familiar. *Shit, it can't be!* He rolled over to his belly, and looked towards the sound. Emmy was in the arms of a tall dark-haired man, his long black hair cascading over her as he kissed her. "Just my luck!" Eric cursed softly. He walked away as fast as he could towards home.

Agitated, he crossed Divisadero's streetcar tracks and densely wooded bikepaths, avoiding mid-afternoon traffic. On Hayes he pushed through sticky sweet, billowing marijuana plants. *Maybe I ought to smoke a little something,* he thought, anger coursing through him.

An old woman tended the plants, pinching buds and trimming branches that were clogging the right of way. Not far off, clouds of smoke and laughing voices drifted from open Bay windows. A reggae bass line rumbled out of the same place. A topless young woman with long dreadlocks was dancing in the window. Two large men danced on either side of her, both with their hands on her torso, all with long dreadlocks swirling into one great mass of tangles. They handed a giant spliff back and forth. The girl smilingly invited him to join them, arching her back to emphasize her pert little breasts. "No thanks," Eric grinned back, "but I'd love a hit…"

One of the men leaned into the window. "Why'n'cha c'mawn in mahn? Eet's a pahrtay!" He laughed.

"I'm heading home, but thanks anyway." The girl produced another fat joint and tossed it to him. He fished it from the bush where it landed, and gave a small bow of thanks.

He cut across the Panhandle, ducking discs and avoiding dogs playfully nipping at his heels. He bummed a light from a reveler enjoying the afternoon sun, and after a taking a deep hit, he passed the spliff around. By the time it came back to him, it was down to the last 20%. He bade the group farewell and took the last with him. He walked through the Page Mews gate, relieved to know that at least he was not going to run into Emmy.

"Hi Eric, howzit twirlin'?" Tanya was at the solar oven as he entered the yard.

"Everything's spinning along I guess," he said, deeply stoned, with a note of resignation.

"Oh come on! It's such a beautiful day! And I see that you're not at work!" she said with a wink and a smile. Her muscular arms were bulging as she lifted the big flat bread shovel and began moving loaves around in the oven.

"Hey, have you met my new honey, Melinda?"

"No, is she here?"

"Riiiiiight there!" Tanya pointed to a woman barreling out of a door. She was square-shouldered, carrying a large container of bread dough, covered in a towel. As she drew near, Eric could see a big whale tattoo covering her left shoulder, her olive skin and Roman nose leading him to assume she was Latina or Italian or maybe Jewish.

"Hey Mel, this is Eric—remember I told you? He has the room down the hall."

"Sure!" She slung the bowl of dough onto the table and offered him an enthusiastic slap.

"Baking bread?" The tantalizing bread smell in his altered state was making him powerfully hungry.

They laughed. "Yes we are, but not the usual... Here, take a look." Tanya opened the oven and pulled out a loaf shaped like a big penis. Chortling, she shoved it back in and pulled out another, which seemed to be two women in a 69 position, but it was kind of hard to tell.

"X-rated loaves?" Eric asked, puzzled.

"For the Folsom Street Fair tomorrow. We're going as bread maidens!" and Tanya giggled impishly. "You going?"

"My friend Anita is taking me. But what's the deal?"

Melinda grabbed Eric by the wrist. "You mean you've never been to the Folsom Street Fair?"

"Nope. Never heard of it until a few hours ago."

"Oh man, I WISH I was going for the first time! That's always the best!" and she looked at Tanya and they both laughed.

"I guess the joke is on me," said Eric, irritation rising. "What exactly is the story about this fair?"

"I can't believe you've never heard of it," said Tanya again. And then she launched into a brief history, how the fair was almost 200 years old, the storied leather and sex parties. "And yes, there's plenty of sex, you'd better believe it!" her eyes danced with excitement.

"Well, sounds like fun," he said without much conviction. "Is it a costume thing?" he worried.

"You might say that," laughed Melinda. "But not really."

That wasn't much of an answer, but he gave up asking and went upstairs. It was intriguing that Anita asked him to accompany her. Maybe that was a good sign. In his room, he opened windows to the afternoon breezes and laid down on his bed. But he was restless and not in the mood to waste a beautiful afternoon indoors.

"Vyne!" and down it rolled. "Messages!" and there were several, one from his parents, one from Kathy, and one from Victoria Matthews. His parents were sending him a chatty greeting for no particular reason. He quickly composed a similar response.

"Everything is fine. I just wrapped up a big arson case. I like the Public Investigators'. My co-workers are the dew. The work is either quite interesting, or horribly boring. Next I'll learn about biology labs! Ugh! Anyway, I'm fine. Give my love to everyone."

"Victoria Matthews!" he called, and she quickly took form on the leaf's surface.

"Hi Eric! It was great to run into you again. I don't know anyone here, so you can imagine my surprise when I found you. Are you busy Friday night?"

Tonight? Hmmm.

"There's a concert at the Civic Green after the parade. Want to get a bite and go? I'm not sure I'll be able to check messages, so I'll be at Market Pond, near the Church Street pier, around 5 o'clock. I'll probably have a drink or two and hang out until the parade starts at 6. Meet me there if you want. I'm looking forward to getting together again!"

He actually didn't have any plans for the evening. Meeting up with Victoria and having dinner, music, the Friday parade, it all sounded quite civilized and fun.

Lastly, he checked his message from Kathy.

"Hey Eric, I just realized that your three month Tryout is over. I want you to start an Apprenticeship. Let's talk on Monday."

Decision time! An Apprenticeship! That was a three-year commitment, not three months. Three years seemed like forever. But he liked working with Kathy and the rest, especially with Anita now. He thought he'd probably go for it, but it was very hard to decide, especially for such a big commitment. *No need to decide right now. I've got all weekend.* But he was feeling pretty good again. *Things aren't so bad.*

* * *

It was after 10:30 the next morning when he woke up in his bed, a deep foggy hangover clouding his senses. He tried to remember the night before. He had gotten extremely stoned in the late afternoon, then more later in the evening with Victoria. "Oh shit!" The evening's embarrassing events started coming back to him. Meeting Victoria at the Market Pond had been fine. But he was so stoned that he found it difficult to converse. Luckily Victoria was quite a chatterer, but as the evening progressed, it got worse.

He groaned as he remembered, much later, falling into the fountain in the Civic Green after whirling a little too enthusiastically to Belle and the Bluebells. "Oh maaaan," he put his hands on his pounding head. Trying to focus across the room, he discovered his crumpled wet clothes piled in the corner. *Victoria must think I'm an idiot!* The horrible memory of sitting in cold water, fountain spray pouring a cold, bracing mist over him, made him miserable. He struggled to remember how he'd gotten out of the fountain, who else had been there. *Victoria? She wasn't there, I don't remember her! Maybe she didn't see me fall.* Then he remembered. She had left a while earlier, not shit-faced drunk like he was. She had been pleasant enough on departure.

Chingale! She's not my type anyway! He forced himself into the bathroom, staring into the mirror. He shaved his blotchy growth of a beard, and stood in the hot shower for 20 minutes. He dressed slowly, wondering if he should be wearing silk or leather, even though he didn't have anything like that. "It's just a street party, after all. It can't be that big a deal what you wear!"

He clattered down the back stairs over to Trixie's kitchen, planning to hurry to Angelo's in time to meet Anita. First though, he needed coffee. At the hot tubs he ran into Angie and Gerald, having a mellow morning soak.

"Where're you rushing off to?" asked Gerald.

"Meeting a friend. She's taking me to the Folsom Street Fair."

"Oh HO!" Gerald and Angie both exclaimed together, laughing.

"What IS the deal with this anyway?"

"You'll see," said Angie in a sultry tone, with an unmistakeable prurient smile.

"I feel like the only person in the whole town who doesn't know what's going on!" Eric said, exasperated.

"You'll have fun—I guarantee it!" said Angie. "Say, what's the latest on Robertson?"

"I guess he's on the run... I hope he's already left town. There's some concern that he may start another fire as a farewell gift."

"Really? I'd think he'd be pretty easy to stop after all that publicity, no?"

"Who knows? If people aren't paying attention, they may not know what he's up to."

"My sister told me about treating him in Citrus Heights," she shook her head. "What do you do about someone like that?" They all shrugged, unable to understand why anyone would start fires.

"If he doesn't leave on his own, I guess there will probably be a trial. Where do people get exiled to from here anyway?"

Gerald piped up. "There's a ranch near Susanville on the other side of the mountains, way way north of here. I think there's a place in Baja too. They definitely send 'em far from here!"

"I gotta get a cuppa coffee," he apologized as he left them behind.

"Have fun at the Fair!" Angie teased.

Eric scowled as he walked away, sensitive to what he felt was her insinuation that he was inexperienced. Which he was, and that only made it worse!

He walked into the kitchen, where Trixie was busily cooking something for later in the day. "Mmmm, smells great! What is that?" he asked.

"It's a lentil stew. You gonna be around for lunch?"

"Nope. Heading to—"he bit his tongue, "—downtown, to meet a friend." He got coffee while Trixie sprinkled cumin into the stew. He scuffled through the swinging door into the dining room and stopped abruptly.

"Oh, uh, hi," he mumbled. Emmy and her new boyfriend were sitting at the opposite end of the room, sharing a plate of toast and coffee.

"Eric!" Emmy called nervously, "This is Jan." He waved and smiled through his long hair, a small goatee lending a sharpness to his chin.

"Hi," he waved back, and immediately retreated to the kitchen, saying nothing more. His heart felt heavy as he quickly gulped down his coffee. He thought about the times it had been him at the table with Emmy in a similarly fuzzy morning state. In the backyard he went over to a bench under some lemon trees and sat by himself, trying to get composed before leaving. His hangover had diminished, and the memories of last night were fading too. He wasn't angry with Emmy, but seeing her with Jan filled him with self-pity. He gazed at Gerald and Angie nuzzling each other in the hot tub. Another couple that he didn't know came out of the easternmost building in the Mews, also looking quite lovey-dovey. He rose abruptly and made for the bike rack. Laughter peeled upstairs from Tanya and Melinda. In a minute he passed through the Wiggle's western gate and joined dense inbound traffic.

In five minutes he hit the Sans Souci Bridge and finished the last straightaway to Angelo's. He parked his bike, looking for Anita. He looked right past her at first. Then her roguish smile caught his eye.

He couldn't believe it was her! Her hair had been braided into dozens of small braids, then those too had been tightly braided together. She was wearing an incredibly tiny, skintight dark blue suede miniskirt with matching spike-heeled boots that went over her knees. Her midriff was bare and she wore a blue suede halter top, her bosom bulging from it. Uncharacteristically she was wearing bright red lipstick. She wore elbow length blue gloves too. His chest tightened anxiously as he approached her.

"I've been waiting for you." She gave him her best *femme fatale* look.

"Goddam Anita, I can't believe it's you!" He gave her cheek a kiss, grazing her midriff with his hand like violating a boundary.

"Uh-uh, pal," she said raspily. She put one hand on his crotch and pressed her mouth into his in a long violent kiss.

When she let him go, he was completely aroused and gasping for breath. "Anita!" he said in a sing-songy tone, "I had no idea!... Hey, you didn't tell me to dress up."

"Honey, don't you worry! *Everything* is available at the Folsom Street Fair."

He rode behind her, ogling her surprisingly perfect ass while she awkwardly pumped her pedals in highheel boots. More and more people were appearing in similar get-ups. The streetcars were overflowing with men and women dressed as sexual predators. He had never seen anything like it. They made a right on 11th Street and crossed Mission Plank Road, where they deposited their bikes at the velome. She grabbed him by the elbow and tottered along on her impossibly high heels, pointing out other outfits on the way. Loud music echoed nearby from a live stage. At the corner of 11th and Folsom they came to the Oasis, a sprawling pond surrounded by palm trees and café tables.

"We're meeting Jeremy and his boys here," she announced. Multitudes thronged the street in front of the pond. A half dozen Adonis's cavorted in the water. Another group of men in various states of undress were busily making out, groping and fondling each other along the banks of the pond. "He's probably here somewhere already," Anita said, pouting provocatively in a way he'd seen before but had never interpreted correctly until now.

"Well, well, well!" boomed Jeremy behind them, his hands landing on Eric's shoulders at the same moment. Startled, Eric twisted around but all he could see were three large bellies bulging against stark white shirts with shiny brass buttons and leather suspenders. He leaned forward to get a better angle on Jeremy and two other guys who looked like triplets. Anita was laughing uproariously and soon all the bellies were jiggling along with her, surrounding Eric with a deep, throaty laughter.

"So my dear, you've brought us a live one, eh?" Jeremy boomed. His companions shook with laughter. They were wearing formal shirts with cufflinks and bowties under their studded lederhosen. They wore frilly hats too, and eye makeup, maybe even rouge on their cheeks—Eric wasn't sure. They were quite a sight, three men shaped like bowling pins, waddling about in lederhosen, laughing like circus clowns.

Eric realized he was the object of their unspoken designs, and he was seized with a wave of fear. "Wha-Wha-What d'you have in m-m-mind?" he stammered, which only made them laugh all the harder. Anita stood up, assuming her full posture and power.

"My gawd Anita!" Jeremy exclaimed. Eric was gulping for air, awestruck again at Anita's transformation.

"OK boys, back off!" she snarled with a laugh, "he's mine!" Eric felt momentarily relieved, and then a new wave of anxiety.

"Anita," he whispered, "what's going on?"

She smiled at him coyly, stroking his arm reassuringly. "It's all in good fun, don't worry!"

He sighed and decided to go with the flow as best he could.

"Come along my dear," Anita took him by the hand. Jeremy and his companions, Ron and Moe, bounced along behind, distracted by the gorgeous men lining the streets. Eric was shocked by the brazen sexuality on display all around him. In upstairs windows there were men going down on each other for all to see, frequently cheered on by small knots of observers on the ground. In an adjacent sun-filled alley the ground was covered with red velvet material, apparently over mattresses. People were sprawled in every imaginable position. Eric stared in as Anita pulled him along.

"We can go back there later if you want. But first—" and they came to a storefront and entered. Jeremy, Ron and Moe decided to continue on. "Anita, Bear's Lair at 2, okay?"

She gave Jeremy a blue-gloved thumbs up and they disappeared. "That'll make this a little less pressured," Anita declared. "They are fun, but we need a few minutes to set you up."

The proprietress noisily crossed the wooden floor in her own spiked heels, a strange slithering noise accompanying her shimmying walk in a skintight black rubber dress. Her big blonde hair cascaded down her back and over her shoulders. She winked conspiratorially.

"Jerri, help me out here."

Jerri dragged Eric to the back. It dawned on Eric that Jerri was probably a man. Her hips were very straight and her shoulders square, plus her grip was strong. Her voice confirmed it, a strange in-between sound, neither female nor male.

"Let's see..." Jerri put her long golden fingernail to her lip. "Try this," handing him a black vest. Frantically she pulled out more items while Eric felt Anita's gloved hands slowly slipping his clothes off. *Why fight this?* He donned the new clothes. Standing before the mirror, he frowned at how white his skin was, and murmured something to that effect.

"Hey, don't complain about your best feature!" admonished Anita with a giggle.

Jerri came up with a flourish, "Here, this will complete the 'look'." She gave Eric a broad-rimmed swooping black hat. Eric admired his image, surprised and pleased. He wore a fishnet shirt which stretched tautly over his chest, obscuring his skinniness. The black vest went over the shirt, and very tight, brown leather pants fell over ornately engraved cowboy boots. Around his neck they'd snugly attached a buckled choker, with some rings hanging down from it. "What's this for?"

"You'll see," Anita cooed breathily in his ear, thrusting her breasts into him as she stood close, rubbing one hand on his ass and the other on his bulging cock, grinding her own crotch into his hip. He was getting very turned on. He was completely surprised at the new Anita. He watched her in the mirror, amazed, and finally just laughed out loud. "I can't believe you!"

"What?!?" she pulled back, putting her hands on her hips. "You don't like?"

"No, of course I do!" And he pulled her into a kiss, duplicating her violent embrace earlier at Angelo's. Jerri clapped her hands loudly. "Okay, okay, I guess this works, huh? Just remember me later," and she clicked and swished into the back.

"Is she a she or a he?" asked Eric in a soft voice.

"Does it matter?"

"Well... yeah, kind of."

"Both."

He didn't know what to say to that.

"C'mon!" Anita suddenly led him into the street, where it was getting denser by the minute. A small dell of n'oak trees grew next to the shop on Folsom, and as they passed under, they heard the grunting and groaning of sex coming from them. A transparent treehouse sat in the branches, where five men were chained together in a circle of sex. Judging by the sounds they were all near climax. "Keep going," Anita pushed Eric along.

Soon enough they came to an outdoor labyrinth, and once they entered, she urged him to stay close. "It's incredibly easy to get separated and lost in here. If we stick together, it won't matter how long it takes."

Inside the sunwashed labyrinth they came upon one bacchanalian scene after another. Both of them were getting extremely turned on by the intense sex on view at every turn. Finally, they came to an empty cul-de-sac, this one had a big soft lawn on the ground, and a harness floating from a hook in the wall, as well as a stump-shaped table. Anita let out a soft yelp, and yanked Eric towards the table. She threw herself over the table, thrusting her ass into the air.

Ravenous with lust, she discovered that Eric didn't get it. She rolled on to her arching back, pulled her legs up and spread them wide. She had nothing on under the skirt. "Give it to me!" she implored, "god what are you waiting for!! GIVE IT TO ME!!"

He started fumbling with his pants but couldn't undo his button. "Aaargh! What the hell!?!" Anita leaped forward, tearing at his pants. She was going to tear them off, but miraculously got the zipper moving. In seconds she had pulled his pants down and taken him in her mouth, fully erect. Gasping with pleasure she resumed her original position over the table. This time he needed no further encouragement and in seconds he was plunging in and out of her, completely lost in sexual frenzy. They both came within a minute, exploding in loud moans.

Eric leaned over Anita's back, dropping his head, gasping for breath. Tittering invaded his consciousness and he turned to see a half dozen spectators watching approvingly, one man stroking the erect penis of another.

"Great!"

"Beautiful—you guys are just beautiful!"

Anita had a dreamy look, smiling and enjoying the accolades. Eric zipped up his pants as quickly as he could, sheepishly acknowledging the compliments. The watchers went on their way.

"Hey Anita, how ya doin'?"

"Woonnnderful!"

He stroked her thighs, and she began spreading her legs. Soon they were at it again. After the second bout, they made their way through the labyrinth, watching others for a while, and finally an hour later, slipped out one of the side gates. They stumbling along happily arm in arm.

"I need a drink!" Anita demanded.

"Whatever your heart desires!"

"Let's go over there," she pointed to the Bear's Lair. Dozens of potbellied men were coming and going from the bar, many balding, very hairy, mostly wearing plaid shirts, bluejeans, and cowboy hats. At the bar, they ordered cranberry vodkas.

"THERE you are!" boomed Jeremy. "Eric! You look mahhvelous! And you both look like you've been *busy*!" He gave an exaggerated wink.

"How about you Jeremy? Where are Ron and Moe?"

"Just left actually. I think they're heading to the Dungeon, but we're not meeting up until dinner." He hinted that they'd had a spat.

"Come along with us!" Eric insisted. Then he looked from Anita to Jeremy and spread his hands, realizing he didn't have a clue what they should do next. They went up to the second floor to sit in the window and finish their drinks.

"So how do you like it?" Jeremy asked Eric.

He shook his head, dreamily. "I can't believe it. But I especially can't believe Anita!" and he kissed her, stroking her thigh under the table.

"MMMPHFF!" Anita pulled away suddenly, jumping up and pointing out the window. "FIIIRE! FIIIIRE!" she shouted at the top of her lungs. Everyone within earshot in the broad parkway stopped at the call. A plume of smoke rose behind the buildings across Folsom and the acrid smell was filling the air. It was probably in Clementina Alley.

FIRE! The call raced through the fair, and hundreds of volunteer fire fighters stopped whatever they were doing and rushed into action.

42.

A warm sun shone on the early October Saturday, people thronging the streets. He maneuvered through streetcar passengers to the second deck stairs, furtively glancing from side to side. He disguised himself with a gray scarf and sunglasses. Two days ago his picture was splashed all over the papers. From the rear corner seat he stared at passing fruit and vegetable stands. Produce grown in nearby street gardens was stacked under the fluttering green flags of the Garden Party.

At the top of the streetcar he could better see the higher reaches of the street. Banners hung from rooftops and strange sculptures oozed from rooftop to rooftop hiding the practical windmills and solar panels that all buildings sported. An oversized human-shaped figure appeared on a façade dating to the mid-20th century, waving a big Garden Party flag in its hand. It took Nwin a second to make sure it wasn't really someone climbing the building. Now they passed under the ubiquitous banner that he particularly hated: "No One Wants To, so We All Have To… Do Your Annuals!"

If I never see that again, it'll be too soon, he thought darkly. He tried to estimate how hard it might be to reach up and pull it down, but thought better of it.

They cruised over the Broadway Bridge on Polk, a small pond filling the gulley beneath them. After they crested the hill, Polk became even more busy with people on Saturday morning errands. In the distance a long transparent tube soared through the air, bicyclists darting back and forth in it between Cathedral and Nob Hills. Nwin contemplated the first Velobrij, built to save cyclists having to ride down and then up again. The Garden Party had been fighting them in general, while the Transit-Firsters were arguing about where to build them. This was the prototype, cutting out Polk Gulch between the two hills.

His attention was redirected to a huge banner advertising "The City's Premiere Public Sex Party! Folsom Street Fair, Saturday, October 6, noon-midnight." Nwin had never been to it. Jimmy's report had discouraged him. He was not at all interested in gay sex, in fact it put him off. Jimmy said it was very loose and unpredictable. *Shit, I ought to go and check it out. What the hell?* figuring he *could* control who he let touch him.

It was still a few hours before the Folsom Street Fair opened, so he decided to have breakfast. He took the spiral staircase to the streetcar's lower level. As he neared the exit an old lady gasped loudly and everyone fell silent. Slowly he turned, certain that everyone would be staring at him. The streetcar halted just as he realized the people behind him were looking at a couple already promenading in their outrageous outfits for the Folsom Street Fair. Everyone was buzzing, some approvingly. A few wolf whistles erupted. The old lady whose gasp had focused everyone's attention was still shaking her head.

Nwin made for the shadows of a small copse of n'oak trees in the intersection at Sutter. Under the trees, he checked if anyone was watching him, but saw nothing. He skirted the Sutter gardens, crossed the veloway and passed a patch of beautiful, ready-to-harvest pot plants. San Francisco was bursting with a new marijuana crop. It was hard to go anywhere and not notice the sweet sticky smell of fresh pot, either growing or being smoked. Nwin tended to smoke socially without thinking much about it. But it had been a week since he'd spent the night at Rita's, and he hadn't had a puff since then.

He absent-mindedly pulled some dense buds off as he walked by, wishing his mother hadn't found him at Rita's. Rita had been furious that his mother had tracked him down at her place, and when he tried to explain, telling her about the P-I's case, she became even more agitated.

"You're hiding out *here*? Why don't you clear your name if you had nothing to do with it?" she demanded suspiciously. He left without trying to explain any further. She slammed the door behind him. That night he'd docked near *Immersion*, and walked up to his tree for the sunset. He'd already lost the place on Alamo Square, so he had no place to go. *Chingale, I'll camp out for a few days.*

Tables filled a small courtyard just off Sutter, the sun streaming down on one corner of it where a couple sat with their steaming coffees. Nwin picked an empty table in a dark corner, pulling off his scarf as he sat down. A strange mural graced the wall of the adjacent building, a large horse's head smiling garishly, baring a set of improbable teeth. "The Toothsome Horse" was the café's name.

A thick-maned blond man appeared with an apron tied around his waist. He delivered a tray of eggs and fruit to the couple in the sunshine. They hardly registered their breakfast's arrival, they were so enraptured with each other. Nwin sat back, rocking in his chair towards the wall, his arms folded as he focused his free-floating hostility on the anonymous couple across the way.

"What can I get you?" asked the waiter. He was deeply tanned and wore a delicate golden filigree choker. Nwin scowled at him unconsciously, rocking forward with a thump.

"Gimme a cappuccino and scrambled eggs."

The waiter turned soundlessly and disappeared, unimpressed by the surly young man. Luckily for Nwin, the waiter was not up on the news, and did not recognize him. He turned his attention back to the couple, irritated that the two lovebirds were so lost in each other. Perversely, he wanted them to look over and recognize him.

Finally they were eating their breakfasts, speaking in soft voices out of Nwin's range. The man's fork dropped from his hand and he sat back, staring across at Nwin. The man began whispering urgently to his companion, who looked over at Nwin and raised her hand to her mouth. Then they looked down at the food and began eating quickly, as though they wanted to get away.

Nwin, realizing that they didn't want to confront him, grew cocky and disdainful. He was on the verge of taunting them when the waiter returned with his order, bringing him back to reality. The waiter's wrist bore a beautiful bracelet, matching his fili-gree choker. Nwin looked up at him, assuming that he was gay.

"Going to the Folsom Street Fair?" he asked aggressively.

The waiter said nothing and began to retreat.

"Hey! I asked you a question!" Nwin was teetering dangerously out of control, and the waiter, sensing it, was anxious to get out of his range. He disappeared indoors. Nwin started to rise from his seat when he observed the couple looking at him fearfully.

"What's your problem?" he demanded.

"Nothing. Nothing, man," said the guy, and he and his girlfriend got up abruptly and walked quickly out of the café.

"Chingado!" snarled Nwin at their backs. "Good riddance!" He began wolfing down his scrambled eggs, throwing down his coffee just as quickly. When he was done, he rose so suddenly that he knocked his table over. The plate and cup shattered on the flagstones of the courtyard. Nwin stood there, breathing heavily, staring at the mess. Rage got the best of him and he kicked as hard as he could but missed, swinging over everything. He turned to face the café. The waiter peered out of a window, but Nwin's glare chased him further inside out of sight. "Chingin' coward!" Nwin flipped him off and walked out.

He walked hard, instinctively heading uphill. He didn't know where he was going and it didn't matter. His earlier concern for being seen had evaporated and he glared at everyone, defying them to challenge him. He zig-zagged up the hill, cutting through gar-den courtyards, slowly getting himself under control. As he drew near the Velobrij's out-let on California at Leavenworth he stopped a short distance from the transparent tube. He hadn't been through it yet. Clanging in the background was a cable car, lumbering up the hill, visible through the transparent tube behind the cyclists who were mostly arriv-ing at the eastern end, far fewer having climbed Nob Hill for the ride west to Gough.

Once stopped, his mood began to change quickly. The rage had spent itself, and his defiant cockiness vanished. Once again he felt isolated and vulnerable, sure that he was about to be recognized and confronted. Seeing two guys emerging from the Velobrij that he vaguely knew from his days at the Pyramid he ducked sideways into a stairwell. An old lady was just coming down the stairs with her miniature terrier.

"G'morning, young man! How are you on this lovely day?" she sang to him in a melodious voice.

Nwin was startled at the unnaturally musical greeting, and when he saw how eld-erly the woman looked, he was even more surprised.

"Good morning," he returned, stepping back down off the steps to get out of her way.

"Isn't it just beautiful?" she said as she toddled onto the path, admiring the blooming bushes and vibrant greens of the gardens that filled Leavenworth just below California. Her dog yapped and pulled at the leash. "Ferdy, calm down!" The old lady looked at Nwin, her gaze piercing his shell. "Are you alright?" she asked, touching his arm.

He jerked backwards, eyes wide.

"Oh ho!" she chortled. "Don't be afraid of me! A hundred and thirteen, and still a threat! Ho ho!"

He forced a smile and shoved his hands into his pockets. He walked a short dis-tance up the hill.

"Just a minute!" she called after him. "Would you mind giving me a hand?"

He stopped and slowly turned around. The old lady stood there waiting, giving him a mischievous smile. She extended a hand towards him and he dutifully returned with his arm.

"What brings you out here on this beautiful Saturday morning?" she sang to him again. "You seem to be a lit-tle loooossst."

He laughed at her operatic approach to conversation, and tension flowed out of him. She seemed to notice too, and laughed along with him.

"Lost? Me? Not a't'all!" he replied in a low voice, mimicking her musicality with a staccato rhythm. They covered the fifteen meters to California, near the Velobrij. A couple on a tandem appeared, turning from Jones onto California, beginning their descent into the tube. Up close Nwin could see that it wasn't an enclosed tube, but a circular plastic bridge with open sides. It swayed, responding to the wind and weight of dozens of cyclists traversing it.

The old lady was checking it out too. "I don't know if I could stand to go in there," she said, shaking her head. "Looks frightening!"

"You mean because it's not stable?"

"I like my feet on the ground!" she said emphatically, abandoning her musical-in-the-making.

"It might be fun," suggested Nwin, seeing its utility and convenience, but also the sheer pleasure of soaring through the sky on a bike, unhindered by traffic or gravity.

"You sure you're okay?" said the old lady, peering into Nwin's face. "You don't look so good…"

"Thanks, but I don't want to talk about it."

"I've been around a loooong time," she said, a weariness creeping into her voice. "You, on the other hand, have a long life ahead." Her voice hardened, her alert eyes flashed, and she wouldn't let Nwin go. "A public trial can be a wonderful experience… the accused can clear his name, or the truth of a complicated situation can be revealed, or the public can offer forgiveness—sometimes all three!"

He pulled back, horrified, realizing that this deeply wrinkled old woman knew who he was.

"Don't worry about me. Keep an open mind. Accept a path to reconciliation or resolution, or at least a chance to move on. No need to hide, no need to fear. Have a nice day, Mr. Robertson!" Her iron grip and remarkable strength belied the frail woman she'd been up to now. He couldn't leave until she was finished with him. She pulled him down to kiss him on the cheek with her leathery lips. Then she let her dog Ferdy lead her back to the gardens, yapping furiously. She didn't look back.

Nwin watched for a moment, and then he walked up the hill, sweating and confused. He felt nauseous and dizzy and sat down on another staircase. He squeezed his eyes shut as tightly as he could. *Breathe, breathe, breathe*, he counseled himself. The old lady was terrifying. Her advice seemed to come from another world. *Reconciliation? Forgiveness?* It was impossible to imagine, and besides, *I want out, not in!*

A boisterous group poured from an apartment building, dressed in scanty and transparent get-ups. They gathered across the cable car tracks, laughing and hooting at each other.

The revelers unfurled a large banner to lead their procession, evidently to the

Folsom Street Fair. "Nob Hill's Naughtiest!" with a smaller line of type saying "Huntington Harem." The latter name graced their building too. The last stragglers clattered out of the lobby, and they finished tying themselves together with all sorts of ribbons and chains. A few donned fruit-laden gags and colorful blindfolds, four played trumpets and one strange hooded character with a big whip herded the rest along. With a huge crack of a whip, the next cable car shuddered forward and carried them down California, past the Velobrij and the Leavenworth gardens.

His dizziness and nausea passed, thanks to steady breathing and the distraction of the Huntington Harem. He headed past the crumbling ruins of Grace Cathedral, through the gardens at the top of Nob Hill, and stopped in front of the Mark Hopkins at the corner of California and Tailor. Tourists jammed the venerable old hotel, dozens prepared for the Fair.

So this is where they bring people who just got here, thought Nwin, standing aimlessly on the opposite corner staring at the bustling scene. He had been over Nob Hill from time to time, but somehow had never noticed the tourists and newcomers at the Mark Hopkins. Mentally halfway out of town, he was drawn to the transient energy of the place. He walked across the crowded cobblestones towards the ornate iron doors. Some locals in puffy renaissance costumes bowed deeply and opened the doors for him as he approached, which unnerved him. He stared into the chaotic lobby where more tourists were milling about in various types of "sexy" clothes. The two doormen looked at him expectantly but he retreated from the courtyard and started down the steep slope of Tailor.

* * *

How long had he been in this sunny room under the open skylights? He groped in the corner for his clothes. Garments were piled deep, and he pulled out one thing after another, recognizing nothing. He used someone's shirt to wipe the sweat and ejaculate from his torso and legs.

Gasping and groaning, three couples copulated with fresh energy on the opposite side of the room. Dozens of others were spread across the floor in various states of exhaustion and delight. Legs and arms wrapped impossibly under and over each other, one body indistinguishable from the next.

He felt wobbly after coming again and again during the past couple of hours. *Where was that girl who brought him here?* Nowhere to be seen. *And who were the others? Who knows?* It was his first time sharing a room with strangers having sex. He watched a gay couple in the corner going at it and it left him cold. He remembered one hairy face kissing him at some point, but he'd turned away when he felt the beard. *Who cares? It doesn't matter.*

He finally found his clothes and went into the alley through the back door. He shoved his hands in his pockets, thinking about getting something to drink. He found matches. Across the alley was a dumpster, full of trash, sitting against the back of a large wooden building. He looked up and down the alley, and observed just a few people, including a small group busily having sex under a tree. Unthinking, he moved automatically towards the dumpster, and before he knew it, he'd thrown a flaming match into the dumpster. Nothing happened. He threw in a second and a third. Wisps of smoke began to rise. Flames slowly began eating through the dumpster.

His breathing was short and fast as he backed away, furtively glancing down the alley. No one paid any attention. He admired the slowly building conflagration, flames leaping out of the dumpster, scorching the wall of the building behind it. Then the building was on fire and the flames grew rapidly, voraciously devouring its wooden corner. "FIRE! FIIIRRE!!" The call sounded from somewhere. Then it was everywhere, people yelling "FIRE!" running to and fro, bells clanging in the distance. He leaned against the wall, watching the scene unfold as though he were in a dream, hypnotized by the wall of orange flame dancing up the side of the building.

A wall of people came rushing from 6th Street, clad in all manner of kinky outfits. Hoses were dragged into the alley. Already naked volunteer firefighters had one hose pouring water on the burning building from the rooftop across the alley. Others blasted the dumpster and the corner of the building with extinguishers but the flames had leaped too high to be stopped.

Nwin began to walk calmy through the frenzied crowd, a lone figure fighting the current of onrushing humanity. "Hey! STOP!" boomed a voice, and suddenly two figures took shape in front of him. He tried to sidestep but they matched him, refusing to let him pass. Several potbellied guys in lederhosen chugging up a moment later to back them up.

"What's your problem?!" he demanded, not interested in playing anyone's game. The man grabbed one arm and the woman the other. Nwin thrashed back and forth violently, throwing them both off and creating space around himself. He ran towards the fire, submerging himself in the hundreds of people focused on the burning building. Panicky, he looked to see if they were still after him, but he couldn't tell.

Seeing an opening towards the other end of the alley, he dodged through the multitude. Behind him he could hear "Stop him! Stop that man!" but the people he was running past weren't making the connection. In a few seconds he popped onto 5th Street running at full tilt. In no time he re-entered the densely packed Folsom Fair, everyone buzzing and pointing at the smoke but paying him no attention. Surging with adrenaline, he ran all the way to 4th and turned south. He didn't stop until he came to the wall around Russ Gardens. Spent, he stopped near dense bushes to look for pursuers, but saw no one.

Slowly he followed the wall to the 5th Street gates. A steady stream of celebrants passed and he easily blended in with the people heading to the ferry dock. He glanced back towards the Fair and concluded from the small plume of smoke that it must be under control now. The big clock in the Gardens read 5:25.

"I can't believe I was there for that long!" He boarded a northbound ferry. "Back to my hole for one more night! Then Sayonara San Francisco!"

43.

Beer steins and plates crashed as everyone on the 2nd floor reacted to Anita's scream of "Fire!" Eric, Anita and Jeremy scrambled into the rushing throng on Folsom. Fighting through bodies, straining to get to 6th Street where they could cut around to Clementina Alley, Anita yanked Eric abruptly into a dark bar.

"This way! There's a back door on Clementina."

There wer few patrons in the murky bar. A bartender mopping the counter and one very besotted woman sprawled at a corner table watched them lurch by.

"Everyone's out there already! There's nothing you can do!" the bartender called after them.

Anita was having trouble running in her high-heeled boots, but she held Eric's arm tightly. Eric, for his part, was lost in the adrenaline of the moment. He was strangely aroused by the intensity of Anita's hand digging into his arm. In the panicky rush to reach the fire, he hadn't stopped to think about how utterly unprepared he was to do anything useful. He had never fought a fire before.

They made it through a cluttered passage behind the bar to a big metal door, swinging it open, almost smashing people running by. Smoke billowed 100 meters east. Water poured across the alley on to the fire. They were propelled by the crowd towards the fire.

"Hey, STOP!" yelled Eric, staring in astonishment at the tall dark fellow coming towards them. Nwin Robertson walked towards them as if he were a salmon struggling up a furious stream. A torrential mob poured around him as he pushed into the oncoming flood.

They stepped in front of him. He tried to move to the side. They matched his movement.

"What's your problem?!" he snarled. Nwin Robertson clearly did not recognize Eric or Anita. Anita and Eric spontaneously grabbed one arm each. Robertson furiously thrashed back and forth, releasing himself from their grip. Before Eric could react again, Nwin Robertson turned and ran through the crowd, escaping their grasp. They ran after him for a minute or two, but he eluded them. By the time they got to 5th Street he was nowhere to be seen.

"Goddammit!"

"Chingale! Where'd he go?" Anita exclaimed, totally out of breath, bending down with her hands on her knees, trying to catch her breath.

Eric was too angry at having lost Robertson to notice Anita's butt, fully revealed once again. But his anger and frustration soon ebbed and he began to feel that he'd failed. He stood leaning on the wall, sinking into despair.

"He's gone. Let's go back and see how they're doing with the fire. Looks like it must be under control," Anita was pointing down the alley where people were dispersing and the smoke was subsiding. She looked at Eric, but the passionate cowboy she'd been riding the past few hours was gone, replaced by the drooping sad-faced boy she was used to from work. *I guess it was too good to last.*

"Hey, c'mon," she put her arms out and he came into them, hugging her tightly. He spoke in a tiny voice.

"Anita?"

"What is it, Eric?"

"I should've caught him."

"It's not your fault, we *both* had 'im. He got away. It's not our job to catch him, after all."

"I don't understand. It doesn't make sense."

"What do you mean?"

He pulled back, trying to maintain his composure. "We spent the last three months figuring out that Robertson is the arsonist. He comes to our office, denies everything, and disappears. Then we find him, completely by accident, leaving the scene of a fire."

"We don't know if he had anything to do with it!"

"I know. But seems probable, doesn't it?"

Anita shrugged.

"I'm not sure what I'm doing as a Public Investigator. It doesn't seem very effective, to say the least."

"You're upset. Let it go. You're meeting Kathy tomorrow to talk about an Apprenticeship?"

Eric nodded.

They began walking up the alley, towards the ash-filled puddles and burned rubble where the firefighters were putting out the last smoldering ruins. "You need a good night's sleep. Tomorrow you can decide what you want to do." She could see that he was pretty upset. "You want to get a drink and head back into the party?"

He shook his head. Eric's sexual appetite was already overfulfilled. He felt silly in his leather outfit and he looked at Anita in her get-up and wished he could be in a quiet room with her, or perhaps sitting in a sunny meadow under a tree—not in a muddy alley dressed in sex clothes. He sighed and walked away from Anita disconsolately.

"Uh, Eric?"

He stopped and turned. "Sorry... I feel sick to my stomach..." They had had an awful lot to drink and smoke during the past few hours, compounded by a heady dose of adrenaline. "I think I'd better head home. What do you want to do?" He was hoping she would say she wanted to go home with him. She once again pouted in a provocative way. But he wasn't able to shake off his despondency. The shock of the fire and Robertson's appearance and subsequent escape had brought him back to reality with a thud.

"I'll see you Monday, then, okay?" Anita gave up on Eric getting back into the swing of the Folsom Fair. But she wasn't going to let him stop her. The annual orgy was one of her favorite events of the year, and it wasn't half over!

* * *

On Monday, Eric entered Kathy's office.

"How was the Folsom Street Fair?" She peered at him, a wicked gleam in her eye.

Eric was embarrassed. "Yeah, it was fun," he mumbled, but didn't elaborate. Kathy didn't press him either, seeing that he was uncomfortable. Eric told her about the fire and Robertson.

"Don't be so hard on yourself, Eric. There are no police!" she admonished. "You did your best. Besides, sounds like Anita's yell was at least partly responsible for the quick response that helped keep the fire under control, no?"

Eric shrugged, feeling a powerful combination of shame and fear.

"Kathy, I—" but he choked up. She waited patiently, saying nothing.

"Look, about that Apprenticeship..."

She came around her desk, realizing with surprise that he wasn't going to automatically move on to an Apprenticeship. She put her hand on his shoulder.

"Eric, what's going on?"

He looked up at her, confused and frightened. Kathy gazed at him sympathetically.

His voice was deep and gravelly as he spoke. "I'm not cut out for this work. Like this biological lab case you put me on... I don't want to investigate inventors!" he sighed. "Plus, well... Anita and I went to the Fair together... and..."

Kathy grinned. "Ahhh HA!" she folded her arms and sat on her desk. "So you don't like the idea of working with a romantic partner?" she guessed.

Eric nodded. "I don't know where I stand." He ran his hand through his hair. "I mean, I *think* we started something! But maybe it was just the Fair..."

Eric was obviously overwrought, circuits overloading.

"Eric, you need a break. Take a few weeks off. You should get out of the city... you've been working hard."

His head hung between sagging shoulders. "Yeah, I guess so..." He'd been dreading this meeting but it hadn't been so hard. He wanted to take the Apprenticeship but his confidence was at low ebb. He got up abruptly and gave her a hug, which she returned stiffly.

"I'll be back in two weeks, okay?"

"Sure, Eric. Go and have some fun. Take Anita on a trip!" Kathy suggested.

He scowled. "I'd like to, but..."

"Hi you guys!" Anita was standing at the door.

"Speak of the devil!" Kathy laughed.

"Wha-? Me?" Anita stood in the door, no sign of the vixen she'd been on Saturday. Her hair was hidden under a Slugs hat and she wore a loose-fitting plaid shirt, no make-up, black jeans and her ever-present muddy sandals. Her feet were dirty, too. She looked down at herself unconsciously, as though she was also thinking about the contrast between Saturday and today.

Kathy briskly strode to the door. "I'm going for a coffee. Catch ya later." She gave Anita's arm a squeeze and a look hidden to Eric as she passed her.

Anita walked straight to Eric, who stood up. She flowed into his arms, knocking her hat off. His whole demeanor changed as he wrapped his arms around her. He began kissing her forehead and cheeks, and she squirmed under the onslaught, but smiled sweetly, enjoying the affection. When he stopped for a moment, she looked into his eyes, her own bouncing gaily.

"That was a wave, Eric. You surprised me."

"*I* surprised *you*?!" They both laughed. He told her about Kathy's suggestion that he take a vacation before starting his Apprenticeship.

"Eric?" Anita stood back looking at him carefully. "Does Saturday make it harder to work with me?"

He nodded.

"Shit—I was afraid of that," Anita walked to the window. "That was selfish of me."

"No! I didn't know what I was in for, but I went along with you all the way. Believe me—I have no regrets!"

"But it ruins a job you were enjoying..."

He looked at her appreciatively. "Frankly, I'd much rather be involved with you than investigating."

She turned from the window to see if he was sincere. "I don't want you to have to choose." He stroked her neck, touching her softly. She melted into his arms and a long deep kiss.

"Will you take a trip with me Anita?"

Her lips were inches from his. "Yes, but only if you promise to not let it interfere with being a P-I."

"It's a deal," he grinned. "Do you know the way to..." He tried to remember the name of some other place he had wanted to visit. "...San Jose?"

"My cousin lives in a big co-op down there, a place full of inventors. It's not right in San Jose but close. I have a standing invitation." She grinned at him. "I can even take you to see my plaque in the Hall of Fame!"

Eric and Anita walked out just as Kathy returned with her coffee.

"So what are you lovebirds going to do?"

"We're going to San Jose! See you next month!" and off they went.

* * *

Nwin waited for an elderly couple to finish feeding pigeons close to his hidden campsite. When they finally left, he emerged, rolled up his sleeping bag and closed his dufflebag. He stretched and ran through his brief exercise routine. The sun was somewhere up there behind a gray overcast sky. Sunday, October 7, 2157. Everything felt inexplicably altered. He was floating. He wasn't hungry at all.

At the dock just east of *Immersion*, he noticed the last few stragglers emerge from the underwater all-night club. He found *Hot 1* where he'd left it a few days earlier, bobbing in the Bay. Tossing his bags in, he noticed that the skiff was wrinkled around the edges, a sign that it needed some fuel pellets. He walked over to the storage box on the wooden pier and grabbed a half dozen 'phylls to feed to *Hot 1*. He steered over oddly still waters in the morning grayness. The boat's skin, freshly nourished, grew taut and even seemed to blush as he gained speed, pushing *Hot 1* to its 25 knot speed limit.

He patted the stern of his skiff. "We've had some fun, together, eh?" he muttered as he sped along. "I hope someone puts you to good use after I'm gone."

It didn't take long to curve around North Beach and get to Pier 1½. Waiting at the dock, as promised, was an unimposing ship. "*The Republic of Texas*" graced the stern beside a limp red, white and blue flag. Nwin stopped in the Bay to look at the ship. The city loomed behind it: the bright orange pyramid where he'd lived, the Dominoes falling into each other, the Tweezer Towers further west, Rincon Towers to the south. Gray morning light gave everything a slightly dull quality. Sunday morning traffic was light. Few ferries or taxis were moving and practically no barges. Nwin stared at the city where he'd spent his whole life, the only place he'd known, and felt no sorrow, no doubt. He was ready to leave. He was dying to get away from San Francisco!

With renewed certainty he flipped up to the docks, tying up *Hot 1* near Pier 3. He hoisted his bags painlessly, and walked unsteadily over the bobbing dock towards Pier 1½. A dozen others were already lined up at the gangway to the ship, where two men were screening them. On the ship's deck Nwin could see Nance and some men he didn't recognize at the railing, looking down at their recruits. He made eye contact with Nance but she was stony-faced so he made no gestures either.

No nonsense, no bullshit... I like that.

"Wait here," said a sailor gruffly, a tall broad-shouldered guy in a peacoat, thick mustache and eyebrows obscuring his deepset eyes. A burly blond in front of him was getting questioned. They stopped him just out of earshot.

"OK, you're next."

Nwin approached the boarding ramp. Two men stood in front of him, one with a clipboard. The one in charge was a hawk-faced man with a mottled gash running from his right cheekbone to below his jaw. His pale blue eyes betrayed no emotion.

"Your name?"

"Nwin Robertson."

The guy with the clipboard found his name on it. He nodded silently to his colleague.

"Does anyone know you're here?"

"No."

"Do you know why you're here?"

Nwin was taken aback by the question. Nance had been vague at best.

"I have an idea."

Hawk-face grimaced, or maybe he smiled. Nwin's answer was deemed sufficient.

"Pass," they waved him aboard.

Once aboard the ship, he was confronted by a row of men and women in black jumpsuits. The man closest to him pointed to a stairwell, so Nwin climbed down into the hold. Below deck, he was immediately met by a square, grizzled sailor.

"Over there!" he said in a too-loud voice. Nwin's eyes adjusted to the dim light and he joined the others along the wall at the end of the line.

"Chingin' nigger! What's HE doin' here?" spit the burly blond who had preceded him up the ramp. Nwin was startled to hear that kind of talk, something he'd never experienced. The two men to the other side of the blond muttered under their breath.

"WHAT DID YOU SAY?!" The sailor that had been herding them into position stepped aside as a uniformed officer appeared behind him. He walked authoritatively across the floor directly to the young man who had uttered the complaint. He stopped inches from the face of the complainant and then stared unblinking into his eyes.

"Sailor! I asked you a question!"

The blond straightened up, cast a glance at his compatriots he'd boarded with, and spoke clearly. "Sir! I said 'chingin' nigger' sir! 'What's he doing here,' sir!"

The officer stared at him, his face hardening. Suddenly a muffled crack sounded, and the blond's mouth opened, his eyes widened, and he slumped dramatically to the floor.

"Bobby!" the man to his side fell to his knees, reaching for his fallen brother. Simultaneously, the man beyond him lunged for the officer, who slammed him in the temple with the butt of his gun. He crumpled to the floor, his shoulder in the pool of blood draining from his slain brother. The three brothers were now two. The one conscious brother was sobbing over the dead body, cowering beneath the terrible rage of the officer.

"We will not have any racist bullshit on this ship, is that clear?"

Everyone except the three brothers stood at silent attention along the wall. The whimpering brother pushed his unconscious sibling away from the blood. "You killed Bobby," he wailed. "How could you?"

"SILENCE!"

The officer paced back and forth staring into the faces of his new recruits. Each one was terrorized, but some looked it more than others. Nwin was inscrutable in the face of the horror that had just taken place.

"Some of you seem to think that you've joined an outfit involved in some fairy-tale race war. Well get over it!!" The officer stalked back and forth furiously. "I am Captain Ortega. This is the Northern Division of the Reagan-Pinochet Army. Our aim is simple. We are fighting for freedom, complete individual freedom—freedom for everyone, regardless of race, creed or color. We will destroy communism!" He folded his hands behind his back as he paced, completely oblivious to the dead body at his feet, the pooling blood, or the quietly sobbing brother sitting over his two siblings, one dead and the other unconscious.

"Our army has begun the final struggle. The front line of the war is currently in Chile, but it won't be long before we've opened fronts across the planet."

The deranged captain promised to reveal more soon. "First we have to get out of this sad little town with its pathetic people. When we've reached the high seas, we'll tell you more. For now, you will each be assigned to a bunk and given a job to do. We'll be watching carefully over the next few days to see who has come to fight... and who hasn't," he finished ominously. The recruits stood immobile. Finally the captain pointed at two recruits. "You two, take the body to the foredeck and deliver it to the infirmary. The rest of you..." and he looked up and down the line at his recruits, "Jones here will show you where your bunks are. Settle in and we'll call you up when we've cleared the Golden Gate."

The captain headed towards the door but suddenly spun around. "Robertson!"

Nwin jumped, standing as straight as he possibly could.

"Follow me!"

Nwin followed the silent figure up a spiral staircase to the deck. The ship was moving now. Already the city was receding as they rounded Telegraph Hill. The captain walked to the bow where several crew members were watching their progress. Nwin was startled when one of the dark figures turned around and it was Nance. *Commander Anna N. Kzyzcynski* read the badge on her chest.

"Mr. Robertson, we meet again!" she said with a grim smile, extending her hand. He started to slap it, but she grabbed his hand with an iron grip and shook it in a traditional handshake. "Sorry about that racist shit. I warned our agent about recruiting white supremacists, but I guess he tried to slip a few in, anyway." She twirled gloves in one hand as she began pacing. "I understand the Captain has already taken some remedial action," she glanced at the Captain. "I don't think we'll have any more backwards behavior on *this* ship!" Looking hard at Nwin she continued. "We like your initiative and ... shall we call them 'native skills'?... With that in mind, are you prepared to accept an officer's commission?"

"Me?" He stood erect, gratified that he'd been singled out, already feeling loyalty to Nance and the rest of them.

"Granted, it's just a beginning. We'd like to appoint you to lead the new squad of recruits as we begin training. Do you accept?"

Immediately Nwin replied, "Yes m'am!" his chest swelling with pride.

"Very well. I'll brief you on your responsibilities and the chain of command. Please wait for me at the stern of the ship."

He made his way along the outer deck as the *Republic of Texas* steamed past the south tower of the old Golden Gate Bridge, green and tilting precariously over the bluffs where the road had once been. The windmills were standing quietly in the calm air of the morning. He reached the stern, and leaned over the railing. In the wake of the ship a small flock of seagulls swooped up and down. Glancing at something that caught his eye to the side, he observed a small pod of dolphins prancing around in the outbound tide.

The *Republic of Texas* hit full speed now and the Golden Gate shrank behind him. *Complete individual freedom*, he thought. He liked the sound of that, especially after a lifetime of San Francisco's urgent coddling, always pushing him to do his share... *No more goddam Annuals!* He stared at the widening ocean, San Francisco disappearing into the nondescript shoreline. Gripping the railing, he waited to be told what to do.